THE LAST ORCHARD

HUNT

❀ Created with Vellum

he bank's interior was immaculate. From its polished white marble floors to the crystal chandeliers that hung from the ceiling, every square inch of the financial institution was bathed in decadence; all of it monitored by a pair of armed guards by the revolving front doors.

It had an open layout inside, with the tellers situated to the left, protected by bulletproof glass where they handled the queue of customers' withdrawals or deposits.

All walks of life waited in line, all of them on their phones save for an elderly woman who waited patiently, both hands clutching her large burgundy purse with dollies etched across the side, smiling to herself while the man behind her argued and raised his voice on the phone.

"I told him fifteen times that the deadline was this afternoon. Just get it done!"

The rest of the bank's open floor was comprised of ornate wooden desks built from oak and stained a rich, dark brown, where the loan officers examined proposals. By checking a box on a form with a simple flick of their wrists, they had the power to bring dreams to life or kill them before they had a chance to take their first breaths.

A mixture of handshakes and tears brought the conversations to an end, though not all the applicants walked away without pushing back.

"Thirty years!" An old man stood, shoving his chair back, his voice and the screech of the legs of his chair turning every head in the bank. "That's how long I've given my business to this bank."

"Sir, you need to calm down." The fortysomething suit behind the desk raised his palm, trying to soothe the old man like a child, then tossed a quick glare at one of the guards, and the sentry approached quickly and soundlessly.

"I missed two payments, and only two! I already told you I can pay it back."

The banker leaned over the desk. "Then pay it."

"Because I can't do it in the time you've given me!" The old-timer slammed his fist onto the table, causing a few pens to fall off the banker's desk. "My family has been on that land for five generations! What right do you have to take it away? We worked that land! We've helped feed this state and this country for over a century!"

The banker remained emotionless. Cold. "You've defaulted on your loan. And we're well within our rights to take control of your assets. It's all outlined in the details of your mortgage."

"But you can't—"

The security guard seized the old man's arm from behind. Surprise and shock flashed across the old-timer's face. He stared up at the big brute, his pleading eyes useless against the guard's apathy.

The banker stood once the guard had the old man secured, and he leaned forward and planted his knuckles on the desk. "You will have until the end of the month to pay the remaining balance of your mortgage, or your family will be escorted off the property."

And with the flick of the banker's eyes, the security guard dragged the old man away from the desk.

But the old man didn't go willingly. "Get your hands off me!" He jerked his arm but was unsuccessful in his escape attempt, and the guard yanked the old man harder toward the door.

"C'mon, you mother—"

The security guard froze and whipped his head around quickly to the stranger that had grabbed him.

Charlie Decker kept a firm grip on the security guard's arm, blocking his path toward the bank's exit. The pair stood eye to eye, both just a hair above six feet tall, though the guard had the weight advantage.

A light tic at the corner of the guard's eye prompted Charlie to remove his hand. He wasn't in the mood for an altercation, especially not before he had a chance to plead his own case to the bank.

Charlie kept his voice low, and while the bank had grown quiet, only the guard and the old man heard him speak. "I'd like to think security here would handle folks with a little more dignity."

The guard flared his nostrils but then noticed the number of phones pointed in his direction, ready to make him the latest viral video.

The guard released the old man but then thrust a finger in his face. "You walk out of here without a word. Understand?"

The old man grimaced, but he nodded, the weathered lines from all the years of manual labor etched along his face like worn wheelbarrow paths. He turned to Charlie. "Thank you."

Charlie nodded. "You've still got until the end of the month. I'm sure you've done more with less."

The old man cracked a smile, exposing a missing tooth on the left side of his mouth. He shook Charlie's hand. The calluses on both men's palms were part of their identity.

Then Charlie watched him leave and glare at the security guard on his way out.

Charlie returned to his seat in the waiting area, ignoring the expressions of shock from the other customers. He picked up the folder he'd dropped on the floor when he saw the growing altercation then waited patiently to be called.

The old man was one of hundreds of farmers that had gone belly-up. It was the nature of the business—adapt or die. It was a trend that was becoming more common among the farmers in the area. If you couldn't compete with the large farm conglomerates, then it was game over.

Most families were lucky to get back what they owed, and a best-case scenario involved walking off their land without any debt. But that was a rarity.

"Mr. Decker?"

Charlie lifted his head and flashed a smile at the loan officer dressed in a sharp blue suit, white shirt, and red tie. He was clean-shaven and had a fresh tan but didn't smile.

"Nice to meet you."

Charlie extended his hand, and the banker regarded it for a minute, almost as if he was making sure it was clean. Once Charlie's hand passed inspection, the banker reciprocated the handshake.

"Have a seat, Mr. Decker." The banker kept his attention on the papers on the neatly stacked piles of documents on his desk, then glanced to the folder in Charlie's hands. "I see you came prepared."

"Yes, sir," Charlie answered, repositioning himself in the chair. The plastic seat wasn't comfortable, but he suspected that it was designed that way.

"Your visit today is for a loan application for your..." The banker flipped through the pages, unable to finish his thought.

"Orchard," Charlie said, happily filling in the blank.

"Yes, orchard." The banker accentuated his frown the further he dove into the orchard's financial history.

Charlie cleared his throat. "It's no secret that smaller farms just don't have the same profit margins as the larger corporate farms, but we're more agile than those big guys, which allows us to adapt more quickly." Charlie set the folder on the banker's desk. "My plan outlines a more efficient and streamlined approach for harvesting, which in turn will allow for better marketing because we're producing a better product." He pressed a finger on top of the pages. "We're rebranding our orchard and opening it up for tours, and I already have vendors lined up for a weekly weekend farmer's market. We'll also have an events department for weddings and parties. And once we're able to purchase the upgraded processing equipment, we'll be able to double our daily output."

The banker picked up the folder, and Charlie took the nods as a good sign. "You'll be funneling the projected revenue into the payments for the new machinery and renovations?"

"Yes, sir, and those projections are very conservative." Charlie inched toward the seat's edge. "I think those margins will increase to the low teens by the third quarter after operations are up and running. I've also developed relationships with local bakeries and grocers to help supplement our demand, and I've received a lot of positive responses. There's definitely an interest for our product both locally and nationally."

The banker nodded but never broke from the stoic nature of his posture or expressions. And the longer the banker remained silent, the more Charlie's stomach soured.

Finally, reaching the end of Charlie's documents rather quickly, the banker closed the folder then leaned back in his chair, hands clasped together over his stomach. "You've put together a fine presentation. Your numbers look solid, but I don't share your optimism about your margins increasing so quickly."

Charlie chewed the inside of his cheek and nodded. "Our property is well maintained. Our nurseries are promising, and our cover crop—"

"Your orchard's financial history doesn't paint a pretty picture." The banker shifted in his chair, the stiff suit limiting his mobility as he stretched his neck. "Every loan that this bank has extended to your farm has been met with late payments and extensions. And despite the rosy figures you put together, you failed to account for the toxic debt that your orchard has accrued over the past forty years."

"I understand that, and if you look at my reinvestment numbers, you'll see that I include paying off that debt from the profits—"

"Mr. Decker, even if you managed to scrounge together enough funds to pay the minimum payments on your debt, which is doubtful, those numbers just aren't profitable for our bank."

Charlie lingered at the edge of his seat. He clasped his hands together and chewed the inside of his cheek, gathering his thoughts. "I know that my family's orchard doesn't have a history of consistent payments or profits and that this bank has granted us a lot of leeway over the years, and I don't want to take advantage of that generosity—"

"It wasn't generosity, Mr. Decker." The loan officer planted his elbows on the table, his small, beady pupils boring into Charlie's rich hazel eyes. "It was bad business. And it's not a business this bank will be continuing." He pushed Charlie's folder across the table.

Charlie stared at the weeks of work inside that the banker had discarded.

"Next!" The banker raised his hand toward the waiting area, and another hopeful applicant rose from their seat and stepped into the lion's den.

Charlie headed for the exit, remembering his family's prior experience with bankers coming to the farm to collect. It was never the same people twice, but they all had the same look. They'd drive down the dirt road in a dark-colored luxury sedan, kicking up dust and not getting out of the car until that dust had settled.

Charlie watched them complain about the dirt that would collect on their suits and polished shoes as they scowled and turned their noses up at everything that he had called home.

All the bank saw was numbers on a spreadsheet. They didn't see the toil, the sweat, the blood that Charlie's family poured into their land, which was why they fought so desperately and passionately to keep it.

But what he wanted the bankers to see was something that couldn't be shown in a PowerPoint or spreadsheets or business proposals. And it was something that the bankers who came out to their orchard never stuck around long enough to see.

It was watching something grow. Months, and sometimes even years, of constant nurturing. You couldn't see all of that in five minutes of assessing land. Hell, you couldn't see all of that over the course of a long weekend. It was only when you woke up in the morning, on a normal Tuesday, after fifteen years of living on the farm, and you walked out and caught the sunrise in the field and, for the first time, really felt the warmth on your face.

The same warmth that fed the trees and the earth that grew the very crop you were trying to harvest. It was all connected.

When Charlie passed the security guard, the big man snickered. "Don't forget your dignity."

Charlie ignored the quip and stepped through the revolving door and into the busy weekday Seattle afternoon, squinting from the sunlight.

Hurried pedestrians passed Charlie, most of them on

their cell phones, and two of them knocked into Charlie as if he weren't even there.

After a few steps, Charlie stopped and turned back toward the bank.

Seattle Credit was carved in gold letters, and a pair of thick marble columns stretched from floor to ceiling. The structure looked Romanesque and ancient compared to the Starbucks and H&M stores on either side.

Hesitant, Charlie removed his phone and made the call that he'd been dreading all day. It rang seven times before his mother finally answered.

"Charlie? Son? Can you hear me?"

"Hey, Mom," Charlie said, stepping out of the sun and into the shade of a nearby tree surrounded by a fence and concrete. "Is Dad with you?"

"Yes. Hold on. I'll put you on speaker. Okay, can you hear us now?"

"How's the weather over there?"

Charlie pulled his ear away from his phone, laughing at his father's boisterous greeting. "It's fine, Dad."

"So how'd it go?" his dad asked, his tone masked with trepidation.

Charlie exhaled. "No one approved the loan."

"Not even Seattle Credit?" his mother asked.

Charlie glanced back up at the bank's moniker. "Nope."

His parents' silence was louder than any words they could have spoken, and Charlie headed for his truck, parked on the street a few buildings down.

"So what options does that leave us?" his mother asked.

"Not many," Charlie answered. "I'll look at the books again and see if there is any other capital that we missed that could be used as collateral, but it's going to be hard to find."

"It's all right, Charlie," his father said, that hearty voice still optimistic even with the deadline fast approaching.

"They'll have to drag me off this farm cold and dead before I leave!"

"Oh, Harold, stop it," his mother said. "Well, we love you, honey, and we'll see you at home. Drive safe, okay?"

"I will."

Charlie pocketed his phone, trying to rid himself of the lingering taste of the lie on his tongue. He'd already been through every asset that his parents owned. Every leaf and blade of grass was accounted for, and he knew checking the books again wouldn't yield any hope.

He might be able to try some other banks throughout the state, but after the dozens of doors slammed in his face, he didn't expect a different outcome anywhere else. Seattle Credit had been his last hope.

Charlie loved his family, and he loved the orchard where he grew up. For the past four years, it was all he'd focused on. He'd attended one of the best agro-business schools in the state, and after graduation, he was confident he was equipped with the tools he needed to save the farm.

But his parents had driven them too far into debt, and despite their arduous hours and tireless work ethic, they could barely break even. And while their yearly losses were small, they added up after four decades. It was just too big of a hole to climb out of.

The only option left was the one option he hadn't discussed with his parents, and that was to sell before the bank took everything. They might be able to break even then find work somewhere else, but he knew that his father was serious about never leaving his land. He had too many roots set deep into that ground. If he uprooted them now, he wouldn't survive the transplant somewhere else.

Charlie walked the three blocks to his truck, which was parked in a space on the side of the road. Cars zoomed past, and as Charlie approached his truck, he noticed a green paper pinned down on his windshield by one of the wipers. "Dammit."

He snatched the parking ticket off his windshield and checked the meter, finding it expired by only a minute. "Unbelievable." He crumpled the ticket in his fist and searched for the parking maid but found no one in uniform. "When it rains, it pours."

Charlie fished the keys out of his pocket and stepped toward the driver's side door. With his mind still lingering on the ticket, he didn't see what caused the scream from across the street. But he glanced up in just enough time to watch the sedan veer from its lane of traffic and make a beeline straight for his truck.

2

The harsh crunch of metal preceded the shattering of glass and the din of the car horn as Charlie half jumped and was half thrown from the driver's side door of his truck.

He thrust his arms out to catch himself against the sidewalk, which greeted him stiffly, and his palms scraped across the grainy concrete, drawing blood. His knees hit next, the pain sharp and hot, which he tried to diminish by rolling to his side, the momentum spinning him a few rotations before the world was finally upright again.

Bones aching, Charlie struggled to his feet, his senses overwhelmed with pain and light and screams, compounded by a symphony of car collisions that echoed down the street.

People scattered from the sidewalks as drivers lost control of their vehicles and swerved into parked cars, signs, meters, trees, and buildings.

What few cars managed to stay on the road smashed into each other, creating a chain of wrecks that stretched to the horizon.

"Jesus," Charlie whispered under his breath and slowly turned his attention back to his truck and the sedan, which had crushed together, the metal crinkled like an accordion and the windshield shattered, transformed into crushed white glass.

Charlie hurried over to check the driver behind the wheel and found the air bag had been deployed. The driver was leaned back in his seat, disoriented. A nasty gash ran across his forehead, and blood dripped down his face.

Charlie tugged at the handle of the car door, but it only opened a crack. The collision had smashed the metal around the doorframe, preventing it from fully opening.

"My head," the driver said, sounding confused and his voice ragged. "I can't feel my head."

"Hang on. I'm going to get you out." Charlie wedged himself in the narrow opening of the door. He planted both feet, squared his hips, and pushed.

Metal groaned and cracked, and the muscles along Charlie's arms trembled, his cheeks reddening from the effort.

The door opened a few inches, the progress slow, and Charlie doubled down, offering one last push. The metal gave way, and the door opened wide enough to reach the driver.

Charlie unbuckled the driver, who had blood dripping into his eyes from the gash, then grabbed his arm. "Nice and slow now." He pulled the driver out of the wreck, the man's large belly scraping against the steering wheel, and Charlie leaned him up against the car. "How are you feeling?"

"My head," the driver repeated, lifting his hand to touch the wound, but Charlie stopped him.

"It's fine," Charlie said. "Just a cut."

Charlie examined the rest of the driver. He was overweight, his neck wobbly like a turkey neck. He was bald save for a few wisps of hair that sprouted from the very top of his scalp. He wasn't old. Charlie guessed midthirties.

"Just stay put." Charlie reached for his phone, hoping that

it hadn't broken when he fell to the sidewalk, and glanced down both ends of the road. "What the hell is going on?"

Charlie finally retrieved his phone from his pants pocket but discovered the screen was black. He pressed the power button, and still nothing. He frowned and looked back at the driver, who was wobbling from side to side, the blood drying to his face and shimmering beneath the sunlight.

"Let's get you off the road." Charlie took the guy's hand and led him to a bench near one of the storefronts. He then rushed over to his truck and grabbed a towel from behind his seat.

"Here," Charlie said, placing the towel in the guy's hand.

The driver pressed the rag to his face, smearing the blood before finally removing enough for him to see. He glanced down at his shirt and tie, both stained red. "I can't go to my meeting like this. Shit!"

Charlie shook his head. "I don't think anyone is going to that meeting." He looked at the nearest store. "I'm going to call for help. Just stay put. I'll be right back!"

"Yeah," the driver said, grimacing as he touched the cut on his forehead. "No problem."

Charlie entered a small FedEx office. The lights were shut off, and the patrons inside were staring in confusion at their phones, all of them blank. Just like his.

Charlie weaved around the frustrated customers and headed for the cashier behind the counter, whose jaw hung slack as he stared through the storefront window at the chaos outside.

"Hey," Charlie said, waving his hand in front of the employee's face.

The cashier pulled back, surprised by Charlie's intrusion. "Can I help you?"

"I need to use your phone," Charlie answered.

"It's dead, man." The cashier gestured to the store. "Everything's shut down." He tapped on the register, which did nothing, to help prove his point. "Sorry, pal."

Charlie spun around and found the rest of the customers staring out the window like the cashier, their bodies silhouetted by the sunlight.

"Hey, are you all right?" the cashier asked.

"What?" Charlie saw that the employee was staring at his hands. Charlie glanced down and found the driver's wet blood on his fingers. He rubbed his fingertips together and felt the hotness and slickness of the blood and smelled metallic scent, and his stomach lurched.

No power. No phones. Drivers losing control of their vehicles. It was more than just a power outage. It was as though the world had stopped spinning.

Charlie stepped back outside. The crowd along the sidewalks had grown, and people were gawking at the wrecks that dotted the road. He looked at the driver he'd left on the bench, and the man was moaning in discomfort.

"Hey," Charlie said, kneeling at the man's side. "How are you holding up?"

The man tilted his head to the side, his tone deadpan. "Like I got in a car wreck."

Charlie smirked. "The phones are down, but we need to get that cut on your head looked at. Can you walk?"

"How far?" the man asked.

Charlie gestured to the south. "Seattle General is about five blocks away. Probably a ten or fifteen-minute walk." He looked back at the big guy, who was now staring down the road in the same direction, dreading the trip on foot. "Think you can make it?"

"Do I have a choice?" he asked, grumbling.

Charlie stood and extended his hand. "Come on. I'll help you."

The man regarded Charlie's hand then finally grabbed it so he could help him off the bench, and slung his arm around Charlie's shoulder as he wobbled, unsteady on his legs.

"What's your name?" Charlie asked as the pair started their slow limp down the sidewalk.

"Mel," he answered. "Short for Melvin." He then turned a sharp eye at Charlie. "But only my mother gets to call me Melvin."

"I'm Charlie. Everybody just calls me Charlie."

Mel rolled his eyes at the attempted humor and used his free hand to stem the blood flow from his gash.

People shouted at one another about who was at fault. People with confused expressions and slack jaws stared up at the dark stoplights. Desperate hands gripped dead phones.

The longer they walked, the more people stepped outside, crowding the streets, gazing out over the wrecks. Confusion spread through the thickening crowds like wildfire, though reactions varied.

Arguments were shouted between strangers over the wreckage of vehicles, concern flitted between friends over their disabled phones, and the steady hands of parents wavered as they attempted to calm their children's fears. And the fears only grew worse with size of the crowds.

Twice, Charlie was shouldered by men and women running past them. Their paths were directionless. It was motion without purpose, and every time someone in the crowd started to run, two more joined them.

Uncertainty spread through the street like a virus, a herd mentality taking control, and it wasn't long until Charlie and Mel were fighting against the panic, their pace too slow for the growing desperation of the mob.

"Gah! Hey, watch it!" Mel looked behind him at a kid who wasn't looking and had slammed into Mel's big body. "What the hell has gotten into people?"

Charlie's senses heightened, his mouth going dry as he shook his head. "I don't know."

"Got to be something with electronics," Mel said.

"What do you mean?"

"I tried using my phone while you were calling the cops. And before I crashed, the power steering and car engine shut off. All of that stuff is run by computers, right?" Mel peeled away the towel and examined the fresh blood then grimaced. "Christ, it just won't stop bleeding."

But while Mel was focused on his wound, Charlie lingered on those words. There was definitely a connection. But he knew of nothing capable of turning every piece of technology off like a flip of a light switch.

"Gah! Hang on." Mel shuffled to a stop, forcing Charlie to halt as well. His breathing was labored, and his cheeks had gone pale. "I just need a minute." He gestured to a nearby windowsill, and Charlie helped him over.

Mel collapsed back against the window, his head thumping against the tinted glass, and he shut his eyes. "How much farther?"

Charlie placed his hands on his hips, and the growing crowds forced him close to the window with Mel. They'd barely made it a block. "It's close."

"My head just won't stop throbbing." Mel leaned forward, but Charlie pushed him back to an upright position.

"Just keep pressure on it," Charlie said. "You might have a concussion."

"Christ, I think I'm going to be sick."

This time, Charlie let Mel hunch forward but kept pressure with the towel over the cut. But while he held Mel, Charlie still couldn't peel his eyes away from the panicked pedestrians.

It was as though everyone had caught the same scent in the air, pushing them toward the edge. The longer he and Mel remained out and exposed like this, the worse Charlie's anxiety grew.

"We should go." Charlie spoke quickly, and his heart

pounded in his chest. He looked down both sides of the street then grabbed Mel's hand and pulled him off the ledge.

"Whoa, man. Take it easy." Mel tried to resist, but he was too weak to fight back. "My head is killing me, my back hurts, I'm tired, and I don't—"

Several quick pops created a forced silence in the crowded streets. Every head turned in unison toward the commotion coming from a few blocks down.

Charlie frowned and squeezed Mel's arm tighter. "Was that…"

Gunshots and screams broke the silence, this time triggering a massive tidal wave of pedestrians into a sprint, clamoring over one another and flooding the streets.

Bodies flew past Charlie and Mel, nearly knocking the pair over as the ripple effect was exacerbated by more people screaming and running, all brought on by more gunshots that grew louder and drew nearer.

"Oh my god," Mel whispered with trembling lips.

But as the tides of chaos heightened, Charlie kept his eyes focused on the cross street two blocks down. It was the source of the flood of people, and while fear gripped Charlie, his curiosity forced him to watch. He needed to see what it was. He needed to see what they were facing.

"Charlie, c'mon!" Mel tugged harder, and Charlie relinquished a step. "What are you doing?"

Charlie looked back toward Mel and saw the fear spread across the man's face, the exposed gash on his forehead, and the sea of bodies flooding past them on the sidewalk. But he turned to face the source of the gunfire just in time to witness the masked men emerging from the street, shooting at anything that moved.

3

Flashes ejected from the rifle muzzles in rhythm with the gunfire. The masked men fired without mercy, without hesitation.

Random members of the fleeing crowd dropped, their bodies flung forward, and they crashed into the pavement and lay motionless as the gunmen advanced down the street, widening their kill zone.

"Charlie!"

Mel's voice broke through the daze of anger and fear that muddled Charlie's senses, and pulled him back to the present.

"C'mon!" Mel tugged at Charlie's arm, and they joined the streams of retreating human targets screaming in a stampede of chaos away from the wolves on the hunt.

Charlie fell into stride with Mel. The big man moved quickly now, the sudden burst of speed and endurance derived from a release of adrenaline.

Charlie turned at the waist, away from the screams, gunfire, gunmen, and death as they progressed down the street. They needed to get off the main road and out of the shooters' path.

18

Charlie skidded to a stop, forcing Mel to stop with him. Bodies slammed against them, and people scrambled to get around the pair, nearly trampling the two of them in the process.

"Where are you going?" Mel asked.

Charlie tugged him down a side street, steering them away from the crowds and their unchoreographed escape, and pushed a reluctant Mel down a dark alley, the tall buildings on either side blocking out the sun.

"Just keep going." Charlie shoved Mel toward the light at the end of their dark tunnel, and just before they reached the end of the alley, Charlie turned back to find the crowds gone.

For a few seconds, it was nothing but empty roads, then another gunshot announced the shooters' presence, and the line of masked men filled the alleyway's narrow view of the street.

One of the masked men pivoted toward the alley and stopped when he locked eyes with Charlie, and time slowed.

The gunman aimed at Charlie, who spun around and pushed Mel harder and faster toward safety at the alley's end.

Sunlight was only steps away when gunshots thundered, and Charlie turned a sharp right out of the alley and onto the street, his speed and momentum sending both himself and Mel to the concrete.

Both men landed violently on the hot pavement, but Charlie scrambled to his feet first and pushed himself back up against the wall of the building near the alley's exit.

"What the fuck, man?" Mel wallowed on the pavement like a walrus, flopping over from his belly to his back with a strained effort.

Charlie peered around the corner, only a sliver of his skull viewable from the other end of the alley, but the army of monsters in masks had already passed, the thunderous gunshots and terrified screams fading farther north.

Charlie pulled away from the end of the alley and kept his

back flush up against the wall. He shut his eyes, his heart pounding in his chest, and the heat from the sun overwhelming his senses.

"Hey!"

Charlie opened his eyes and looked at the hand on his shoulder then at Mel, whose face was covered in a fresh coat of crimson.

"You all right?" Mel wiped at his face, but his sleeves were already so covered with blood he only succeeded in spreading the blood instead of ridding himself of it.

"Yeah," Charlie said, pushing himself off the wall. "I'm fine."

Charlie stepped out into the street, his attention focused south. More car wrecks dotted the roads, but the streets were less crowded, at least by the living.

Bodies were sprawled out over the pavement, facedown, faceup, blood seeping from their clothes and running over the roads like a river.

"I can't see shit, man," Mel said, and he started to cry, smearing blood over his eyes. "I just want to go home."

"You need stitches," Charlie said. "The hospital's close. C'mon." Charlie grabbed Mel's arm and placed it back over his shoulders, then he led him down the sidewalk.

Charlie kept his attention everywhere but on Mel. He didn't want them to get snuck up on, and the last thing he needed was another surprise.

But while the gunfire died down and the screams faded, Charlie noticed other sounds replacing death and fear. The crash of glass.

The large window of a retail store full of clothes on the opposite side of the street was suddenly smashed with a rock. Dozens of hands reached for anything they could grab, then the people sprinted away with their loot.

Two men wearing saggy gym pants, sneakers, and tank tops quickly flung open the passenger-side door of an E-

Class Mercedes and grabbed whatever they could carry then sprinted to the next car, where they repeated the process.

More glass shattered along the storefronts that Charlie and Mel passed, and the number of bodies scurrying from shattered windows to shattered windows multiplied.

Clothes, bags, jewelry, electronics, food, liquor—anything and everything that could be carried in arms and hands was trucked away from the stores as fast as the people carrying them could flee.

"Christ, people are losing their minds," Mel said, breathing heavily and struggling to keep pace with Charlie's strides.

The number of people joining the looting multiplied. It was like an airborne disease, the symptoms violently contagious and infecting anyone that was close.

"Just keep your head down and keep moving." Charlie kept hold of Mel, forcing the big man past his point of failure. But as they neared the hospital, the crowds thickened, the world devolving into violence and chaos.

Charlie veered into the road, weaving around the never-ending line of car wrecks that clogged the streets.

"Help!"

Charlie frowned. "Did you hear that?" He glanced left and right, still propping Mel up.

"I can't hear, I can't see, and I can't fucking walk anymore, man." Mel sagged lower, and Charlie struggled to keep him upright.

"Please! Help!"

Charlie's ears perked up again. The cry for aid had been faint and muffled. "There." He spun another few degrees and looked past a bad wreck where a cluster of men scurried past with their arms crammed full of clothes.

Charlie shuffled Mel over to a nearby SUV and propped him up against it, ignoring the big man's questions as he darted over to the source of the cries for help.

"My daughter! Please, help!"

Charlie followed the woman's voice to a car turned over on its roof. The doors were mangled, and half of the roof had caved in. Charlie dropped to his hands and knees, peered into the shattered driver's side window, and found a bloodied woman in a business suit.

She cried when she saw Charlie. "My daughter." Her voice wavered, and she tried to turn around, but the wreck had pinned her in. "I can't see her." Her lips quivered. "I can't hear her."

"Just hang on, ma'am." Charlie investigated the back seat and saw a pair of legs lying motionless on the ceiling.

The rear driver's side door was completely sealed off, so Charlie hurried around to the other side and slammed into a young man sprinting in the opposite direction.

"Fuck you, man!" the kid shouted but didn't stop running, and Charlie didn't bother to stop, already on his hands and knees on the other side.

And when Charlie ducked his head low enough to get a view of the back seat,.

"*Is she okay?*" the mother asked, shouting from the front seat.

"She's fine." Charlie couldn't fit his whole body inside the small sliver of space, and his arm scraped against some pieces of glass, drawing blood, but he managed to grab hold of the girl's calf and pulled.

Charlie made sure to move the girl slowly and carefully, unsure of the type of injuries that she might have but knowing that he couldn't call an ambulance to help him figure it out.

Carefully cradling the girl in his arms, Charlie was able to find a pulse, and he noticed that she was still breathing.

He ducked his head back into the rear seats. "I think she's okay, just knocked out." Charlie carefully laid the girl down.

"I'm going to come in and get you, all right? Just hang on." And then he caught a whiff of something.

The mother coughed, as smoke billowed from the engine.

Charlie ducked his head into the car again, his movements harried. "Just hang on!" He would have jumped in to get her out right away, but he didn't want to risk the girl by putting her in danger even more.

Charlie scooped the little girl into his arms then sprinted back to where he'd left Mel and breathed relief when he found him in the same spot. He put the girl down next to him before he could even react then ran away.

"What the hell are you doing?" Mel asked.

Charlie turned around at the waist. "Just watch her!"

A crowd gathered as the plume of smoke rising from the car's belly worsened, but despite the screams for help coming from inside the overturned vehicle, nobody moved.

Charlie skidded to his knees again and reached his arm through the smoke, which was already starting to sting his eyes as he groped for the woman's shoulder. "Grab onto my arm!"

Fingernails dug into his skin, and Charlie pulled. The first hard yank was met with resistance and a harsh yelp from the woman.

Charlie released her arm and poked his head inside, sweating from the heat of the fire. The smoke thickened, and struggling for breath and with his eyes burning, he looked up at the seat and found the woman's legs were pinned beneath the dash.

Charlie pressed his hand against it and pushed, and the plastic cracked but refused to budge. He let go and hacked, struggling to breathe. He backed out and noticed the flames spreading closer.

The sight of the fire nearly made him flee, unsure if he would be able to pull her out in time and unsure if it would matter. But just when he was about to turn, a man appeared on his left, shouting something at him.

"What?" Charlie asked, coughing through his reply.

"We'll pull her out together!" he shouted then dropped to a knee.

The pair reached underneath at the same time, and Charlie stopped his new partner before they made the same mistake that he did.

"She's pinned, so we need to wiggle her free from the dash! Push up as hard as you can." He turned to the woman. "Ma'am, you need to pull your legs out as quick as you can. Okay?"

The smoke grew so thick that she couldn't speak, save for coughing, but she managed to nod.

"One, two, three, pull!" Charlie pressed up with all of his might, and the stranger did the same. This time, the dash buckled, and the woman was freed. "Get her out!"

The pair grabbed her arms, tugging her out of the driver's seat just as the flames engulfed the rest of the car.

Smoke steamed off of the woman's pants and shirt, and she wallowed from side to side, hacking and coughing so hard that she vomited. Charlie looked away from the woman and toward the fire, which had completely consumed the vehicle.

"My daughter." The woman grabbed Charlie's arm, pulling his attention back toward her.

"She's okay," Charlie replied, helping the woman pick herself up off of the pavement. "But we need to get you two to a hospital. You probably have smoke-inhalation damage." He took her over to her daughter, who had thankfully woken up, and the world around the mother dissolved as she cried and hugged her child.

Charlie smiled as he stood next to Mel, who stared at the fire now blazing from the car.

"You're one crazy son of a bitch, you know that?" Mel asked then laughed as he slapped Charlie's shoulder.

But while the good deed filled Charlie with pride, the continuing dissolve of society around him returned the itch to keep moving. "C'mon. We still need to get to the hospital."

"Oh good," Mel said, taking Charlie's arm. "I was beginning to think you'd forgotten about me."

he remainder of the journey to the hospital revealed the widespread nature of whatever event had taken place. A cloud of chaos and confusion had descended upon the city, and while Charlie had hoped the hospital would act as a place of order and stability, those aspirations were dashed when they finally arrived.

Charlie stopped at the edge of the parking lot, which was filled with people hunched over their engines, scratching their heads. People rushed in and out of the open doors, the entrance of the hospital dark and ominous compared to the sunny afternoon.

"What are you doing?" Mel asked, slurring his words due to exhaustion. "We're here. Let's go."

"I don't know if…" Charlie shook his head. "Never mind." He looked behind him, checking on the mother carrying her little girl. "How are you holding up?"

The little girl rested her head on her mother's shoulder. Both of their faces were covered with soot. The mother's business clothes were torn and ragged, and she coughed as she nodded. "We're okay." She adjusted her little girl in her arms and kissed her forehead.

Charlie weaved around the cars in the lot, overhearing the conversations of the baffled motorists.

"It won't even turn over." A man was hunched over his sedan, fingers black with engine grease. "It was fine this morning."

A pair of women two spots over had the hood of their van propped up. "The battery was just changed, so it can't be that."

Her friend flapped her arms at her sides. "Terry, I need to get to work."

"Well, what do you want me to do, Charlotte?" She fished her phone out of her pocket and waved it in front of her friend's face. "Car doesn't work. Phone doesn't work. We're out of luck!"

Charlie hastened his pace. While the parking lot hadn't boiled over into the same chaos as the rest of the city, Charlie felt it simmering, and he didn't want to be there for when those first bubbles spilled over.

Following a flood of other people inside, Charlie blinked a few times so his eyes adjusted to the fading light.

Nurses hurried between patients and doctors, each of them pulled in a hundred different directions. Questions and screams funneled together, the noise inside the ER of the hospital akin to a stadium roar.

All of the lights in the ceiling were out, and from what Charlie could see, the hospital had no power.

"That can't be possible," Charlie said. "They have generators, backup power supplies. What the hell is going on?"

"Jesus," Mel said. "I should have just gone home."

Charlie spotted an open chair and walked Mel over and gently set him down in it. The mother and daughter followed.

"I'll get someone to look at you," Charlie said.

"Thank you," the mother said.

"I'm not going anywhere." Mel groaned then collapsed into a puddle of exhaustion in his seat.

Charlie weaved around the nurses and patients, his eyes locked onto the back of a nurse who happened to be the only one behind the counter.

"Excuse me, ma'am. I have a—"

"Patricia!" The nurse spun around, looking right over Charlie's left shoulder, and extended a folder that almost scraped Charlie's cheek. "Room twenty-five!"

"Thanks!" A hand reached past Charlie's face.

"Ma'am, if I can just—"

"Mark!" The nurse looked to her left, her hair blocking out most of her profile. "Two-two-seven needs their insulin within the next hour."

"Thanks, Liz!"

The nurse finally spun around from the filing cabinets, and heaved a stack of papers onto the desk where Charlie waited. She worked her fingers along the edges of the files, separating them quickly and efficiently.

"Miss, I need—"

"Just one minute, sir." Liz held up her finger, her attention still focused on the paperwork.

Without thinking, Charlie reached over the desk and snatched the nurse's wrist.

Liz snapped her head up, flinging the bangs off of her forehead, while a few strands framed a pretty, tanned face with green eyes that flashed anger.

"I have a man who needs stitches, and a little girl and her mother who need to be checked for smoke-inhalation damage." Charlie spoke calmly, but it did little to calm the nurse's anger.

Liz yanked her arm back hard, and Charlie relinquished his grip. "You always touch things that don't belong to you?" She returned to her paperwork, quickly flipping through the file.

A doctor appeared from behind the side entrance to the station, never fully coming to a stop as he passed through. "Liz, I need—"

"Five hundred milligrams, and make sure you have someone keep an eye on her. She tends to seize up after a treatment!"

Charlie continued to lean over the counter. "I know you're busy, but there are people that need to be looked at out here."

"And there are people who are already here that are dying because we don't have any power and our systems are down —shit." Liz quickly tossed aside a file and pressed her hands to her temples as she shook her head.

Another doctor appeared from the opposite direction. "Liz, you find it?"

"No, it must be in the basement."

"All right, I'll send someone else down."

Liz peeled her face away from the folders, defeated.

"Please," Charlie said. "It'll only take a minute."

Liz regarded Charlie, her hands on her hips, then nodded. "I'll find a room."

"Thank you," Charlie said.

With the amount of people running around, Charlie was doubtful that they'd be able to find any open space, but Liz secured a bed with a curtain and an additional nurse to help with Mel's stiches while Liz gave the mother and daughter oxygen.

"What is it?" the little girl asked, scooting closer to her mother for protection.

Liz held up the oxygen mask that was attached to the large green tank that she'd dragged into the room. She moved closer so the little girl could see. "It's not as scary as it looks. See?" She placed the mask over her face and took a deep breath. She smiled when she pulled it away and held it up for the little girl to try. "It'll help make you feel better. Get rid of that cough."

"It's okay, sweetheart," the mother said, urging her daughter to try.

The little girl grabbed the mask from the nurse's hands and held it for a little while before she hesitantly placed it against her face then giggled after her first breath. "It's like wind."

"Yup," Liz said. "And that wind will blow that smoke right out of your lungs." She winked up at the mother as the girl did as she was told, and the more the little girl inhaled, the more she laughed.

"Might want to pass some of that over here," Mel said. "I could use some of the good stuff."

"Sir, I need you to stay still." The nurse repositioned Mel's head to face forward.

"Sorry," Mel said.

Charlie stood in the doorway to the room, and Liz walked over to him as the mother and daughter passed the oxygen back and forth. "Thank you."

"It's my job," Liz said.

"I know, but still."

Liz nodded, picking at the dirt beneath her nails. "And what about you? Any injuries to report?"

"I'm fine," Charlie said.

"So, what, you're one of those tough guys that don't like doctors?"

Charlie laughed, shaking his head. "No, ma'am."

Liz wrinkled her nose. "Ugh. Don't call me ma'am. Makes me feel like my mother." She poked her head around Charlie and out into the hallway, which remained busy. "You know, ten minutes after the power went out and everyone's phones went down, I saw some nurses and doctors just walk out and leave." She shook her head then turned to Charlie. "Not everyone would have done what you did for these people."

The little girl on the cot giggled, fogging up the oxygen mask. Charlie smiled. "People want to do the right thing. They just get scared sometimes."

"Yeah, well, I should get back to work." Liz placed her hand on Charlie's arm and gave it a squeeze. "Don't forget to take some of that oxygen—"

Charlie frowned as he watched the confusion spread over Liz's face as she glanced down the hall.

"What in the world?" Liz asked.

Charlie spun around and saw hospital staff and patients flood through the double doors and out of the ER, glancing behind them on their sprint.

Gunfire thundered, accentuated by the narrow hallway, and whatever semblance of order remained in the hospital dissolved into hysteria and chaos.

People burst from their rooms, clogging the hallway as they joined the massive retreat from danger.

Charlie quickly moved toward the cot and grabbed the mother and daughter off the bed. "We need to go!"

Mel, Liz, and the second nurse followed Charlie out of the room and into the hallway, ducking and shuddering with every gunshot.

People randomly hurried into rooms, seeking shelter, but Charlie didn't stop moving forward and prevented anyone from his group doing the same. Hiding was a mistake.

"This way!" Liz appeared on Charlie's left, motioning for people to follow her, and Charlie steered his people in the same direction.

Before Charlie turned the corner at the end of the hallway, he glanced behind himself one last time.

The masked men left a wake of bloodied bodies as they marched down the hall, opening doors and firing into the dark rooms.

Fear propelled everyone forward, and among the people in the crowd, Charlie saw a familiar face.

"Mel!"

The big man ran as fast as his body allowed, the fresh stitches on his forehead barely holding together as he fell farther and farther behind in the pack. He stretched out his arms as if Charlie could reach him from the fifty feet that still separated them. "Wait!"

Gunfire forced several more bodies to the floor, arms flailing forward and blood welling up from the wounds on their backs.

Tears broke loose from Mel's eyes and streaked down his face, cutting through the dried blood as he struggled for breath.

"Run, Mel!" Charlie lingered by the corner in the hallway, the terrorists closing in, moving quickly as they pumped bullets into the backs of innocent victims, while the cowards smiled behind the anonymity of their masks.

Angered by the sight of so much needless carnage and death, Charlie took a step toward them, and if it weren't for the hand that pulled him back, he would have been killed.

"We need to go!" Liz shouted, struggling to keep Charlie from rushing into the madness.

But Mel was close. Charlie stretched out his hand and grabbed the big man then yanked him around the corner, evading the lead that collided with the wall.

"Go!" Charlie shoved Mel forward, following Liz through the hallways, and with every additional turn down the winding hospital halls, Charlie lost his sense of direction. He was in Liz's hands now.

"Not much farther," Liz said breathlessly as they sprinted through the halls. She periodically pounded on doors and shouted to anyone they passed to find the nearest exit. Some people listened. Most didn't.

The noise of gunfire faded the farther they ran, but even with the distance between them and the killers, no one stopped running until they reached the emergency-exit doors.

Sunlight flooded the dark hallways, and streams of people poured out of the hospital building, sprinting away from the danger inside.

Charlie slowed to a stop, mostly because Mel and the others had stopped to rest.

"*What the hell is going on?*" Mel screamed, and his cheeks flushed bright red. "They're just... *killing people!*" He ran his stubby fingers over the thin wisps of hair on his scalp. He spun in circles, hyperventilating.

"Mel," Charlie said, his arms passively stretched out as he slowly approached. "Calm down. You need to keep it together."

Mel smacked Charlie's hand away. "We're already dead, man! We're already fucking dead!" He shuddered and turned away.

Charlie looked at the rest of the group and found similar expressions of distress. They needed to get out of the city. All of them.

"He's right," Charlie said.

"Wh-What do you mean, 'he's right'?" The mother with the little girl held her daughter tighter and shook her head. "You really think we're going to die?"

Charlie hesitated, choosing his words carefully. He didn't want to provide additional panic, but he didn't want to give them false hope. "The city is falling apart, and I haven't seen any person in authority since the bullets started flying. No cops, no ambulances, nothing."

"So what are we supposed to do?" Liz asked. "Where do we go?"

"Out of the city," Charlie answered. "Stay with any friends or family and get away from populated areas." He pointed to the hospital and the city beyond. "Those monsters are attracted to densely populated areas."

"Our apartment is in the city!" the mother cried. "We don't have anywhere else to go." The daughter whimpered, and the mother held her tighter. "Shh. It's okay, baby. I didn't mean to yell."

Whispers of fear and doubt circled the group, and Charlie wasn't sure if his next move was the smartest, but he did know that it was the right thing to do.

"I have an orchard," Charlie said, his voice cutting through the group's chatter and once again turning their attention toward him. "It's east of the city. My family owns it, and we have plenty of space. Anyone is welcome to come with me if you don't have anywhere else to go."

"Really?" the mother whispered. "Oh, thank you!" She rushed over and flung her arms around Charlie's neck. "Thank you so much."

The mother slid off of him, and Charlie smirked, hoping that the heat flushing his cheeks wasn't too obvious, then looked at Mel and Liz.

"My hotel was in the center of downtown, and home for me is back in Chicago, so..." Mel shrugged. "Guess I'm with you, cowboy."

Charlie turned to Liz, whose attention was on the hospital. He walked over to her. "What about you?"

Liz paused, taking a moment, but eventually nodded. "Yeah. Okay. Getting out of the city sounds like the best option."

Charlie nodded then led the group away from the hospital. "We better get going. It's a full day's walk on foot."

"Great." Mel exhaled, shaking his head. "Because I haven't done enough of that today."

5

*S*eattle's skyline grew smaller behind them, and the landscape transformed from skyscrapers and tall office buildings to family homes in local neighborhoods.

But the blackout that plagued the streets of downtown Seattle had spread to the suburbs. Charlie watched as neighbors convened with one another, everyone unable to answer the question that raced through their minds.

How did this happen?

Their group caught a few stares from the locals as they passed, but the area was far less violent and dangerous than the city's epicenter, at least for the moment.

Mel checked another car parked in the middle of the street. "Dammit." He slammed the door shut and stomped his feet, his arms like noodles at his sides. "How can none of them work?" He rolled his head around on his neck then fell back in line next to Sarah and Adelyn, the mother and daughter, both of whom hadn't done a tenth of the complaining that Mel had.

"How much farther?" Mel asked.

"I told you it was a hike," Charlie answered.

"You'd think that we were dragging him along by force."

Liz kept her voice low and walked on Charlie's left. She'd kept pace with him since the hospital.

"Didn't strike me as the outdoorsman type when I found him." Charlie smirked, and Liz mirrored the expression.

"I didn't get a chance to thank you for this," Liz said, keeping her eyes on the ground. "So thank you." She looked up at him. "I don't know many people that would take a bunch of strangers to their home. Especially not under these circumstances."

"Couldn't just leave you guys with nowhere to go," Charlie said matter-of-factly.

Liz laughed. "Yes. You could have."

Charlie watched the dimples appear on both sides of Liz's cheeks. He liked her smile. "Are you from around here?"

"No," Liz answered. "I moved here from San Diego three months ago. Seattle General had an opening for a management position for nurses, and I threw my hat in the ring."

"So you got it?" Charlie asked.

"No, but they liked me enough to offer me more money than my old job, so I packed up and moved." Liz shrugged and twisted her fingers, which Charlie noticed were devoid of any rings. "There wasn't anything keeping me in the city besides the job."

"I visited San Diego once. It was nice. Did you grow up there?"

"No. I was an army brat, so we moved around a lot. I've lived in Germany, Tennessee, Texas, Florida, California, and Hawaii."

"I've never left the west coast."

"It must have been nice to grow up in one place," Liz said, a glint of nostalgia in her voice. "I always wondered what it would have been like to set roots down."

"I couldn't imagine living anywhere else." Charlie shut his eyes, feeling the warmth of the sun on his back. "It's nothing but greenery that stretches to the horizon."

"It'll be nice to get out of the city." Liz inhaled as though she hadn't breathed in days and brushed her bangs out of her eyes. "I could use a change of scenery."

Mel appeared between them, huffing labored breaths. "So, what do you guys think is happening? I mean, it must be terrorists, right? Probably Muslims or something?"

"And you could tell that from the masks over their faces?" Liz asked.

"Yeah, maybe I could." Mel rolled his eyes. "It's no secret who hates this country."

"Let's not jump to conclusions," Charlie said.

Sarah positioned herself on Charlie's right. Adelyn was asleep on her shoulder. "Do you think that those gunmen had anything to do with the power going off?"

"And how the hell did they manage to turn my phone off?" Mel fished out his mobile and pressed the button repeatedly. "Some kind of internet virus or something?"

"When do you think everything will turn back on?" Sarah asked. "And why haven't we seen the military or—"

Charlie stopped, holding both hands in the air. "I have just as many questions as you do, but right now, what's important is staying mobile and staying alive. We'll have plenty of time to figure this out later, but right now, let's just keep our heads cool and focus on what's in front of us. Getting out of harm's way. Okay?"

Sarah nodded quickly. "Yeah."

Mel grumbled, shoving his phone back into his pocket. "Whatever."

Charlie started walking again, and silence fell over the group. He knew they were just scared. And the more fear you pumped into somebody's heart, the wilder they were going to become. It was simple survival instincts, and whenever people started harvesting those primal thoughts, shit was bound to hit the fan.

The sun sank lower in the sky, and conversation died down.

When they made it out of the second neighborhood, Charlie decided it was a good time to stop and check the pulse of the group. And to make sure that Mel didn't pass out from exertion.

"How's everyone doing?" Charlie asked.

"I can't... move." Mel collapsed onto the hood of a parked BMW, and his shirt pulled up and exposing his white, hairy belly.

"I'm thirsty, Mommy," Adelyn said.

Sarah pushed the sweaty bangs off her daughter's forehead and softly shushed her. "It's okay, sweetheart. We'll be done soon."

Charlie glanced around and spotted a convenience store down the road. "Does anyone have any cash?"

"I do," Mel answered, only lifting one arm from the Beemer's hood.

"Left my purse back at the hospital," Liz said.

Charlie gathered the cash, and with his own money, they had close to one hundred bucks. "I'll get us some water and snacks. Any special requests?"

"Fritos," Mel said. "And a Mountain Dew, and a Starbucks double-shot espresso!"

With the orders filled, Charlie headed over to the convenience store while the group parked under the shade of a nearby tree.

Charlie approached the convenience store warily. The bars along the windows of the building were a sign of the neighborhood. The parking lot was empty, but the door was propped open.

Charlie paused at the entrance, peering inside. "Hello?"

No answer.

Hesitant, Charlie crossed the dark threshold.

The inside of the store was just as empty as the parking

lot, and minimal sunlight shone through the tinted windows, exposing the looted aisles. Charlie stared at the cash in his hand, feeling foolish for even bringing it.

"Right." He stuffed the money back into his pocket and picked up a basket by the door.

Charlie headed for the coolers first. Although the power was out, the drinks inside were still cool. He piled as many bottles of water as he could into one basket then perused the snack aisle, where he loaded up on jerky, nuts, and the limited fruit selection, which consisted mainly of bananas.

With the basket overflowing, Charlie was about to head back toward the front to grab another when he heard a voice.

"Please." It was a frightened whisper, breathless.

"Quiet!"

The order was followed by a harsh slap, and Charlie set the basket down. He crept along the aisle, searching for anything heavy that he could use as a weapon, but the snacks and household items didn't provide many options.

A bottle of bleach caught his eye, and he removed it from the shelf, unscrewing the top as he inched closer toward the whimpering moans.

"I already told you there's no money in the—"

Another slap, this one harder than the first. The whimpers worsened.

The noises led Charlie toward the back corner of the store. He paused at the end of the aisle, his shoulder against the wall. He turned slowly and saw an elderly woman by a safe, blood on her lip.

"Open it!" The gunman pointed a revolver at the old woman, anger and greed in his eyes, and the old woman started to turn the dial on the safe. Then Charlie made his move.

He flung the bleach into the man's face, charging at him in the same motion. But the chemicals hit the gunman's eyes before he could aim the pistol at Charlie, who tackled him to the floor.

Both men tumbled over one another, Charlie landing on top and pinning the robber down.

"Jesus fucking Christ, it burns!" The robber clawed at his eyes but kept them shut, his skin reddening from irritation.

Charlie flipped him over on his stomach and clamped his hands together. "Don't move!" He quickly searched the floor for the gun but found it in the weathered hands of the old woman, who had it aimed at the thug who had tried to rob her.

"Easy," Charlie said. "Lord knows he deserves it, but you don't want something like this on your conscience."

The old woman grimaced. "He needs a lesson in manners." She adjusted her trembling grip on the pistol.

"You're right." Charlie stood, arms still outstretched as he moved closer to the woman and the gun. "But right now, what we need to do is make sure that you don't do anything..." Charlie placed his hand on the gun, and the woman looked at him. "You'll regret."

With both of Charlie's hands on the pistol, the old woman finally let go, and he breathed a sigh of relief.

"I can't see!" The robber squirmed on the floor, crying and thrashing. "I can't fucking see!"

Charlie grabbed the kid by the scruff of his neck and picked him up off the floor. "You're lucky to be breathing. Now move!" He shoved the guy forward, gun in hand, and marched him out the front.

Charlie wasn't sure what he'd do, but he knew that he couldn't kill him.

Outside, Charlie shoved the guy down the street, and he stumbled blindly, still clawing at his eyes.

"What the fuck am I supposed to do now?" he shouted, spinning around, unable to find Charlie.

"You run and be thankful that you still have your life." But when the man didn't move, Charlie raised the pistol and fired a shot into the air. The man sprinted off, tripping over himself, and Charlie watched him until he disappeared down an alleyway.

Charlie stared down at the gun then flipped the safety on before tucking the weapon into his belt. He spun around and found the old woman staring in the direction that the robber had fled. "Are you all right?"

The old woman nodded then wiped the blood from the corner of her mouth. The name tag on her vest read Arlene. "Thank you."

"You're welcome." Charlie turned back to his group of people, all of them staring at him in confusion over what they'd just witnessed. He turned back to Arlene. "Think you'd like to join us?"

"Sure."

Arlene followed Charlie to the group, and introductions were made, but while they talked, Charlie glanced back down the road, and he wondered if he had made the right decision.

6

Like the rest of them, Arlene was now an orphan of the city. She had a small condo in a high rise on the outskirts, but after hearing the horror stories they'd told of what they'd encountered, she decided to join them on their journey toward the orchard.

And while the group kept most of their attention ahead of them, Charlie couldn't keep his eyes in one direction for very long.

"Hey." Liz appeared at Charlie's side, tapping his elbow with her nearly empty water bottle. "You've been awfully quiet. Everything all right?"

Charlie nodded, but his eyes glanced toward Arlene, who was helping Sarah with Adelyn.

Liz noticed his glance. "She was lucky that you were there."

"That's what bothers me," Charlie said.

"Why are you beating yourself up about it?" Liz asked. "She's safe now."

"Is she? Are any of us?" Charlie clenched his jaw before releasing the tension. "Is this what happens to people? Something goes wrong, and we lose our sense of decency?"

Liz turned and looked back at Arlene and hugged herself, rubbing her arms. "Fear makes people do crazy stuff."

"No," Charlie said, shaking his head. "What I saw in that man's eyes wasn't fear. It was lack of consequences. He didn't think he'd get caught."

The pistol was still in Charlie's waistband, and he became more aware of its presence.

"I should have let her shoot him."

"Hey." Liz stepped in front of Charlie, stopping him and blocking his path. "Stopping someone from killing isn't a bad thing."

Charlie shook his head. "I'm not sure about that anymore." He stepped around Liz and wondered how long they could stay alive in a world with no rules or laws.

Liz caught up to him. "You don't get to decide who lives and who dies, Charlie. You're not some judge, jury, and executioner."

The words caught Charlie off guard, and he remained frozen in place as Liz walked on, joining the others up ahead.

Charlie watched them walk a while then lowered his gaze to the outline of the pistol beneath his shirt.

"Hey! Farm boy!"

Charlie looked ahead and found Mel waving his arms at a crossroads up ahead.

"Where to now?"

The road had reached a dead end, forcing the group either left or right. He looked left at the steep incline of the mountain terrain then to the left, where the road took them through a neighborhood.

"Don't tell me we're lost," Mel said. "Jesus Christ." He spun around in a circle then shook his head. "The one time I come to Seattle, and it decides to implode on itself."

"Charlie?" Liz asked.

Charlie kept his voice down. "Left is quicker, but the terrain's more difficult."

Mel scoffed and walked away, flinging his empty water bottle into the woods. "Great. It's either longer or harder."

"We need to get to the farm before nightfall," Charlie said. "Left will get us there quicker."

"That gets my vote," Arlene said.

"Whatever you think is best, Charlie," Sarah said.

"I don't care," Mel replied.

The group looked to Charlie to make the final decision, and he nodded. "Left it is, then."

With the sun fading behind them, the bottles of water were passed around, and their stash disappeared. Knowing that they were losing daylight, Charlie hastened his pace, but not everyone was able to keep up.

Liz jogged up to him. "Hey, Mel and Arlene need a break."

"We need to make up time. We can't stop every time someone needs a breather." Charlie kept his tone short and didn't relinquish the pace he'd set.

"I understand that, but we've been walking all day, and not everyone can keep up," Liz said, stiffening her tone.

"Well, then they can find another place to stay."

"Hey!" Liz grabbed Charlie's arm and whipped him around, forcing him to stop. "You were the one who asked them to come along. You were the one who told them that they had a safe place to stay."

"Yeah, well, I didn't realize I'd be the only one doing the heavy lifting." Charlie flung Liz's arm off of him and restarted his trek, but she wouldn't let him go.

She blocked his path. "What the hell is wrong with you?"

"Open your eyes, Liz!" Charlie yelled, and she backed up. "You really think all of this is going to get fixed in a couple of days?"

Liz continued her retreat, and the rest of the group caught up.

Charlie laughed, his resolve cracking under the weight of

everyone that had piled onto his back. "What the hell do you think is going to happen a day from now? Or a week? We've been walking all day, and you know what I *haven't* seen aside from robbing and looting and attempted murder? Cops. Military. First responders of any kind. And you want to know why?"

"Charlie, stop it."

"Because they're taking care of their own families and friends!" Charlie shouted, his volume quieting everyone in the group, even Mel. "Which is what I should be doing, but no, I had to play the goddamn hero!"

"That's enough." Arlene stepped forward. "You will not talk about us that way, young man. You offered to help, and if we have been a burden, then we will relieve you of that burden."

"Arlene, wait." Liz rushed after her.

Charlie was unable to hear their hushed conversation.

"You really know how to inspire the crew, Captain," Mel said, still catching his breath, his hands on his hips, then plucked the sweaty collar off of his chest.

"Not now, Mel."

Mel leaned forward, his stance aggressive. "You think you're better than us, farm boy? Well, you can take that little country accent all the way to your inbred family!"

It happened quickly, the rage rushing over Charlie and blinding him to his actions. It wasn't until he heard Liz's screaming that he realized he was on top of Mel the big man's face was disfigured.

Charlie looked at his raised fist, which had matching blood dripping from its knuckles. He stared at it for a moment then stood and backed away from Mel as Sarah and Arlene walked over to check on him.

"I'm sorry. I—"

Liz shoved him hard. "What the hell are you doing?"

Charlie looked at his trembling, clenched hands and then

at Mel. He shook his head, his mind spinning and his heart pounding. "I-I don't know."

"Fuck you, man!" Mel stumbled to his feet and shrugged off Sarah and Arlene's help. "I don't need this shit!"

"Mel, wait!" Liz attempted to follow, but Mel refused to slow down. Wherever the big man was going, he was going alone. She spun around and stomped her way over to Charlie then shoved him hard enough to push him back.

"Are you happy now?" Liz shoved him again, harder than the first time, before he even had a chance to answer. "Manage to get all of that off your chest? Huh?" She shoved him hard again.

"It's not worth it, honey." Arlene came up behind Liz and gently but firmly pulled her back. "C'mon. Let's go."

The words hurt, but it was the look in their eyes that stung worse. He had just joined the ranks of the same bastards that they were trying to escape.

Long after the group had left, Charlie stood there, staring at the blood on his hands, still in shock at the way he'd snapped.

After all of that talk about society collapsing and no law and order and people doing whatever they wanted, he had sunk into the same cesspool as the rest, and by the time he finally looked up, Liz and the rest of them were gone.

Slowly, Charlie turned toward home.

His pace was slow, and he struggled to keep his face forward. He continued to steal glances behind him.

But every time he did, he forced himself back around, reminding himself that he barely knew those people. He had a family to get back to, a home waiting for him.

Charlie dwelled on that thought for a moment, wondering what his parents would think about his actions. He knew what his mother would say, that he should turn around and apologize until he convinced them to keep going.

But it was his father's voice that frightened him. Harold

Decker was never a man who took handouts, and because of that, he was frugal with giving things away. And despite knowing that, he knew that his father would have knocked him flat on his ass for treating those people the way he had.

Charlie stopped, his boots scuffing against the pavement, and he turned. The road behind him turned through hills and trees, and alone in the quiet of nature, he knew that he'd made a mistake.

He took a single step forward, and his foot landed on the asphalt at the exact same moment the gunshot rang out.

 he sound had traveled far, the gunshot nothing more than a faint pop. And while the first gunshot froze him stiff, the second triggered him into action. He sprinted forward, legs churning up the pavement, and the decline offered the aid of gravity.

A million different scenarios raced through his mind, and they multiplied and grew more horrific the farther he ran.

He listened for more gunfire, but the world had quieted to the smack of his boots on the ground and the labored breaths from his exertion. By the time he reached the crossroads where they departed, Charlie had to slow down. He glanced toward Seattle, knowing that they probably wouldn't have gone back to the city. No matter how upset they were, he didn't believe they'd head back into a warzone.

With the west not an option, Charlie squinted to the south at the neighborhood they had walked away from when they turned left at the crossroad.

Twilight had descended, making it hard to see, and he headed toward the neighborhood, checking down the sides of houses, searching for Liz or Arlene.

Unlike the other neighborhoods they passed, Charlie saw

no one on the porches outside their homes, and most of the cars in the driveways looked as though they hadn't been used in weeks.

Most of the homes were run-down, and foreclosure signs were plastered on several doors.

Charlie jogged three more blocks, glancing down each street but staying on the main road. Every street he passed, hope appeared then vanished when he found them empty.

They hadn't been separated for that long, and the deeper Charlie moved into the neighborhood without finding them, the more anxious he grew.

Finally, he stopped.

Charlie spun in circles, no longer sure of where to go or what to do. He wanted to scream out their names, but giving away his position to whoever had fired the weapon wouldn't help anyone.

Exhausted, he took a seat on the stoop of a nearby house. The windows were boarded up, and a stack of foreclosure papers had piled up on the porch.

Charlie looked at the neighboring houses on either side and saw similar notices posted on the doors. Half the neighborhood was like that.

He stared at the red foreclosure lettering, remembering all of the notices he had stacked back home at the orchard. What did all of those pieces of paper mean now? Maybe this had turned into a blessing. Of all the ways to keep the orchard, this phenomenon hadn't even been on his list.

Charlie stood, and a nasty pop echoed from his knees. He shook out the pain that followed. His body had finally grown irritated from the day's activities. And while a lifetime of work on the farm had left him in good shape, the day's extraordinary events had put an unusual amount of wear and tear on his body.

Charlie limped the first few steps but then fell back into an easy stride by the time he passed the second house. To the west, the sun had completely dipped below the horizon, and twilight had ended.

Voices caught his attention ahead, and Charlie slowed to listen.

Laughter. It was faint, but it was laughter. He walked toward it, keeping quiet, and moved off the center of the road and onto the sidewalk then the yards of houses, so he had better cover.

The best-case scenario was finding Liz and the rest of them at a friend's house, laughing and eating. He'd apologize, and everything would be fine.

But the closer he moved and the louder the laughter grew, he knew that it wasn't his people. The laughter was wild and laced with anger.

Charlie approached the house at the corner of the street slowly then craned his head around and crouched low.

He saw three men five houses down the street. Each of them was seated in a folding chair on the front lawn, beers in their hands.

And while their conversation leaned on the side of rambunctious, Charlie didn't see anything that made him believe that they were dangerous. That was until one of them stepped outside.

"Yo! You go and take care of that fat dude?"

"Bitch, he's facedown in the ditch. He ain't getting up." The man who answered lifted his drink to his lips, laughing.

The man to his left, shirtless and with a large tribal tattoo on his shoulder, mocked his friend. "Yeah, you're a real tough guy, huh?" He took a drink. "A fat guy and an old lady. Just a killer!"

Laughter burst from the group, and "the killer" flipped his middle finger at the group.

"Whatever," Killer said. "At least we got those girls, right?"

"Yeah, if we can get close enough without them scratching our eyes out."

"Well, you boys just don't know how to treat a lady right." Killer set the drink down then clapped his hands together. "Dr. Love is coming through!"

The rage that coursed through Charlie's veins was so violent that he couldn't stop shaking on his retreat from the corner. And the more they laughed, the tighter he squeezed his fists.

He reached for the pistol in his waistband, and while his first instinct was to turn the corner and charge down the street, firing off as many rounds as he could before those bastards had a chance to realize what was happening, he shoved that instinct back down to the pit of his stomach.

Gun still in his hand, Charlie took off back down the street he'd just come up in search of Mel and Arlene.

Charlie retraced his steps as quickly as he could, but he couldn't remember any ditches that he'd seen along the way. He imagined that the group had run into those guys somewhere along the neighborhood, so they had to be close.

But it wasn't until Charlie reached the beginnings of the run-down housing district that he saw the ditches running along either side of the road. He rushed over and found that they were deep, a steady stream of water and trash trickling through them, and he checked the right side first.

Charlie looked left then right but found nothing down in the dirty water as far as he could see. He rushed to the opposite side and checked again. The first look to his left, he saw nothing, and when he quickly turned his head in the other direction, he thought he saw nothing again. But he stopped himself and strained his eyes at a pair of lumps that had started blocking trash and water.

"Oh my god." He sprinted down the road, his eyes never coming off of Mel and Arlene's backs. Both of them were lying facedown in the ditch.

Never breaking stride on his run, Charlie dropped the

five feet into the depths of the ditch, splashing the warm, dirty water up his pant legs, and dropped to a knee.

"Arlene," Charlie whispered her name, his voice catching in his throat, as he carefully flipped her over, and he immediately jumped back.

Arlene's head wobbled, and the bones along her broken neck ground and cracked against one another as her dead eyes fell on him.

Charlie sat there for a minute, just staring at Arlene's blank expression. Growing up on a farm, he had seen life and death, but he'd never had that experience with a person. At least not this up close and personal. The harsh snap of Arlene's neck represented violence Charlie had never seen before.

Slowly, Charlie pulled his eyes away from Arlene and looked at Mel. He made sure that he didn't touch or step on any part of Arlene, but when he got closer to him, he already saw that he was dead.

The back of Mel's head was bloody, as if he'd been hit with something before he was thrown down here. The blood on his skull hadn't dried because of the water, and there was a light tinge of red that continually washed downstream.

But just to make sure, Charlie pressed his fingers against Mel's neck. No pulse.

He looked at the gun in his hand then turned to Arlene and Mel one last time. "I should have stopped you. I should never have lost my temper. I should never have let you even come this way." A tear squeezed through the anger and rolled down his cheek, and he quickly wiped it away.

It was the only one Charlie let fall, then he quickly climbed the dirt-packed wall of the ditch and returned to the road. His wet jeans clung to his legs like a second skin.

He sprinted back down the street and refused to let Liz and Sarah and little Adelyn succumb to the same fate. He was going to get them out of that house, no matter what.

8

*D*ripping with sweat and stinking of the ditch, Charlie skidded to a stop at the end of the same street corner where he'd seen the men in the yard, which now held nothing but empty chairs.

He retreated behind the house on the corner and stepped into the overgrown grass of its backyard. Four fences separated Charlie from the house where the girls were being held, and he moved quickly over the first two, which were both chain-link and only three or four feet tall.

The third fence was wood and taller than Charlie, but it had a side door.

The fourth fence was similar to the third, but this one only had an exit to the front of the house.

He scanned the fence, looking for cracks that offered him a view of what he'd encounter on the other side. The backyard was empty.

Before that changed, Charlie tucked the revolver in his pocket then pulled himself up and over the fence and landed hard on the balls of his feet, then he kept low on his sprint toward the back of the house.

He paused near the back door, reaching for the revolver

and catching his breath. He slowly reached for the doorknob but found it locked.

"Shit."

Carefully and quietly, Charlie crawled around toward the far side of the house and undid the latch on the gate's exit from the backyard. He opened the gate only a crack and peeked at the other side.

He found the side yard clear of people, and he saw a potential entrance point. A basement window at ground level was cracked open. It looked big enough for Charlie to squeeze through, and he hurried over to check.

As he moved closer, he found the window smaller than he originally envisioned. But he opened it all the way, he was able to square his shoulders up and stick his head inside to get a better view.

It was dark, but after he blinked a few times, he saw the basement was crammed with boxes and old furniture.

Charlie backed out then shimmied into the window feet first, his back to the ground. His wet jeans scraped against the concrete sides, and when his legs were inside, his back started to pinch due to the harsh angle. He shimmied faster, trying to rid himself of the pain in his back, but he became stuck when he tried to pass his shoulders through.

He stuck his arms straight back, narrowing his shoulders as much as possible, and gravity did the rest of the work, pulling him down until he landed awkwardly on concrete.

Charlie winced, a harsh burn running down his right side, and when he pressed his palm against the pain, he felt something wet. When he examined his palm in the darkness and wiggled his finger, he was able to make out the dark crimson of blood.

A piece of jagged metal had cut him down his left side, from love handle to armpit, and while the slash only broke the first layer of skin, the length of the scrape had produced a significant amount of blood.

"Leave her alone!"

Charlie snapped his head up toward the ceiling, the rush of adrenaline overpowering the pain. He followed the screams and laughter toward the staircase that led up to the first floor of the house.

The door at the top of the stairs was cracked open, and Charlie tightened his grip on the pistol at his side. He counted four men that had been in the front yard, but there could be more inside.

Another scream. More laughter. Muffled cries.

He planted his foot on the first step of the staircase, testing it for noise. When all his weight was applied and no sound was made, he moved to the second, then the third, keeping a steady pace all the way to the top, where he paused.

Sweating and shaking, Charlie shut his eyes and tried to calm his unsteady hand. He needed to keep his wits about him if he was going to make it out of this alive. He inhaled deeply, held it, then exhaled slowly.

His muscles relaxed, and his heart rate lowered. It was now or never.

Charlie opened the door all the way, not bothering to check inside first and hoping to catch the bastards off guard. The revolver was exposed first, his arm outstretched, and then he stepped into the narrow hallway.

It was empty.

Doors lined both sides, and more laughter echoed from up front, but the cries for help were coming from inside the room down the hall and on the left.

Charlie paused at the door and positioned his ear close to the wood. The whispers inside were unintelligible, and he gently placed his hand on the knob. He turned it slowly, wincing with every little noise triggered by his movement.

When he couldn't turn it any more, Charlie leaned his weight against the door. His heart hammered in his chest so hard that he was convinced everyone in the house heard him.

But when the door finally opened and no one had come barreling out of the room to attack him or yelled from the living room, Charlie realized that it was all in his head, and all of those concerns erased when he saw Sarah on her back on the bed, her t-shirt off, but still wearing her bra and jeans, and a man towering over her, his back to Charlie.

"You want to keep your daughter safe?" the killer asked. "Then you do what I tell you to." He unbuckled his pants.

Charlie seized the moment and charged forward and cracked the pistol on the back of the man's head then tackled him onto the bed and wrapped him in a choke hold.

The killer's cheeks turned purple, and he bucked his hips, but Charlie squeezed tighter, knowing that if the man cried for help, they were all dead.

The killer gurgled, but then, slowly, he started to fade. The fight went out of him, and he passed out.

Exhausted, Charlie let him go then turned to Sarah, who was shaking on the bed, unable to form any coherent words.

"Sarah." Charlie barely spoke above a whisper and tried to get her off the bed. "We need to go. Where are Adelyn and Liz?"

"The living room." Sarah finally spit the words out, and she started to cry. "They have her there. Please, Charlie. You have to get her."

Charlie hushed her and nodded. "I will. But I need to get you out. Come on." He led Sarah by the hand into the hallway. He brought her toward the basement door then motioned her to go down. "There's a window. Crawl out and wait for me there. If you hear anything, then I want you to run down the street, east, as far as you can, and I'll catch up."

"But my daughter—"

"I will bring her to you," Charlie said. "I promise."

Reluctant, Sarah descended the stairs, and Charlie turned his attention to the living room at the end of the hall.

Charlie moved quickly, unsure how long the killer in the room would be passed out. He didn't know what he'd do, but he understood the time crunch.

"Hey, Ronnie! You need some help in there, man?"

The voice drew closer, and when the man rounded the corner of the hallway, drink in hand and smiling, Charlie raised the gun and fired.

Blood and liquor stained the carpet as the man and his cup crashed to the floor. With his cover blown, Charlie charged forward and was in the living room before the rest of the gang could react save for tossing their hands in the air.

"Don't move!" He shifted his aim between clusters of the men. He counted six then saw Liz and Adelyn tucked in the corner, Liz crying as she quickly picked the girl up. "Liz, Sarah's outside. Go now."

With everyone else distracted by Charlie and his weapon, Liz scurried out the front door, leaving him alone with the six men in the confined space.

"Everyone get facedown on the floor, hands behind your heads," Charlie said, his voice shaking due to the adrenaline pumping through his veins.

The group remained seated, their expressions ranging from fear to contempt, but none of them moved.

"Do it now!" Still no one moved, and Charlie began to sweat.

"You going to shoot us, boy?" One man stood slowly, his eyes locked on Charlie. "I don't even think you've got enough bullets in there for everyone, so what happens when you run out?"

Charlie grimaced, finger inching over the trigger. Six men, four bullets—the math wouldn't end well, not for him at least.

"I don't want any more trouble," Charlie said, his mouth dry. He retreated toward the hallway and the basement door.

"I think you're just talk." The leader snarled, taking a single step forward. "I don't think you've got the balls to pull that trigger on all of us."

"I said don't move!" Charlie screamed, whipping the pistol in a forward motion, but the threat went unheeded.

And as the first man stood, the others slowly rose, feeding into their leader's boldness, and it wasn't long before they were all on their feet. Charlie was out of options.

He fired. The bullet screamed from the barrel of the revolver and dropped the leader.

The rest of the men charged, and Charlie pivoted his aim and fired again on his retreat toward the basement door. The bullets bought him some time, but he needed to move quickly.

He headed for the basement door and slammed it shut on the way down, leaping the stairs two, three at a time. When he hit the bottom, he spun around and fired back up at the basement door, forcing the men to stop, and then beelined it for the window, which was still open.

Charlie jumped, thrusting his head and shoulders through the window, and he clawed frantically at the grass as he pulled himself from the basement.

He rolled out just as the men reached the bottom, and he sprinted toward the road. He didn't look back when his feet hit the pavement, but he was two houses down when the gunshots fired behind him.

Ahead, he saw Sarah and Liz with Adelyn. He screamed at them to keep running, and at the last second, Charlie turned his head around and watched three men with pistols chasing after him.

He fired one last shot then didn't look back, and he didn't stop running.

9

"*J*ust keep going!" Charlie pushed them forward, continuing their sprint away from the neighborhood. He looked back twice as he steered what remained of their group to safety, and finally, after seven blocks, the chase ended, but Charlie didn't let up their pace until Sarah couldn't move anymore.

"I just need to stop," she said, clutching Adelyn. "I'm sorry." She collapsed with her daughter on the curb, holding her tight.

Charlie and Liz remained standing, and he grabbed her arm. "You all right?"

Liz nodded quickly, her movement jerky and uncoordinated. She was still in shock. "I'm fine." She looked around, making sure they were alone.

A million words funneled through his mind but vanished by the time they reached his tongue. In his silence, Charlie kept staring down at the pistol still gripped in his hand. He'd held it for so long that it was as if the weapon were glued to his hand. It had become an extension of him.

The world had changed, and it seemed that he had unknowingly changed with it. But how much further would he have to go? How much more would he have to give up in order to survive? What else was it going to cost?

"We should really keep moving," Charlie said.

Sarah nodded then stood.

"Do you need help holding her?" Liz asked.

"No," Sarah answered. "I'm fine."

With their pace slowed to a brisk walk, they faded deeper into the night, as silent as the world around them.

It didn't take long for the trio's pace to transform to a crawl, and with the night in full swing and them out of the neighborhood, Charlie knew they needed to camp somewhere.

Twice, Charlie caught Liz dozing off, and she jerked awake, quickly looking to see if he noticed.

Charlie glanced around. Their surroundings were nothing more than woods, night already upon them. "We'll stop at the next building we find."

Liz and Sarah nodded in agreement, and after another half a mile, they came across an abandoned gas station that looked as if it had been shut down for years.

"That'll work," Charlie said.

The pumps were rusted, and the overhang that had once protected the customers from the weather had collapsed.

The glass along the front windows had grown dirty and cloudy with time, but the door was unlocked, and Charlie stepped inside first to make sure the coast was clear. The last thing he wanted to do was have to use that weapon again. His hand started to shake at just the thought of it, and he was glad that Liz wasn't there to see it.

Aside from some broken glass, rusted car parts, and some overgrowth sneaking in through the cracks of the building, it was empty.

Charlie stepped out and found Liz shivering near one of the pumps and staring down at her feet while Sarah rubbed Adelyn's back. "It's clear."

Sarah entered first and took a corner of the room, then Liz stumbled over, swaying from side to side, as she continued to hug herself.

Charlie entered last, shutting the door behind him. "Probably best to stay up here near the cash register and out of the garage. I don't think I can get those bay doors shut."

But when Charlie looked at Sarah and Adelyn, the mother and daughter were already passed out in the corner.

Charlie sat down, and Liz joined him by the door.

"Mel tried to stop them," Liz said, keeping her voice low and staring at a patch of concrete. "I didn't think anything of it at first, just some boys talking tough. And then one of them pulled a gun. I don't know why, but Mel just wouldn't stop shouting at them. It was like he snapped." Her lips quivered. "They forced him on his knees." A tear fell, but she didn't wipe it away. It hung from her jawline for a few seconds then crashed to the ground. "When they went for Sarah and Adelyn, Arlene was the first to try to stop them, but they were too big. Too strong."

Charlie wished that she would stop. He didn't need to hear how they had died. It was hard enough finding them the way he had on the side of the road. "Liz, you don't—"

"They wanted to leave Adelyn, but I grabbed her," Liz said. "Sarah wouldn't stop screaming. She pounded her fists against them as hard as she could, but they just laughed." She frowned then cleared the phlegm growing thick in her throat.

She scrunched up her face again as if she were going to cry but then reached for Charlie's hand and squeezed tight.

Charlie stared into the frightened and wide eyes looking up at him, and he reciprocated the touch. She was warm, and the heat transferred across his chest to the opposite arm.

"I shouldn't have let you guys leave," Charlie said.

"It wasn't your fault," Liz said.

"It was."

Liz moved closer to Charlie and held his face. "No. It wasn't."

But the reassurances didn't erase what he'd done or what he'd failed to do.

"Hey," Liz said, but Charlie refused to look at her and forced her to pull his face toward her. "We chose to leave you. Got it? And despite all of that, despite all of the weight we put on you to get us out of trouble, you still came back to look for us even when we didn't want you to. I can count the number of men in this city that would have done the same thing on one hand." She held up her palm, all five digits lengthened and spread wide. She had beautiful hands.

"I don't know if the blood will wash off," Charlie said.

Liz nodded. "I was working my residency down in San Diego the first time I saw someone die on the table." She leaned her head back against the wall, the supple flesh of her throat moving with every word. "Car wreck. Hit and run. He was a homeless guy. Couldn't tell his age other than he was old. Had a beard down to his chest, all matted with blood. He was in bad shape before the car even hit him, and his abdomen had swelled from the internal bleeding." She lifted her hands as if she were holding a pretend needle. "When the doctor instructed me to relieve the pressure, I couldn't keep my hand still. He yanked the needle out of my hand and shoved me aside, and I just stood there. The other nurses seemed fine, unfazed by the fact that this guy was quickly dying on the table." She frowned. "He was all skin and bones too. Gaunt and hollowed cheeks. Probably hadn't eaten in days. But just before the doctor was getting the paddles ready to bring him back, he woke up, gasping and choking for breath. Every cough sprayed blood over him and anyone that was close, including me." She touched her chest as if she could still feel the splatter. "But he turned his head as he struggled for air, and he looked at me. I'm not sure how long we locked eyes, but it felt like an eternity. And while the rest of his body had wasted away either by drugs or alcohol or time, his eyes were still bright and fresh, like he was seeing for the first time." She paused, reflecting on the moment, then shook her head quickly. "He didn't make it through surgery. Shattered spleen and ruptured kidneys, and at least six vertebras were snapped in his lower back. Even if he survived, he would have been confined to a wheelchair for the rest of his life."

"Do you ever get used to it?" Charlie asked.

"I did," Liz answered. "I never thought I would, and I swore to myself that I wouldn't go numb like all the older nurses and doctors, but it happened." She shrugged. "I guess it's the only way for our minds to cope after trauma."

"I couldn't do what you do, Liz." Charlie shook his head. "Not in a million years."

Liz smiled, mild sadness in her eyes. "Yeah, you could."

But Charlie only shook his head. "I'm not the person you think I am. I just try to do the right thing."

"You're exactly what I think you are."

Silence shrouded over them again. The pair remained close, the heat in their bodies rising, each a breath away from giving in, then Sarah stirred in the corner, pulling them out of the moment.

"You should get some rest," Charlie said.

Liz nodded and lay down.

10

*I*t didn't take long for Liz to pass out, and Charlie's gaze switched between her and the view of the road. He brushed the bangs off her forehead but then quickly withdrew his hand.

Watching Liz sleep only made the longing for Charlie to catch his own shut-eye worse. But a sense of duty flooded through him, and he felt the need to protect her. After all, it was what he'd been doing since they left the hospital. And if he was being honest with himself, that was the way he liked it.

It was a refreshing change of pace from some of the women he'd dated back in college. He understood the need for independence, but after a lifetime of watching his parents interact with one another, he also understood that having a partner meant being able to pass the baton.

If you were tired, they stayed up. If they got sick, then you brought them soup. And when a patch of cows wandered from the neighbor's pasture at two o'clock in the morning—which, even for a farmer, was early—through the fence that you had begged them to fix for the past eight months and woke up your pregnant wife, who could barely sleep anyway, you got your ass out of bed and got those cows away from your house.

Charlie smiled, remembering that last story was one of his dad's favorites. He recited it any chance there was an opportunity, because that night, Jon Berkin—the neighbor who owned the cows—landed face-first in a pile of cow shit. His father said that karma did exist and it was a cruel son of a bitch.

The point was that you couldn't be strong all of the time, and that was okay. People were fallible, and they were going to screw up eventually. Charlie had done it enough to know the truth in that statement.

The longer Charlie sat by the door, the more he started to doze off. Twice, he caught himself snapping back awake, and he had to fight the impulse to wake Liz up to have her be on watch. He just needed something to keep his mind busy.

He opened the revolver's chamber and counted the bullets. Two.

He plucked them out of the chamber and rolled them around in his hand, repeating the process of unloading and reloading until that became like counting sheep and only worsened his desire for sleep.

Unsure of the time, Charlie finally rested his head against the wall near the door, at least keeping his body in front of the only entrance, and finally dozed off.

While he was sure he went to sleep instantly, Charlie had no idea how long he was out before he was woken by a mechanical rumble.

He reached for the gun, his heart rate spiked, and his vision still blurred with sleep. Once he realized there was no one there, he looked at Liz, who was still asleep nearby, and Sarah and Adelyn in the corner.

The rumbling outside grew louder, and Charlie frowned when he saw the pair of headlights coming down the road. It was a car.

Charlie stood, hand still on the grip of the revolver, and peered through the clouded glass.

The headlights grew larger, and the tension in his body tightened the closer they moved, and just when it grew so tight that he couldn't stop shaking, one of the headlights from the vehicle highlighted a man walking nearby, wearing camouflage.

Charlie squinted, double-checking to ensure that he hadn't imagined it. Then he saw the other men marching along the road. They were all dressed in camouflage, all of them wielding rifles.

Soldiers. American soldiers.

Laughter escaped Charlie's lips, and he opened the door and rushed out to the convoy, that fear and tension immediately transforming into joy and excitement. "Hey!" Charlie shouted, waving his hands and turning the convoy's attention toward him, along with their guns.

"Don't move!"

"Get down!"

"Drop the weapon!"

The orders were barked with a violence that forced Charlie to freeze. He held up his hands, and the vehicle's lights pivoted in his direction to blind him.

The soldiers repeated their orders, and Charlie placed the revolver on the ground then lay down on the pavement just as he was instructed to do, putting his hands behind his head.

"I'm not one of the bad guys," Charlie said when he felt hands pat down his back and legs.

"All clear, Lieutenant."

The concrete was rough against Charlie's cheek and still hot from baking in the sun all day. When he lifted his face off the ground, he caught an eyeful of the AR-15 barrel aimed at his head. "I just wanted to ask for some help."

"Help?" The voice preceded the thump of boots, then a man crouched down to Charlie's level. "Son, you need a lot more than that." He laughed and shook his head. "If this boy is part of the terrorist group, then I'm Paul McCartney. Get 'im up."

The orders were swiftly followed, and Charlie was peeled off of the concrete and lifted upright. He blinked and found the man who'd spoken to him, the one the soldiers had addressed as Lieutenant.

"You out here by yourself?" the lieutenant asked.

"No, sir."

"And where is the rest of your party, and how many are there?"

"Three. One of them is a little girl. They're asleep in the station." Charlie gestured back to the run-down building where they'd sought shelter.

"Sully, go check it out." The lieutenant stepped closer as Sully jogged over to the building, then examined the revolver that his soldier had confiscated. "This your weapon?"

"No," Charlie answered.

"You find some trouble on the road?"

"Yes, sir," Charlie said. "Lost a couple people along the way."

The lieutenant nodded. "A lot of that going on." He looked past Charlie's left and saw Sully bringing Liz, Sarah, and Adelyn out of the building.

"Three, just like he said, Lieutenant," Sully said.

"Everyone all right?" the lieutenant asked.

"I'm fine," Liz said, her voice cracking as she was brought over to the rest of the circle, then looked at Charlie. "You?"

Charlie nodded.

"You can let him go, boys," the lieutenant said.

The two pairs of hands restraining Charlie relinquished their hold, and he rotated his shoulders, glad to have his mobility back. He rubbed his wrists as Liz inched closer to his side, and the soldiers returned to their ranks, leaving only him, Liz, Sarah and Adelyn, and the lieutenant.

"What's going on?" Charlie asked.

"We were attacked," the lieutenant answered.

"By who?" Liz asked.

"The last intel we received before our communications went down was activity off of the Korean peninsula. The Chinese had maneuvered a considerable amount of their forces toward the North Korean border. We think that it might have something to do with that, but we're not sure."

"Mommy, I'm still tired," Adelyn said, rubbing her eyes.

"I know, baby," Sarah replied.

"Why is the power out?" Charlie asked. "No cars, no phones—how could they have done that?"

"We think we suffered an EMP strike," the lieutenant answered then explained when he saw the confusion on their faces. "Electromagnetic pulse. It's a device that fries any electrical circuits within the radius of its blast."

"But there was no explosion," Charlie replied.

"It's a pulse sent through the air. It's soundless and not dangerous to humans," the lieutenant said but then turned around toward the city. "Until the aftermath, that is."

"So nothing works?" Liz asked.

"Anything with a computer chip is down for the count. And considering that pretty much everything we rely on has one built inside, you can see why there was so much destruction."

"Oh my god." Charlie stepped back and turned away from the lieutenant. He looked back at the decrepit and broken-down gas station, and it was as if he were looking into the future now instead of the past. "How big?" He turned back around to face the lieutenant. "How far widespread was the blast?"

The lieutenant hesitated, and it was the only preparation that Charlie had for what came out of the lieutenant's mouth next. "It's the whole country."

"Jesus," Liz said, the word escaping in a breathless whisper.

"We managed to find some old Humvees at the base that still worked, and our CO told us to head into Seattle and secure the city. He figured that's where most of the damage would be done."

"We barely made it out of there alive," Liz said.

Adelyn grew fussy, and Sarah struggled to calm her down.

"Ma'am, you can have her lie down in the Humvee if you want," the lieutenant said.

"Thank you." Sarah smiled then walked over, escorted by one of the soldiers.

"Well, we'd offer you a ride, but I don't think you'd enjoy the destination. But—" He spun around and grabbed a bottle of water out of one of his men's packs. "We'll get you loaded up with some rations."

Charlie was just about to protest and tell the lieutenant that he was already close to home when the first gunshot erupted in the night.

"Get down!" The lieutenant immediately shoved both Charlie and Liz toward the protection of the Humvee. And while he screamed a few other orders at them, Charlie couldn't hear it over the roar of the gunfire.

He and Liz ducked low next to the aged armored vehicle, both of them covering their heads with their hands. With his back against the door, Charlie felt the vibrations from bullets, and when he looked toward the front of the vehicle, he found the headlights highlighting two soldiers that had already fallen in the firefight. And Sarah.

It took a moment for Charlie to realize that Adelyn was still on the ground, next to her mother, screaming her head off, but he scrambled to the front and yanked the little girl out of harm's way.

Liz grabbed hold of Charlie's shoulder, turned him

around, and screamed in his face, though he could barely hear her. "We need to go!"

Charlie nodded in response, keeping Adelyn close to his chest while the little girl screamed for her mother.

He poked his head over the doors and peered through the windows on their retreat, and he saw the flashes of the gun muzzles in the fight. "There's too many." Charlie pulled Liz back from the rear of the Humvee, shaking his head. "We won't make it!"

"Well, we can't just sit here!" she said, ducking from a bullet ricochet off the Humvee's roof.

"We don't have a choice!" he said, screaming. "There's too much random fire!"

A few more minutes into the firefight, the lieutenant returned behind the cover of the Humvee, breathless and reloading his rifle, accompanied by only three of his men.

"I'm out, Lieutenant!"

The lieutenant tossed a magazine past Liz and Charlie's faces, and the solider quickly reloaded.

"You guys need to make a run for it," the lieutenant said. "I don't know how many out there, but we won't be able to hold them off for much longer."

Charlie and Liz hesitated, and more bullets thudded against the Humvee. Liz grabbed hold of Charlie's hand, and he reached for the revolver in his belt.

"We'll give you some cover fire," the lieutenant said, positioning himself at the back of the Humvee. "On three!"

Adelyn screamed, and Liz's grip on Charlie's hand tightened.

"One!"

Charlie tensed.

"Two!"

More gunfire made Charlie shudder, and he twitched forward in a false start.

"Three!"

With one hand holding Adelyn and the other holding Liz's, he didn't let go of either as they sprinted toward the forest.

"This way!" Charlie steered them to the left of the old gas station, the cacophony of gunfire still tearing apart the night air, and when they veered in that direction, Charlie felt Liz stumble, yanking his arm back.

She didn't yelp or scream, and Charlie simply tugged at her arm, pulling her forward.

"C'mon! Don't stop!" He knew that they were both tired, but they needed to keep going. They needed to escape.

Pavement gave way to grass and rocks, and Charlie led them into the woods and to the safety of the thick cover of trees, which also slowed their pace.

"Charlie," Liz said, her voice faint.

"C'mon. We need to keep going." He felt her hand go limp in his, but he clamped down harder. "Just keep moving!" But he only made it a few more steps before Liz finally collapsed, dragging Charlie and Adelyn down with him.

On the ground, Adelyn squirmed out of Charlie's reach, and he spun around and found Liz on her side. He slid down the rocky terrain and dropped by her side.

"What's wrong?" But then his eyes traveled down to her hand, which was clamped down over the right side of her abdomen.

"Just go," Liz said, and she started to cry.

Charlie reached for Liz's hand and slowly peeled it off to reveal the blood blotching her shirt.

he scent of blood was thick in the air. Every breath that Charlie inhaled was heavy with the metallic heat that had splashed over Liz's stomach and onto his hands, which he studied with horrific fascination. Even with the glow of the moonlight and stars overhead, it was hard to see the blood in the dark. But he could feel it, and he could smell it, and when he rolled his fingertips together—

Gunfire pivoted Charlie's attention to the south. The flesh around his eyes twitched, and it wasn't until the second round of rapid gunshots that he ended his paralysis. He turned back to Liz, who wouldn't stop shaking and gasping for breath. He grabbed hold of her hand, the blood slick and warm against both of their palms.

Charlie quickly pressed her hand back over the wound, keeping his own hand over hers, and applied pressure. "You're going to be okay."

Liz winced, and her body started to go into shock. "I don't… think…"

"Tell me what I need to do." Charlie's voice danced between excited and nervous. She was a nurse. She could just give him instructions. "Tell me how I can help you."

Liz shut her eyes, and even under the moonlight, she looked extremely pale. "Keep pressure." She opened her eyes and stared at Charlie, and he saw blood forming at the corner of her mouth. "I won't make it without a doctor."

"There's a doctor near the orchard. He's a vet, but he'll be able to help."

"I can't walk that far."

"We're not going to walk." Charlie reached for her other hand and placed it firmly over hers.

He rushed over and found Adelyn still crying in the woods. He picked her up, trying to soothe her but failing, then placed her next to Liz. "I'll be back."

"Hur-ry..." Liz choked out the word.

He squeezed one final time then released her hand and turned quickly in the dirt and leaves of the forest. Every gunshot that thundered on the road below pounded through his chest. The heavy drum of war hastened his pace, and he weaved through the trees, careful of the steep decline of the hillside.

Soil and loose rocks gave way, and Charlie slid a few feet before catching himself on a nearby tree trunk. He straightened, checked his footing, then returned to his descent, leaving behind his bloody handprint in the darkness.

Through the dense brush and trees, Charlie saw the back of the abandoned gas station where the soldiers had found them. Closer to the fighting, Charlie heard shouts echoing during the lulls in gunfire, coming from both sides, though he couldn't understand any of them.

He left a trail of blood as he gently ran his hand over the rear wall of the gas station on his path toward the road. He slowed as he neared the corner, carefully craning his head around to get a better look.

The Humvee was positioned at the intersection of perpendicular roads that traveled in front of the gas station.

He turned back toward the woods where he'd left Liz and Adelyn. He didn't have time to waste.

Charlie scanned the area one last time, still unable to see the enemy firing from cover, and sprinted for the Humvee.

He was only aware of his steps, his breaths, and the gunfire on his sprint. Bullets zipped past and collided with the rusted pumps and metal garage doors of the station. On the run, Charlie forgot to grab the weapons from the soldiers and focused only on the man leaned up against the Humvee, reloading a magazine into his rifle.

Charlie slammed against the Humvee doors, the pain numbed by the adrenaline caused by the bullets vibrating against the other side of the armored military vehicle.

Beads of sweat covered the last soldier's face, and Charlie gawked at him, the rush of battle and the fear of death so intense that he had forgotten why he'd come here in the first place.

It wasn't until the soldier grabbed Charlie by the collar, pulled him close enough to smell the stink of his breath, and screamed, that he realized it was the lieutenant.

"Grab one of the guns!" The lieutenant shoved Charlie off him then positioned himself near the Humvee's tailgate, having to move aside another of his fallen comrades to be in a position where he could return fire.

Charlie watched the lieutenant's body vibrate from the recoil of the rifle then spun around to where the second pair of soldiers lay in the road. His side scraped against the rough metal doors, and he half crouched, half crawled toward the Humvee's front bumper.

At least three feet of open space lay between Charlie and the rifle lying across the dead soldier's chest. The lieutenant was the only man left.

Charlie shut his eyes, and the tension in his muscles grew painful as he hesitated before his attempt at the final push. Finally, he lunged, scrambling for the rifle in a mad dash.

The three feet of open road between the rifle and the Humvee exposed him to the enemy, and bullets puffed up bits of asphalt in Charlie's peripheral.

He fumbled his fingers around the rifle's stock and gave it a hard yank as he quickly retreated back toward the safety of the Humvee. But just when Charlie stepped behind the Humvee's engine, a harsh tug yanked him back into the kill zone.

At first, Charlie thought the soldier had woken, but the soldier was still dead, and Charlie saw that the rifle's shoulder strap had caught on the corpse's arm.

The soldier's face was turned away, but Charlie caught the stench of death and blood, which covered the dead man's arms and legs and torso as he hastily removed the snag with one final yank.

More gunfire and bullets shredded the soldier's leg, and Charlie ducked back down and checked the weapon. It took him a moment to find the chamber, but he opened it, cleared the jam, then shut it. He squeezed the weapon tight, as if his strength could crush the steel and carbon in his hands.

"We need to leave!" the lieutenant shouted from the Humvee's tailgate. "We're overrun!"

"The woman I was with! She's been shot! We need a ride east to my farm!"

The soldier squat-walked over the dead and joined Charlie near the front. "Nearest working medical facility is back at the base." He reached for the chests of his fallen comrades and yanked the dog tags from their necks then reached over Charlie and snagged another then shoved them into his pocket.

"She won't make it that far," Charlie said. "My neighbor is a vet, retired, but he'd be able to help." More gunfire, and Charlie ducked.

"Where is she?"

He gestured toward the woods behind the old gas station.

The soldier nodded. "All right. Go grab her." He reached around to his pack and removed a red stick with a clear plastic cap on the end. "Just pop this when you're ready for pickup." He pointed to the left side of the gas station. "Extraction point is there. Got it?"

Charlie gripped the flare in one hand and nodded.

Then the gunfire ended, and a foreign voice emerged from the dark forest on either side of the road.

The soldier smacked Charlie's shoulder. "*Go!*"

Charlie sprinted toward the gas station, sliding his arm through the rifle strap, and kept low, attempting to dodge the bullets. He didn't look back on his run, and he made sure to keep the gas station between himself and the gunfire.

On hands and knees, he climbed his way back up the mountainside. The night made it difficult to see, and a moment of panic gripped him when he couldn't find them again, but luckily, Adelyn was still crying.

Charlie followed the child's voice then dropped to his knees at Liz's side. Adelyn quickly crawled into Charlie's lap, burying her face into his chest. "It's all right, sweetheart." He gave Liz a gentle shake. Her eyes were shut. "Liz, are you still with me? Liz?"

She opened her eyelids only a sliver. "Is Adelyn—"

"She's fine," Charlie said then placed his hand over Liz's wound. "I just need you to hang strong for a few more minutes. All right?"

He knew that he'd have to carry both of them, and he was lucky Liz was small. He positioned Adelyn in one arm then heaved Liz over his shoulder, her arms and head lolling lazily and without control. "Just hang on."

Charlie moved as quickly down the mountain as he could but chose his footing carefully because he knew a tumble down the mountainside this time could be deadly for all of them.

Gunfire then a heavy percussive blast stole Charlie's

attention from his path down the side of the mountain, and he saw a plume of smoke rise off somewhere in the trees.

With his arms burning, and struggling to balance Liz and Adelyn, Charlie veered toward the extraction point.

He waited until he reached the bottom of the hillside before he set Liz and Adelyn down then popped the flare.

Red smoke plumed into the air, then the gunfire was silenced by the roar of the Humvee's engine.

Charlie craned his head around the corner and saw the Humvee reverse. He scooped Adelyn back up in his arms again and waited until the back of the Humvee was past the back of the building.

He opened the back door and set Adelyn inside first as gunfire peppered the Humvee's front.

"C'mon, man. Hurry it up!" The lieutenant was frantic behind the wheel, keeping low behind the dash. The windshield was nearly shattered, making it almost impossible to see anything out of it.

Charlie scooped Liz off the ground and laid her down in the back and jumped in. "Go!" He slammed the back door shut as they sped forward and kept both himself and Adelyn ducked low, keeping one hand on Liz to keep her stable.

"Just keep your head down!" the lieutenant screamed up front.

The gunfire eventually faded, and Charlie poked his head up to check the view from the back window. A pair of men emerged from the thick haze of smoke, firing as they grew smaller in the distance until they vanished.

"How's she doing?" the lieutenant called from up front.

"She's lost a lot of blood." Charlie checked her pulse and found a faint beat. "She's unconscious." He lowered his ear to her nose, where he felt puffs of air from her nostrils. "But she's breathing."

"Just make sure she stays that way," the soldier shouted. "You know CPR?"

"Yeah." Charlie turned around so he could face the soldier.

"There's a first aid kit tucked back there somewhere," the soldier said. "Has some gauze and clotting powder."

Adelyn screamed while Charlie searched the back of the Humvee and found the red first aid box underneath a spare flak jacket. He flipped the top and ripped the bag of the clot powder open. "I just pour this stuff over the wound?"

"That's the idea," the lieutenant answered.

Charlie ripped open Sarah's shirt and wiped away some of the blood. He dumped the powder in, and Liz groaned, her stomach contracting as if it stung.

"How long do I keep on this road?" the lieutenant asked.

"Until the next intersection," Charlie answered, setting aside the bag of powder, then picked up a red-faced Adelyn and gently patted her back. The child was so overwhelmed that she didn't even know why she was crying anymore. "Then you'll take a right. After that, you'll want to stop at the second house on the left."

"Copy!"

Charlie slowly rocked Adelyn back and forth. "It's all right, sweetheart."

"Mommy!" Adelyn cried. "I want Mommy!"

The words cut through Charlie's heart as he remembered Sarah's body lying on the asphalt behind them.

"Shh. It's okay," Charlie said then looked at Liz. "We're okay."

The lieutenant kept his foot on the gas, and with no traffic on the roads and not many roadblocks, they made good time.

The Humvee chewed up the miles quickly, and it wasn't long before they turned down Dr. Wilburn's drive.

The lieutenant was out his door first and hurried around back to help Charlie.

"Take the kid," Charlie said, passing Adelyn over to the soldier.

With his hands finally free, Charlie scooped Liz from the Humvee then rushed toward the front door. "Doc!"

The adrenaline that Charlie had used to push himself this far started to wane, and his grip on Liz slipped.

The door opened, and Dr. Wilburn tied closed his robe, fatigue and confusion spread over his face upon seeing the motley crew on his doorstep. "Charlie? Oh my god. What happened?" He stepped aside without protest as Charlie and the lieutenant entered.

"She was shot," Charlie answered. "The bullet is still inside."

"Let's get her out to the table," Doc said, hurrying toward the back of the house, then he led them outside to the small barn that acted as his operating table for the animals.

Doc quickly laid a blanket down over the steel top and gestured for Charlie to put her down. He checked her pulse then examined the wound. "Clotting powder?"

"Yeah," Charlie answered, breathless.

"Okay." Doc stepped away. "Keep an eye on her while I get my tools. Either of you have any medical experience?"

"No," Charlie answered.

"Limited," the lieutenant replied.

"Sterilize your arms," Doc said. "Hot water and soap."

Doc stepped out, and the lieutenant set a still-crying Adelyn down then washed up in the sink.

Charlie approached the table and reached for Liz's hand. The past twelve hours replayed in his mind like a broken record. He squeezed her hand. "I'm sorry, Liz." He lingered by her side until Doc returned with his tools and his wife, Ellen.

"All right. We'll need to move quickly." Dr. Wilburn set down the tools. "Ellen, can you take the little one for us?"

His wife was a short woman. Her hair was done up in a perm, dyed brown, though there were streaks of white starting to show at the roots. "Of course." She scooped the girl up off the floor with practiced ease and went out of the room.

"Charlie, what's your blood type?" Doc asked, unraveling his tools.

"Um, O-negative," he answered.

Doc gestured to the lieutenant, who was drying his hands. "Can you draw blood?"

"Yeah."

"Needle and bags are in that drawer," Doc said. "Make sure you grab some gloves."

Charlie sat down and let the lieutenant work, but his eyes were focused on the limited view he had of Liz. And as the needle pressed into his vein, Doc made his first incision to retrieve the bullet from Liz's gut.

12

---

*D*awn broke on the horizon, and the early-morning sunlight pierced through Doc's front living room window. Charlie had fallen asleep while sitting on the couch, the sunlight from the window behind him silhouetting his features. He twitched in his sleep, his dreams reliving the previous day in Seattle.

He saw Mel and Arlene in the ditch, the pair tossed aside like garbage. He saw the men he killed in the house when he rescued Liz, Sarah, and Adelyn, but in his nightmare, the body count was much higher. And finally, he saw Sarah covered in blood, illuminated by the bright headlights of the Humvee. She looked at him, crying.

"Take care of her," Sarah said. "Don't let her die."

And suddenly, Adelyn was in Charlie's arms, and they were both covered in her mother's blood—

"Charlie?"

He jerked awake, his breathing accelerated and sweat beading on his forehead. He blinked and straightened up on the couch, wiping the sleep from his eyes until Dr. Wilburn's figure materialized in front of him. "Doc." He cleared his throat. "How is she?" Then panic struck Charlie, and he stood, his legs wobbling, as he frowned. "Is Liz all right?"

Doc raised his hands. "I just checked on her, and her vitals are fine." Dark circles were under his eyes. He sighed. "It will take some time before she's fully recovered, but everything looks good so far. But." He held up a finger. "We're in uncharted territory here. I don't have the proper tools to check for other signs of internal damage she may have sustained from the injury. I may have missed something."

"Right," Charlie said, nodding. He took a breath then looked around the living room. It was warm. "What about Adelyn?"

"She's asleep with Ellen," Doc answered, smiling.

"Where's Liz?"

Doc stepped aside. "Bedroom. Down the hall on the left."

"Thanks." Charlie stepped past him.

"And Charlie."

Charlie turned.

"I need to know what's happening out there." Doc gestured out the window, but Charlie knew he wasn't referencing his front yard. "We haven't had power since yesterday at lunch. Car won't work, my phone—"

"I know," Charlie said. "It's like that everywhere."

Doc took a breath. "Right. Just find me after."

Charlie nodded and walked down the hall toward Liz's room. He passed another room with an open door and found the soldier sprawled out on top of the sheets, still dressed in his bloodied uniform, passed out on the bed.

He had questions, but he didn't even know where to start. He left the lieutenant to his rest and carefully opened the last door on the left, the hinges groaning from his intrusion.

Liz was on her back beneath the covers. The doc had set up an IV on the far side of the bed, feeding the liquid through a tube and needle that funneled into her arm. She was asleep, the only sign of life the subtle rise and fall of her chest with each breath.

Charlie approached her bedside like a gentle breeze on a spring afternoon. As he towered over the bed, she looked small and fragile from his point of view. And while he wanted to be optimistic about her recovery and the fact that she had survived the surgery, he understood the reality that Doc was trying to convey.

All their modern conveniences were gone. No hospitals, no surgeons, no power, no help. Not wanting to disturb her anymore, Charlie turned to leave but paused one last time at the door, looking at the girl in the bed, then gently closed the door.

When Charlie returned to the living room, the lieutenant had woken and was talking to Doc and Ellen, the three huddled in confidence.

"Charlie," Ellen said, smiling. "How are you feeling?"

"I'm fine, Mrs. Wilburn." Charlie joined the huddle, wedging himself between Ellen and the lieutenant. "I'm sorry for waking you up last night."

Ellen dismissed the apology and gently patted Charlie's cheek. "I'm just glad you made it out of the city." She gestured to the soldier. "Dixon was just telling us about what happened."

The lieutenant was wide-eyed despite just waking up, though Charlie figured the man was used to waking up quickly in the military. And he suddenly realized that this was the first time he'd learned the man's name and shook Dixon's hand. "Nice to meet you, Dixon."

"Likewise, Charlie," Dixon replied, but there was no smile on his face, and when both men retracted their hands, they each looked at the dried blood on them. Dixon broke away first. "There were a few more units coming from my base just north of here. I was going to take the Humvee up there and inform my CO what we ran into."

"All of this because of some electronic blast?" Ellen asked.

"Yes, ma'am. The only intelligence we've received is that there were insurgents penetrating the city and that there may be additional sleeper cells activated around the country." Dixon crossed his arms. "My mission was to secure the eastern region of Seattle and establish an FOB."

"FOB?" Charlie asked.

"Forward operating base," Dixon answered. "It would be a rallying point from where we could take the rest of the city."

"My word." Ellen placed her hand on her chest and looked at her husband. "Ronald, there could be a lot of people that need help out there."

"Does your base have doctors?" Doc asked.

"We have a few, but I'm not going to turn down extra help," Dixon answered.

Doc turned to his wife. "It might be good for us to go. The base is probably the safest place we could be right now."

"And what about the girl?" Ellen asked.

"I've done all I can for her. Aside from changing the bandages and giving her pills, there is nothing else for me to do." Doc turned to Charlie. "I'm sorry."

"I understand." Charlie nodded in compliance and briefly considered tagging along, though he knew his parents wouldn't agree. "Think you can watch Liz and the girl for a bit? I wanted to head over to the house. My folks are probably worried."

"Of course, dear," Ellen said.

"How long will you be?" Dixon asked.

"No longer than an hour," Charlie answered.

Dixon grimaced but nodded. "All right, but don't dawdle. The sooner I can report back to my division about what I saw, the sooner we can retaliate."

Charlie headed for the door but stopped to turn around again. "And thank you again, Doc, Mrs. Wilburn."

Once outside, Charlie cut across the lawn, his pace quick

as he headed out onto the empty and worn road. The closer Charlie moved toward home, the faster he walked, and terrible questions sped through his mind.

What if those terrorists had made it to the orchard? What if his parents had been hurt? It wasn't as if they could drive anywhere or call anyone. His father didn't like to admit it, but he was getting older, unable to move around the way he used to. And any injury sustained now could become life-threatening.

The worry grew, and Charlie broke into a sprint. His lungs and muscles burned, a brief surge of adrenaline providing the needed boost for the rest of the journey home. The orchard fields appeared on his left, the early-morning light highlighting the rows of green that stretched up the hills on the horizon and toward the sunrise.

Just the sight of the trees made him feel better, and his body lightened. A few seconds later, he saw the barn then the house.

Charlie turned up the gravel drive and saw his dad's truck parked in the grass near the porch, exactly where it had been when Charlie left the day before. He leapt up the steps and shouldered open the front door.

"Mom? Dad?" Charlie yelled for them through gasping breaths. He was lightheaded from the run and the abrupt stop.

"Charlie?" It was his mother's voice, coming from the back.

"Mom!" Charlie cut through the kitchen and stepped out the screen door and found his mother eating breakfast outside. "Thank god." He swooped down from the steps and engulfed his mother in a hug.

"Charlie, my god, what happened to you?" His mother pulled back to get a better look at her son. She grabbed his hand and stared at the dried blood. "Are you all right?" His mother patted his chest, checking for wounds that didn't exist.

"I'm fine, Mom. Are you all right?" Charlie asked, snatching her hands and keeping them steady in his. "Where's Dad?"

"We're fine, but your father and I worried when you didn't come home last night." She freed her left hand from Charlie's hold and gently touched a bloodstain on his chest. "Are you sure you're all right?"

"Yes," Charlie asked. "Where's Dad?"

His mother spun around and gestured toward the barn. "I don't know. He's fiddling with something. He didn't even come to bed last night. He wouldn't say it, but he was worried too. We lost power, and so did the Bigelows down the street." She bit her lower lip and frowned. "You're sure you're all right?"

Charlie exhaled relief and nodded. "Yeah, I'm okay. Really." He finally addressed the blood that covered his hands and clothes. "It's not mine. A nurse was shot. She's down at Dr. Wilburn's house."

"Shot?" His mother tilted her head to the side, repeating the word as if she didn't recognize it.

"Charlie!" Harold Decker waddled out of the barn, his sleeves rolled up, still dressed in the same overalls and shirt that he wore yesterday, and broke out into a meandered jog.

"Dad." Charlie met him more than halfway, and the father and son embraced, Charlie burying his face into his father's shoulder.

Harold leaned back, grasped Charlie's face with both hands, and took a good look at his son. "Your mother was worried sick." He kept his eyes on the blood.

"It's okay, Dad. The blood's not mine." Charlie removed his father's hands, and his mother walked over to join them. "Listen, something happened in the city."

"I'll say," Harold exclaimed. "Everything in the house went dead. Even that cell phone you gave me."

"The land line wasn't working either," his mother added.

"Cars, power, everything is down. Seattle is at a standstill right now, and the people responsible are just… shooting anything that they come across."

"Oh my god." Mary clasped both hands over her mouth then looked at Harold. "I told you I heard shooting last night."

"Is that what happened?" Harold touched the blood on his son's chest, his expression shifting between grief and rage.

"Dad, I told you, I'm fine." Charlie looked past his father and toward the barn from where he'd emerged. "What were you doing in there?"

"C'mon. I'll show you."

The barn was two stories, with the second floor running around the perimeter of the barn, keeping the middle open. It was mostly for storage. His dad had built it for his mother, who had seen one just like it in some farming magazine. And that was just how their relationship worked. Mom would say something, then Dad would do something about it. They'd been married for thirty-eight years.

Harold motioned them over to his workbench, where tools and an old radio sat open and exposed. "I managed to get it working early this morning. Wanted to know what in the hell was going on out there, but the only thing I can get is some emergency broadcast signal playing on loop. That and static."

Charlie reached for the dusty and aged radio. The back cover was torn off, exposing the tubes inside. It was old technology, which matched what Lieutenant Dixon explained to him about the EMP. He looked at the back of the barn and a faded blue tarp. "If this works, then maybe—"

The radio ended the monotonous emergency broadcast and blared a high-pitched din followed by a stern voice. "And now, a message from the President of the United States of America."

"My fellow Americans. I'm speaking to you from a secure facility where my administration is hard at work to solve our broadening crisis. If you're hearing me, please pass this message along to anyone else that you can, because as you know, all modern communication devices have been rendered useless. Currently, the entire United States power grid is down. Emergency systems have been disrupted, along with basic utility services such as water and sewage."

Charlie couldn't look away from the speaker and the radio, and the chatter between his parents was washed out by his thoughts.

"Over the past twenty-four hours, I have been in contact with my generals, Cabinet, intelligence advisors, as well as several experts in the civilian fields, and I can tell you with confidence that we know and understand what happened. Our country was attacked using an electromagnetic pulse, most commonly referred to as an EMP. It has rendered any device that uses a CPU to function completely useless. And while this has affected every person across our great nation, I am here to tell you that we do have a solution, and it will be unfolded to the general public within the coming weeks. Until then, I ask that you remain calm, help one another, and above all, remain the hearty, law-abiding citizens that you are. Thank you. And God bless the United States of America."

The high-pitched whine returned, then a rush of static, and finally, the repeated loop of the emergency broadcast system came back online.

Charlie kept staring at the radio after the broadcast was over, wrapping his mind around what the president had just said. "In the coming weeks?" He frowned. "How in the hell are people supposed to last for weeks?"

His dad offered a cynical chuckle. "That's code for they're

still working on a solution, but they don't want to say that they don't have anything. We're going to be on our own for a while."

"Well," his mother said after remaining silent. "I suppose all we can do is just carry on." She smiled gravely. "No sense in worrying about something that we can't control."

"Your mother's right," Harold said. "Best thing we can do is keep things going here as best we can. After all..." He started toward the barn's exit. "People still need to eat, right?" He cracked a grin then clapped his hands together once the way he did whenever he was done with a conversation.

While Charlie admired his parents' attitude about the situation, they hadn't seen what he'd seen or experienced what he'd gone through getting out of the city. And if those terrorists decided to make their way farther east, away from the suburbs and into rural country, then they'd only bring death and pain with them.

---

*C*harlie stepped out of the barn, choosing to take the radio with him in case there were any updates, though his father didn't expect any further help from the folks over in DC. As he made his way back toward the house, he saw Mario and a few other orchard workers arrive on their bikes out front.

Charlie raised his arm in a friendly wave, and Mario reciprocated. If he hadn't known Mario for ten years, he would have been surprised that the middle-aged farm hand showed up for work after a day like yesterday. The man was relentless.

"Howdy, Mr. Decker." Mario smiled widely, his fake Southern twang muddled with his native Mexican accent. He always enjoyed addressing Charlie like that.

"Hey, Mario." Charlie bear-hugged Mario in lieu of their normal handshake. It was good to see him and the other guys alive. While Mario and the others didn't live in the city, Charlie had seen enough death to make him fear that it could stretch anywhere. "Everything all right at home?"

Mario nodded. "Family is fine. No power, though. The kids aren't liking that since they're staying home from school, but Maria will keep them busy." He turned to Harold. "Do you know what's going on?"

"Some kind of terrorist attack," Harold said then gestured to Charlie. "Started in the city, and I guess it's working its way east."

Nervous chatter flitted between the men, their Spanish quick and startled.

Worried, Mario turned to Charlie. "Really?"

"Yeah." Charlie stepped closer. "I have a soldier down the road at Doc's house. We were with his unit when we were attacked. I'm going back over there now, but it might be a good idea for you to bring your families here. We have the well working, and provisions." And deep down, Charlie thought that having some additional numbers on their side wouldn't hurt.

"You think it's going to get that bad?" Mario asked.

"It already is." Charlie began to turn but stopped himself. "If you have rifles or guns, bring them and whatever provisions you have."

Mario shook his head, and Charlie started his way up the road. All of it was surreal, and it felt as though weeks had passed since he left for Seattle yesterday.

The world had changed in the blink of an eye, and while he didn't know what to expect next, he understood what would happen if those bastards made their way to the orchard. He felt anger simmering in him, just thinking about it.

Charlie stopped on the road, watching Mario and the other workers return home, and looked up toward the apple groves. The haze of early morning had burned away, and sunlight streamed down over the endless sea of green that rolled over the hills.

The sight brought a smile to his face, and he veered from the asphalt and made his way up toward the hill. As the ground beneath his boots shifted from concrete to grass and dirt, the stress and worry that had plagued him throughout the morning began to fade away.

The leafy branches of the apple trees cooled him from the summer sun, and he shut his eyes as he took a deep breath. Soil, tree, and the sweet scent of fruit grazed his nostrils. It cleansed him of the concrete and smog of the city.

Any place with life was where Charlie wanted to be, and the orchard was always teeming with it. He stretched out his arm and ran his fingertips along the tree bark, the rough texture familiar.

Apples dangled overhead, and Charlie grabbed the closest one. It was firm, the pink lady ripe in his hand. He took a bite, and his mouth exploded with flavor.

The taste awoke hunger, and he realized that he hadn't eaten anything since yesterday morning. He devoured the apple and plucked another one on his walk through the orchards. A trail of apple cores followed him through the trees, and the walk helped clear his head.

The orchard had always done that for him. The land and the trees were as much a part of him as his beating heart. He'd spent endless summers and seasons running through these trees. He grew them, harvested them, climbed them— his history was written here.

When Charlie reached the edge of the orchard, he looked back at the long rows he'd passed through and smiled. It was good to be home.

He descended the hill and broke into a jog on his way toward Doc's house. He found Dixon outside, puffing on a cigarette. He still hadn't changed out of his army fatigues, and the sunlight exposed the blood and dirt on his uniform.

"Everything all right?" Dixon asked, squinting in the sun's brightness. A shade of black stubble had appeared on his face, and his cheeks and neck were lined with red smears. His comrade's blood.

"Fine," Charlie answered. "What's the next move?"

"Retaliation." Dixon took a deep drag then exhaled, his body language relaxing as he deflated in the process.

"How far away is your base?" Charlie asked.

"An hour's drive." Dixon ground out the cigarette on the porch then flicked the tiny butt down the concrete path that cut through the front yard.

Charlie pointed toward Seattle and the road that they had come from. "The terrorists that gunned down your unit and shot Liz were heading this way. It might be nice to have some military support over here."

"I don't know if I can convince my CO to come and protect a bunch of farmers." Dixon stood, his knees popping in the process. He grimaced as he cradled his lower back and twisted, trying to loosen his muscles. "We deployed most of our ground forces on missions into the city."

Charlie turned to look back at the Humvee parked in the drive. Like Dan's fatigues, blood shimmered off the armor in the sunlight, and he got a better look at the bullet holes that dented the sides and transformed the windows into crushed glass, a grave reminder of what was potentially heading their way.

"I want you to take the girls," Charlie said, looking at Dixon. "Think you can manage that?"

Dixon nodded. "We'll find room for them at the base."

"Thank you."

Charlie headed inside and found Ellen with an awake Adelyn in the kitchen, eating Cheerios, then headed down the hall and back to Liz's room, where he found Doc checking her pulse.

"You might have some nausea from the medication, but if it gets too intense and you start vomiting, we'll have to take you off." Doc delicately returned Liz's wrist to the bed. "You're already dehydrated, and this summer heat won't be doing you any favors. The pain will be a little worse, but it's better to be safe than sorry at this point."

"Thank you," Liz said, her voice barely above a whisper.

Doc leaned close. "You're a strong young lady." He turned then smiled when he saw Charlie in the doorway. "Don't stay too long. She needs her rest."

Liz smiled when she saw Charlie. Her skin was pale and shiny with sweat. The bangs of her black hair clung to her forehead in stringy lines, and her lips had lost their color. But those green eyes were still as vibrant as they had been back at the hospital.

"Hey," she said.

"How are you feeling?" Charlie approached with hesitant steps, as though if he pressed down too hard on the floor, it might burst the stitches running down her abdomen.

"Tired." Liz tried to adjust herself in bed but grimaced and stopped just as quickly as she started.

The pain that flashed across Liz's face made Charlie close the gap between himself and the bedside. He dropped to a knee and cupped her hand with his. Her skin was cold.

"It hurts to breathe," Liz said.

"That's what happens when you get yourself shot."

Liz formed a thin-lipped smile then gave the lightest squeeze of his hand. "The doc said you got me here just in time." Her grip tightened. "I guess I owe you again."

"I'll put it on your tab." Charlie smiled but was unable to hold her gaze. It was something about her eyes that twisted him up inside. Staring at them for too long stoked a fire that he wasn't sure he could control. A part of him was afraid to let it burn, because he knew that once it started, it might not stop.

But there was another part that wanted to know what would happen if he let it burn.

"I talked to the lieutenant." Charlie lifted his eyes and met hers once more. "You and Adelyn are going with the doc to their military base."

Liz retracted her hand.

Charlie fumbled his fingers for a moment. "I think it's for the best."

Liz nodded. "You're probably right."

He lingered for a moment then stood. He walked toward the door then turned back and found Liz already asleep. He watched the slight rise and fall of her chest, and that fire in his stomach grew angry. He was angry with himself for letting her get shot, and he was angry about the masked evil that put the bullet in her stomach in the first place.

Charlie returned to the living room, where Doc and Ellen were sitting on the couch, playing with a still-sleepy Adelyn. "You two going to be able to handle her?"

"I think so," Ellen answered, bouncing Adelyn on her knee.

"We're going to pack some things up and leave in the next hour," Doc said.

Charlie shook Doc's hand. "Good luck."

"You too."

"You and your parents should come, Charlie," Ellen said. "It's not safe here."

While Charlie knew that Ellen had a valid point, he also knew his family. And himself. He'd spent so much effort getting home, he wasn't about to leave it now.

Hell, he had spent all day yesterday getting turned down by every bank in Seattle at just a shot of trying to turn things around. He'd poured buckets of blood, sweat, and tears into that place, and whatever he'd put in, his father and mother had put in one hundred fold. His soul was in that land.

"I can't," Charlie said.

"I told her you wouldn't go for it." The doc tickled Adelyn's stomach, but she only yawned at the motion.

"Take care of yourself, Charlie," Ellen said.

"I will."

Charlie walked outside, knowing that if he lingered in that house any longer, he might change his mind about going. Because while he'd only met her yesterday, he'd already grown used to having Liz around.

"I'll try to bring some help," Dixon said, dropping the rag he'd used to clean off the Humvee.

"I'd appreciate it," Charlie said. "Keep them safe."

"I will."

Charlie glanced back at the house one last time then headed for the road. But he didn't even make it past the driveway before he stopped.

The bright sunlight made it hard to see, but the shapes were unmistakable. Masked men armed with rifles emerged from between the trees.

Charlie counted two, four, then ten, then lost count after a dozen. He turned around and found Dixon already by the house's door, waving for him to follow and trying to remain silent.

But the silence broke with the sound of gunfire.

14

*T*ime stood still, and Charlie remained frozen at the end of the driveway to the rural road outside of Doc's house. He saw the masked gunmen emerge from the woods down the street, but his mind refused to acknowledge their reality.

"Charlie!"

Charlie turned toward Lieutenant Dixon who was already at Doc's front door, rifle in hand.

"Move your ass!"

Charlie sprinted toward the house, and then disappeared through the open doorway just before Dixon slammed the door shut behind him.

Dixon peeked out of the curtains, keeping most of his body hidden. "Fuck." He quickly retreated from the window. "They'll sweep the house, then move on. Everyone needs to hide, and everyone needs to stay quiet."

Doc and Ellen, who still had Adelyn in her arms, stepped out of the kitchen.

"The cellar," Doc said. "It's around back, and I can lock it from the inside."

"How many entrances does it have?" Dixon asked, checking the magazine of his rifle.

"Just the one," Doc answered.

"Go."

"What about Liz?" Ellen asked, clutching Adelyn tighter in her arms.

"I'll take care of her," Charlie said.

Doc led the two girls toward the back, and Dixon shoved a pistol into Charlie's hands.

"Don't use it unless it's a last resort," Dixon said. "Let's go get Liz."

The weapon was heavy in Charlie's hand, and memories of the men he'd killed back in Seattle flashed in his mind like lightning. The blood, the flash of the barrel, the screams-

"Charlie!"

He looked up from the pistol and found Dixon waiting outside Liz's door in the hallway.

"C'mon!"

Charlie hurried down the hall, pushing the memories from his head. Liz was unconscious, and Dixon was at the window, peeking outside.

"Shit," Dixon said, quickly transitioning from the window to the far side of Liz's bed. "We won't have time to get her to the cellar before they walk inside. We need to hide her now." Dixon gestured toward the closet. "Help me put her inside."

"Are you serious?" Charlie asked. "We can't just shove her in a closet."

"You'll be in there with her." Dixon gestured to the gun. "Anyone opens the door, you shoot them."

"That's not the smart play—"

"We don't have time, Charlie." Dixon took a breath and gathered his thoughts. "It's a scouting party. They won't send more than three men inside."

Foreign voices brought both of their attentions toward the window. They were out of time. Charlie rushed to help

98

Dixon lift Liz from the bed, taking the IV with them, which was thankfully short enough to pass through the closet door.

Charlie shoved aside clothes and shoes, making room for the two of them, and they set Liz inside first, then Charlie.

"Just stay here and keep quiet." Dixon shut the door, and Charlie watched him scurry out of the room through the narrow slits of the closet door.

The groan of the hinges at the front door sounded and was followed by the light patter of boots against the hardwood. The terrorists whispered to one another, their words inaudible even if Charlie understood the language.

Boot steps echoed from all around the house, some growing louder and closer, others becoming quieter.

Charlie positioned his body in front of Liz and aimed the pistol at the crack of the closet door, then placed his finger on the trigger.

Hushed foreign accents whispered in the hallway, and Charlie's heart skipped a beat when the hinges to the bedroom groaned.

Liz moaned behind him, waking, and Charlie quickly reached around and placed his hand over her mouth, praying that the gunman didn't hear her.

Charlie tensed and squinted through the narrow slits of the closet door. The barrel of the gunman's rifle penetrated the room first, followed by the pair of tan and weathered hands that held it. Despite the summer heat, the terrorist wore long sleeves and pants, with boots. The clothes were well-worn, the elbows and knees sporting holes from use.

Only one soldier entered the room. He paced around the bed, checking underneath as he circled to the opposite side. He reached for the bottle of pills that Doc had set on the nightstand, and then pocketed them.

Liz moaned again through Charlie's fingers, and Charlie's stomach twisted as the terrorist turned toward the closet.

Charlie adjusted his aim to make it level with the terrorist's chest, but then wondered if the gunman was wearing body armor. He'd only get one shot, maybe two the moment that door opened, and he needed to make them count.

The gunman's shadow grew larger, blocking out the light of the room. Charlie held his breath, using every ounce of strength and concentration to keep the pistol steady in his hands.

Seconds would decide the fate of Charlie and Liz's souls, and just when the gunman had his hand on the door, and Charlie was about to squeeze the trigger, a heavy thump echoed somewhere in the house.

The terrorist released the closet door knob, and then called something out in his language before he stepped toward the hallway. He lingered for a moment, called again, then disappeared.

Charlie exhaled, and then turned around to check on Liz. "You all right?"

Liz nodded, but even with the limited light, Charlie saw the pained expression on her face.

"Just hang on, because I—"

Three quick gunshots thundered in the house, and Charlie jumped, his heart skipping a beat. Two more gunshots, then a scream.

"Charlie!"

He stepped out of the closet quickly, turning to catch a brief glimpse of a terrified Liz on the floor, clutching the gauze covering the wound on her stomach. "I'll be back." He shut the door before he saw her reaction and raised the pistol as he headed for the hallway.

"Charlie, living room, now!" Dixon's scream was accompanied by another hard crash, followed by grunts and groans.

Charlie hurried down the hall, his vision tunneled at the end of the pistol. And when he finally stepped from the hallway and into the living room, he saw a dead terrorist on the floor, and another one grappling with Dixon on the rug.

"Shoot him!" Dixon spit the words out, his face reddened as he choked the terrorist.

Charlie squeezed the trigger, his adrenaline pumping so hard that he didn't even bother aiming. The first bullet screamed from the barrel and missed wide left. He lined up another shot, then squeezed the trigger again.

Blood spurted from the terrorist's shoulder, and the fight ran out of him. Charlie aimed to shoot again, but Dixon bucked the masked gunman off him and brandished a knife that he sliced across the terrorist's throat.

Dixon stepped back as the masked enemy clawed help-lessly at the blood cascading down the front of his shirt, his efforts futile as blood pooled on either side of his head on the floor.

A few final muscle spasms and the man lay dead.

"We need to move." Dixon shoved Charlie back toward the hallway, then checked the front living room window. He patted down the gunmen, taking their rifles and ammuni-tion. "C'mon, let's grab the girl before the rest of them show up." He gave Charlie another shove down the hall, but he stood his ground.

"Wait." Charlie rushed to the gunman with the slit throat, then reached into the pocket that held the stolen pills. He tried not to look at the wound but found his gaze pulled toward the gruesome sight. The wound was wide, ear to ear, and with the terrorist's neck tilted back, the wound opened wide enough to expose bone.

"Charlie!"

"Yeah." Charlie pocketed the pills, then followed Dixon down the hallway and into the room where he was already helping Liz out of the closet.

"Do you think you can stand and walk a little?" Dixon asked, balancing the weapons he stole off the terrorist while throwing Liz's left arm over his shoulders.

"I think so," Liz answered.

Charlie swooped in on her right side and propped her up. The three of them walked down the hallway and then out toward the back door where Doc and Ellen had run.

The burst of sunlight and warmth smacked Charlie's face like a brick wall, and he turned left, spotting the pair of basement doors Doc had told him about.

"Here, take her." Dixon passed Liz fully into Charlie's arms and then knocked on the doors. "Doc! Ellen! Open up!" It was quiet for a little bit longer, and then metal scraped on the other side of the door, and it cracked open.

"Everyone all right?" Doc poked his head out first, alone.

"We're fine." Dixon helped pass Liz to Doc, and then Charlie carried her the rest of the way.

The inside of the basement was lined with canned foods and some of Doc's old vet equipment. Ellen had Adelyn on some blankets, and when she saw Charlie carrying Liz, she quickly set some blankets down for her as well.

"How is she?" Ellen asked, helping Liz onto the floor.

"She's in and out of it," Charlie answered, setting her on the blanket, Liz's eyelids fluttering as she groaned the moment she hit the pavement.

An engine revved out front, and Charlie headed toward the stairs, finding Dixon at the corner of the back side of the house. Charlie stepped out of the basement and knelt at Dixon's side.

"What is it?" Charlie asked.

"They're taking the Humvee," Dixon answered.

The engine faded, heading down the road, and Charlie's eyes bulged from the realization of where they were heading next. "The orchard." Charlie stepped from behind the house and sprinted into the open field, praying that he could get to his parents before the terrorists.

15

*C*harlie led Dixon through the orchard, the pair concealed by the trees to the gunmen on the road. The journey back through the trees was a stark contrast from his earlier trek. Peace and tranquility had been replaced with anxiety and nerves. But the familiar terrain boosted his confidence. He knew every nook and cranny of the property.

Sweat dripped down Charlie's forehead and stung his eyes. He wiped the sweat on his sleeve, then glanced down to the road. While he couldn't see all of the terrorists on their death march toward the house, he was able to hear them, along with the stolen Humvee. They'd moved the old military vehicle to the front of the pack, most likely for cover.

Dixon grabbed Charlie's shoulder, pulling him to a stop once the house was in view of the orchard. "How many entrance points does the house have?"

"Just front and back," Charlie answered.

"All right, we'll head through the back." Dixon stepped forward. "You stay behind me and watch my back, got it? But do not shoot unless you're seen. We have the element of surprise, and the moment we lose that, we lose our advantage."

Charlie nodded and flexed his grip on the stock and the pistol grip. He eyed the house and the surrounding trees, praying that the workers had already left to get their families.

Charlie followed Dixon down the slope toward the house, continuing to use the trees for cover until he couldn't use it anymore.

Dixon paused at the orchard's edge and knelt, holding up his hand, and Charlie mirrored the lieutenant's motion as he dropped to a knee as well.

"Ten o'clock." Dixon pointed through the trees, and Charlie saw the Humvee pull into the driveway, surrounded by six armed men. "Bastards are still wearing those masks."

Charlie lifted the rifle in his hands, peering through the scope. He lined the crosshairs up on one of the gunmen's chest.

"Let's move," Dixon said. "Stay close."

They used the house as cover, staying directly behind it. Charlie struggled to keep the rifle steady in his hands on the run. He'd never been a good shot on the move.

Dixon sidled up on the left side of the back door, and Charlie landed on the right. The rumble of the Humvee's engine drowned out the voices of the terrorists on the front side of the house. Dixon reached for the door handle and then cracked it open, leading with the end of his rifle as he stepped inside, and Charlie followed.

Adrenaline heightened Charlie's senses, tensing his muscles as he entered the kitchen. It was an odd feeling, breaking into his own home.

The front door opened before Charlie and Dixon exited the kitchen, and the pair ducked behind the wall that separated the kitchen and the front living room.

Slowly, Dixon peered around the corner, and then just as quickly as they hid, he darted forward once the pair of terrorists moved deeper into the house, one heading down the right hallway and the other turning up the stairs.

They kept low to avoid being seen through the front windows. Dixon positioned himself at the base of the stairs while Charlie peered through the window in the front door.

The Humvee continued its slow procession down the road, still escorted by the terrorists marching their way farther east, spreading their shadow of death.

Another tap on Charlie's shoulder pulled his attention away from the window, and Dixon motioned up the staircase for himself, then hand-signaled for Charlie to follow the terrorists on the first floor.

Dixon ascended the steps, and Charlie made his way down the first floor hallway, rifle up. He moved slowly, each step carefully placed to minimize noise.

His parents' bedroom door was open at the end of the hall, and he saw a shadow moving about inside. Charlie raised the rifle, approaching the door, and right before he reached the bedroom, screams erupted on the second floor.

Charlie glanced up, and the terrorist sprinted from the room, turning Charlie's attention back to the gunman. The pair locked eyes. Because his rifle was already aimed, Charlie fired first, sending the terrorist to the floor where he lay lifeless.

"Charlie!" Dixon shouted from upstairs.

Charlie hurried to the second floor, following the commotion down the tight hallway. He tensed the closer he moved toward the room where Dixon shouted for aid. He had his finger over the trigger and burst into the room.

Dixon was on top of the gunman, both men with each other's hands around their necks. Red-faced, Dixon glanced at Charlie. "Knock him out!"

Charlie flipped the weapon around and butt-stroked the terrorist's head as hard as he could, ending the masked gunman's pathetic crawl for help. He looked up from the unconscious man and frowned in confusion at Dixon. "What are you doing?"

"I want at least one of them alive," Dixon answered, catching his breath and rubbing his neck. "They're heading toward a location, and I want to know where." He slung the rifle over his shoulder and then restrained the man's ankles and wrists. "Let's find your folks."

Charlie checked the rest of the hallway, finding the rooms upstairs empty. His anxiety growing, he descended to the first floor and checked the master bedroom, stepping over the dead terrorist in the hall, but found no one inside.

Spinning in circles, Charlie shook his head. "They're not here. I don't—" He stopped, staring out the back door where he had a view of the barn.

Without another word, Charlie sprinted outside, leaving Dixon behind.

"Charlie, wait!"

The doors to the barn were closed, and Charlie screeched to a stop, wedging himself between the narrow gap and shoving the heavy doors open. Light flooded the dirt floor, and Charlie frantically searched the darkness. "Mom? Dad?"

Charlie lowered his rifle, the tip of the barrel scraping against the dirt. He spun around in circles, his nerves frayed.

"Charlie."

The voice echoed from a darkened corner in the back left of the barn, and his father's hulking figure emerged from the darkness, his mother close behind.

"Thank God." Charlie sprinted toward them, forgoing the rifle, and then flung his arms around each of them. "I was—"

"Umjig-iji mala!"

The foreign accent tickled the hairs on the back of Charlie's neck and he spun around, keeping his body as a barrier between the gunman and his parents, though his father made for a big target.

The terrorist blocked the entrance, shaking the rifle threateningly. "Naelyeowa!"

Charlie eyed his rifle on the ground between himself and the terrorist and cursed beneath his breath for dropping it.

"Please," Charlie said. "We don't want any trouble. We—"

"Naneun ne muleup-e malhaessda!" The terrorist screamed and again, threateningly waved the rifle in his hands.

"Get behind me, boy," Harold said.

But despite Charlie's father tugging at his shoulders, he didn't budge.

The terrorist closed the gap and then kicked Charlie's rifle behind him, erasing the slim chance of Charlie reaching for it. And as the terrorist shouted again, stepping closer, Charlie clutched his parents' hands tight.

The gunshot that rang out sent a shudder through Charlie's body, and a coldness spread from the base of his skull and down his spine all the way to the soles of his feet.

His parents' fingertips dug into Charlie's shoulders, and he waited for the pain to follow, but it never came. Slowly, he opened his eyes, and he saw the terrorist face down in the dirt.

Dixon stood at the barn's entrance, rifle still aimed at the dead man on the floor. He approached, patted him down, then snagged Charlie's rifle out of the dirt.

"I told you to wait," Dixon said, then tossed Charlie his rifle. "Might want to hang on to that next time."

Charlie's mother flung herself into Dixon's arms and hugged him tight. "Thank you." She peeled her face off his chest and kissed his cheek. "Thank you so much."

Harold slapped his big palm on Dixon's shoulder. "Good shooting, Lieutenant."

Screams pulled their attention toward the barn entrance.

"They've got more coming," Dixon said, heading toward the barn's back exit. "Let's go!"

But Charlie shook his head. "We'll never make it in time on foot." Charlie turned to the backside of the barn, his eyes lingering on a lumpy blue tarp, then he turned back toward Dixon. "Take my parents to the north side of the orchard."

"Charlie, no!" His mother lunged for him, but he was already out of reach.

Charlie flung the blue tarp off a pair of dusty dirt bikes and slung the rifle strap over his shoulder. He straddled the seat, pumped the primer, and squeezed the clutch. He took a breath. "Please work." He dropped his heel down hard on the starter.

The engine sputtered, but it didn't start.

The voices outside the barn grew louder.

Charlie jumped and then slammed down on the starter again, and this time revved the throttle. The engine roared to life.

His mother screamed once more, and Charlie looked back one last time to see Dixon holding his parents back.

"Get them to safety, I'll draw them away!" Charlie released the clutch and the tires spun out, kicking up dirt as Charlie rocketed forward and burst out of the double barn doors.

The sudden exposure to sunlight blinded him, but his vision adjusted quickly as he sped down the slope toward the house.

The old bike rattled violently in his hands, and when he reached the back side of the house, a cluster of masked terrorists burst from the far corner.

Charlie turned a hard left, evading the gunfire that chased him to the front of the house.

Wind whipped violently against his cheeks, and in the blink of an eye he was out in the front yard, then the road, the soldiers that had been at the back of the house just now stepping into the front yard.

The stolen Humvee was a quarter of a mile up the road. Keeping hunched low on the bike, Charlie twisted the throttle, turning left and heading toward the east field, which held their nursery.

Smoke from the bike's two-stroke engine pilfered through the air and the scent of burnt rubber blasted Charlie's senses.

More gunfire broke out to his left, and again he made himself as small a target as he could muster, speeding through the trees, catching the harsh slap of a few branches along the way.

Charlie quickly checked behind him and saw the soldiers taking the bait.

A smile broke up the left side of his face, and he cut a hard left, digging up a rivet of black soil, before rocketing up to the next level of orchards.

The harsh incline nearly flung him off the back of the bike, but Charlie leaned forward to regain his balance. Gunfire and screams chased him, roaring above the whine of the sputtering two-stroke engine growing hot between his legs.

Streaks of green and black blurred in his peripheral, and for a moment he was transported back to the summers of his youth when his father let him ride around the orchards after chores were finished in the afternoon. The sunlight shone down like gold in the evening here, and it made everything twice as beautiful as he could have ever pictured in his own mind.

But the moments were brief and passed quickly as the noise of gunshots and foreign screams drowned out what good memories he was able to harvest in the shitstorm that currently surrounded him, and Charlie just focused on going as fast and as far as he could.

16

*O*nce the orchard ended and melded into the untamed wilderness to the north, Charlie killed the engine and stashed the bike in the trees, then doubled back toward the north field, keeping to the forest for cover.

Charlie didn't like leaving the bike behind, and he didn't think that anyone would find it, but he didn't want to draw attention on his return home. And after his long trek from Seattle, Charlie understood the importance of transportation.

Covered in sweat and parched by the time he reached the halfway point at the barn, Charlie stopped for a moment to splash some water on his face from the hose that ran from their well.

Charlie splashed the cool water generously, coating his face and neck. Once revived, he headed toward the north field.

Water ran down his body beneath his shirt during the rest of the trip, helping to keep him cool. But by the time he reached the north field, the water had evaporated and a fresh coat of sweat covered his skin.

"Dixon?" Charlie raised the volume of his voice. "Mom? Dad?"

The longer Charlie walked along the northern fence without finding his parents, the more poisonous his thoughts became that entered his mind.

What if a stray soldier had stumbled upon them like the one who'd found them in the barn? What if Dixon took off and left his parents behind and his father was currently face down in the dirt alongside his mother? What if his dad had gotten into a fight with Dixon after Charlie took off and—

"Charlie!" His mother burst from the trees, tears streaming down her cheeks and her arms spread wide as Charlie hopped the fence to greet her.

Their bodies collided and his mother clawed at Charlie hungrily. She grabbed hold of his face and forced his gaze into her eyes. "Don't you ever do something like that again, you understand me? Ever."

Dixon and Charlie's father appeared next. Dixon had given his dad one of the rifles, and the old timer looked like a modern-day version of Paul Bunion who'd traded the axe for a rifle.

Charlie hugged his father, the pair clapping each other on the back twice the way they'd always done. "Everyone all right?"

"Your father twisted his ankle trying to chase after you." Martha cast an accusing glare at her husband, who dismissed the accusation with a wave of his hand.

"I'm fine." And as if on cue, he wobbled slightly on the bad leg. "Just need to walk it off."

"We did walk," Martha said, then shook her head and tossed her hands in the air. "I really don't know what to do with either of you sometimes. It's almost like you enjoy getting hurt." She crossed her arms, giving them another angry glare. "Foolishness."

Charlie looked to Dixon. "Where do you think they're headed?"

Dixon tucked his rifle's stock beneath his arm. "The nearest strategic target for them to hit would be the air force base north of here, but they're heading east."

"The power plant," Harold said. "It's east of here, over in Mayfield."

"But the power's already out," Martha replied.

"I know one way we can find out," Dixon said. "That soldier is still tied up in the house, and I have a few questions for him."

"You can use the barn," Harold said.

Dixon nodded his thanks and headed toward the house.

"I'll be over in a second." Charlie looked back toward Doc's house, then to his parents. "I'm going to check on Doc, Ellen, and Liz."

"Liz?" Martha asked. "Who's that?"

"The nurse," Harold answered, grinning.

Charlie rolled his eyes and then gestured toward his dad's ankle. "Just don't trip on the way down, old man."

Harold laughed and took Martha under his arm. "Never happens when you've got the support of a good woman."

Charlie didn't let his dad see his smile, and as he headed toward Doc's house his thoughts circled Liz.

After everything that had happened over the past thirty-six hours, he couldn't be too sure that he wasn't rushing into something troublesome. He barely knew the woman, though he couldn't deny their connection.

Charlie shook his head, pushing the thoughts from his mind. He was going too far down the rabbit hole. First thing was making sure everyone was still alive, and the second priority was keeping it that way. And they were in a better position than most of the folks in the city.

Both the basement and cellar were stocked with food items, and the forests that surrounded them provided plenty of opportunities for hunting and fishing. Plus, Mario, their head worker, worked on the boats in Seattle's port before trading his sea legs for land. He'd be able to help out on that front. And while Harold was aging, he was still a better shot with a rifle than Charlie.

Charlie knocked hard twice on Doc's cellar doors, the harsh bangs echoing into the fields behind him.

Light footsteps preceded the sound of a lock, and the doors were pushed open, Doc squinting from the sunlight.

"Everything all right?" Doc asked.

Ellen popped her head up behind him. "We heard the shooting." Ellen clutched her hands together tightly, keeping them close to her chest.

"Everyone is fine." Charlie smiled and looked past the pair of them and into the darkness below.

"Liz is fine," Doc said, noticing Charlie's worried expression. "The little girl too."

"Some of the workers are coming back with their families and staying at the orchard," Charlie said. "You're more than welcome to join."

"No, we're fine here," Doc said, then looked back down to the darkened cellar. "Probably best if Liz stays here too, so I can keep an eye on her."

Charlie nodded, but the fact that Liz would no longer be close cut him a little deeper than he expected. "Yeah. Probably for the best."

"Adelyn can stay too," Ellen said, and then frowned. "She keeps asking for her mother, but I haven't answered." She trailed off, hoping for Charlie to fill in the blanks.

"She died, just before we got our ride here," Charlie said.

Ellen brought her hand to her mouth, stifling a gasp.

"Does the girl know?" Doc asked, the old man's face slack.

"No." Charlie rubbed his eyes, unsure of how to navigate that conversation. "At least, I don't know if she understands."

"Best not to put it off for too long," Doc replied. "Kids that age are perceptive."

Charlie swallowed. "Right."

Ellen and Doc stepped aside, letting Charlie down the steps. He pumped his hands, trying to get a grip on his heart rate, which had skyrocketed on his way down. His heart caught in his throat, and he stopped on the last step, spying Adelyn on the floor next to Liz, holding her hand as Liz slept.

It'd been only hours since Sarah was gunned down in the streets to the south. They were so close to escape. All they had to do was get in the Humvee. A minute sooner, or even a minute later, and things would have been different.

Adelyn saw Charlie on the staircase. "Where's Mommy?" Her eyes watered, but no tears fell, and when Charlie offered no answer, she looked back at Liz.

Charlie looked back up to Ellen and Doc, hoping for some words of encouragement, or advice, but he only saw their silhouettes at the top of the stairs, sun and blue skies in the backdrop. It was too beautiful a day for such bad news.

Charlie stepped onto the concrete floor and walked over to Adelyn, the little girl's attention still focused on Liz's hand. He crouched in front of her, struggling to find the words.

"Adelyn," Charlie said. "There's something that we need to talk about."

"What?" Adelyn asked, keeping her head down, exposing the light blonde curls at the top of her head made even messier by the previous day's events.

Charlie opened his mouth, but then closed it. He pinched the bridge of his nose, closing his eyes. He couldn't do this. He wasn't built for something like this.

But then a warmth touched Charlie's hand, and he looked to his left, finding Liz with her eyes cracked open. She slid her hand around his wrist and applied pressure.

Charlie looked back toward Adelyn, the little girl glancing up at him now. Her eyes were wide, the hazel coloring around her pupils so bright it looked like they glowed, and through Liz's touch, Charlie gathered his courage.

"Adelyn, your mommy is gone," Charlie said.

"Where did she go?" Adelyn asked.

"She died. Do you know what that means?"

Adelyn kept her face tilted up, but looked away, thinking it over, then nodded. "It means she's gone forever."

"Yeah." Charlie trembled, and Liz squeezed his wrist tighter. "That's what it means."

Adelyn lowered her head and then crawled over to Charlie. She climbed into his lap, resting her head on his arm.

Charlie looked to Liz, eyes watering, and then back to Adelyn, gently placing his hand on her back, the heat pulsating from the little girl akin to a furnace. Charlie stayed there until Adelyn fell asleep, Liz still holding his hand.

Charlie wasn't sure if he'd done the right thing, but seeing as how it made Liz smile, he figured he could have done worse. But with that news delivered, Charlie headed back to the barn, hoping that Dixon was able to get some answers out of their prisoner.

* * *

THE TERRORIST WAS TIED up in a chair, his chin pressed into his chest. Dixon had a bucket of water, and Charlie and Harold stood off to the side, letting the lieutenant do his work.

With a quick jerk of his arm, he flung the water into the terrorist's face, and he woke with a gasp and cough. Dixon set the bucket down, and then hunched forward with his hands on his thighs. "Good afternoon."

Water dripping from his face, and disoriented, the terrorist spit in Dixon's face. Dixon retaliated with a harsh backhand, and the terrorist grunted in anger. He screamed and thrashed in his chair, and Dixon stuffed a dirty rag into the enemy's mouth, muffling the panicked cries for help.

Dixon then brandished a knife and he pressed it against the terrorist's throat. The thrashing stopped.

"That's better," Dixon said. "Now, I have a few questions for you. If you answer me, then I don't hurt you. If you don't answer me." Dixon applied a little bit of pressure. "Then I cut you. Okay?"

The terrorist only stared at Dixon, motionless.

Dixon removed the gag, but not the knife. "What are you doing here?"

The terrorist's breathing grew labored, and he looked left, staring at Charlie and Harold.

"Hey!" Dixon forced the man's gaze back toward him. "What. Are. You. Doing. Here?"

The terrorist forced the top right of his mouth to twitch. "Uli modu jug-ilgeoya—"

Dixon dug the tip of the knife into the man's leg, and he erupted into screams and spasms. Blood flowed from the point of penetration, and Charlie stifled a gag at the sight of the squealing pig.

"In English, please," Dixon said, removing the blade.

Exhausted and disoriented, the terrorist only laughed as he looked Dixon in the eye, his English broken but understandable. "You die." He turned to Charlie. "All of you die. American scum."

"Where were your men going?" Dixon answered.

When the terrorist only laughed and muttered another spout of Korean, Dixon stabbed him again, and the hostage flailed in pain.

"Where!" Dixon repeated, this time refusing to remove the knife. "Is it the power plant? Is that your play? Tell me!"

Finally, the lieutenant removed his blade, more blood spilling from the terrorist's leg and splashing into the dirt.

But the hostage only shook his head. "We will not stop." His complexion became pale, his body covered with sweat and blood. "We will win."

Dixon wiped the blade on the man's shoulder then placed it in its sheath. He removed the firearm and then placed it to the man's head. "No, you won't."

Charlie shuddered when Dixon pulled the trigger, and his eyes were still on the gruesome sight of bone and brains spread across the barn floor when Dixon walked over.

Dixon holstered the weapon and then gestured to the blue tarp at the back of barn. "Did I see two bikes under that tarp?"

Charlie finally peeled his eyes away from the dead terrorist. "You're welcome to the bike, but I want something in return."

"Name it."

"Protection," Charlie said. "If they come back, I want to make sure the families out here have more guns than the enemy."

"If the enemy is using the power plant as a rallying point, then that shouldn't be a problem."

It was a phrase Charlie had grown accustomed to hearing over the past forty-eight hours. It was what a few of the bankers who hadn't given him an outright no said when he'd asked for the loans, but he'd been around enough of the finance folks to know 'I'll do what I can' was code for politely getting someone out of their office before they could cause a scene.

"Do I need to gas it up?" Dixon asked.

"No, it's full."

"I'll be back as soon as I can." Dixon picked the bike up, and Charlie and Harold watched him leave.

"You think it's a good idea letting him take the other bike?" Harold asked.

"If it weren't for him, we wouldn't have a bike to even give away," Charlie answered, then looked to the dead man in their barn. "And we're going to need the help."

17

*I*t was evening by the time Mario and the other workers returned with their families, hauling whatever belongings they could carry in backpacks and bags, or wagons and baskets. In total, the Decker Orchard added twenty folks, which included five children.

Martha was at the front door, blankets and pillows ready, greeting them with water and directions toward their rooms. "Maria, you and your kids can take the room upstairs at the end of the hall, it's on the left."

Maria nodded her thanks as she shuffled her kids into the house, the three of them squabbling amongst themselves over a ziplock bag of Fruit Loops. She snatched the bag from her eldest's hands and turned them all to face Martha. "You thank Senora Decker for letting us stay here."

All three children looked up, each of them with brown eyes and jet black hair, speaking at the same time in the same practiced and polite tone. "Thank you, Senora Decker."

Martha smiled. "You're very welcome. And you listen to your mother while you're here, and make sure you give her the help that she needs." She ushered them forward and then winked at Maria as she walked past.

"Everybody here?" Charlie asked, sneaking up the porch.

"I think so," Martha answered. "Your father has the men around back." She crossed her arms, and the smile she wore for the children faded. "He's showing them the rifles."

Charlie nodded, then walked around the house instead of through it, letting the families get settled.

Harold Decker was a smart man, and a proud one. Both were requirements to run your own business, especially when it came to farming. But laced between those virtues was a stubbornness that had cost Harold more than he would have cared to admit over his lifetime.

And while Charlie was certain his father could hold his own, he'd seen the kind of weaponry the terrorists were wielding firsthand. Rifles and shotguns could only do so much against automatic AK-47s, assault rifles, and grenades.

The barn doors were open, and Harold had Mario and four other men gathered around one of his work tables. He held a rifle, keeping the chamber open and showing them how to reload.

"It holds three, so you'll need to make your shots count," Harold said. "Anyone have any experience with firearms before?"

Heads shook in response, and Harold waved it off.

"We'll do some practice in the morning."

"Hey, Dad."

Charlie stepped up from behind them, garnering nods of respect as they made a space for him at the opposite end of the table where his father stood. Every rifle they owned was spread across the stained and splintered wood. Remingtons, Rugers, Winchester, each of them in a different make and model than its counterpart.

Harold picked up the Remington .223 and extended it down the table to Charlie. "You want to show them how it works?"

Charlie grabbed the rifle, the weapon a good weight in his

hands. He glanced up and found every eye on him, including his father, and he set the rifle down. "Could you guys give me a minute with my dad?"

The group nodded. Mario led his crew, shaking Harold's hand before they left, each of them again giving their thanks for their family's hospitality before turning for the house, their Spanish growing softer until it disappeared.

Harold set the long-rifled Winchester down and wiped his palms along the front of his dirty overalls. "Everything all right, son?"

"Dad, we need to think about how we're going to handle this," Charlie answered, planting both palms on the table.

Harold looked at him. "That's what I was showing Mario and the others. Those guys are coming back and we need to be prepared."

"And we will be, but we don't have a platoon of soldiers at our backs." Charlie stepped around the table, walking toward his father. "We have a group of farm hands that have never fired a weapon in their lives."

"Well, we're going to show them how to use it first!" Harold tossed his hands up. "Those boys need to know how to defend themselves."

"I'm not disagreeing with you, but I know how you get, and I know what's going to happen if those guys come back." Charlie pushed himself off the table and stepped around the side. "You'll want to charge full steam ahead, and it's going to get you, and anyone that goes with you, killed."

"This is our home, Charlie!" Harold roared, then pointed east. "They're just a bunch of cowards in masks too afraid to show their faces."

"Dad, you heard the same conversation with that fighter that I did," Charlie said. "They are trained military forces, and they will not quit their mission. If they do come back, then we need something better than charging full steam ahead. We need a strategy." He took a breath. "And that's something we should talk about before we start shoving guns in people's hands."

Charlie studied his father's expression, unsure if there was a hint of agreement beneath that stoic glare.

"It's important for us to have a united front on this," Charlie said. "Mario and the rest of the crew are going to look to us, and if they don't think we're on the same page, then their trust in us will start to waver. You're always telling me that strong leadership requires cooperation amongst management, right?"

Harold shifted his weight back and forth between his legs, and Charlie hoped that throwing the old man's wisdom back at him would help bring him around. "Never thought you were listening when I said that." He relaxed a little bit, but his expression retained its frown. "You think that your military friend will make it back?"

"I think if he can come back, then he will," Charlie answered.

But Charlie knew that Dixon was limited to the orders his commanding officers gave him, and the military had to think of the whole, not the individual. And if Charlie's little stretch of farmland wasn't a strategic area to secure, then Charlie and his family would be on their own for quite a while. But he was hoping the power plant at Mayfield would change that.

"So," Harold said, regarding his son. "What kind of unified message will we be sending?"

Charlie swallowed the ball of nerves caught in his throat then crossed his arms. "The biggest advantage that we have is the knowledge of the area. We know the land, we know the people. We'll establish a lookout schedule, someone always keeping watch, round the clock. And we only engage in a fight with the enemy if we know we can win. The moment those guys see our inexperience, they'll bum rush us."

"Do we have the numbers for round the clock guards?" Harold asked.

"It'll be some long days, but we should be able to manage if everyone pitches in to help." Charlie planted his fists on his hips and exhaled, as if he could feel the work already beating him down.

"We'll have to get a handle on our food stock," Harold said, sliding into Charlie's line of thinking. "The moment supplies start to run low, we're going to be in trouble." He gestured toward the house. "With all of those folks in the house, we'll blow through our cellar pretty quick."

Charlie nodded in agreement. "We can hunt in the woods, and Mario spent some time on the fishing boats, so maybe he could help us set nets in the river." He turned to his father. "We should say something before everyone goes to bed tonight."

Harold nodded and clapped his son on the back. "I think I'll leave that to you, my boy." He laughed. "I've been waiting for you to run the show since you got back from college." He threw his arm around his son's shoulder and squeezed him into his body. "Glad to see you wanting to be a leader, son."

Charlie mirrored his father's smile. "Thanks, Dad."

"I'll meet you inside."

He watched his father stumble toward the house, his big body swinging back and forth. His dad didn't get around as well as he used to, and truth be told, he couldn't do much around the farm other than supervise, but no one made a fuss about it. There wasn't anyone else that Charlie knew who had worked harder than his father over the course of his lifetime.

Harold had poured tireless hours into the land that surrounded him. Day in and day out for nearly forty years, starting at fifteen when he dropped out of high school to help his family with the orchard full time.

Charlie would have done the same if it hadn't been for his

parents. He still helped, of course, but not at the sacrifice of his schoolwork. His parents had placed a big bet on him when they sent him off to college. And it was a bet that was finally paying dividends, at least up until yesterday.

The EMP had thrown their future into a different type of uncertainty. It was uncharted waters and filled with dangers that Charlie couldn't even imagine.

When Charlie returned to the house, he heard the chatter from their new guests through the back-screen door before he even stepped inside. He paused at the back steps, listening to the voices inside. And despite the hardship of the day, he smiled at their laughter.

Charlie entered, finding Mario, the workers, and their wives gathered in the living room, the women sitting while the men stood. It was Mario who noticed Charlie first and hushed the group.

"I hope everyone is settled in," Charlie said.

"We are," Mario said. "Thank you, Senor Decker."

"Yes," Maria replied, echoing her husband's thanks. "We are very grateful for your family's generosity."

"It's our pleasure," Martha said, smiling next to Harold. "And you're all welcome to stay as long as this…" she waved her hands around through the air as she struggled to find the words, "thing goes on."

"And do we know how long this will last?" Mario asked, acting as the mouthpiece for the other workers. "No power? No cars? Nothing? This—" he frowned, struggling with the pronunciation. "E-M-P, caused all of this?"

"The truth is we don't know how long this is going to last," Charlie said. "But we should be planning for the long term."

"But the power will come back on, right?" Antonio stepped from the corner of the room, hands in his pockets, his open shirt exposing the harsh tan lines from the neck up.

"We don't know that either," Charlie answered. "And I'm

not going to give you answers that I don't have. The power is off. But, we do have food and water here, which I can tell you is a lot better off than most of the people I saw on my escape from Seattle. We have provisions in our cellar, and the forest holds plenty of game. But there is a bigger threat than just the power being shut off."

Charlie crossed his arms and stepped closer to the center of the room.

"The people responsible for this are dangerous," Charlie said. "If they come back, they're not going to leave us alive."

"You want us to fight them?" Antonio asked, bunching up his face in a grimace. "But they're trained killers."

"We're not going to look for a fight," Charlie answered. "But we're not backing down from going a fight. We'll have security on watch twenty-four hours, which means we'll all need to be trained in using firearms."

"We will do what we have to," Maria said, her tone firm as she grabbed hold of her husband's hand. "Right, ladies?"

The other wives offered the same hardened expressions as Maria, and Charlie was glad to have Mario and his wife here. They were good people, and they'd be invaluable at bridging any language or culture barriers that they were bound to run into during their time together.

"It'll also be important for us to conserve as much of our supplies as we can, because while we'd all like for this to be over quickly, we need to ensure we're preparing for the long haul." Charlie gestured to beyond the walls of the house and to the orchard outside. "We have a lot of acreage out there to maintain. Other people might need help, and I want to make sure we're ready to do that if the time comes." He took a breath, everyone leaning into him now, every pair of eyes watching him intently. "Our strength comes from working together." He looked at each of them in turn. "I'm well aware of the sacrifice it takes to leave your home, and all of us will have to sacrifice more before this is done."

A wave of nods washed over the rest of the faces, and while Charlie felt good about their desire to believe in him, he hoped that translated into believing in themselves just as much as him.

"Thank you," Charlie said. "Now we should all probably—"

The distant pop of gunfire silenced the room, and every head turned toward the window. It was too far away to be any danger to them, but that didn't lessen the expressions of horror that rippled through their faces.

Another series of harsh pops pulled Charlie outside, and the rest of the crew followed suit. The commotion was coming from the east where the terrorists had marched.

"That's Mayfield," Harold said, standing in the back by the door with Martha, who huddled up next to her husband.

"They would have to pass the Bigelow farm," Martha said as she looked up at Harold. "Do you think they're still there?"

"Don's a smart man," Harold answered. "He wouldn't do anything rash."

"I'm not so sure about that." Charlie listened to the continued pops on the horizon. And just as suddenly as the gunfire started, it stopped.

The silence that followed was more deafening than anything that Charlie had experienced. It was like the air had been sucked out of everyone, the environment around them transformed into a vacuum. And while Charlie stared at the horizon, unsure of what he was waiting to hear, his feet backpedaled into the house, the rest of the group stepping aside.

18

*B*efore he realized it, he was back in the barn, grabbing one of the Remingtons and spare magazines, which he shoved into his belt. When he looked up, Mario was by the table.

"You don't have to come," Charlie said.

Mario switched his attention from Charlie toward the weapons on the table. He picked one of the Winchesters up, grabbing some of the bullets and shoving them into the chamber, just like Harold had shown him.

"We never got to the shooting portion of the lesson," Charlie said.

Mario gestured to the end of the rifle's barrel. "Just make sure it's pointed at the bad guy, right?"

Charlie nodded. "That'll work."

The pair marched off into the fading evening light, keeping to the orchard for cover on their path toward the Bigelows' farm. The pair churned up soil until they reached the open space between the Deckers' land and the Bigelows.

Panting, Charlie raised the rifle and peered through the scope, magnifying the Bigelows' house. "Front and back doors are open." He shifted to a nearby window, but it was too dark to see anything inside.

"Are they still in the house?" Mario asked.

Charlie removed his eye off the scope, then lowered the rifle. "I don't know."

The Bigelows grew cabbage, which didn't provide any cover on their sprint through the field, but Charlie didn't see the enemy lingering in the fading light.

Charlie slowed when they approached the house. "Stay behind me." He headed toward the back, hoping to throw any of the terrorists off guard should any be lurking behind.

The Bigelow house was one story, but sprawled out over a larger space, which would make searching the house difficult seeing as how there were dozens of places to hide.

"Watch our backs," Charlie said, whispering behind him.

"Got it, boss."

Charlie poked the end of his rifle barrel into the open back door and the darkness inside the house. He resisted the urge to call out to Don or Amy, or any of the kids inside. If they were hiding and there was still someone else in the house, then he didn't want to give away their position.

But the top step of the three-tiered staircase that led into the back sunroom of the house, which was completely screened, groaned loudly when Charlie stepped on it, the noise made worse by the deafening silence of the night.

Both Charlie and Mario froze, curses running through Charlie's mind at machine-gun fire pace at his own clumsiness.

A series of hushed voices followed Charlie's foot faux pas, and they were coming from the shed that sat on the back left side of the house. Charlie headed over first, Mario following, both men keeping their weapons up and aimed, fingers on the triggers.

The noises inside the shed ended before Charlie reached

the door, and he looked behind to Mario, gesturing with his free hand to keep a lookout. Mario nodded.

Charlie turned his attention back to the shed's closed door. He reached for the handle, wrapped his fingers around the black bar, paused, took a breath, and then pulled hard.

A quick rush of air smacked Charlie's face when the door opened, and he lunged inside the darkened space in the same motion, his foot thudding against the concrete floor. But as Charlie scanned the tiny space through the sight on his shotgun, he found it empty save for the sacks of tools and chicken feed that lined the floors and tables.

Charlie lowered the rifle and frowned. He blinked a few times, making sure he wasn't missing anything in the darkness. He turned toward the door where Mario was still watching the exterior when another noise caught his ear.

A shuffling, in the corner of the shed, coming from the sacks of chicken feed. Charlie stared at the space, then slowly approached. He prodded the sack of corn with the end of his rifle, but there was nothing but feed inside.

Charlie glanced at the floor, then lifted one of the feed sacks and found the outline of a door etched in the concrete. Charlie set the rifle aside and then removed the rest of the feedbags until he finally revealed the door underneath.

A handle rested on the left side, but when Charlie pulled, it wouldn't give way. He knocked on the door, leaning close to the cracks provided. "Amy?" He paused, waiting for a response. "Amy, it's Charlie Decker, are you down there?"

A few seconds passed, and there was nothing. Then a shuffling noise, and a heavy thunk, and Charlie stepped back as the door in the floor cracked open. A pair of eyes stared at Charlie, and then the door opened the rest of the way.

"Charlie? Thank God." Amy extended her hand and Charlie helped her up and out of the hole. She wrapped her arms around him, but then quickly pulled back. "Did you see Don?"

"He's not down there with you?" Charlie asked, glancing into the hole and finding their three boys huddled at the bottom, looking up at him in the darkness.

"No, he-he brought us out here, and locked us inside, and then I heard all of that gunfire and I—" She covered her mouth with her hand and then looked past Charlie and Mario and toward the house.

Before Amy did anything rash, Charlie grabbed her by the shoulders and pulled her back to the present. "You need to stay here with the kids, and I'm going to go and find Don, all right?" He gestured back toward Mario. "I'm going to leave Mario here with you to watch your back. Just stay here with the kids."

Charlie backed out of the shed, instructing Mario to position himself inside, and then headed toward the house with his rifle raised.

It would have made sense for Don to head for the woods on the backside of his property, but Charlie wasn't sure if he would have made it that far in an open field. And if he did, then Charlie assumed Don would have returned by now, unless he was still leading the terrorists on a wild goose chase through the trees. Charlie knew he couldn't cover that much ground, so he decided to search the house and see if Don was inside.

The back screen door groaned when Charlie entered, his eyes already adjusted to the darkness inside.

An old oak table, chairs askew around the imperfect rectangle, sat near the door. Charlie cleared the dining room and then transitioned toward the living room where a long, three-cushioned sofa sat against the far wall with two love seats positioned on either end of the room, giving the open space a sense of structure.

"Don," Charlie said, whispering. "Don, it's Charlie." He stepped lightly over the blue carpet, leaving behind tracks of dirt from his boots. He glanced down, finding other dirtied prints already crushed into the carpet, no doubt left behind from the terrorists when they swarmed inside.

But when Charlie reached the end of the living room that dumped into the foyer by the front door, which was open, he noticed the three bullet holes on the adjacent hall and the Bigelow family picture that lay shattered on the floor.

Moonlight helped guide Charlie's path as he headed toward the bedrooms of the house, and when the heel of his boot slipped across the wooden floors, he glanced down to find a smear of blood. He frowned, dropping to a knee, and noticed the other droplets that dotted the floor and trailed all the way to the end of the hall.

Charlie stood, adjusting his grip on the rifle, and then hastened his pace down the hall. "Don." He repeated his neighbor's name with his harsh whisper, his voice growing louder and bolder the farther he headed down the hall. "Don."

The blood droplets ended at the end of the hallway to an open door and a bedroom, and Charlie's heart jumped into his throat as he turned the corner, unsure of what he might find inside. His eyes settled on Don's body on the floor of the room.

Charlie lowered the rifle, setting it aside as he quickly knelt by Don's side. "Don?" Blood covered his leg and both hands lay motionless on his stomach. He pressed his fingers against Don's neck, trying to stop himself from trembling so he could get an accurate reading of the man's pulse.

Finally, Charlie's hand steadied and he felt the lightest bump beneath his fingertips, and then Don stirred, his eyes fluttering open in time with a guttural moan from his lips.

"Don, can you hear me?" Charlie repeated the question, but Don's only reply was the same low growl. He placed his hands over the wound on Don's leg, then reached for the sheets on the bed. He tore them down and quickly wrapped

Don's leg to help stop the bleeding, smearing crimson over the pale blue sheets.

Charlie turned back toward the door, confident that they were alone in the house and that the terrorists were already long gone down the road. "Mario! Mario, I need help, now!" His voice cracked, and he was surprised by the urgency in his volume and tone. He turned back toward Don. "Just hang on, buddy, we're gonna get you some help. Just stay with me, okay? Do it for Amy and the kids. They need you, Don."

Don fluttered his eyelids, then worked his lips as if he were going to speak, but only a raspy breath escaped from the depths of his chest.

Charlie shook his head. "Try not to talk, Don. Just hang on." He applied firm pressure to the wound on the gut and was about to scream for Mario again when the man came bursting through the door, his eyes widening with a mixture of horror and shock at the scene in front of him. "Get something we can carry him on. We need to take him to Doc's house."

Color drained from Mario's face as he gawked at Don, the rifle gripped lazily in his right hand, the barrel aimed at the floor.

"Mario!" Charlie shouted, pulling the farmhand's attention toward him, the pair locking eyes. "Something to carry him on, or he's not going to make it."

Mario nodded, his body twitching in the same adrenaline-filled spasms that Charlie felt. He stole one last glance at Don before he disappeared down the hall.

Charlie held Don's hand in his own and gave it a squeeze, as if he could transmit some of the life flowing through his veins into his neighbor. There had already been so much death, and it had spread throughout their community like wildfire. And the longer Charlie sat on the floor with Don dying and bloodied next to him, the angrier Charlie became.

19

*M*orning arrived quickly, and Charlie rolled uncomfortably in the spare cot that he'd pulled out from the attic. He sat upright and rubbed the sleep from his eyes.

When he lowered his hand, he caught sight of the dried blood on his knuckle. He stared at it, thinking of Don.

Mario and Charlie had managed to get Don over to Doc's house, leaving the old vet to work on another body while Charlie went back for Amy and the kids. But after the kids were secured at the house, Amy went to Doc. He wasn't sure if she came home during the night and even more unsure if Don had survived.

Doc hadn't been optimistic about Don's chances when Charlie and Mario brought him over. He didn't say it in so many words, but the grave expression didn't bode well for his neighbor.

Charlie rubbed his face, the stubble along his cheeks scraping against his palm. By the end of the week he'd have the beginnings of a beard, and the prospect of so much hair on his face during the middle of summer was making him sweat just thinking about it.

Charlie's knees popped as he stood. The violence and recklessness of the past forty-eight hours had ravaged his mind and body, so he descended to the first floor in search of coffee.

Thankfully, Charlie's mother was already awake and had the old pot belly stove working out back. She had just clanged the door shut, letting the wood inside burn and heat the top.

"Hey, boy," Martha said, planting a kiss on her son's cheek. "Hear anything from Doc about Don?" She stepped back inside the kitchen and grabbed a pot, then poured some water she'd already retrieved from the well and placed it on the warming stove top.

"Not yet," Charlie said. "I was going to get ready to head over there in a minute."

"Well, your father is already up. He pulled out that damn iron stove from the back of the barn and set it up for me. He's out passing some bacon and eggs around to the folks that we put on guard duty last night. We've got some left if you're hungry. I ran over to the Bigelows' chicken coop and grabbed a couple eggs, and the bacon is actually more like jerky, but it does the job."

"Coffee first," Charlie said, still struggling to keep his eyelids open.

With her hands planted on her hips, the water boiling for coffee, and the near obliviousness of her attitude toward the danger that was surrounding all of them, Charlie found it hard not to laugh at his mother. But he kept his lips tight and planted a kiss on her cheek once the coffee was done.

The rest of the house was up by the time Charlie headed toward Doc's house, but he made sure the rest of the farm hands knew which posts they were relieving for the ones still out in the fields.

"How long will we be out there, boss?" Hector asked, one

eye squinted shut and his dirty white shirt untucked from his dirt-stained jeans.

"We're working in eight-hour shifts, that way everyone gets a chance at some sleep," Charlie answered. "It'll be a little tricky during the day with some of the chores, but we'll be all right running a skeleton crew for a while."

Hector flashed a thumbs up, and his youngest daughter ran up behind him, squeezing his legs, as she smiled up at her father, who picked her up and swung her around in the air.

Charlie appreciated everyone's positive outlook and the kindred spirit atmosphere, but he knew that the close quarters would eventually wear down on people, which made the prospect of having Doc's house and even Don's place as a backup for beds good.

The rest of the kids spilled outside, no doubt thankful for the open space after being cooped up in that house with twenty other people. But while the farm hands' kids were outside, Charlie noticed that the Bigelow boys weren't. If Don hadn't survived the night, then Charlie needed to figure out a plan for Amy and the boys.

The sun had burned away the rest of the grey in the sky, and morning was in full swing by the time Charlie reached Doc's house. He was about to enter unannounced but stopped himself. He stepped back and then knocked. He wasn't sure of any rule changes in this new world order, but he decided it best to maintain social etiquette.

Ellen answered the door, still dressed in the same clothes that Charlie had seen her wear yesterday.

"How is he doing?" Charlie asked, stepping inside while Ellen shut the door behind him.

She shook his head, hugging her shoulders. "He did what he could, but Don lost so much blood, even more than Liz. And the two bullet wounds added a lot of trauma. He was able to get the bullets out and stitch him up, but he's not sure

Don is going to make it." She exhaled. "He's on borrowed time."

Charlie's stomach tightened. "Is Amy still with him?"

"Yeah, poor thing. She stayed up with him all night," Ellen answered. She nodded toward the hallway with the bedrooms. "You can go and check on her, but she hasn't said a peep since Doc finished sewing Don up." She frowned, shaking her head. "I think she's still in shock."

Charlie nodded and then took a closer look at Ellen, who hugged herself tightly with a concerned expression glued to her face. The woman looked like she'd slept about as much as Charlie had. "How are you holding up?"

"Hmm?" Ellen arched her eyebrows in surprise, Charlie's question pulling her from her daydream. "Oh, I'm fine. Just tired. Doc hasn't been sleeping well, and when he doesn't sleep well, neither do I. We're attached at the hip like that." She smiled sadly, trying to convince Charlie that she really was fine, but it was a mask that Charlie had seen people wear a lot over the past two days. And he imagined that it would be a mask people would grow accustomed to wearing over the coming weeks, or even months, if things remained bad.

"Anything you and Doc need from the orchard you just ask, all right?" Charlie said, placing a firm hand on Ellen's shoulder. "I mean it."

Ellen patted Charlie's arm and nodded. "You're a good man, Charlie."

After Ellen disappeared into the kitchen, Charlie headed down the hallway, passing Liz's room, who he found still fast asleep in her bed, Adelyn curled up by her side. He stopped, watching the pair of them sleep. A sense of purpose flooded through him, knowing that the pair had no one else to depend on save for Charlie. He smiled and then headed toward Don's room, finding the door cracked open.

Even though the door was open, Charlie knocked softly. "Amy?"

When no one answered, Charlie poked his head though the crack in the door. Amy kneeled at Don's bedside, elbows planted on the mattress, and her hands clasped together as she stared at her husband.

Charlie pushed his way into the room but didn't go farther than the threshold, where he got a good look at Don in the bed. His eyes were closed, and his lips were lightly parted. He lay still and unmoving, save for the light rise and fall of his chest. The sheet covering his body was pulled all the way up to his chest, leaving only his shoulder, neck, and head exposed.

Amy didn't acknowledge Charlie's presence, but he wasn't sure if it was because she hadn't heard him or if she didn't want to talk.

"Amy?" Charlie asked.

Amy turned, surprised, and then wiped her nose, which was red from crying. "Charlie. I'm sorry, I didn't—"

"It's fine," Charlie said, gesturing for her to stay put as he walked to the foot of the bed. "How's he doing?"

"Doc says he's fighting it," Amy answered, smiling.

"He's always been stubborn," Charlie replied.

Amy laughed. "Yeah." She reached for her husband's arm and squeezed. "Thank you for last night. If you hadn't come, if you hadn't gotten him here in time—" She shook her head, fighting back tears. "I don't know what would have happened."

Charlie smiled, but looking at Don's pale complexion, he wasn't sure if he got the man here soon enough.

Wood groaned by the door, and both Amy and Charlie turned to find Doc standing in the doorway. He wore his blue robe, hands in his pockets, those dark circles under his eyes even deeper than yesterday.

"How are you doing, Amy?" Doc asked.

"I'm fine."

Doc nodded, then walked over to Don, checking his pulse.

Amy frowned in concern. "Is he okay? Is—"

"He's fine for now, my dear." Doc removed his hand from Don's neck and then looked to Charlie. "Why don't we let them rest."

"Sure," Charlie said, then followed Doc out of the room, shutting the door behind him.

The pair remained silent on their walk into the living room, but Doc crossed his arms and paced nervously with his head down.

"You all right, Doc?" Charlie asked.

"No, Charlie," Doc answered. "I'm not." He finally collapsed onto the couch by the front living room window. The same couch where Charlie had passed out that first night back from Seattle when he wasn't sure if Liz would survive.

Doc rubbed his hands together, thinking. "I don't have any more antibiotics." He looked at Charlie. "I gave the last of my dosage to Liz. And while I tried to sterilize everything—" He shook his head, the frustration mounting, and he stood. "I don't have the necessary equipment to deal with treating humans, Charlie. My knowledge is rudimentary at best."

"You've kept two people alive," Charlie said. "You're doing a great job."

"Well, if I don't get more supplies, I don't know if I can keep them that way."

Charlie turned back toward the hallway where Liz and Don slept, still recovering, still fighting for the chance at tomorrow. He turned back to Doc. "There's a hospital over in Mayfield. I could get whatever you needed and bring it back."

Doc shook his head. "Charlie, that's exactly where those men were headed. It's too dangerous."

"If that's what we need to keep them alive, then that's what I'll get," Charlie said. "Just tell me what you need."

Doc hesitated for a moment, but the medical professional in him eventually won out.

It didn't take long for Doc to compile the grocery list of needs and wants, which Charlie made him list separately. The names on the list were so long and so hard to pronounce that Charlie didn't even try. All he'd need to do was make sure the names on the medications matched up with the ones that Doc had written down.

"Now, they'll most likely have some kind of lock or security system in place for the medications, but if it's anything electronic—"

"Then it makes my job easier," Charlie said. "What's the likelihood that the hospital staff will still be there?"

"Depends if the generators are working or not," Doc answered. "Though I can't imagine they'd still be on after something like this."

With the list tucked into his back pocket, Charlie walked back through the orchard, the sky still blue and vibrant, though clouds had started to form, foreshadowing rain.

"Charlie!" Harold waved at his son from a few rows up in the trees. "Give me a hand for a second."

Charlie jogged over to his father, keeping the ladder steady as Harold plucked a few good ones clustered at the top branches.

"Your mother wanted to have the kids help her bake some pies," Harold said, stretching his big arm up for the last apple, which he plopped into the bucket. "She thought it might help keep their minds off of things."

Charlie stepped out of the way as his father descended the ladder.

"Plus, we get some pies out of the deal, which will last for a little while." Harold clapped the dirt from his hands and smiled at the bucket of Honey Crisps.

"It's a good idea," Charlie said.

"Yeah." Harold shifted his attention from the bucket to the

rest of the orchard, the long and separate, elevated rows that comprised their property. He smiled. "Nothing like picking fruit straight from the tree. Makes you feel connected to the world."

Charlie nodded. It was simple but beautiful.

"How's Don?" Harold asked, popping their peaceful bubble and thrusting them back into reality.

"Doc needs more meds to keep him alive," Charlie answered. "I'm going to the hospital in Mayfield and see what I can find."

Harold nodded. "You know when your grandfather passed away and I took over, it was a different time. He died young, and I had so many doubts about myself and whether or not I could keep this place afloat." He scuffed his heel against the dirt. "I did what I could, but I know it wasn't enough."

"Dad, what are you talking about?" Charlie gestured to the fields. "Look at this place."

But Harold only shook his head. "You've done more for this place over the past five years than I did after close to forty. Your mother might not let me read the accounting books, but I saw the notices in the mail. Overdue, Past Due, Late." He chuckled. "Just never could get it exactly right." He finally looked at his son. "But you're not like that. Never have been. Got your mother's brain, thank God."

A red flush crept up Charlie's neck and warmed his cheeks. It was rare that his father was ever sentimental. He cleared his throat.

"I never got the recognition I wanted from my father, and I know that I'm not one to express myself very well, but I didn't want you to think that I wasn't so damned proud of you."

Harold swiped his big hand at the corner of his eye, and Charlie smiled. He'd seen Harold Decker cry only twice in his lifetime. The first was when Charlie was eight, when his grandmother had passed away. The second was right now.

"I love you, Dad," Charlie said.

Harold cleared his throat and swiped at his eyes one more time before he turned around and smiled. "Love you too, son." He wrapped his boy in a bear hug, and then picked up the basket of apples. "Grab that ladder."

Bowlegged and tired, Harold carried the apples down the row of trees while Charlie trailed behind, letting the old bear take the lead. He knew how hard it was to admit that his tenure as boss was ending, but as far as Charlie was concerned, there was still only one opinion that mattered in this place. And it belonged to that gentle giant ahead of him.

When Charlie returned to the house, he packed up some food and water and started his trek toward Mayfield. His mother begged him to take someone, but Charlie didn't plan on walking.

Charlie found the dirt bike where he'd left it in the woods after he'd led the terrorists on a wild goose chase and checked the fuel. He still had three quarters of a tank, enough to get him to Mayfield and back with some to spare.

Charlie tightened the straps of his backpack and then hopped onto the seat of the dirt bike, pressing down hard on the kick starter, revving the two-stroke to life.

Wind blasted Charlie's face, cooling the sweat that had already formed on his body, the shirt and pants sticking his chest and legs.

Charlie glanced at Don and Amy's house as he passed, knowing that both of them were counting on him to retrieve the medicine Doc needed to keep Don alive.

And while he had the rifle slung across his back and the pistol on his belt, Charlie still hadn't determined how he was going to handle any pushback from anyone other than a masked gunman.

The world and its resources were going to get considerably smaller over the next few weeks if things didn't improve, Charlie had no doubts about that. Which was why he had hoped Dixon would make good on his promise and return with a military escort that would help alleviate the self-policing state that would inevitably follow.

But Charlie focused on what was ahead of him. Two lives, and who knew how many future lives, depended on it.

---

*T*he walk from the bridge where Charlie ditched the dirt bike to Mayfield was just under thirty minutes. He stashed the bike before town because he didn't want to give away the element of surprise should there be more terrorists nearby.

Charlie stuck to the woods on his trek but made sure the road never strayed too far from view. The walk was made longer by the rocks and hills and curving paths of the mountainous terrain.

But nature brought the added serenity of peace and calmness in a world that had become decidedly louder and scarier.

Charlie had always enjoyed the quiet, which had set him apart from a lot of kids he went to school with. When he was little, his teachers always used to tell his parents that he was aloof, or absentminded, but he'd just always been introspective.

There was something about the quiet that helped extract Charlie's thoughts. It allowed him to dig deeper, examine all the sides, turning the idea over in his mind.

Darker clouds rolled in above his head, and while he was

thankful for the reprieve from the sunlight, he didn't want to get caught coming back in the rain. Time wasn't on his side, and rain would only slow him down, even with the dirt bike.

Thirsty, Charlie reached into the side compartment of his pack for a bottle of water. He paced himself, knowing he had another one, but wanting to ration it for the walk back or if he was forced to stay longer than he would have liked.

He pressed the bottle water on the back of his neck. He tilted his head back, letting the cool water droplets run down his neck. When he opened his eyes, he saw the road sign for Mayfield, so he returned the bottle to his pack.

Closer to town, Charlie's senses were heightened, and he kept a keen lookout for any guards that the terrorists might have stationed in the area. After all, it was what he'd done on his own farm.

Flashes of Seattle peppered his mind, and just like the big city, the little town was at a standstill. Charlie kept hunched forward, his muscles poised to strike at any movement. But like the town ahead, the forest that surrounded him was deadly silent.

Charlie hovered near the tree line, using one of the big maples for cover as he scanned Main Street.

Cars were stopped dead in their tracks, though the number of vehicles that clogged the road in Mayfield were significantly less than the thousands of vehicles that had broken down on the streets of Seattle.

Charlie removed the rifle from his shoulder and used the scope for a better look at the buildings and the sidewalks. He maneuvered the crosshairs over the town, expecting to find some people, but the streets were empty.

Charlie lowered the scope. The ghost town ahead of him was somehow worse than finding it overrun with the terrorists.

Charlie kept the rifle in his hands, then emerged from the

woods. He moved quickly, rushing to the cover of the first building, which was an antique store.

The mountains were littered with them, bursting at the seams with hipsters and couples who wanted to score something unique for their loft or home back in the city.

Charlie peered through the darkened front windows, finding the inside void of any ransacked looting or destruction that was so prevalent in Seattle. He'd always believed that small-town folks were different, and he was glad for the affirmation of that not changing when times got hard.

Hunched forward, both hands gripping the rifle, Charlie hurried toward the hospital near the edge of town.

Gusts of wind jingled bells and wind chimes that stretched along the front porches of the businesses along Main Street. Every building was separated by a narrow alley, barely wide enough for a single car to make it through, which led to the personal parking lots for the business owners and employees.

Charlie paused at every alley, checking to ensure he wasn't ambushed by friend or foe, and when he stepped onto the front porch of a florist's shop, the pump of a shotgun froze him in place.

"Drop the rifle, friend," a man's voice said. "Off to your left, and do it real slow."

Charlie did as the man asked, setting the rifle down.

"And go ahead and slide that pack off your back," he added.

Charlie again complied, setting his backpack next to the rifle. He kept his hands raised in the air and kept very still.

"Good. Now turn around, nice and slow. Keep those hands up," the man said.

A lump caught in Charlie's throat just before he was able to make out the image of the middle-aged man aiming the shotgun at him, surprise flashing over both of them.

"Holy shit, Charlie?" Doug Collins lowered the shotgun, his jaw dropping in the same motion.

Without a word, Charlie walked over to Doug and the men wrapped each other in a bear hug.

Charlie smiled. "Good to see you."

Doug was Charlie's height, but ten years older. Charlie had grown up with Doug's younger brother, Billy, who joined the Marines after high school. Three months into his first deployment, a roadside bomb took out his convoy in Afghanistan.

Doug laughed. "You too. Is everything all right? The orchard okay?"

"We're all right," Charlie answered, going back for his weapon, which he holstered. "I was heading to the hospital for some supplies. Don Bigelow's hurt pretty bad, and Doc needs some medicine to keep him alive."

Doug wiped his palm along the rough red stubble that crawled over his cheeks and neck, ending at his Adam's apple. "Shit. That's not good."

"I know, it's sort of a time crunch, so—"

"No, I mean going to the hospital," Doug said. "It's at the end of town and it's crawling with those fuckers who stormed through here yesterday. They shot anything that moved, or anything that didn't." He looked out into the streets. "Me and a few others got the bodies out of the road and turned them over to their families if they had any. The rest we covered out back, but we need to get them in the ground soon before they start to rot."

Charlie followed Doug's gaze into the streets and the carnage that lingered behind. Blood stains were still on the pavements from where the bodies had been removed, and a few rays of sun illuminated the bullet casings that littered the pavement, which stretched down the length of Main Street.

Doug glanced around them, nervous. "We should talk inside. C'mon."

Charlie followed Doug around the backside of the building and Doug knocked on a pair of metal cellar doors, paused, then knocked twice.

A few seconds later and a lock turned on the inside of the doors, and after they opened, the end of a rifle poked through.

"Charlie?" Mr. Collins scrunched his face in disbelief and then stepped out of the cellar, extending his weathered hand, which gripped hold of Charlie's with a firm tenacity that didn't match the aged man it belonged to. "Good to see you, boy."

"You too, Mr. Collins."

"Well, better get back inside before those bastards pick us off with whatever snipers they have hiding in the area." Mr. Collins waved his big hand and turned back down the steps of the cellar, Doug letting Charlie go in first.

The basement was cool and dark, save for the few candles that they had burning, and it was just the two of them down below, but Charlie didn't expect anything different. The pair had always been loners, especially after Doug's mother passed away. It was right after the death of Billy. That was a rough year for the Collins family.

Mr. Collins collapsed in a chair, setting the rifle across his lap and rubbing his left knee, wincing as he worked his knobby fingers over the surrounding muscles. "Your family hold up all right?"

"Yes, sir," Charlie answered.

"He's heading to the hospital," Doug said. "Don Bigelow's hurt and Doc needs some supplies."

"The vet?" Mr. Collins exclaimed. "Christ, things must be bad if Doc has swapped farm animals for people on that steel slab of his." He ended the work on his knee and then leaned back into the chair. "Hospital's locked up pretty tight. Not sure you'd find anything if it wasn't though. Those masked folks have probably pilfered that place clean."

Charlie leaned forward, hoping to learn more about the foreign enemy that had invaded their homes and communities from the pair of roughnecks in the basement. "Do you know how many men they have?"

Mr. Collins sucked in his lower lip and glanced toward the ceiling, as if he were counting them individually. "I'd say around three hundred."

Charlie popped his eyes open in surprise. "Three hundred? The group that came down our way couldn't have been more than a dozen, maybe two."

"They've been coming through the woods," Doug said. "They're in those same sizes you described, but they've been arriving during all hours of the day and night."

"Bastards have stationed themselves off the road toward the electric plant," Mr. Collins said. "They've occupied any building near it and killed anyone that tried to stop them." He snarled as he shook his head in a manner of disgust. "They've got machine guns for Christ's sakes, the people out here don't have that kind of weaponry!" He huffed, his breathing growing labored and his cheeks reddening the more he thought about it.

"Your blood pressure, Dad," Doug said. "Just take it easy."

Mr. Collins tugged at his shirt collar and grumbled to himself, and Doug turned to Charlie.

"What about you?" Doug asked. "Hear anything?"

The expressions on the Collins' faces ranged from disbelief to laughter when Charlie brought the pair up to speed.

"All of Seattle?" Doug asked.

"From what I could tell," Charlie answered.

"And how long has that lieutenant been gone?" Mr. Collins asked.

"A little over a day now," Charlie answered. "But I really do believe he'll come back."

"So long as his CO doesn't have a problem with it." Mr. Collins bit the end of his fingernail and bounced his right leg, thinking. After a moment, he nodded to himself. "We need to get organized. There's no guarantee that help is on the way." He pointed at Charlie as he looked to his son. "He's got the right idea. He's getting ready."

"Dad, we tried getting people to do something, and it didn't work." Doug leaned forward and then backpedaled toward the steps that led up to the cellar doors. "There's maybe only another dozen or so people that know how to shoot around here, and half of them are long gone."

"We fight with the men that we have," Mr. Collins said, his voice challenging his son.

"Against three hundred trained soldiers?" Doug waved the notion away. "You're out of your god-damn mind."

"Doug's right, Mr. Collins," Charlie said. "We won't stand a chance in a fight against that many numbers, even if we had more. But we can gather supplies."

Doug slouched, a pained expression on his face and a slight whine to his voice. "Charlie, I just told you how many men they've got down at that hospital, and now you want to go running straight into that? You just said yourself that fighting them head-on isn't a good idea."

"I'm not talking about fighting them, I'm talking about getting the supplies we need, and then getting out." Charlie stepped closer to Doug. "We know this area better than they do. We can do it."

Mr. Collins stood, pushing the chair back behind him, the legs scraping against the old wooden floors. "He's right, boy. We can't just sit around. Action is what we need. It's a tough pill to swallow, but medicine that's good for you never tastes that way."

"Says the man who won't take his heart meds," Doug said, spitting the words back at his father. He leaned back against the wall, shaking his head, raising his eyebrows at Charlie. "You really think that this is a good idea?"

"It doesn't have anything to do with how good or bad the

idea is," Charlie answered. "It's what we have to do to survive. Plain and simple."

And just like that medicine Mr. Collins talked about that tasted so bad going down, Charlie knew that the hard truth he'd just spoken was equally as bitter.

21

*T*he journey between the cellar and the hospital was short. Charlie let Doug and Mr. Collins lead the way. They kept to the back side of the buildings on Main Street until Charlie convinced them the woods were a better source of cover.

The thick brush, rocks, and unlevel terrain slowed them even more, but Charlie was more comfortable in the concealment that the forest offered.

The three men bunched up together as they neared the hospital, and Charlie peered through the scope of his rifle to get a better look.

Mayfield's hospital was small compared to the big facilities in Seattle. It was three stories and was a near-perfect rectangular box.

A pair of bodies lay outside the back entrance.

"No terrorists," Charlie said, performing another scan, this time keeping his motion slower, making sure that he didn't miss anything. "If we can sneak through the back, I think—"

A pair of masked men stepped into Charlie's line of sight, walking down the hospital's west perimeter. Both were armed, though their posture was relaxed. He followed them around toward the back, where they entered the hospital.

"Shit." Charlie lowered the rifle. "Two of them just walked inside."

"Only two?" Mr. Collins asked. "That's manageable."

"We can't assume that they're inside alone," Charlie replied.

"Goddammit," Doug said, muttering under his breath. "So, what do we do now?"

Charlie tucked the rifle's stock under his arm, tapping the chamber with his forefinger. A crease was set in his forehead, the way it always did whenever those hard thoughts traveled through his mind. "We'll circle around to the other side, check and see if there's another entrance, or if they've got more guards stationed."

"Well, let's keep moving," Mr. Collins said. "Every time we stop, my damn knee freezes up."

Luckily the backside of the hospital had a nice wooded area and provided the threesome with plenty of cover on their journey toward the east side of the hospital's perimeter, which they found clear of terrorists.

"And you're sure they don't have anyone stationed out front?" Charlie asked.

"I was down here just before you walked into town," Doug answered, his tone dancing between confident and perturbed. "Ain't nobody sitting out front."

Charlie nodded, flexing his grip over the rifle in his hands. It was as sure of a bet as he was going to receive in these conditions. "We keep quiet when we're inside, only speaking if we have to. Doc said the meds and equipment he needs would most likely be on the first floor in the center of the hospital, away from the patients and waiting rooms. We get what we need, and we get out."

The Collins men nodded in agreement, and this time Charlie took the lead as he quickly darted from the woods and toward the hospital's back entrance. It might have been a risk going through the same door that they watched the enemy enter, but it was already a confirmed point of entrance, and if they were going to get into a gunfight, Charlie would rather it happen sooner rather than later.

They clustered together at the door, and Charlie reached for the handle, looking to Doug and Mr. Collins, who nodded they were ready.

Charlie stepped inside the darkened hall without hesitation, scanning the narrow corridor, and found it empty.

"I have eyes on the left," Doug said.

"I've got our backs," Mr. Collins said.

"I'll take right," Charlie said.

The trio moved forward in unison in a triangle formation, and every room that they passed with a closed door sent a shiver down Charlie's back. But it wasn't until they'd passed the hallway's halfway point that he realized why everything was so unsettling.

"It's quiet," Charlie said.

Doug frowned. "Yeah. So? The staff probably ran for it when the power went out and those gunmen showed up."

Charlie shook his head, glancing at the doors up ahead. "A hospital doesn't just have a staff, they have patients."

As the realization washed over Doug's face, his cheeks turned a shade of green. "Jesus Christ."

Charlie turned toward the nearest door. He approached wearily, the rifle sagging lower the closer he moved. It was cracked open, the darkness inside masking the interior.

He took three steps inside. The air was damp and a smell graced his nostrils. The scent was foul, but he resisted the instinct to turn away.

After a few seconds, Charlie's vision adjusted, and he blinked away the darkness. Objects took shape: a table, chairs, an empty bed, and a curtain that was pulled back and concealing the other half of the room.

Charlie stepped toward it, his movements slow but methodical. He outstretched his arm, his fingers grabbing hold of the end of the curtain, and then slowly pulled it back, revealing the bloodied body on the bed.

It was a woman. She was old. Her eyes were still open, and the wound on her chest had dried and crusted with blood, covering not just the gown that she wore in her final moments, but also the bed, the wall, ceiling, and floor.

Several life support machines were lined against the back wall and on either side of the woman's bed, and Charlie wondered if she was even alive when the murderers gunned her down.

"Charlie?" Doug's voice was quiet and sheepish, and he lingered at the doorway, staying in the hall. "You all right?"

Charlie stared at the blank expression on the old woman's face, and anger simmered below the calm and calculated surface of his thoughts.

Charlie pulled the curtain back, sealing the woman away. He stepped back out into the hallway, gun still lowered, and continued his trek down the hall, but Doug jumped in front of him, blocking his path.

"Whoa, hey, are you all right?" Doug asked.

"No, Doug, I'm not all right, but we have a job to do, so why don't you get the hell out of my way so we can do it." Charlie kept his voice down, but it didn't lessen the sting from the venom laced with every word out of his mouth.

"Hey, man, you're the one who wanted to come inside here," Doug said, refusing to back down. "What did you think you were gonna see, huh? You saw what it was like out in the street."

"Knock it off, boys," Mr. Collins said.

But the old man's words rolled off of Charlie like water on a seal. He stepped forward, that rage simmering beneath the surface starting to boil.

"I was in Seattle when they attacked, so you don't have to

tell me what those bastards can do," Charlie said, starting to lose control of the volume in his voice.

"I said enough," Mr. Collins said, stepping between the pair. "This isn't a competition of how much shit we've waded through."

Charlie knew the old man's words were true, but they didn't calm his anger. And just when that inertia pushed him past the point of no return, gunfire and shouts echoed down the hall.

All three of them ducked. Mr. Collins was the first to return fire down the hall, which provided them enough time to press forward and dart down a cutaway from the main hall.

A few more retaliatory shots were fired from the terrorists at the front of the hospital, and just when Charlie was about to turn the corner and fire, he caught sight of a body on the floor just left of his feet. It was a nurse, and the woman's face was turned up toward the ceiling, a wound in her chest and stomach, similar to the elderly woman he found in the room.

The sight of the scrubs brought Liz to the forefront of Charlie's thoughts. It could have just as easily been her on that floor.

"Charlie, no!" Doug reached for Charlie's arm, but his motion was too late, and his fingertips were only able to scrape against Charlie's sleeve.

Exposed in the hallway, Charlie fell into the tunnel vision that his rifle's scope provided. The magnification thrust him down the hall, and he squeezed the trigger, and for the first time since he encountered the enemy, they weren't wearing masks.

It was an Asian man, and he was young. Charlie's age, or even younger. A mixture of anger and surprise was plastered over his face, the rushed courage that only the pumping of adrenaline could provide. It was the same adrenaline that coursed through Charlie and had propelled him to the place he currently stood.

But the force controlling Charlie's adrenaline was rage, and it burned through whatever empathy he had for the young man at the end of the hall. For all Charlie knew, he could have put a bullet in that old woman in her bed. Or the nurse that lay at his feet. Or a dozen other corpses that littered the hospital tile. The boy made his choice. And Charlie had made his.

The bullet went through the young man's left eye, dead center, bulls eye. Charlie didn't even feel the recoil from the gunshot, and his hands worked deftly over the bolt action as the bullet casing dropped to the floor and Charlie chambered another round.

The second terrorist at the end of the hall fired, his shots wild and quick, more concerned over quantity of bullets than their accuracy, hoping dumb luck and the spray would bring Charlie down, or at the very least cause him to run.

But Charlie kept a steady pace forward, eye still glued to the scope, and smoothly brought the crosshairs over to the next target. It was like chasing a deer. Charlie had done it thousands of times with his father, and all those trips had finally come in handy as he pulled the trigger.

The bullet screamed from the rifle and struck the terrorist's chest, dead center. Blood spurted, and the man's expression transformed from unadulterated rage to cold shock with the snap of a finger, then collapsed to the floor, skidding forward.

Charlie lowered the rifle, but he didn't stop walking toward the dead men on the floor, the one he shot in the eye staring up at the ceiling through what one good eye remained to him. The second was face down, but still moving.

Charlie aimed and fired again. The bullet cracked against the man's back, and the contact caused the man's torso to convulse, one final spasm before he lay motionless on the tile.

Blood pooled from beneath the man that was face down, and Charlie didn't stop walking until his boot stepped into the growing puddle.

Charlie stared down at the man he'd killed. The rage and adrenaline had run its course and hollowed out his bones in the process, and something took its place. He couldn't name the feeling, he only knew it was slowly creeping through him, filling the void that the kills had left behind. He didn't know what it meant, but he understood that he had fallen from the edge and passed to another side.

Killing was making a choice. Death over life. And over the course of however many hours, and days, weeks, or even years that he'd contemplate the decision he made in that very moment, the hard truth was that he had just taken his first step down a path and a road that provided no quarter and offered no relief. If it was peace Charlie Decker hoped to find one day, it would always elude him.

Hands spun him around, and Charlie reached for the pistol at his hip, hand clutched tight over the handle, but he froze when he saw Doug's shocked expression.

"Christ, man, what the hell?" Doug asked, taking a step back.

Mr. Collins simply stared down at the dead men, then after a moment, he looked at Charlie. The old man kept his feelings hidden, and if there was something that he wanted to give away, he didn't. He simply cleared his throat and adjusted the rifle in his arms. "If any of their friends were around, they were bound to hear that, so we better make ourselves scarce."

"Yeah, let's get the hell out of here," Doug said.

"We're not leaving without the supplies." Charlie spoke with a finality, not leaving the subject up for any further discussion.

"Christ, Charlie, this isn't some kind of macho thing, all right? I don't want to die," Doug said, dropping the façade.

"Then go back to your cellar." Charlie didn't wait for a response, heading deeper into the hospital. He wasn't leaving without those meds, and he didn't care if he had to do it alone.

But after a minute, Charlie felt a presence on either side of him, and he looked back to find both Doug and Mr. Collins flanking him. Neither wore a smile. They'd donned masks to conceal their emotions, like the terrorists themselves. It was all business now, though Charlie didn't have a problem with that. He needed them to be on point.

The carnage grew worse the deeper they penetrated the hospital. What light filtered through the windows revealed bloodied walls, bullet holes, overturned medical cots and instruments, and more corpses than Charlie could count.

He imagined it was like shooting fish in a barrel when those bastards walked in. The narrow hallways, lack of security, and general confusion from the power going out was the perfect storm.

It took a sick kind of person to prey on the weak and the sick like these animals had done. And what made the scene so overwhelming, at least for Charlie, was the fact that there were so many of them.

Three hundred.

And each of them were armed and trained, and dangerous to anyone that opposed them. Because despite the fear that Charlie saw in those men's faces, there was also conviction. Conviction to push past the fear and finish the job for the sake of the mission, and for whatever ideals they'd adopted when they decided to kill innocent women, children, and those that never had a chance to defend themselves.

After a series of maze-like hallways, Charlie spotted a cluster of hospital staff bodies piled outside of a certain door.

He frowned, wondering what was so precious on the other side, and then he noticed the lock on the door.

"There," Charlie said, pointing toward the lock.

He hurried over, jiggling the handle, and found that it was still locked. He slung the rifle strap over his shoulder and then bent down to search the bodies. His hands prodded the meaty sides and bodies, the smell and heat coming off them powerful enough to make him gag.

"We're running out of daylight, Charlie," Doug said, his voice cracking with impatience.

"One of them must have a key," Charlie said, turning over the body of a female nurse, then freezing in place when his hand touched the bullet wound on her side.

Blood transferred from the corpse and onto his palm, and Charlie stared at it in shock for a moment before sticking his hands into her pockets. When he found nothing, he moved on to the next.

With the fresh blood on his palm, Charlie left behind prints of his acts as he searched for the keys. Three bodies later and he found them.

"We need to move these bodies so we can get inside," Charlie said, and Mr. Collins and Doug helped him clear enough space to open the door.

Charlie stepped inside and grabbed hold of one of the makeshift shelving racks. He plucked a bottle of pills from a cardboard box and rattled them in his hand, struggling to read the label in the darkness.

"This is it." Charlie placed the pill bottle back on the shelf since the name didn't match what Doc had told him to grab. "Keep a lookout." He set his pack on the ground and then opened the top.

Charlie searched the rows of pills for the names on the list. He found two of the drugs quickly, but the other three took some time. And he double-checked the other stacks of shelving to make sure that he hadn't missed anything.

Finally, with the pills scratched off the list, he moved over to the rest of the supplies. Gauze, bandages, sterilizer, stitches, soft casts, anything and everything that he could fit into his bag he took, and anything that didn't fit, he shoved into a duffel bag that he found in the corner.

Doug and Mr. Collins fidgeted nervously at the door, feet tapping and legs swaying as Charlie hurried to finish his search. He removed the list, double checking to make sure that he hadn't missed anything, which he did.

"We need to find some surgery tools," Charlie said, his attention on the list.

"Well, where the hell do we find it?" Doug asked. "It's not like there's a directory in this fucking place that I can look at."

Mr. Collins gestured down the hall. "I see an ER sign. They probably have surgery tools there."

"Let's go." Charlie picked up the bags and followed Mr. Collins and the signs toward the ER, which was even more of a massacre than the rest of the building.

"Oh, Jesus Christ." Doug turned away the moment they passed through the swinging double doors and into the ER's lobby.

The mass grave of bodies reeked of decay after having sat for almost two days, which was no doubt made worse by the sun shining through the windows. There were easily double the bodies in the lobby than they'd seen in the rest of the hospital.

Charlie did his best to ignore the stench and the gore, and he spotted a separate hallway on the other side of the check-in desk. "There." He pointed and stepped over a leg and an arm from two separate bodies that had fallen next to each other.

Doug and his father followed, and when Charlie shoulder-checked the door into the next hallway, he found the surgery rooms with large viewing windows. The first two rooms had a body lying on the table, but the last one was empty.

"Those poor bastards picked the wrong time to get their appendix taken out," Doug said, passing the window, his head turned toward the carnage like a driver on the road looking at a car wreck, unable to look away. "It's like a nightmare."

"He was asleep when it happened," Mr. Collins said. "Didn't even know what was happening to him, probably."

Doug winced. "I don't know if that makes it better or worse."

"In here." Charlie stepped into the empty surgical room.

Charlie opened drawers, the metal tools inside clanking from his quick movements. He searched for the specific instruments Doc wanted, but even with the descriptions he was given, it was hard to identify the tools he needed versus the tools he didn't.

Charlie tossed a pair of prong-looking clamps back into the drawer, shut it, then moved onto the next one. He remembered Doc telling him that the knives would be clustered together, most likely wrapped and layered in heavy cloth.

"Hey," Doug said, calling from the hallway, refusing to enter the room. "You find what you were looking for?"

"Not yet." Charlie shoved aside different items, still unable to find the tools, and then moved onto the next drawer.

"Charlie, we—"

"I know." His motions became more frantic and less calculated. His fingers fumbled nervously inside the drawers, twice scraping his hands against pointed tips, but still finding no knives. "Fuck." He slammed another drawer shut, and just when he opened the next drawer, a commotion broke out inside the ER.

Charlie, Doug, and Mr. Collins all turned their attention

toward the door that led into the ER and the foreign voices on the other side.

The hurried speech and heavy stomp of boots spiked Charlie's adrenaline, and while Doug and Mr. Collins raised their weapons, Charlie returned to his search of the drawers, the voices and the commotion in the ER propelling him to move faster. His fingers scraped against fabric in the back of the drawer.

Charlie yanked the thick stack of cloth out, able to feel the outline of tools inside. He unwrapped the cloth, finding the knives Doc needed. He stuffed the cloth into his bag, then spun around toward Doug and Mr. Collins. "I've got it, let's go—"

The doors to the ER opened, and four men stepped inside, then immediately stopped at the sight of Doug, Mr. Collins, and Charlie.

"Geudeul-eul jug-yeo!"

Bullets were exchanged, each of them retreating away from one another as they fired round after round, flashes from the tips of their rifles illuminating the darkened hallway like strikes of lightening.

Once the terrorists were shoved back into the ER, the trio turned for the back of the building and broke out into a sprint, leaping over the bodies that lined the floors.

Charlie used the broken emergency exit signs to help guide them toward safety, but because it was so dark, he missed a few, which led them toward dead end hallways. Sunlight filtered through one of the rooms.

"A window." Charlie hurried inside, passing the corpse in the bed, and then reached for the locks on the window sill. He lifted it, then ripped the screen out.

Voices grew louder, angrier, and sounded as though they were in the adjacent hall. With the window opened, Charlie stepped to the side and let Mr. Collins through first. He and

Doug helped him over the sill, and he landed awkwardly on the grass outside.

Doug was next, and Charlie raised his weapon toward the door when he heard voices in the hall, the shouting echoing off the ceiling and walls. He slid the pack off his back and tossed it outside once Doug had passed through, and then quickly backed toward the window, dropping his rifle at the last second and then heaving himself through.

He hit the ground with a thud, then quickly scooped up his rifle and pack, including the duffel bag, and headed toward the woods as quickly as they could.

Right before they reached the trees, gunfire thundered behind them, and they all ducked instinctively. They weaved in serpentine motion through the trees, and even with his backpack and the duffel bag, Charlie still charged to the front of the pack. He didn't stop running until the noise of the gunshots disappeared and he found himself alone.

Charlie panted, his chest heaving with every labored breath. He squinted between the trees and rocks and hills. "Doug? Mr. Collins?" There wasn't a trace of them to be found, and he couldn't even hear their footfalls. He grabbed the rifle and used the scope to search the rest of the woods.

The view through the scope was jerky as he hastily scanned the area. Still unable to locate the Collins men, Charlie removed his eye from the scope and started the trek back. But he only made it a few feet before heavy footfalls to his left caught his attention.

Charlie aimed the rifle toward the noise, unsure of who it could be, but he exhaled a sigh of relief when he saw Doug helping his father down an unsteady path of rocks. "You guys all right?"

"Yeah," Doug said. "Dad twisted his ankle."

Mr. Collins kept his left leg cocked up to avoid putting any pressure on it. "First the knee, now the damn ankle. Might as well chop the whole damn thing off. It's useless."

Charlie helped Doug carry his father down and then found a rock for Mr. Collins to catch his breath. Doug looked back to the hospital they'd escaped.

"I don't think they're going to follow," he said. "They looked more concerned with just chasing us off." He looked to Charlie, then at the supplies in his pack. "You better get back, huh?"

Mr. Collins massaged his leg by the knee and looked to his son. "We'll catch up with you. Don't need to be slowing you down."

"Don't wait too long," Charlie said. "I don't know what they have planned, but if they decide to send folks out to make sure the surrounding area is clear, then it's best we consolidate our strength."

"Yeah," Doug said. "We'll catch up."

Charlie nodded, the adrenaline from the hospital fading, and that hollowness it had carved out in his bones was gone, filled up with a substance that he couldn't name. He turned, walking quickly, then broke out into a jog and headed for the dirt bike.

22

----

*S*peeding past the orchard, Charlie focused on Doc's house up ahead. Above, the storm clouds had grown more ominous, darkening with the fading afternoon light, which made the world outside more evening than afternoon.

Charlie turned the dirt bike up Doc's drive and skidded to a stop, killing the engine, leaving the bike on its side. He adjusted the pack of supplies as he quickly opened the front door.

Doc and Ellen were in the living room, both of them changed out of the robes and pajamas that Charlie had seen them wearing that morning.

"I got everything." Charlie swung the pack off his back, then set it down in the chair. "The pills, the tools, everything on the list." He thrust his hand into the pack and removed the pills, but when he extended them to Doc, he didn't take them. He frowned. "What? Are they wrong?"

Charlie hadn't registered their grave expressions when he'd first entered, but examining them now, he saw that while Doc still had control over his emotions, Ellen couldn't.

Doc walked over. "He's gone."

It took a moment for Doc's words to sink in, and Charlie glanced down the hallway. "Is she still here?"

"Yes," Doc answered.

Charlie handed the bag over to Doc. He hesitated, but then headed toward Amy and the room down the hall.

The door was open and he found her in the same position, kneeling at Don's bedside. It was like she had remained frozen the entire time Charlie had been gone.

"He didn't hesitate last night," Amy said, her voice thick with phlegm, her gaze locked on her husband. "Once he saw those men with the guns, he just grabbed me and the boys and took us to the shed." She laughed, but it was short and humorless. "I always told him that damn bunker was stupid, but when I helped him get the boys down, all of those jokes I made about him installing it were the farthest thing from my mind." She wiped her nose, then returned them to the prayer-like position she'd held them before. "Before he shut the door and sealed us in, he told me not to open the door until morning, no matter what. But when I heard your voice," she shrugged. "I figured it was all right. It didn't even register why it was you coming to get me instead of Don."

Charlie remained close to the door and kept quiet.

"I mean things like this just don't happen, not here." Amy shook her head. "It should have just been a bad dream, a terrible dream, and any moment I'd wake up in bed next to Don, and I'd go back to sleep. But when Jimmy started crying, I knew it wasn't a dream."

Amy finally turned to face Charlie, her eyes rheumy and red, though she retained a stoic expression. It was like the grief had just become a part of her natural state, and the coldness in her eyes froze Charlie to the core.

"I held his hand the whole time he was on Doc's table," Amy said. "I held on for so long, Charlie. Fourteen years we've been married, did you know that? Three beautiful boys, a home, and every year on our anniversary he'd always tell me that he wanted nothing else but another forty years, just the way we have it now—"

Amy stopped, choking on her own grief.

"I know he's gone, but I can't let go." Amy squeezed her husband's hand harder. "I can't let go."

Amy buried her face into the mattress, crying.

Charlie walked over, placing a gentle hand on her shoulder. "It's all right, Amy." He knelt by her side, staying with her until she cried herself into exhaustion, and she let Charlie carry her out of the room, that last veil of strength pulled back and discarded.

Charlie said nothing as he found the next empty room and placed Amy on the bed, where she passed out.

Charlie closed the door to Amy's room, and when he turned toward Don's room, he saw Doc pulling the sheet over the body before he joined Charlie in the hallway.

"In my thirty-five years practicing veterinary medicine, I've heard quite a few people grieve whenever a sick pet or animal with sentimental value had to be put down." Doc's voice cracked and he bowed his head, the loose skin from his neck wobbling as he gave a gentle shake. "But I've never heard a woman cry like she did." He exhaled. "Best to keep her here until she's had a minute to calm herself down. Don't want her to frighten the boys."

And then, as if the moment of humanity had passed between them, Doc turned to Charlie, switching gears immediately. "We'll need to determine what to do with the body. Cremation would obviously be the most efficient method, but if Amy prefers him to be buried, then we'll need to do it quickly. With no air conditioning and in this summer heat, the body isn't going to keep for very long, and I don't think that will help Amy or the boys in grieving for their father. Plus, there's the sanitary aspect to contend with."

"Right," Charlie said. "I'll ask Amy what she wants to do

when she's calmed down a little. The boys are fine for now, they're back at the house."

"Good. Good." Doc mirrored Charlie's nod. He took one last glance at Don in bed and then placed his heavy hand on Charlie's shoulder. He gave it a firm pat and walked away.

Charlie lingered in Don's room for a minute, trying to remember the last time he'd seen his neighbor. It had probably been a week ago, maybe two. Don had come over to the house to borrow a table saw, trying to fix something one of the boys had broken, but Charlie couldn't remember what it was.

And while Don had been upset over what his boys had done, the father couldn't help but smile when he brought up their names and started bragging about how his oldest had hit a double on his Little League team last Saturday, or how his youngest managed to eat an entire tube of cookie dough last night right under their noses.

Don had been a good man, and a good father.

While Charlie couldn't predict the future, he doubled down on his resolve then and there. No one else was going to die on his watch. There wouldn't be any more sheets pulled over the faces of the people he cared about.

* * *

AFTER CHARLIE HELPED Doc wrap up Don's body with the bedsheets, he placed him out back, then walked into Liz's room and sat with her, the pair holding hands.

"Don makes four," Charlie said, counting the number of people that he'd lost under his charge. The number had plagued him for the past hour.

"It's not going to get easier," Liz said. "But you do get used to it."

Charlie gently massaged the top of her hand. She had

long, slender fingers, and while she was tired, he knew there was strength in those hands.

Adelyn's giggles drifted through the living room. It was the first time either of them had heard the little girl saying anything since Charlie delivered the news.

"You did good with her," Liz said.

Charlie nodded, praying that he never had to bury a little one in the ground. He wasn't sure if he could come back from something like that. "How did you deal with it? Watching people die at work?"

"Everything happens so quickly in the hospital, especially when I worked the ER. All you could do was jump from one patient to the next and treat them with the skill, knowledge, and supplies you had in the time you had them. And then you moved on."

Charlie turned toward the bedroom window, the curtains open, giving him a view of the road out front. "One of the worst things that can happen to a farmer is rot." He frowned. "It's contagious, and it spreads, and it can affect the very soil the plant was growing in." He gestured toward the window. "There was another orchard a few miles south of us, kind of a competitor over the years, but they were good people. About eight years ago one of their trees contracted the rot, and they thought they caught it in time. They removed the tree, inspected the soil, and then checked the rest of the trees to make sure it hadn't already spread. And after their due diligence, and not finding anything, they thought they were free and clear."

The creases in Charlie's forehead deepened as he remembered the news articles that came out after the farm had gone under.

"But the one thing they didn't check was the water lines that were feeding the trees," Charlie said. "A fungus had grown into their water supply, and by the time they realized what happened, the whole damn farm was infected. They couldn't salvage a single tree, and the soil was so bad that they were buried in debt even after they sold everything."

"That's terrible," Liz said.

Charlie nodded, then looked away from the window and back toward Liz. "I remember what it did to the family. It was like the rot had gotten into them too. They just withered away and died like the land they'd live on and worked for so many years. I don't know what happened to them afterward. Moved to Kansas, or Iowa, somewhere like that. But I do remember feeling ashamed after they left."

"Why?" Liz asked.

"Because I was just glad it didn't happen to me," Charlie said. "I wouldn't have thought to check the water supply, hell, no one would. It was an act of God." He squeezed her hand. "That kind of event changes you. It shakes you down to the core, strips away everything else save for the bones you were born with. And I didn't understand that until now. I didn't understand how something that big could linger." He bowed his head, doubt creeping back into his mind. "What if I can't shake it?"

"Hey," Liz said, and when Charlie didn't look up, she placed her fingers beneath his chin and lifted his face to meet her gaze. "You might not shake it. But that's not necessarily a bad thing. Use it. Have it make you stronger instead of weaker. Re-define that feeling to suit you, instead of having it define you."

Charlie leaned his cheek into her palm and shut his eyes, then kissed her wrist and pulled back. "Thank you."

"You're welcome," Liz said. "And you would have thought to check the water."

Charlie smiled. "How do you know that?"

"Because you're smarter than you think, Charlie Decker."

The pair smiled at one another, and if Charlie didn't have a thousand other items on his to-do list, he would have stayed with her all day.

"I'll let you get your rest." Charlie let go of Liz's hand and headed toward the living room, finding Amy playing with Adelyn on the floor, the mourning wife smiling at the little girl's playful antics.

Ellen and Doc watched the two from the couch, and when Charlie entered, Doc stood and walked over.

"Let me talk to you out back," Doc said.

Charlie nodded, lingering at the sight of happiness that had grown rare over the past few days. He finally joined Doc and found the old vet with a cigarette to his lips.

"Don't tell Ellen," Doc said.

Charlie raised his eyebrows in surprise. "I didn't even know you smoked."

Doc took another drag and nodded. "We're living in a surprising world now." He turned to Charlie, shaking his head. "You did what you could. Even if you made it back with the supplies, I don't think he would have survived."

Charlie nodded, but Doc's words didn't make him feel any better about it.

"How do you want to handle the body?" Doc asked.

"I don't know," Charlie said. "I thought I'd leave that up to Amy."

"Not to sound like a miser, but the sooner we get him in the ground, the better." Doc took another drag. "The last thing that family needs is to remember the stink of Don's body when they buried him."

Charlie watched Doc smoke for a minute and then looked up at the darkened skies threatening rain. It was a rain he had hoped for back in Seattle when he had just stepped out of the bank. Rain washed everything away, made it new again.

"Hey."

Charlie and Doc turned toward the back door, surprised to find Amy standing behind the screen.

"Everything all right?" Charlie asked.

Amy nodded, her eyes still red from crying, but she forced a smile. "I was thinking about burying Don back by the big oak tree on the edge of our property. It'd be nice for the boys to have a place where they can go and visit him."

"Of course," Charlie said.

"It's a wonderful idea, Amy," Doc said.

Amy smiled and then returned to the living room.

Doc dropped the cigarette on the small patch of concrete outside the back door. "You need help taking the body over?"

"I'll have Mario help me," Charlie answered.

Doc chuckled. "I guess that's the nice way of saying you don't think I can carry him." He clapped Charlie on the shoulder. "But you're probably right."

After Doc walked inside, Charlie lingered outside the back of the house, then walked to the dirt bike and headed home.

He chose to walk, instead of ride, wanting to conserve the fuel. Plus, he didn't mind the alone time. Everything had been full throttle for him over the past few hours, and he needed a break.

Thunder cracked in the distance, the noise rolling toward him in ominous waves, and Charlie's gaze wavered between the sky, the forest, the pavement, and the rifle on his shoulder. Over the course of the past two days, he'd carried a weapon on him more than any other time in his life. And in that time frame, it already felt a part of him like his hands.

When Charlie neared the house he ditched the dirt bike on the back side of the house, then entered through the back door, kicking the dirt off his boots on the staircase before going inside.

The kids' laughter pulled Charlie into the living room, where he found them setting up a board game. The workers filed in after him, each of them tracking dirt into the house.

A series of apologies were uttered to Martha, the grown men bowing their heads like little boys who knew they'd done something wrong, the shame as clear on their faces as their nose and mouth.

Charlie watched the men interact with their families, all of them speaking in their native Spanish. He imagined that was most of their communication at home, and Charlie was glad that they all felt comfortable enough to speak it here.

But as he watched the families cluster together in the living room, he was pulled from the moment by a tug on his left pant leg. And when he looked down and saw Don's youngest staring up at him, Charlie's stomach soured.

"Where's my mommy?" Dillon Bigelow asked. His face was covered in freckles, the bright orange of his hair a floppy mess on his head. He had his mother's eyes, and Charlie remembered Amy back at Doc's house, waiting for him to return with Mario or one of the other workers to carry her husband back to their house to be buried.

Martha came up behind Charlie, piggybacking onto Dillon's question. "Yeah, how's Don doing? Did you get Doc what he nee—" She cut herself off when Charlie turned his head to look at her.

Martha glanced down at Dillon, and then to his older brothers who were playing with Mario's kids on the rug. She cleared her throat and then squeezed Charlie's shoulder before she took hold of Dillon's hand and led him over to join his siblings.

Knowing the longer he waited to put it off, the worse it would be, Charlie caught Mario's attention and beckoned him into the kitchen.

The weathered field hand placed both hands on his hips like he did whenever he listened intently, striking the serious tone which had granted him the authority and respect of the position his father had given him. In all respects, Mario was the right hand at the orchard. Without him, it fell apart.

"Don passed," Charlie answered.

Mario simply nodded, the news registering slowly on his face.

"I need you to come and help me move the body back to their house. Amy wants to bury him there. We'll have a service when she's ready."

Mario nodded, and they headed to Doc's house. Moisture clung to the air, the rainfall just a matter of time, and neither of them spoke on the walk back to Doc's place. Charlie suspected that Mario was mentally preparing himself for carrying the body of a dead man. That's what Charlie was doing.

"Around here," Charlie said, gesturing toward the back.

When they entered the house, Ellen and Amy were in the kitchen, their conversation whispered and soft spoken. She smiled when she saw Charlie.

"I wasn't sure if you wanted to come when we took him over," Charlie said.

"I'd like to," Amy said.

Mario kept his head bowed. "I'm sorry for your loss, Senora."

Amy smiled. "Thank you, Mario."

With Don still wrapped in the sheets, Mario grabbed hold of Don's feet while Charlie took the shoulders. The pair lifted in unison and then started the journey back.

But almost as a sign of respect, neither man tired. It reminded Charlie of the funeral processions that were escorted by police, never stopping for red lights or stop signs, until they reached the final resting place.

Barely halfway to the house, and Charlie felt his back and arms burn. His legs wobbled, but he made it a point to never show how much exertion he was putting toward carrying her husband's body. He didn't want her to think that it was a burden. She had enough to worry about.

By the time they reached the house, Charlie couldn't feel his arms anymore. He was thankful that she wanted to bury him by a tree on the edge of the property. And despite wanting to drop the two hundred pounds of weight, Charlie and Mario set him down gently, and then took a single deep breath. He turned to Amy, unsure of what else he could say, but she spoke before he had a chance.

"Ellen said that the boys and I could stay at their place," she said. "I thought it might be best to wait until tomorrow morning to bury him. Maybe at sunrise."

"That's a fine idea," Charlie said.

"Yes," Mario replied. "Very beautiful time of day."

Amy smiled. "It was always his favorite. Loved to be the first one up to catch the sun rise." She hugged Charlie and then kissed his cheek. "You're a good man, Charlie." She offered the same thanks to Mario, then disappeared toward the house.

23

*C*overed in dirt, and exhausted, both Charlie and Mario lowered Don's body into the grave, then headed back to the house. Charlie thanked Mario for the help and let the field hand retire to the comfort of his bed. But a light coming from the barn caught Charlie's attention.

Charlie wandered back toward the old structure, the sound of static growing stronger the closer he moved. When he entered the barn, he found his father at one of his work benches, fiddling with the tube radio that they'd listened to when they'd been told about the EMP from the President.

"Dad?" Charlie asked. "What are you doing?"

Harold sat hunched on a stool, holding the radio with one hand and a screwdriver with the other. He'd torn the back off the radio and was tinkering with the parts inside.

"I can't find a channel that works on this damn thing," Harold said, his attention on the device. "The Emergency Signal stopped."

Charlie joined Harold by his side, then peered into the same innards of the radio that his father was looking at, trying to find out what the old bear was doing. "Dad, I don't think it has anything to do with the radio."

"Maybe," Harold said. "But I'm trying to increase its range." He gestured to the old walkie-talkie next to some spare parts. "Might come in handy if we can reach someone out there."

Charlie nodded, then paused, knowing that his father hadn't heard the news about their neighbor. "Don didn't make it, Dad."

The tinkering stopped, and Harold leaned back from the radio. He was silent, then finally looked up at his son. "How's Amy?"

"She's taking it as well as anyone could take it," Charlie answered.

Harold dropped the screwdriver and wiped his palm down his face. "He's got three boys."

"I know."

Charlie crossed his arms, and the Decker men lingered in silence.

"Dad, I wanted to get your advice on something," Charlie said.

"Fire away." Harold continued tinkering, his ear cocked toward his son.

Charlie took a seat on a stool on the other side of the table, and his father looked up from behind the radio knowingly while his fingers continued to fiddle with the tubes. The glance was quick.

"There are three hundred of those terrorists sitting in Mayfield right now," Charlie said. "Probably even more than that, and with the potential for more on the way." He reached for one of the spare parts on the table, a slim plastic tubing that he rotated between his fingertips. "If they decide to come back this way, they'll overwhelm us, no matter how many guns we have."

"Mm-hmm," Harold said.

Charlie set the plastic tubing down and drummed his fingers on the work bench. So far he'd been able to bury the thought and idea that manifested itself ever since he returned from the town, made even worse by Don's death, which he figured would haunt him for many nights to come.

"We should consider leaving," Charlie said.

Charlie braced for the mass bravado that his father would bluster his way. He stared at the old wood of the work bench, the boards splintered and splattered with all kinds of paint and veneer from decades of use, chipped away by hammers and chisels that missed the mark for the project he was working on.

But there was no outburst, no cry of defiance from his father like Charlie had expected. Instead, his father only nodded, continuing his work on the radio.

"If that's what you think we need to do," Harold said.

Unable to speak, the shock so intense that Charlie wasn't even sure he'd heard his father correctly, he worked his mouth like a car trying to start, but unable to catch.

Harold laughed. "Not what you were expecting to hear?"

"You'd be okay with leaving?" Charlie asked.

Harold set the screwdriver down and transferred the nervous energy he used on the radio onto his hands, squeezing them together tightly, his knuckles swollen from arthritis. "I think I must have told you the story about how your grandfather started this place a thousand times." He smiled fondly at the story, and Charlie nodded.

"You said that he forged land documents so he could buy the land with collateral he didn't have," Charlie said. "And when the bank found out about it, the loan officer was so embarrassed about the mistake that he didn't press charges and let him keep the deed to the acreage."

"Dad always said that a man is his own worst enemy." The big smile that spread across Harold's face slowly disappeared as he bowed his head. "I think that sentence grows truer the older I get." He sighed and leaned back off the table. He looked past Charlie and out the barn doors toward the house. "I've never wanted anything more my whole life than to work this farm and to raise a family. You and your mom were the best things that could have ever happened to me. And however good I thought things could become in my imagination, they were better. Much better."

"I thought I'd have to pull you from this place kicking and screaming," Charlie said. "It was the reason you sent me to school, why I tried so hard to get another loan from the banks, it was the basis of everything that we tried to do."

Harold grimaced. "Sometimes I think I let myself get wrapped up too tight with that idea," he said. "It was like I believed if I lost the farm, then I lost who I was, and that's just stupid. I know who I am." His confidence returned the more he spoke, as if he were verbally finding his footing, growing bolder the longer he made it without collapsing into nothing. "And I shouldn't have passed that burden on to you."

"Dad, you didn't pass on any burden," Charlie said. "You did so much for me, and for Mom, and for this place. Without you, none of it would even happen, and I sure as hell wouldn't even exist."

"I suppose I did play a small part in your conception," Harold said, that grin spreading wide across his face. "But I'm not willing to let my family and friends die for something just because I'm afraid of who I'll become if I don't have an orchard to run anymore." He shook his head, shoulders rounding forward as he exhaled. "No. I'm not going to do that." He locked eyes with his son. "Stay, fight, it's up to you." He stood and then stepped around the table, placing that big bear paw on Charlie's shoulder. "I told you before that this is your show to run. And I meant it."

Charlie stood and hugged his father, burying his face into his dad's shoulder the way he used to do as a boy whenever he was carried around from being too tired to walk.

All the while the static from the radio played, spitting out the same white noise. And then it cut out completely, replaced by a single high-pitched beep that lasted for a few seconds, and then stopped.

Both Charlie and his father broke from their embrace, each of them staring at the radio with a foreboding sense of doom etched on their faces. It had something to do with the sudden noise, and then silence, and then, without warning, a voice echoed through the speaker.

"My fellow Americans, I speak to those of you fortunate enough to hear my message with a heavy heart." The president's voice was weathered and grave. He sounded nothing like the man who'd spoken the day before. It was like someone had stuck a knife in his gut and the life was slowly draining out of him while he spoke. "The terrorist threat to our country has grown more dangerous than previously imagined. We have learned that the insurgents have congregated near or around major utility structures. My advisors believe, as do I, that this is a strategic move to prolong our days without power and communication. Therefore, to expedite our recovery process, I have made it a priority for any active military, reserves, retired, or deactivated men to take up arms and fight to reclaim those facilities. Without them, it could take years for us to pull ourselves out of this mess. But be warned. We've already had reports that even after successful breaches into those facilities, they have been wired with explosives to bring the structures down should the enemy be forced to retreat. I repeat that it is imperative that these water plants and power plants must be retaken without catastrophic structural damage. So I ask you, my fellow citizens, that if you have the ability to fight, then do so. We as a nation have always been strongest when we are one people. A united front is what we require to emerge from these desolate and desperate times. God speed. And God bless the United States of Amer—"

Static returned, cutting short the President's message in

eerie fashion, and continued to play as Charlie and Harold stared at the radio.

"I guess that means Dixon will be on his way back," Harold said.

"Charlie!"

The scream came from the house, and Charlie quickly stepped from the barn, his father not far behind. He saw his mother coming out of the back door, stumbling toward him in a shambled sprint, and Charlie hurried toward her, cutting her off before she had a chance to distance herself from the house.

Charlie grabbed hold of her arms, then glanced past her at the door. "What happened?"

"Doug Collins," Martha answered, spitting out the words between breaths, then pointed back toward the house. "His father's hurt, they need Doc."

Before his mother could even finish her words, Charlie sprinted into and then through the house, the concerned faces in the living room nothing more than a blur as Charlie rushed past. He spilled out onto the front porch and found Doug with his father in a wheelchair, slouched forward.

Both of them were covered in blood, though the majority of it looked to be from Mr. Collins, who sat motionless, the only sign that he was even still alive the faint rise and fall of his chest.

"Charlie—"

"Doc has all of the supplies," Charlie said, helping his friend move his father's wheelchair before he could even finish talking. "How long has he been like this?"

The pair fell into a steady jog, pushing Mr. Collins as fast as they could without throwing him from his seat.

"Man, you don't even know what the hell is coming." Doug shook his head.

"Doc!" Charlie screamed when they moved closer to the house, and the old vet hurried outside.

"What happened?"

"Stab wound," Doug answered.

Doc checked his new patient's pulse, then flashed a light in Mr. Collin's eyes, who batted him away in frustration. "All right, let's get him inside."

Charlie guided Doug and his father to what had become the operating room in the garage and the same large table that they'd placed Don on, and Charlie prayed that they wouldn't have similar results.

"Be careful with him," Doc said, scrubbing his hands and arms down with disinfectant.

Charlie and Doug did as they were told, but a gush of blood spurted out over the floor, and Mr. Collins wailed in pain, writhing in defiance on the table. He gritted his teeth, and Doug grabbed his father's hand, their grip firm and tight and covered in blood.

"All right," Doc said, opening some of the supplies that Charlie had brought back. He cut the shirt open along the front and revealed the gnarly gash that had been carved into Mr. Collin's abdomen.

Doc stared at the wound with a mixture of fascination and trepidation, but he didn't let the emotions linger long.

"What's his blood type?" Doc asked, cleaning the wound of blood.

"Uh-um, AB positive, I think?" Doug answered.

"And what are you?" Doc asked, still continuing his work.

"I-I don't know," Doug replied. "O negative I think."

"Ellen!" Doc screamed for his wife, and she appeared almost instantly, already heading to the disinfecting station before Doc told her what he needed. "Get a line going from Doug here and draw blood, we'll need to do a transfusion."

All the while Charlie kept his eyes on Mr. Collins, a man who had been alive and well only a few hours ago, with his biggest complaint being that his knee was swollen and his ankle was sprained. The color had disappeared from Mr. Collins' lips, and his eyelids started to close.

Ellen steered Doug away from his father and sat him in a chair, then rolled up his sleeve.

"Is he going to be all right?" Doug asked, wincing as Ellen pricked his arm with the needle.

"I don't know," Doc answered.

"Jesus Christ," Doug replied, his words growing thick with grief.

Charlie crouched to a knee next to Ellen and pulled Doug's attention away from the operating table. "Doug, what happened? Did the soldiers come back? Did they see you?"

"They just started torching everything," Doug said. "I guess maybe they thought there were still too many survivors from their first sweep, so they wanted to clean house or something, I don't know."

Charlie frowned. "They burned the town?"

"They went from building to building, dousing them with gas, but eventually the fires caught," Doug answered. "And then they just sat there and watched the buildings, guns in their hands, and shot anyone that came running out." The muscles around his eyes twitched. "Some of them were on fire. But the bastards didn't shoot them. They just let them burn."

Charlie leaned back, then looked to Mr. Collins. "How did your dad—"

"We heard screams coming from one of the houses, so I went in and grabbed a woman who was trapped," Doug said. "Dad was watching the exit, making sure that none of the bastards snuck up behind me and put a bullet in my head. But when I came out, coughing and hacking, we headed for the woods, where we were surprised by two of the terrorists. The woman ran off and Dad managed to shoot one of them, and the second didn't have a gun, and he just lunged forward." He frowned. "I didn't see what it was at first." He shrugged. "I just thought maybe he punched my dad. But after I shot him, I turned around and saw Dad on his back—" His lower lip quivered and when he shut his eyes, tears streamed down his face. "He was holding his guts in."

While Doug struggled to regain his composure, Charlie tried wrapping his head around the fact that the terrorists had torched Mayfield.

Doug wiped his nose. "The town was up in flames as we were hobbling away. I kept us to the woods for as long as I could, but I knew that he wouldn't be able to walk all the way here, so I found that wheelchair and shoved him in it and just started pushing as fast as I could."

With that much burning, Charlie was surprised he hadn't seen the smoke or a kind of glow on the horizon, but then again, it wasn't like it was something he was looking for.

"I think they're coming, Charlie," Doug said, finally looking away from his father and at Charlie. "I think they're gonna burn anything that's in the area. We saw clouds on the horizon. They were everywhere."

"No power. No communications." Charlie extended a finger for each one, ticking them off like a list. "No food." He spoke to himself, the realization washing over him. Farm land was just as much a resource as power.

"Charlie!" Amy screamed from the front of the house.

Charlie rushed toward her, finding her in the front door-way, leaning against the frame for support, gazing out into the night.

"Amy, what are you doing—"

But when Charlie joined her outside, his jaw dropped.

The blaze was high, even from the long distance where they stood. It was the Bigelows' property.

And from the light of the flames, Charlie saw the darkened figures marching down the road. The terrorist army from Mayfield had made their way toward them, and the next house in their sights was Charlie's orchard.

24

*C*harlie sprinted for the orchard, turning back to Amy on the run. "Get everyone and tell them to head for the woods!"

Legs and feet aching, and his lungs burning, Charlie waved his arms, screaming at everyone that stood outside of the house, gazing at the flames in the distance.

"To the woods! Get to the woods, now!"

Gunfire interrupted Charlie's orders and the first wave of soldiers appeared in the darkness. Behind the men with guns were a separate unit of men with flamethrowers, torching the first trees on the edge of the Decker property.

Mario and Harold ushered everyone toward the woods, the women clutching their children, and Martha helping to shepherd Amy's little ones.

Breathless, Charlie skidded to a stop outside of the house, tugging at Mario's shoulder. "Did we get everyone out?"

Overwhelmed by the action, Mario shook his head. "I don't know. I—"

"Dillon!" Amy screamed. "Where's Dillon? Dillon!"

Charlie turned toward Mario as he jogged toward the house. "I'll get him, just get everyone to the forest! Go!"

Amy's screams faded when Charlie entered the house. "Dillon? Where are you?" He searched the first floor, checking the living room and bedrooms, closets and kitchen. He flung open cupboards, checked behind furniture, and only when he was sure the first floor was clear did he head upstairs.

Charlie hurried down the hallway. "Dillon!" But just before he checked the next bedroom, a bright orange hue caught his attention from the window at the end of the hall, and Charlie was drawn to it, like a moth to flame. "Oh my god."

Flames spread across the east field, the fires alive and dancing toward the house. It was an ocean of fire, smoke rising into the night sky.

Soldiers headed toward the house, and Charlie turned from the window and headed for the room to continue his search for Dillon.

"Dillon!" Charlie hunched low, creeping through the room. "Dillon!"

A whimper, and Charlie turned on his heel. The closet. Charlie hurried toward the door and flung it open. Dillon was tucked in the corner, curled into a tight ball with his face buried in his hands, shivering and whimpering.

Charlie exhaled in relief and then snatched Dillon from inside. "It's okay, buddy."

Dillon wrapped his arms around Charlie's neck, burying his face into Charlie's shoulder, and then Charlie headed down the stairs and out the back of the house.

Outside, the heat from the fires that surrounded him blasted his face immediately, and Charlie froze at the sight of the flames moving toward the house, the fire reflected in Charlie's eyes. The barn out back was already up in flames.

The roof caved in on itself, sending up a massive plume of embers that danced against the night sky, and as the structure collapsed, so did Charlie's heart. From the second-story window, he was able to see the east fields set ablaze.

All of the trees, the fruit, the life that had grown here was being devoured by the sea of fire, which was growing larger and more powerful with every bit of life that it consumed.

Running on fumes, fueled only by adrenaline, Charlie sprinted past the burning barn. He didn't dare look left or right, focused only on the darkness of the forest ahead.

"Charlie!" His father's voice broke through the noise of the chaos, and Charlie focused on that familiar timbre to guide him away from danger.

He found Harold near the edge of the clearing, the fires from the orchard illuminating his father's massive figure.

"C'mon, son." Harold guided Charlie and Dillon into the safety of the forest, and it wasn't until Harold took his hand off Charlie's shoulder that he finally collapsed to the floor, letting Dillon go, digging his fingers into the black soil of the earth, which offered a cool relief from the heat he'd just escaped.

"All right, let's get you up," Harold said, pulling his son out of the dirt and standing him upright. "It's better to be on your feet than all fours after something like that."

Charlie wiped the saliva dripping from his chin with the back of his hand, and when he looked around him, he saw the frightened expressions in the darkness, illuminated by the fire.

Mario and the rest of the workers were there, along with their children and Dillon's siblings. His mother was the first to separate herself from the group and wrapped her son in a tight hug.

"Oh, thank God." Martha squeezed him tight and then gently prodded his face and body, searching for any injuries he might have sustained. "Are you all right?"

Charlie gently took his mother's hands. "I'm fine."

With his mother by his side, he turned to look at the fires

raging through the fields. It was taking everything. Crops, the house, the barn, equipment, supplies, it all burned.

"Thank God we got everyone out," Martha said.

But as she said that, Charlie looked to the west, toward Doc's house, and the people that he'd left behind to come and save his own family. "Liz."

Charlie headed toward Doc's house, keeping to the tree line, deaf to the questions of his family as he ran away.

The smoke from the fires made it difficult to breathe, and the exertion only worsened the funnel of black death into his lungs as he drew closer toward Doc's house. Closer towards Liz.

Once clear of the orchards and their fires, Charlie saw the dark figures still marching down the road, their sights set on Doc's house, ready to burn it to the ground like everything else.

No longer caring if the terrorists saw him, Charlie veered from the cover of the forest and into the open fields of Doc's property.

With the foreign voices growing closer to the front of the house, Charlie entered through the back, stepping through the kitchen as he traversed the darkened and seemingly abandoned home. "Liz? Doc?"

He checked the rooms, finding them empty, and then headed toward the garage which acted as Doc's makeshift operating room. It was empty as well.

Glass shattered somewhere in the house, and Charlie headed back into the living room, then screeched to a halt when he found it ablaze.

More crashing sounds of glass erupted around the house, and Charlie retreated toward the kitchen, the fire's intensity rivaling the sun. He screamed Liz's name one last time, but his cries were drowned out by the collapse of a few of the beams in the living room.

Charlie leapt from the danger and then sprinted out the

back door, retreating into the night as Doc's house burned. The flames stretched high into the night, adding to the embers that drifted through the night sky like fireflies.

"Charlie!"

He turned, finding Doug Collins deep in the field.

Charlie sprinted, and by the time he reached him, he dropped to his knees, exhausted, and then vomited, trembling on all fours, the hot, sour taste of bile in his mouth.

Three heaves and he was done, his body trembling and his eyes watery with his nose dripping snot. He moved away from the stink of the bile and then flopped onto his back, staring up at the night sky, which was promptly interrupted by Doug's face.

"C'mon, we need to keep moving," Doug said, reaching for Charlie's arm and practically pulling Charlie up on his own.

"Liz, is she—"

"She's fine," Doug said. "Everyone made it out in time. Doc's finishing up stitching up my dad in the woods. C'mon."

Doug headed toward the tree line, but Charlie lingered behind, taking a moment to catch his breath. He turned back toward Doc's house, its fire still blazing and the horde of terrorists responsible returning to Mayfield.

He then looked left, finding a sea of fire that was once the orchard fields he played in as a child, then worked as a man. The horror of the scene was a conflict to the beauty of the fire.

Thunder clapped and a few seconds later, the first burst of rain fell onto his face, and Charlie closed his eyes and let the cool droplets cleanse him of the ash and soot that covered his body.

The rainfall started as a light drizzle, but transformed into a downpour by the time Charlie re-turned toward the woods. It took him a minute to find Doug and the rest of the group, but when he saw Liz, he wrapped his arms around her and wouldn't let go.

The concept of time disappeared as he held her, and when Charlie pulled away, the rain had soaked them both. Thunder clapped and lightning flashed, and as the rain fell, it helped to extinguish the fires that had set their world ablaze.

But amidst the thunder and rain, Charlie heard Doc's voice, and while he didn't hear the words, he understood his tone. Charlie turned, finding Doug standing over his father's body.

"I'm sorry, Doug," Doc said. "He just lost too much blood. I did what I could. I'm so sorry."

Doug collapsed to his knees and bowed his head by his father's side. The thunder and rain masked some of his crying, but the harsh screams broke through the night between the moments of silence.

harlie, Liz, Doc, Ellen, and Doug found the rest of Charlie's party in the woods sometime during the night, and the group waited together in the trees, soaked to the bone and shivering. The children had whimpered and cried, but eventually grew so exhausted that they passed out in their mother's laps.

But while others slept in the darkness and protection of the forest, Charlie and his father gazed into the sea of death that was once their home, both helpless against the enormity of their plight.

The rain had helped, but it didn't save much. Smoke rose like steam from the earth, the once-green landscape transformed to black and grey.

Charlie wiped his cheeks, smearing some of the soot that had lingered and refused to be washed away by the rain.

"It's gone," Harold said.

Charlie turned to his father, the despair transforming his father into a different man.

Harold stepped closer toward the burned wreckage. "What'd they do it for?" He looked to his son as if he would know the answer. "Don't they have to eat too?"

Charlie offered a gentle shake of his head. "I don't know, Dad."

"Charlie."

He turned, finding Doug Collins clutching a rifle in his hands with dark circles beneath his eyes that dragged the rest of his face down. An expression of anger glowered on his face, made more ominous by the darkness.

"We need to talk," Doug said, then turned to Harold. "You too, Mr. Decker."

Doug led them away from the rest of the group, inching closer toward the decaying trees that still smoldered. The burnt smell was something that Charlie didn't think he'd ever get out of his nose.

Doug stopped, then adjusted the rifle in his hands. "What's next?"

The blunt nature of the question threw Charlie off balance. "What do you mean?"

"I mean those fuckers came down here and wrecked everything we've ever known." Doug gestured toward Mayfield. "They're murderers. All of them. Look at what they did!"

"I know what they are, Doug, and I know what they did."

"Which is why we need to do something about it!" Doug tucked the rifle's stock in his armpit, and rage reddened his cheeks. "I say we go down to Mayfield and kill as many of those fuckers as we can."

"Doug, your father just died—"

"Yeah, Charlie, he's dead," Doug answered. "And what do you think is going to happen a few weeks from now when we're overrun with those bastards? Hmm? How long are you and yours gonna last out here?" He pointed toward the fields. "They took everything from you! And you're not going to do anything about it?"

"We don't have the manpower," Charlie said. "We go after

them, everyone dies. That's not what your father would have done, and it's not what he would have wanted."

Doug smiled. "That's where you're wrong. You didn't know my pops like I did. He would have come up with this plan himself. This is exactly what he would have wanted."

"He's right, son," Harold said.

Surprised, Charlie turned toward his father. "Dad, we don't have the upper hand here. It's not a smart move."

"It's not about being smart," Harold said. "And it's not about having the upper hand." He pointed toward Mayfield. "It's about letting those monsters know we're still here. It's showing them that we still have fight left in us."

"Dad, this isn't— I'm just as angry about—"

"It's not about anger," Harold said. "At least not for me." And to his father's credit, the big man did seem eerily calm. "When the Japanese attacked Pearl Harbor, the President had the military perform an immediate counterstrike in the heart of Tokyo. The mission targeted one of their military factories, but the outcome was nothing more than a small dent in the grand scheme of things. But FDR and his generals understood exactly what I understand now." He stepped toward his son, towering over him the way he did when he was a boy. "We need to let them know we're still here. We need to let them know that we can't be run out so easily."

Charlie was speechless. He hadn't expected his father to side with Doug so quickly, and so willingly. But then again, his father had always been rash. It was that mentality and those quick decisions that had put the farm in so much disarray and trouble in the first place.

"No," Charlie said. "That's not what's happening."

"No? What do you mean no?" Doug puffed up, his cheeks getting so red they were nearly purple. "You don't get to tell me what to do, so you can go fuck off if you're too coward to face those bastards head on."

"You and I both know that I'm not the coward, Doug," Charlie said.

Rage propelled Doug's attack, slamming himself into Charlie and sending the pair of them rolling across the wet and blackened earth.

"You son of a bitch!" Doug raised his fists high and brought them down hard.

Charlie rolled left and right, arms up to protect himself from the blows, then bucked his hips upward, twisting Doug off him, sending the pair on another roll down the hill. When they came to a stop this time, Charlie landed on top.

Charlie punched Doug's ribs, and Doug countered with a jab that Charlie dodged. He worked the ribs again, and with every blow Doug's fight went out of him. It wasn't until Harold stumbled down and managed to heave his son off of Doug that the fighting stopped.

"What the hell are you two doing?" Harold stood between Charlie and Doug, the rage billowing out of the old man like a smokestack. "We have enough trouble going on without you two trying to pull each other's heads off!"

Charlie jumped up from the soot, flakes of ash falling from his body.

"The only way we get through this is if we work together," Harold said.

"Oh, really?" Charlie asked, turning toward his father. "Is that what we're going to do when we march to our deaths in Mayfield?"

Harold raised his finger to Charlie. "Don't speak to me in that tone, boy."

"I should have spoken to you in that tone a long time ago," Charlie said, spitting the words at his father. "If I had, then maybe you wouldn't have run this place into the ground. Maybe I wouldn't have had to travel from bank to bank like a beggar trying to salvage our home!"

"Watch your mouth, son." Harold spoke in a low tone,

which was more akin to a dog's growl than a human's warning.

But while Charlie recognized the warning, he didn't heed it. "You talk about how those men burned our farm, but how much money did you torch because you were too stupid to run a business? Huh?" He gritted his teeth. "You buried us in a hole that we've been desperately trying to climb out of, and I'm not going to dig you out anymore. I'm done!"

Charlie marched back toward the forest where everyone had gathered to watch the encounter. His mother was the first to break apart from the pack, but when she came down and tried to stop him, he simply shrugged her off.

Mario and the rest of the workers looked away, and Charlie headed deeper into the woods in search of quiet and solitude.

What happened wasn't his fault, and despite his best efforts, maybe he just couldn't be the one to lead them out of trouble. He knew that they were all looking to someone to give them hope, but he didn't have any more hope to offer. The well had run dry.

* * *

Dawn broke over the mountains and the horizon as Charlie wandered deeper into the forest, gravitating toward the familiar sound of the river's rushing water.

He spotted the river through a pair of trees and walked to the river's edge then splashed into the water, no longer caring about the condition of his boots.

The river started up in the mountains, and even in the dead heat of summer, it was always cold. As a kid, he and his friends used to see who could stay in the water the longest before they froze and had to get out. It was a game that Charlie had played with Doug and his younger brother Billy.

Charlie hadn't thought of Billy Collins in a long time.

After Billy's funeral, Doug and Charlie came down to the river with a case of beer.

They talked about their childhood and all the stupid shit that Billy did in high school. Of the two Collins boys, Billy was always the wild one.

The pair sat there on the riverbank until the sun went down, and just before they stumbled back to their respective houses where they'd black out until the morning, Doug paused, wobbling on two feet and staring out onto the river.

"You know my dad always liked Billy more," Doug said, his tone dismissive. "I mean I know he loved both of us, but he always liked Billy more. The old bastard even said it out loud once when he was drunk. I brought it up to him one time and he said I was full of shit, but I know what he said. Deep down, I think he knew too."

"I'm sure your dad liked you plenty, Doug," Charlie had said, trying to pull his friend out of the rabbit hole he was tunneling for himself. "You and Billy were just different. That's all."

But Doug just stood there, his back to Charlie, staring out over the river, which had turned to liquid gold from the fading sunlight.

"I know we were different," Doug said. "I know my dad liked me too. It's just…" He slowly turned, empty beer bottle dangling from his fingertips as he swayed left and shrugged. "I just know he liked Billy more is all." He flung the empty beer bottle into the river and watched it splash.

It was funny, the memories that returned whenever you visited a place. It was like a portion of whatever happened anywhere on planet Earth was permanently carved into that section of the earth. And thinking about the sheer number of events that took place on this planet, Charlie figured that just over the course of human history alone, there were enough scars on Earth to make it unrecognizable.

But what happened to those memories of places that no longer existed? What happened when a place that held so much of who you were was just wiped off the map, or transformed into something that you could never see again in the same light?

All the holidays, and birthdays, and family gatherings that they had on the property were distorted now, hazy from the smoke that had choked the life out of those memories and left them charred and burnt like the orchard itself. And maybe that's how Charlie would always see it now.

He stared at the water gently flowing downstream. Always moving forward, never stopping.

Motion was life. The constant struggle of growth, and the pain and discomfort associated with it, were a reminder of your existence.

"Charlie?"

The voice was quiet, but familiar, and he turned to find Liz leaning against one of the last trees before the riverbank.

Her hair was a mess and her clothes were wrinkled and dirty, and still damp from their night in the rain. She kept one hand to her side where she'd been shot and then gingerly walked over the smooth stone of the riverbank, careful to keep her balance.

Charlie stood to help her, but she motioned for him to stay put.

"I walked all the way here," she said. "I can make it the last couple of feet."

Charlie still held out his hand, which she accepted when she was close enough, and then the pair sat down together, though Charlie noticed that she kept her distance.

"Your mother is worried about you and your dad," Liz said. "You need to talk to them."

"I know," Charlie said.

Liz glanced out onto the river, the morning rays of light

brilliant against the surface of the water. She smiled. "It's beautiful here."

"It is," Charlie said, exhaling, his mind troubled by the words that lingered on his tongue, begging to be spoken. "I don't know what to do, Liz. I know that when I go back to everyone, they'll expect a plan of what to do next, but I don't have it. We have nothing. No food. No home. If the pumps were damaged in the fire, then we won't have water from the well. No medicine, no weapons. Everything's gone."

"We're still here," Liz said.

Charlie looked at her and frowned. "And you think that's a good thing?" He shook his head then glanced out onto the water. "I should have just gone up in flames with the farm."

"Hey." Liz grabbed hold of Charlie's chin and pulled his face toward her. "Don't go down that road, you hear me? Whatever self-pity that you think you're entitled to doesn't exit, because you haven't earned it."

"I haven't earned it? Liz, I don't have anything left!"

"You have your family and your friends!" Liz pleaded with Charlie. "You don't think crops can be regrown? You don't think homes can be rebuilt? What do you think people do after a disaster? They rebuild, so don't give me that crap that you're afraid, or you don't have any answers, or that people won't want to hear what you have to say." She gestured back toward the orchard. "You're not the only one that's hurting here, Charlie Decker, and you'd do well to remember it."

With her rant ended, Liz grimaced and then clutched at her side as she leaned away from Charlie.

"You really don't pull any punches," Charlie said, sporting a sheepish grin.

"No," Liz said.

Charlie nodded, and then the pair sat in silence for a while, each of them staring out onto the water, the sunlight dancing across the river.

After a few minutes Charlie finally nodded and then stood, wiping the dirt from his jeans. He extended a hand down to Liz, who accepted, and helped her off the ground.

Liz lost her balance, and when Charlie caught her, their bodies were pressed together. Charlie had his hands on her hips, and she pressed her hands against his chest. The pair locked eyes, a flash of heat exchanging between them.

Charlie leaned close and then kissed her. She tasted sweet, like the honey crisp apples they grew at the farm, and she was warm like the sun that baked him during the long days. It was familiar and new all at the same time.

Liz pulled back quickly, grimacing as she clutched her stomach. "Sorry."

Charlie smiled, shaking his head. "It's fine." He took her hand and then walked away from the river and back toward the burnt ash of his home, knowing that it'd be easier to face it with her by his side.

In the woods, the shadows of the branches and trees were made long by the rising sun, and their peaceful walk back to the orchard was interrupted by screaming and shouts.

"Go," Liz said, gesturing for him to run, knowing that she couldn't keep up. "I'm right behind you."

Charlie sprinted toward the screams. But while he wanted to run quickly, his legs were slow and lethargic, exhausted from last night and the long, grueling days.

"Charlie!" Martha shouted, stumbling through the woods, struggling with the uneven terrain.

Eventually his mother stopped, letting Charlie come the rest of the way. When the pair finally met, Martha clung tight to her son's arms, struggling to catch her breath.

"What happened?" Charlie asked. "Did they come back? Did—"

"Your father left," Martha answered, terror filling her eyes, which became watery and red. "Doug too. I don't know where they went."

Charlie released his mother's hands and then sprinted toward the orchard, hoping to catch his father and Doug before they arrived at Mayfield.

26

*C*harlie stepped from the green forest and back into the charred remains of the orchard, smoke still steaming off the trees and that scent of burning wood still clinging to the air like morning dew on grass.

He kicked up puffs of ash on his sprint toward the road, dirtying the back of his pant legs with grey dust instead of the rich dark soil that had provided so much life over the years. On his sprint toward the road, Charlie tried not to look at the charred remains of the field.

A part of him believed that if he ignored looking at the burnt options of his youth, then he'd be able to only remember what it looked like before. It was a child's logic, but at that moment he knew that he wasn't strong enough to do anything more than that.

But he couldn't block out all of the sights, and by the time he reached the road, it felt like all of the memories of his youth and the past twenty-four years had been tainted by the fires that had raged through the night.

Tears in his eyes, Charlie sprinted out onto the road and started his long path toward Mayfield. He considered looking for the dirt bike, but after one glance toward the barn, he knew it wouldn't have survived.

But Charlie didn't make it very far before exhaustion took hold and he was forced to stop. He turned around, the blackened fields of his home and the skeletal remains of the house he grew up in still in view. Charlie dropped to his knees.

The sun beat down on his face, and the clear blue sky was a contrast to the blackened and scorched earth that surrounded him. No matter where he went, that cloud of death followed him. He couldn't shake it, and he couldn't rid himself of it, no matter how hard he tried.

But a rumble to the west caused Charlie to turn his head. He squinted down the road, the noise foreign, but familiar. They were vehicles, a whole convoy of them. An armed convoy. It was Dixon.

Having collapsed in the middle of the road, Charlie squinted from the bright sun. And that was exactly where he stayed as the front vehicle of the convoy stopped a few yards from his position.

The passenger door opened, and boots hit the pavement. Lieutenant Dixon stared down at him and extended a hand. "Christ, Charlie, what the hell happened here?"

Charlie regarded the hand, half of himself still lost in confusion. Then, realizing he hadn't imagined all of this and that the man in front of him was a real as the air he breathed, he grabbed hold of the lieutenant's hand and hoisted himself to his feet.

"They came back," Charlie said, blurting the words out like a mad man, pointing to the burned fields and wrecked homes. "We have to get to Mayfield. Quick."

"That's where we're headed, but I'm not sure you want to join," the lieutenant said, trying to move Charlie out of the Humvee's path. "Mayfield is about to turn into a war zone."

Charlie glanced at the long row of military vehicles, all of them the same old versions that Charlie, Liz, and the lieutenant had ridden in on their escape from Seattle after Liz had been shot. Each of them was filled with soldiers, and Charlie counted at least one hundred.

"War zone," Charlie said, whispering the words to himself. He snapped his attention back toward the lieutenant, grabbing hold of the soldier's shoulders. "My father went there with a neighbor. I have to get them out."

The lieutenant opened his mouth to speak, but then shut his jaw, knowing from the look in Charlie's eye that he wasn't going to take no for an answer. "Get in."

Charlie rode in the very back of the Humvee, and while the driver and the other soldiers eyed him curiously, none of them spoke to him on the drive toward the town.

The cramped Humvee reeked of body odor, and the tin can that they found themselves inside was ungodly warm. It didn't take longer than a few minutes for Charlie to break out into a sweat. He kept to himself on the ride over but listened to the conversation of the soldiers, who spoke as if he wasn't even there.

"What's intelligence say about the rendezvous point?" a soldier with a thick Southern accent asked, sporting black, Buddy Holly glasses that were too big for his face.

"We have another unit approaching from the south," the lieutenant answered.

"What's the likelihood that these bastards just turn tail and run?" another soldier asked.

"Command says the enemy will most likely implode the asset before we have an opportunity to secure, so we need to go in fast and hard," the lieutenant said. "We'll be attacking at the same time as the units from the south, so we'll have to be mindful of crossfire."

"How did you get in contact with anyone?" Charlie asked, pulling everyone's attention toward himself. "Radios?"

"Morse Code," Lieutenant Dixon answered. "But once we

arrive at the location, we'll be basing our assault off of synchronization." He lifted an old pocket watch and then stuffed it back into his pocket. "Someone get him a weapon."

The other soldiers glanced around at one another, questioningly. "Lieutenant, are you sure you want to—"

"He knows how to handle himself," the lieutenant said, not even bothering to turn around. "How the hell do you boys think I managed to make it back to the base in the first place?"

The questions ended and the soldier with the thick black glasses and Southern accent handed Charlie one of the M-16s.

"Just don't shoot me when we're out there," he said, then pressed his finger against the assault rifle's barrel. "And remember that's the dangerous end."

Charlie gripped the weapon, flicking the safety on to make sure he didn't have any unplanned discharges. He'd handled an assault weapon before. His father used to own one, but he sold it a few years back, never thinking he'd need it to fight a war.

The entire ride to Mayfield was plagued with anxiousness. Charlie worried that he'd be too late, that his father and Doug would already be dead on the streets by the time he arrived. But he kept glancing out the window, hoping to find them still on the side of the road, walking toward Mayfield. Since no one saw when they left, it was still a possibility, especially since he knew his father wouldn't be able to keep a fast pace for very long.

Once they passed the road sign that signaled they were less than a mile from Mayfield, the nerves inside the Humvee became electric.

"We secure the perimeter," Lieutenant Dixon said. "Retreat is not an option."

"OOO-RAH!"

The confirmation came in a unanimous chorus, and

Charlie felt it spike his adrenaline. He adjusted his hold on the rifle and told himself that the moment he got out of the Humvee, he'd start searching the buildings for his father and Doug. But he already had a good idea of where they might be holed up.

The hospital at the end of town offered a perfect view for a sniper into the terrorist's stronghold of the power plant. At the very least, from that position they'd be able to determine how many insurgents they were dealing with and how to take as many of them out before they were gunned down.

When they stepped into town, Charlie saw the carnage that the terrorists had left behind. The buildings were burned and charred, some of them still smoldering.

Matching burnt corpses littered the streets, forcing the drivers to weave around the bodies as best they could, but the convoy didn't slow.

"How close, Lieutenant?" the driver asked.

"Until we can't drive anymore," the lieutenant answered.

Every pair of eyes watched the buildings pass, the Humvee forced to slow at the stalled and broken-down vehicles that littered the road. The deeper they went into the town the worse the carnage and congestion became, until the driver was forced to stop completely.

"All right, men, let's move!" the lieutenant said, then flung his door open.

The other soldiers exited the vehicle just as quickly and lined up in formation around the vehicle, awaiting further orders.

Charlie was the last one out of the vehicle, and he circled around toward the back and out of the way. He glanced back at the row of vehicles, all the soldiers recreating the same formation out of the lead vehicle. All of them had their eyes locked onto the surrounding buildings, and the only sound that echoed through the town was the light hum of the vehicle engines that they had arrived in.

And then the first gunshot rang out.

The bullet collided with the lead Humvee, and Charlie and the rest of the soldiers ducked before a barrage of retaliatory fire sent the pair of terrorists retreating to the bulk of their forces.

"Forward!" The lieutenant waved his arm, and Charlie let the sea of soldiers pass him and head down the road while he sprinted for the back side of the Main Street buildings. He figured that if the forces were coming from the west and the south, then keeping to the north would be a safe bet to stay out of their way.

Once Charlie was down a side alley, he kept his eyes peeled, jerking in spasms whenever a random gunshot fired, but he grew used to the noise quickly the more he heard it and the farther he headed down toward the hospital.

Charlie checked down the alleys every few buildings, making sure that he didn't get ahead of the soldiers. The last thing he wanted was to be mistaken as an enemy and shot dead before he even had a chance to save his father.

But the soldiers were moving quickly and efficiently in the streets, and Charlie found himself struggling to even keep up with the soldiers as they hurried toward their objective.

The farther they progressed, the more violent and explosive the gunfire between the two forces became. Charlie kept low, his heart pounding with every step as the hospital building came into view.

He glanced to his right, the soldier's progression forward slowed by a cluster of masked terrorists out of the alley a few buildings down.

One of the terrorists spotted Charlie and fired, forcing Charlie close to the building for cover. He planted a knee and returned fire, but his adrenaline was pumping so hard that it affected his aim, sending the bullets wide left and right.

He waited for them to disappear and then restarted his

trek toward the hospital. Gunfire grew more intense, and so did the screams of the men in battle.

An explosion rocked the earth and sent Charlie stumbling forward on his hands and knees. He whipped his head up in time to see the plume of smoke rising from the direction of the power plant.

Charlie pushed forward. He was less than one hundred yards from the building when another explosion rocked to his right, catapulting Charlie ten feet off the ground where he landed hard on his shoulder, the harsh crack triggering a scream of pain that he couldn't control.

A high-pitched din drowned out the world of sound, and he was unable to hear his own guttural cries. He managed to sit upright and saw that his shoulder had been dislocated. A wetness covered the side of his head, and he reached for it with his good hand and felt blood.

Charlie rubbed the substance between his fingers, staring at it like he didn't recognize it, but then pushed himself off the ground, his hearing slowly returning as he stumbled toward the nearest building. He wandered through the smoke from the blast and slammed his shoulder up against the wall, then jerked his arm up and in, the harsh crack of cartilage and the crippling sensation of pain dropping him back to his knees.

He gasped for breath, then hacked and coughed from the smoke that filled his lungs. His shoulder still ached when he moved it, but most of the motion returned. He stumbled back toward the rifle and picked it off the ground.

The smoke only worsened on his final trek to the hospital, and Charlie coughed, his eyes burning. With the rifle raised and the sounds of war pushing further in the distance, he heard the patter of quick footsteps heading in his direction.

Charlie froze, searching the hazy horizon, but turned too late as the body of a man collided into him, sending them both to the ground. Charlie scrambled to his feet, reaching for the rifle, but the man lunged at Charlie, punching him on the chin.

The pain traveled through Charlie's head, lighting up the back of his brain, but he managed to keep his wits about him and countered the punch with a blow of his own. The pair then locked horns, grappling over the ground, rolling over one another, elbow and knees jabbing at whatever body parts they could reach, and finally Charlie landed on top, his hands wrapped around the terrorist's throat, and squeezed, choking the life from him.

Spit flew from the terrorist's lips, and his eyes bulged from his skull. His cheeks reddened, then turned a shade of purple, and he violently squirmed beneath him, trying to fling Charlie off, but he was too small and Charlie was too big. Charlie offered one final squeeze and then heard the harsh crack of the man's windpipe.

Snot dribbled from Charlie's face, and he heaved breaths, choking on his own saliva. His face was red and sweaty, and he couldn't look away from the pair of bulging and lifeless eyes that stared up and into the blank sky above.

Another round of gunfire erupted into the air, and Charlie snapped from the murderous daze that had taken control of his faculties. He quickly picked up his rifle and then stumbled toward the hospital.

Charlie shouldered open the side entrance and gagged at the stench of the dead bodies that had another day to roast and rot. His heel slipped on blood and guts, smearing it into the already-stained tile floor of the hallways.

"Dad! Doug!" he shouted, no longer caring if he was heard and hoping that they would answer to make his journey shorter. "DAD!" He kept his rifle up and aimed, ready to fire at anything that turned a sharp corner or stepped out of one of the many doors.

He made it all the way to the front of the building where

the ER lobby was located without a single trace of his father. He lowered the weapon slightly. "Shit." He spun around in circles, at a loss what to do next. "DAD!" He screamed, his voice cracking from the anxious strain.

The muscles in his shoulders burned as he struggled to keep the rifle raised. He weaved through the halls, stepping over bodies, the gunfire outside growing louder. When he made it to the east side of the building, searching for the stairs, he glanced out a window.

The scene outside was something out of a movie. The soldiers that Charlie had arrived with were pushing toward the power plant facility, their progress slow but steady.

The terrorists were slow on their retreat but left behind their fallen comrades almost too eagerly. Sunlight high-lighted the patches of red that stained the green grass fields that surrounded the plant, and Charlie wondered how long all of this would last.

A door slammed open down the hall, and Charlie spun around, raising the rifle and poised to shoot. He moved toward the door of the room as the footsteps grew louder, the breathing frantic. Charlie remained hidden by the door, poised to strike the moment the figure darted across the hallway.

An arm came into view, and Charlie charged into the hall, slamming the runner up against the wall. Charlie pinned him using the rifle that he wedged on his throat. The terrorist kicked his legs, battering Charlie's body with the hard toe of his boots, but Charlie didn't relinquish his hold.

A hard kick to Charlie's groin sent him stumbling back-wards, and while the terrorist had no gun, he brandished a knife that he slashed wildly toward Charlie's chest, tearing his shirt.

The next slash came down toward his face, and Charlie was a second too late in his reaction as he leaned back. The tip of the blade sliced open his cheek. The sting was short-lived, and Charlie grabbed hold of the terrorist's wrist, cracking it violently against the wall. The knife crashed to the tile.

The enemy threw three quick rabbit punches, pushing Charlie backward, and then sprinted down the hall. But the punches only pushed him closer to his rifle, and Charlie picked it up off the floor and aimed for the terrorist's back.

Charlie squeezed the trigger, and the gunshot thundered in the halls. The bullet missed, so he chambered another round, then readjusted his aim. He fired again. The terrorist's limbs flung outward right before he hit the tile where he lay motionless.

Charlie turned back toward the direction where the terrorist had run and saw the entrance to the staircase. He hurried up the steps, passing more dead bodies, his senses dulled to the gruesome sights and smells.

"DAD! DOUG!"

He shouted up and down the halls of each floor he passed, but heard nothing, as he ascended higher and higher toward the top floor. He passed over the bodies then scanned the rooms with windows that faced the power plant.

"DAD!" Charlie's voice grew more and more frantic as he neared the end of the hallway's hospital. Maybe he was wrong. Maybe his father hadn't come up here. Maybe their plan had changed. But with only three rooms left, Charlie found what he feared to discover.

"DAD!" Charlie dropped the rifle from his hands and hurried to his father's side, who was collapsed on the ground, his weapon lying next to him. He turned his father on his back and revealed the chest wound and blood that had soaked the front portion of his shirt. "Christ."

"Char-lie," Harold choked the words out, a pool of blood forming in his mouth, his teeth almost pink from the blood.

"It's all right, Dad," Charlie said, trying to keep his voice calm, but failing miserably. "I'll get you some help, I'll—" He looked around the room for anything that could stop the bleeding. He yanked the sheets off the hospital bed and then pressed them against the wound.

His father was too big to move on his own. He might be able to get him on a cot, but he didn't know how he'd get them down the stairs.

Looking around the room, Charlie saw Doug lying in a pool of his own blood, lifeless.

Harold lifted his hand from his side and grabbed hold of his son's shoulder. Charlie grabbed it and held it with his own. His father's strength had disappeared.

"Your mother," Harold said, his body trembling as he tried to spit out the last few words he had left. "Tell her I lo—" He shut his eyes, pain flashing across his face, and he bared his teeth.

But Charlie nodded, squeezed his father's hand so he knew he was still there. "She knows, Dad, but I'll tell her. I promise." He rocked forward and back, the tears falling from his face, the echoes of war beyond the walls of the hospital the background of his final moments with his father.

Harold opened his eyes, which scanned the ceiling in confusion. His breaths shortened and became sharper. When his eyes finally landed on his son, the confusion heightened. He worked his mouth, trying to speak, his eyes bulging from his skull.

"What is it, Dad?" Charlie asked.

Gargled gasps of air bubbled from the depths of Harold's innards, but he couldn't speak. His upper back arched in a spasm, and then landed flat, and he lay still.

"Dad?" Charlie asked, giving his father's hand a gentle shake.

But Harold didn't respond. His chest lay still. His eyes were vacant and empty as they remained staring at the ceiling.

Charlie's cries were silent, the tears streaming down his

face as he lowered his head onto his father's shoulder. And as he drew in a sharp breath, he exhaled a guttural cry that bellowed up from that deep, hidden place inside him.

Charlie lifted his head toward the ceiling. Gunshots drew his attention toward the window. He stood and saw the fight still raging outside. A fight that his father had died for. Charlie clenched his fists, squeezing his hands so tight that his knuckles cracked.

The men below had taken everything from him. His home. His land. And now his father. If he was meant to be surrounded by death, then Charlie decided it was better to be the killer than the victim. He knelt by his father's side and then closed his eyes.

---

27

*T*he gunfire was muffled by the hospital walls and windows and the height from Charlie's position on the top floor. But despite the violent war raging outside, Charlie couldn't pull his eyes away from the blood that stained his hands.

He studied the different shades of claret and its thickness as it traveled along the grooves of his palms and fingers. Every time he wiggled his fingers the blood shimmered, coming alive on his hands. But Charlie Decker was as far away from life as he could get.

Charlie peeled his eyes off of his palms and glanced down at his father, who was dead and bloodied on his back, face turned up toward the ceiling and his eyes glaring lifelessly at the blank canvas of white above them.

The space between Charlie and his father's body was slowly filled with the words that were left unsaid, and then filled the room, and eventually the entire floor. And the words became combustible from the rage and anger that filled the spaces between.

Charlie glanced down to his left where the rifle lay, its black color popping against the white tile. The gun was his lighter, and the moment he picked it up, he would ignite the world around him. It was a fire that his father would have ignited.

Hell, it was a fire that his father did ignite. It was the reason he was lying dead on the top floor of a hospital building. He chose to fight. He did what Charlie couldn't, but that didn't mean Charlie couldn't change his path.

Charlie picked up the rifle, the metal and composite thick and heavy in his hands. Standing, he had a better view out the window and the fight below. Lieutenant Dixon and his men had the enemy surrounded, almost ready to infiltrate the power plant.

Charlie's reflection in the window threw him off guard, the man standing with the rifle unrecognizable to him. Hesitation and uncertainty was replaced with the steadfastness of purpose. And with the foreign enemy crawling over the town where he grew up, Charlie knew exactly how to fulfill that purpose.

He moved quickly from the room and back toward the staircase. His movements were efficient, not a single motion wasted, and before he even realized it, he was back on the first floor and heading toward the nearest exit, which happened to be in the rear of the building.

The cacophony of war blasted Charlie's senses the moment he stepped out of the hospital. He turned quickly, rifle raised and aimed forward.

After one quick overall scan of the field in front of him, marking the position of his American comrades, his vision tunneled to the end of his sight and the rest of the world faded into the gunshots and screams.

Charlie marched toward the front lines, keeping north of the line of soldiers pushing closer and closer toward the power plant's entrance. All Charlie needed to do was keep out of their way and avoid any friendly fire.

He crouched to a knee and aided in the assault on the

plant's entrance where the terrorists had bottlenecked themselves in retreat.

"Forward! Forward! Forward!"

The order triggered motion from the line as the unit continued its assault, and Charlie's heart pounded with the drums of war. His finger worked deftly over the trigger, his aim steady and true.

Through the scope on the rifle, Charlie watched his first kill drop. Blood spurted from the man's chest, exploding out of him like a geyser, his body jerking backward from the bullet's force, and he collapsed to the ground, another corpse added to the pile.

With his target down, Charlie shifted his aim to the next one, his crosshairs lining up over a man's skull. Nothing but the whites of his eyes were visible, his mouth covered with black cloth, and his head wrapped in a similar bandana.

Still marching forward, Charlie's muscles seized up, growing still and calm in the same tenth of a second that he pulled the trigger, which sent his bullet screaming toward his next target, connecting with the left eye.

The bullet exploded out of the back of his skull, snapping the terrorist's head backward before the body dropped to the ground.

Charlie searched for the next target but found the entrance clear save for the pile of corpses that had collected on the ground.

"FORWARD!"

The steady pace of the line exploded into a sprint toward the factory. Charlie hurried alongside the soldiers, the heat of battle so hot and high that none of them noticed the man in jeans, dirty t-shirt, and boots that stood out among the wave of camouflage crashing into the entrance.

Charlie steered clear of the rest of the soldiers, focused only on killing as many more terrorists as he could bring into the view of his scope.

The world darkened when he stepped through the entrance, which opened into a large foyer, candlelight dancing along the walls, shifting the shadows of the men that had entered along the rust-stained metal walls.

Charlie stood off to the side, letting the soldiers file toward the door, still going unnoticed by the military unit.

"Breach, breach, breach." The lead soldier swung the door open, and the soldiers behind him flooded through the gap like a hole in a dam.

Charlie was the last man sucked in, the sporadic pop of gunfire echoing ahead. The hallways and rooms they passed were clear before he even had an opportunity to tick one more notch onto his kill count.

But when the unit passed a hallway, ignoring the darkened path to wherever it led, Charlie stopped. He squinted into the darkness, an eerie calm plaguing him, and an itch to be swallowed up in it.

The military unit went ahead of him, and Charlie slowly inched down the hallway. The farther he walked, the more his eyes adjusted to the darkness ahead. The hallway walls were smooth and barren and stretched high above to an industrial ceiling that was nothing but vent ducts, wires, and tubes.

The hallway curved right, the bend long, keeping Charlie on his toes. When he rounded the other side, he looked behind him, that sensation of someone following him in the darkness unshakeable. It crawled up the back of his neck like an unsuspecting shiver that evoked a tremble that he wasn't willing to give, but his body didn't grant him his request.

The farther Charlie penetrated the darkness and the clearer the images became in that darkened void, the more his paranoia grew.

He became sure that someone was following him.

Charlie kept his head on a swivel, and every turn and scuff of his heels sent the noises echoing into the ceiling. His breathing and heartrate quickened. His fingers tightened their grip on the rifle in his hands, trying to squeeze the metal and crush it in his bare hands.

Doors appeared on either side of him, each of them closed. Charlie glanced ahead and found more that dotted the hall in sporadic intervals. He checked each of them, finding all of them locked.

But still Charlie pressed forward, checking each door, thorough in his search to find more of the bastards to kill. And his diligence was finally rewarded seven doors down, when the handle he pressed down gave way.

Aiming the barrel of his rifle into the crack of the door, he swung it inward, the harsh bang of the door on the wall startling the huddled lump in the corner that threw their hands up in the air.

"Please! Please." The English was accented but spoken clearly.

Charlie stepped forward and pressed the barrel of his rifle against the cowering figure's forehead. The trembling fear running off the man vibrated the weapon in Charlie's hands.

"I don't want to be here, please!"

Charlie frowned. There was something about the figure's voice that threw him off, and with the terrorist's head wrapped in dark cloth that concealed their mouth and their head, leaving only the whites of their eyes visible, he couldn't be sure.

"Let me see your face," Charlie said, gun still aimed at the terrorist's head.

The figure tilted their eyes up from the floor.

"Now!" Charlie barked the order, and the figure flinched from the harsh lash of his tongue.

Slowly, the enemy complied with Charlie's order, removing the cloth. And as the layers dropped to the floor, Charlie felt the aim of his rifle dip with them.

HUNT

It was hard to see the details of her features in the darkness, but the terrorist huddled in the corner of the room was clearly a woman. And it was a turn of events that Charlie hadn't expected.

"Up." Charlie followed the order with a quick tilt of his rifle, and this time the woman obeyed without question. "Who else is down here?"

"Just me." She stared at the floor, keeping her hands raised harmlessly in the air beside her head.

They were alone. The soldiers that Charlie had entered with were gone, and the men that she had fought beside were dead or on the run. He could kill her, and no one would care, no one might ever even know.

But killing a woman, even an enemy, brought forth a conflict that he didn't anticipate facing. He thought of the men he ran into when he first left Seattle, after he was separated from his group. They had taken the women in the group, tried to do acts on them that was worse than death.

Charlie did a quick check of the floor and the walls, finding no weapon. "Spin around. Hands on the wall."

She complied, and then Charlie patted her down, searching for knives or a pistol hidden in her waist, pockets, or boots. But he found nothing. She was clean.

Angry, Charlie spun her back around and then shoved the tip of his barrel closer to her face. "What the fuck are you doing here?"

The woman shivered, unsure if she should answer, until Charlie pressed the barrel against her cheek.

"I-I came with my brother. He smuggled me out and was hoping we could start over here after-" She swallowed, catching her train of thought, no doubt choosing her words carefully. "After all of this was over."

"You know how many people your brother and his friends killed?" Charlie asked. "Do you know what they did to my home? My family?"

The woman cowered, crying. "I'm sorry. I'm so sorry."

Charlie still hadn't taken his finger off the trigger. All he had to do was squeeze. But for whatever reason, Charlie just couldn't do it.

Charlie stepped back and then motioned toward the door. "Keep your hands up and walk slow. Move. Now."

The woman exhaled in relief and nodded quickly as she complied with Charlie's demands. He followed her into the hall, keeping his weapon aimed at her, still ready to pull the trigger should she try anything. A part of him desperately wished that she would try something. But she did nothing.

Charlie directed her out the doors and past the carnage of the dead bodies of her fellow countrymen, and she sobbed harder as she stepped over all the death.

She started speaking in her native tongue, the whispers fast and almost prayer-like as Charlie nudged her along, whenever she stopped and gawked at the death that littered the floor.

Sunlight blinded Charlie when they finally made it outside, and there he waited with the girl, her arms still raised and tears streaming down her cheeks, shaking her head.

"This isn't what I wanted," she said, choking the words out between hysterical breaths. "I never wanted to be here."

"None of us did," Charlie replied, his words surprising him.

The pair waited, frozen in time, stuck in the loop of her crying and Charlie keeping the rifle aimed at the woman's head. The urge to kill her had passed, but he couldn't shake the thought that she was one of them. One of the people that had come to his home and burned everything he had ever known to the ground. One of the same people that had murdered his father.

Charlie wasn't sure how long they waited, but the sporadic gunfire was their only keeper of time, and he was relieved when Lieutenant Dixon marched out of the facility with his men in tow, the soldiers immediately spotting the woman.

"Holy shit, they brought women with them over here?" The voice's surprise was matched by its overwhelming glee. "Smart bastards. Can't tell you how many times I wished I had a woman on deployment."

Looking at her now, Charlie noticed that the woman's fear had glossed over into indifference, and the tears had dried along her cheeks.

Lieutenant Dixon sidled up next to Charlie. "Where the hell did you find her?'

"Hiding in one of the rooms," Charlie answered. "She wasn't armed."

Dixon regarded the woman, the pair locking eyes with one another, and whatever fear the woman held melted away.

"You will not win this fight," she said. "There are more, and they will come, bringing down the fist of God upon your heads."

"Take a look around, lady!" A soldier shouted from behind them. "We killed all your man meat!"

Laughter erupted from the unit, and Dixon turned around, ending the boyish raucous laughter with a single glare. But when he turned around, the woman had only grown angrier.

She started talking in her native tongue, the words quiet and slow at first, but growing louder.

"What the hell is she saying?" Dixon asked.

But Charlie only shook his head, staring at the woman he pulled from the plant as she stared at Dixon. "I don't know."

Her voice grew even louder, and Dixon drew his weapon, taking a step forward as he aimed it at her head. "What the hell are you saying?"

The woman didn't explain and the shouts only continued, echoing into the morning air.

"She's calling her people!" A soldier yelled. "Fucking shoot her, man!"

There was a practiced anger in the woman's words and a boldness that Charlie didn't notice before. The speed of her speech increased and with every repeated syllable, the lieutenant's anxiety worsened.

"Shut up!" Dixon shouted.

And while Charlie's original instincts matched the same angered tone as the lieutenant's, he suddenly wished for the woman to stop yelling or at the very least become quieter. But she wouldn't.

The gunshot fired from somewhere behind Charlie, and he spun around just before the woman collapsed to the floor.

He saw the soldier who fired, standing out as every single head of his comrades looked at him. A mixture of excitement and horror appeared on the man's face.

Charlie spun back around toward the woman who was now lifeless on the ground. With the shouting over and the ring of the gunshot faded, the silence that echoed in the air around them was deafening, which ended with the explosion in the plant.

$\mathcal{C}$harlie couldn't take his eyes off the woman. No one had touched her since the soldier had put a bullet through her gut. The only motion her body offered was the trickle of blood that had spread out over the grass, one final statement to the world.

The explosion had come from inside the power plant. The explosives had been rigged to an egg timer, and while the blast wasn't powerful enough to collapse the structure, Charlie had heard the lieutenant speaking with one of his engineers that a few integral systems had been destroyed.

"Charlie!"

Charlie whipped his head around, still kneeling by the woman's body.

Lieutenant Dixon hovered nearby, staring at Charlie like he'd been calling his name for the past twenty minutes. Dixon motioned for him to come over, and he did so, unaware of how slow he was moving. "You all right?"

"I'm fine," Charlie answered.

Dixon's stare lingered on Charlie for a minute longer, and it was the engineer with the lieutenant that finally restarted the conversation.

"We'll need to check the rest of the building for structural damage, and unless I get some help, it's going to take me weeks." The engineer was a short man and sported a thick black mustache, which added years to the baby-faced cheeks on either side. His hair was the same jet-black color as his facial hair, and his broad shoulders only added to his squat features. "If this place is a priority for reconstruction, then I need the resources to bring it back online."

Dixon nodded and then turned to Charlie. "Any of your boys in the area familiar with electrical engineering, or construction?"

Charlie circled the question, his lag in response time due to his thoughts still transfixed on the dead woman behind him. "I can ask some of the workers back at the orchard, but I don't know if they'll have the formal training you're looking for."

"So long as they're competent with basic electronics, I can show them the rest," the engineer said. "Anything would help."

"You're dismissed, Staff Sergeant."

"Sir."

Once the engineer was gone, Charlie returned his dazed and lifeless expression toward the dead woman. He never learned her name. Not that it mattered.

"I still can't figure out why the hell she would have been inside," Dixon said, staring at the woman. "It's been all men up until this point. The fact that they're bringing people who aren't soldiers over here doesn't sit well with me."

"She came with her brother," Charlie said. "Said that she wanted to start a new life here with her family."

"Christ." Lieutenant Dixon shook his head, his voice a mixture of awe and disgust. "They think they'd just start killing us and then they could carve out something for themselves and everything would be fine?"

But as Charlie stared at the dead woman, that's exactly

what he thought she believed. It was madness, but it was also convicted madness that refused to be denied and would overcome whatever obstacles that were thrown in its way.

"Did you find your dad?" Dixon asked.

Charlie nodded.

Dixon reciprocated the motion at Charlie's extended silence. "I'm sorry."

"If I could have a ride back, I'd appreciate it," Charlie said.

"Do you need help with the body?"

Again, Charlie nodded.

"I'll have some of my guys come over in a second."

"Thanks."

After the lieutenant left, Charlie lingered there alone for a while, and then two men appeared, guns still strapped over their shoulders, one of their uniforms speckled in blood. They didn't speak, and Charlie didn't mind, as he led them over to the hospital.

The pair of soldiers made a few comments about the stench inside the hospital, but they shut up when they saw Harold Decker in the hospital room where Charlie had found and then left him.

"We could probably put him on one of the carts," one soldier said.

"Yeah," Charlie replied.

Charlie didn't help the pair of soldiers carry his father down the steps, and neither of them asked for it. They covered Harold Decker's body with a sheet, and one of the soldiers pointed at Doug's body.

"What about him?"

Charlie grimaced. "He stays."

Charlie led them down, opening doors for them, and shoving bodies out of the way to help make their trek down easier.

The soldiers loaded Harold in the Humvee, and then Charlie climbed into the backseat and the soldiers hopped into the front. He wasn't sure what the pair talked about on the way to the orchard, and Charlie didn't even remember telling them where to go, but he arrived back home at his destination nonetheless.

All Charlie could focus on during the drive back to the orchard was how he was supposed to tell his mother that his father was dead. He ran through the strings of words in his head, rearranging the order of them a thousand times over, and then a thousand times again, but none of it sounded right.

It was like he had been thrust into a bad dream, and no matter how hard he tried, he just couldn't wake up.

"Hey," the soldier said, turning around in his seat up front. "This it?"

Charlie glanced out the window to the smoldering wreckage that was his home and nodded.

Doors opened and the soldiers pulled Harold Decker from the back of the Humvee, keeping him on the cot which they placed on the asphalt.

"Do you need help carrying him up to—"

"No," Charlie said.

The soldiers nodded and then simply returned to the vehicle, turned around, and headed back toward Mayfield, leaving Charlie with his father on the hospital cart with a sheet draped over him in the middle of the road.

Charlie stood there, frozen, long after the Humvee faded on the horizon. He lingered, wallowing in the dead silence that he had always enjoyed his entire life. But it was tainted now, soured by the death that offered it to him as a tool to help him grieve.

He didn't want silence now. He would have taken anything but silence. He wanted to hear his father's bois-terous laugh again. He wanted another story about his youth and the struggles he endured building the orchard. He wanted his father's advice on what to do next, but above all, he wanted the opportunity to speak. He wanted to apologize for what he said the night before when the pair had exploded at one another.

But he'd never have that opportunity.

"Charlie!"

His heartrate spiked at his mother's voice, and he turned to find her stumbling through the ash and blackened, skeletal remains of the trees that had gone up in smoke the night before. Even at a distance, he could see the red in her eyes and the flush in her cheeks. She brought her fingertips to her quivering lips, her attention focused on the body on the cot.

Martha shook her head, jogging forward as she worked her mouth, but found that she couldn't speak the words that struggled to be set free.

Charlie walked toward her, meeting her in the middle of the orchard, and wrapped his arms around her before she could walk past.

"Let me see him," Martha said, blurting out the words, her tone strife with grief. "I want to see him." She lunged forward, but her small frame was no match for Charlie's strength, who easily held her back. "I want to see him!"

"No, Mom," Charlie said, taking the screams and the fists she beat against his chest and arms. "You don't need to see him like that."

Sobbing, Martha collapsed into the dirt, her hands still clawing at Charlie's legs, who dropped with her. He held his mother tight, letting her howls fly up into the air.

And then, one by one, the rest of the people emerged from the orchard, staring at Charlie, then at the cot still on the road, then back to Charlie. It took a while for the sight to register on some of their faces, but when it finally did, everyone began to cry.

But Charlie's eyes searched for only one face among the gathering crowd, and he found her standing front and center of them all.

Liz covered her mouth when she saw Harold on the cot. And then her shoulders bobbed up and down as she sobbed.

Mario and a few of the workers brought Harold to Doc, who started to clean and dress the wounds. His mother ignored Charlie's orders to stay away, a stoic expression on her face as she watched Doc sew up the wounds and clean away the blood. But Charlie could have never guessed at how much that sight would haunt his mother in the months to come.

Charlie found a spot in the middle of the east fields where the burnt carnage was the worst. Every square inch of greenery had been stripped from the field, leaving behind only blackened and brittle skeletons in its wake.

A layer of ash covered the rich black soil that had been the feeding ground for all the life that had once been around him. He stuck his fingertips into the silky grey, feeling the difference between what was dead and the thick soil beneath the ash.

He rubbed the ash between his fingertips, watching the small particles of grey float back toward the ground or be kicked up in a hazy cloud from a gust of wind.

The ash and dirt mixed with the blood still staining his hands. His father's blood.

"Hey."

Charlie didn't turn around at Liz's voice, and he didn't look her way when she sat next to him in the field of ash and death.

"Doc finished with your dad," Liz said. "People want to know when you want the burial to take place. I asked your mom, but she hasn't said a word. She hasn't even left your dad's side."

Charlie didn't answer. He stared at the grey silk he sat upon, wondering if he'd ever be able to get something to grow again. And if he even wanted to try.

"Charlie, you need to—"

"I told him he was a failure," Charlie said. "Those were the last words I said to my father. That's what he heard come from the lips of his only child's mouth. The child he raised, and nurtured, and provided all of the opportunities that he never had growing up."

"But that's not how you really felt, and he knew that," Liz said. "I know I didn't know him very well, but—"

"No, you didn't." The words tasted bitter on Charlie's tongue, and judging by the way Liz retracted her hand from his shoulder, she felt the sting in them too.

After a moment, Charlie shook his head. "I'm sorry." He looked at her, struggling to hold back the tears that wanted to break free.

"It's okay," Liz said, softly. "It's true." She shrugged. "I mean I've been here for what? A few days? We just met, and all of the shit that's happened since Seattle…" She trailed off, looking around at the dead trees. "We haven't had a moment to process any of it."

Charlie smiled. "He liked you. My dad."

Liz's mouth twitched and she wiped her nose, sniffling in the same motion. "I liked him too."

Charlie gestured to the landscape. "Look at this. We have nothing. No food. God knows if our water pump works. The house is gone." He ran his hands through his hair, rewetting the dried blood from his sweat, leaving streaks of red along the sides of his head. "I know what people want from me back there, but I don't know how to give it to them."

Liz frowned. "What do you think they want?"

"Someone to tell them what to do next," Charlie answered. "For someone to give them hope and let them know that it's going to be all right, and that we'll get through this if we just pull together." Charlie clinched his fists and rattled them, then let the tension in them relax. "But I don't have the answers, Liz. I don't think I ever did."

"You get lost in your own head too much, you know

that?" Liz asked. "You don't even give people a chance to actually have them tell you what they need before you let them decide for them." Liz reached for Charlie's face and pulled it toward her own until they touched noses. "The only thing that people want to do right now is grieve with you." She gave him a gentle shake. "Let yourself feel it. Because if you don't, I promise you, it will break you in a way that you can't be fixed."

She kissed him, and while her touch helped pull him out of the darkened corner where he sulked in his mind, he wasn't sure if he could follow her advice. But he knew that he couldn't sit in the dirt forever.

Slowly, Charlie pushed himself off the ground, and even though Liz was still recovering from her gunshot wound, she helped keep him steady when he stumbled on his shaky legs. It was almost like learning to walk again.

The pair passed the burned-down house, and Charlie kept his eyes forward, knowing that staring into the wreckage of his childhood home would only slow him down. And right now, he needed to keep moving. His very life depended upon it. His future depended upon it.

They moved through the west fields, toward the well where Charlie's father had been placed and where his mother still stood by his side, motionless and void of emotion.

"I need to talk to her," Charlie said, stopping both him and Liz. "Alone."

Liz nodded and kissed his cheek before letting him go.

Charlie shuffled toward his mother, who had her back turned toward him, staring down at his father, holding his hand, barely able to wrap her hands around Harold's big paws.

Charlie remained silent, and his mother said nothing even when he stood next to her.

Doc had done a good job cleaning Harold up, making him

presentable for burial, especially considering the limited resources.

The color in Harold's cheeks had already started to fade, but Charlie was glad his father's eyes were closed. There was something unsettling about a pair of lifeless eyes. They were soulless, and eyes without souls tried to collect what didn't belong to them.

"I wish we could put him in a suit," Martha said, her tone surprisingly casual despite the stoic mask she wore as she spoke. "I doubt anything survived the fire, though."

Wanting to ease whatever pain his mother was going through, Charlie nodded. "I can look to see if anything made it."

"You should say something when we bury him," Martha said, keeping her attention on Harold. "I don't want anyone else speaking. Not the workers, no one else."

"Of course," Charlie answered.

Martha then gently lowered her head and kissed Harold's forehead, then placed his hand onto his stomach, folding them together. She stared at her husband, a man who she'd been married for over forty years, someone who she woke up with every morning during that time frame, and someone she laid her head next to at night. Charlie couldn't fathom what losing something like that was like.

Martha turned toward her son, offering no warm embrace or comfort. She had transformed into a piece of steel, cold and unyielding. He'd never seen her like that. It was like staring into the face of a stranger.

"Your father was a hard man, and a proud man," Martha said, her eyes locked onto his. They were so still, balls of concrete wedged into that steel skull. "He died doing what he believed in, and while you may not have agreed with his actions, I did." She stepped closer. "Our world has always relied on moving forward. And after everything that's been thrust upon us, that statement has requested even more respect from us. Be that man, Charlie. Be the man your father always knew that you could be. No more doubt, no more hesitation. You know what you have to do. It's time you do it."

And then his mother walked away, offering no affection after her words, and Charlie was left with the mild sting of reality.

His first instinct was to turn around and talk to her, to run to his mother and hold her and to be held in return, but he pushed the thought aside. Because deep down, under-neath that self-doubt and hesitation that had plagued him most of his life, was the granite of his heritage.

The hard bedrock that his father had bestowed up him and had built a life with nothing more than his will and his hands. Harold Decker made his mark on the world, never asking for permission, and never seeking forgiveness for pushing forward.

It was Charlie's turn to make his mark.

* * *

CHARLIE AND MARIO lowered Harold Decker into the hole the other workers had dug. He was wrapped in a white bedsheet, and Charlie stared down at his father's figure a moment before he lifted his eyes to the living bodies that surrounded the grave.

Everyone had come. Well, everyone that had been with them so far. Some of the men and attempted to comb their hair, making themselves as presentable as they could with their limited resources. Charlie recognized the effort as a show of respect, and it was a gesture that he had forgotten to do himself.

Martha had pulled Liz close, the pair of women clutching hands tightly, both looking to Charlie with the fading sun behind them.

Glancing out at the fields now, with the sun setting and bathing the world in that golden hue Charlie had loved so much, it didn't seem right that he was burying his father on such a beautiful evening.

The would should have been as broken and dreary as Charlie felt, but the sight was just another lesson in the long string of realities that he'd experienced over a very short amount of time.

Charlie lowered his eyes to his father's body one more time, avoiding the stares of the mourners that surrounded him, buying time for the words his mother wanted him to say.

He'd spent most of the day trying to figure them out, but no matter how many times he tried to jot down on the blank page, or how many ways he rearranged the words in his head, they just didn't fit.

So he followed his mother's advice. He plowed forward.

"Three hundred acres," Charlie said. "That's how much land was burned when those terrorists came marching down our road. The fires went up and spread and took everything that we've ever known." He snapped his fingers. "Just like that."

The faces in the crowd remained void of emotion, but they leaned forward, listening intently, wanting to soak in not just Charlie's words, but whatever confidence that they could borrow from him.

"But we're not without our wits," Charlie said. "And we're not without our bodies." He pointed to the blackened and charred fields, made softer by the dying light of the day. "Once upon a time there was nothing out there. No homes. No farms. No signs of life other than the natural essence of the forest. But people like my father saw the potential for what this place could be, and so did Don." He turned to Amy who had her three boys huddled around her, and she offered the first smile from the group. He took it as a sign he was heading in the right direction. And he grew bolder. "This is our home, and no one is going to take it from us. They can bring their men, and their guns, and their fire and death, but it will not be enough to beat us. It will never be enough!" Spittle flew from Charlie's mouth as he spoke, his fervor intensifying.

Charlie focused on the faces around him now. His words had brought forth a strength in them that wasn't there before. And the more he spoke the hotter his own flames burned, every syllable from his mouth feeding the fires.

"This is our home! And we will never give it up!"

29

ONE WEEK LATER

he nightmares hadn't stopped. Every night they replayed, and each time the sickening sour pit in Charlie's stomach worsened. Just like tonight.

Charlie awoke, gasping for air and dripping with sweat. He hands ached from clutching the sleeping bag so tightly. He sat upright, catching his breath, and tried to rid himself of the images of his dead father. He shook his head. "It's not real."

But despite the repeated mantra, Charlie couldn't shake the dreams. Knowing he wouldn't be able to fall back asleep, Charlie dressed, hoping that dawn was near, and he was pleasantly surprised to find the sky gray with early morning. He swiped at the growing scruff on his face and then slicked back his hair.

Charlie stepped around the tents sprawled outside the back of Doc's house, half of which had been consumed by the fires when the terrorists had marched from Mayfield. But the rain that followed had been kind enough to allow Doc to keep some of his home.

It was where Liz and Adelyn slept, along with Mario's children and the Bigelow boys. They were crammed inside that house like sardines in a tin can, and while Charlie may have had to sleep on the ground, he was thankful for at least a little bit of privacy.

The tents were on loan from Dixon. After the battle in Mayfield, he had a sudden surplus of field gear due to the casualties he suffered from the conflict with the terrorists. And the shelters weren't the only items on loan from the newly minted commander.

Charlie reached back inside the tent and grabbed the AR-15 that he kept on his person at all times. None of the adults walked the premises without being armed. It was a rule that Charlie initiated.

With the rest of the group still asleep, Charlie headed toward Doc's back door and found the retired veterinarian awake, sneaking a smoke on his back porch. It was a habit the old man had picked back up, and the number of smokes he was sneaking had increased the longer they'd gone without power.

Doc raised his eyebrows as Charlie approached. Both men kept their voices low.

"How's it looking today?" Charlie asked, his stomach tightening from stress even before he asked the question.

Doc exhaled smoke through his nostrils, and then ashed the cigarette into a small pile of dirt near the back steps. He shook his head. "We have another three days of food. Maybe only two."

Charlie glanced back to the tents, and then to the blackened fields of the orchard. He'd gone through the fields every day since they buried his father, and every time he looked at them, he was reminded of the insurmountable amount of work that lay ahead.

Past the fields were the skeletal remains of Charlie's family house and barn. He had already sifted through the wreckage, but the fires had left little to salvage.

The food stores that Charlie and his family had stashed in

the cellar had been destroyed, leaving them with what food Doc had and what rations that Dixon was able to spare, but he hadn't been as willing to part with his food as he had his weapons.

"Hector and his wife have already been asking about how much we have left." Doc groaned as he stood and his knees popped. He straightened out his back, eliciting another crack. "What do you want to do?"

Charlie peeled his gaze away from the blackened fields and then looked to Doc as the first rays of dawn broke over the eastern horizon. "We'll have to head out. Scavenge."

Doc nodded, pocketed his hands, and then stepped closer to Charlie. "You know what that might mean, right?" He tilted his head to the side.

"I do." And it was one of the reasons why Charlie had dreaded going out in the first place. He hadn't anticipated being so behind the curve. He was supposed to have enough food, water, and supplies to last them for at least a few months while they hunted and fished.

But the three excursions that they made out into the woods for game had been fruitless, and Mario still hadn't completed the nets to use on the river. Time was against them.

Doc gripped Charlie's shoulder, his old blue eyes still vibrant, the mind behind them still as sharp as a man in his twenties. "This isn't the same world anymore, Charlie. We all have to adapt to it."

Charlie nodded, and then both men turned back toward the house at the sound of the back door opening. It was Liz.

"Everyone up?" she asked.

Charlie walked to her, taking her hand and helping her down the stairs. "You shouldn't be up and walking around like that." Charlie took her hand and then pulled her close, kissing her lips and abiding the hunger that went beyond the need for food. But Liz was still recovering, and Doc hadn't lifted his restrictions on certain activities. Both eagerly waited for that day to arrive.

"Doc said that I should be moving around if I can," Liz said, taking a step of independence away from Charlie and toward the rising sun. Once she was away from him, she looked back at him and smiled. "And I can."

"Just don't overdo it," Doc said, returning to the kitchen. "I'll get breakfast ready. If you two are up, then the rest won't be far behind."

"Thanks, Doc." Charlie waited until he and Liz were alone, and then he joined her, gently and carefully wrapping his arms around her waist, enjoying her warmth and the weight of her body as she pressed back against him.

After a minute, Liz turned around, frowning. "What is it?"

"Nothing," Charlie answered.

Liz cocked her head to the side. "Haven't we gotten past this?"

Charlie took a breath and then nodded. He glanced around, making sure that they were still alone, and kept his voice to a whisper. "We only have two days' worth of rations left."

"Can you talk to Dixon?" Liz asked, matching his secretive tone.

"I already did," Charlie answered. "That's where I went yesterday. He said no."

Liz exhaled, her worry suddenly matching his own. She bit her lower lip, chewed on it for a minute, and then nodded. "You're going out?'

Charlie had already tossed the idea around with a few people in the group, the ones he trusted the most. Doc, Mario, and Liz. He would have spoken to his mother about it, but the pair hadn't said a word to each other since the day they buried his father.

Martha Decker had closed herself off, shut down. The

only person she spoke with was Liz, and whatever they spoke about was kept between them.

"I'll take Mario and Hector," Charlie said. "We'll head west."

Liz nodded, trying to hide the worry but doing a poor job.

"I'll be fine," Charlie said, forcing a smile.

Liz studied his face and then pressed her hands on either side of his head, running her nails through his hair. She lifted herself up on her tippy toes and kissed him. "Just come back."

"I will."

Breakfast was uneventful, though there were a few grumbles from the kids about having beans again. Adelyn sat with Liz and Charlie, the little girl becoming their adopted daughter. Adelyn spent most of her time with Liz, and the pair had bonded over the past week.

Charlie had done what he could, but fatherhood wasn't a role he had time to prepare for. It was trial by fire, as was everything now.

After everyone was fed, Charlie pulled Mario and Hector to the side, telling both of them the plan. And while Mario looked prepared, Hector's cheeks had gone pale.

"Grab enough water for a day's hike, along with your rifles and ammunition," Charlie said. "We leave in ten."

The pair of men nodded, both returning to their wives, each of them concerned after their talk.

While they hadn't had any incidents on the orchard yet, everyone had heard the random gunshots that periodically echoed through the day and night. It was a constant reminder of the world's new order.

Charlie returned to his tent, digging up the extra magazines that he'd hidden beneath it, accessed through a flap that he cut out in the canvas floor. He put the magazines in plastic bags to prevent any dirt from jamming the weapon. He placed them in his backpack, and when he stepped out of the tent, he was surprised to find his mother standing outside, waiting for him.

Charlie froze with his hand on the grip of the blade he clipped to his belt. He frowned. "Mom, are you all right?"

Martha Decker remained motionless, her expression stoic, as her faded grey eyes studied the man in front of her. "You're leaving."

Charlie adjusted the straps of his pack and slung the rifle over his shoulder as he walked to his mother. "Mario, Hector, and I are heading out to search for food."

"Search, or take?" Martha asked.

Up close, Charlie had a better view of his mother's deteriorating condition. Her eyes had sunken along with her cheeks, clinging to the shape of her skull. Her arms were bone thin, and the little patches of gray had spread to nearly every strand on her head. In the week since Harold Decker's death, Martha Decker had aged another five years. Grief had changed his mother. And Charlie wasn't sure if the woman who had raised him would ever return.

"Your father knew how to handle a weapon," Martha said, keeping her tone cold. "Do you remember what he taught you, Charles?"

Charlie winced. She had never called him that, not even as a child. It was like being addressed by a stranger.

"I remember." Charlie loaded a magazine into the assault rifle.

"Don't come back empty-handed," Martha said. "Your father wouldn't come back empty-handed." She turned and quickly left, leaving behind nothing but the sting of her words.

Once Mario and Hector had their weapons, Charlie made sure each of them carried two duffel bags to help carry back any provisions that they found.

Goodbyes were said, Charlie kissed Liz one more time, gave Adelyn a hug, and then headed west.

Conversation was kept to a minimum, and Hector and Mario continued to look back toward the orchard even after they were gone. But Charlie kept his eyes forward.

Turning around now meant facing those brittle trees and his failure to protect his family's home. And he'd already had enough reminders about that today.

Charlie stayed alert, constantly readjusting his grip on the rifle in his hands. Every step in this new world was dangerous.

The EMP had robbed people of their decency, casting the surviving population into the Stone Age, forcing people to fight and claw and scratch for scraps.

A few miles west of the orchard and Charlie spotted a cluster of about a dozen mobile homes, all of them raised on blocks, situated on a small clearing off the mountain road.

The people who owned the cluster of units rented them out to anyone that paid cash only, which attracted the type of clientele that usually had legal troubles. Charlie wasn't sure what they might find inside, but he was going to sweep every location until he found food.

Mario and Hector clustered near Charlie by a rocky out-cove just before the clearing for the mobile homes. A nervous energy ran through them, none of them able to remain completely still.

"I'll be the first to enter," Charlie said. "Hector, you follow after me, clearing the left while I handle the right." He turned to Mario. "Watch our backs."

"What do we do if someone is inside?" Hector asked.

Charlie was quiet for a moment, and it was the silence that made Hector drop his gaze, mumbling in hasty Spanish.

"Whatever we find, whatever happens, remember what we have back at the orchard," Charlie said. "We have more to think about than just ourselves." He leaned forward, letting the men feed off of his confidence. "We come back with nothing, and our people suffer."

"We won't come back empty-handed," Mario said, looking to Hector. "Si?"

Hector nodded but still couldn't completely erase the worry from his face.

Charlie faced the mobile units and headed for the nearest one, moving quickly and keeping low on his approach. The old wooden steps that led to the front door groaned from their weight, and every noise caused Charlie to wince.

The element of surprise was their greatest ally, and while Charlie had been able to show Mario and Hector the necessary functions and general safety elements of the weapons they used, none of them were tactical experts.

What little Charlie knew he pried from Dixon. The most important piece of advice was keeping everyone on the same page. Give a person a job, have them focus only on that, and trust that everyone else completed their assignments. Because if that trust failed, then people died.

Charlie burst into the first home, his adrenaline pumping and his brain processing information so fast it barely registered in his conscious mind.

Luckily the room was empty, save for a few broken chairs and a pile of dirty sheets in the far corner of the room. The rest of the mobile home was searched, and they found nothing.

The next three units were in similar condition, and the more the trio worked through the process, the more they fell into a rhythm.

At the fourth unit, Charlie stood opposite of Hector, rifle aimed at the opening of the door crack, and they counted down from three. On zero, Hector opened the door, and Charlie stepped forward.

Once past the entrance's threshold, a force kicked the rifle barrel out of his hands, tackling him into the wall, the motion slamming the door shut in the process.

A random gunshot fired and drowned out the sound of

Charlie choking on his back, squirming to get the upper hand on his attacker.

A pair of bulging and crazed eyes stared down at Charlie, the pair of hands clamped around his neck tightening like a vise. Charlie smacked at the assailant's arms, and then the door swung open and Mario barreled inside, shoving the attacker off of Charlie and knocking him to the floor.

His throat free of the hands, Charlie gasped for air and then rolled to his side, cheeks purple as he hacked and coughed, forcing down the crawl of hot bile that was making its way up his throat.

"There's more outside!" Hector shouted.

Charlie forced himself to his hands and knees, and then grabbed the rifle that he'd dropped to the floor, aiming it at the man Mario had pinned down.

Hector rushed inside, slamming the door shut behind him, and ducked to the floor as gunshots thundered and bullets pounded the flimsy trailer walls.

Charlie flattened himself to the floor as well, and for the moment both Mario and their attacker had suspended their squabbling as they avoided the deadly barrage of bullets.

After a few minutes the gunfire stopped, and Charlie raised his head. He glanced over to Hector, then back to Mario, and finally the attacker who was propped up on the back wall, head cocked to the side, mouth hanging open and motionless. Two red holes punctured his chest, blood leaking from the wounds.

"Come on out!" The voice barked the command, but it was far away, the shout little more powerful than a breeze on a cool day.

Charlie looked to Mario and Hector and pressed his finger to his lips. Slowly, he crawled to the nearest bullet hole and squinted through it.

Two figures appeared, but only one of them was armed.

Charlie maneuvered to get a better look at what he couldn't see, and then saw a third body, also armed.

Charlie leaned back, then held up three fingers and pointed outside. Hector and Mario nodded in understanding.

"Let Frankie out!"

The second voice was different than the first, and judging by the way they were hushed, Charlie suspected that they weren't supposed to speak.

"Come out, now, or we will kill you all!"

"You want your man to come out alive, you drop your weapons!" Charlie shouted, hoping the attackers wouldn't call his bluff.

Silence followed the request and Charlie peered through the holes again, watching the trio deliberate. After a minute, they broke apart, and one of the armed men stepped closer.

"You let him out, and then we let you go!"

"No deal!" Charlie shouted. "Drop your weapons, and then we all walk out together." Charlie kept an eye on the man speaking to him, the only feature he was able to make out the bright red of the man's scruff and the pale skin of his cheeks and exposed arms.

Finally, Red Beard turned toward the other gunman and nodded. The pair dropped their weapons and then stepped back, hands in the air.

"All right, let him out!" he shouted.

Charlie quickly beckoned his men close. "We go out, we pick up their guns, and then we leave through the woods. We move quick, and we only shoot if we have to."

Hector and Mario nodded, panting. Charlie positioned himself by the door. He paused, gathering his courage, and then rushed outside, rifle up and aimed at the three men on the road.

Once all three of them were outside, Red Beard squinted

in confusion. And then the realization slowly washed over his face. "You son of a bitch."

"He was killed in the crossfire," Charlie said, his voice quick and breathless, gun still raised and aimed at the leader while Mario and Hector grabbed the weapons on the ground.

"Bullshit!" Red Beard shouted.

"No one else has to die," Charlie said. "We're going to leave, and the rest of us walk out of here with our lives."

Red Beard spoke the words in a growl, and the man quickly piped down. He turned that anger toward Charlie and lowered his hands.

Charlie stepped forward, aiming for the redhead. "Put them back up, now!"

The order triggered a heightened sense of fear in everyone, eyes glancing between Charlie and Red Beard. Charlie placed his finger over the trigger, praying that he wouldn't have to squeeze it, but with all of his attention focused on the redhead, it was Mario who saw the short, fat man reach for a pistol behind his back.

"Gun!"

Charlie looked away for half a second, but the brief moment was all it took for hell to break loose.

The fat man fired twice before Mario took him down, and the third man charged Hector, who froze, frightened even though the skinny man moved forward with nothing except for his swinging arms and unbridled rage.

By the time Charlie returned his attention to Red Beard, the man had his own pistol drawn, firing on his retreat.

Charlie ducked for cover, crashing behind the nearest mobile home. He found Mario pulling Hector behind another mobile home across from him. Charlie peered around the corner, finding two dead bodies.

Charlie removed himself from cover and hurried out to the road, gun up, ready to fire, but found Red Beard gone.

"Shit." He lowered his weapon, his breathing labored as he spun in circles.

"Charlie!" Mario yelled. "Charlie, help!"

Charlie hurried back to Mario, and when he stepped around the corner of the mobile unit where he and Hector had hid, Hector was on his back and gasping for breath while Mario placed both hands over the wound on Hector's stomach.

"Oh my god." Charlie dropped to a knee and added pressure on the wound.

"What do we do?" Mario asked, looking to Charlie.

Blood poured out quickly despite their attempts to block the hemorrhaging, and Hector's shirt was soaked with crimson, the excess dripping onto the dirt. Doc was the only person that'd be able to help him now.

"We need to move him," Charlie said, looking to Mario. "We'll have to carry him."

Mario nodded, and then both men positioned themselves on either side of Hector. They placed the man's arms over his shoulders, and when they lifted him off the ground, Hector screamed, blood dripping out of his mouth, the man so fatigued and injured that he couldn't even support his own weight.

"Just hang on, Hector!" Charlie groaned through clenched teeth, struggling to support the big man's weight.

They managed to move Hector onto the road, but after only ten yards, Charlie's knee buckled and the three of them tumbled to the pavement. Charlie reached for Hector, trying to lift him up from the pavement, but Mario stopped him.

"He's gone," Mario said.

Charlie looked at Hector's face, and then pressed his fingers against Hector's neck. No pulse. He sat back down on the pavement, staring at the dead man. He bowed his head. "Fuck." He rocked slowly, then tensed. "Fuck!"

Mario reached up and lowered Hector's eyelids, then bowed his head and clasped his hands together in prayer.

Charlie stared at Hector's body, letting Mario speak his piece, and then stood. He walked back to the mobile homes and picked the guns up that the men had dropped. He didn't look at their faces on the return trip; he didn't want to see them.

He stuffed the pistols in his bag, and then slung the rifles over his shoulder. When he stepped back onto the road, Mario stood near Hector, marking himself with the holy cross.

"He's too heavy to carry back," Charlie said. "I'll get Dixon to let us borrow one of the Humvees." Charlie didn't think the newly minted commander would object to funeral duty, but he could be wrong. Generosity was in short supply.

Mario stared at Hector as he passed him. "That's it?"

Charlie kept his eyes ahead and adjusted the rifles on his shoulder. "It's all that's left."

30

ONE MONTH LATER

*T*he parking lot was littered with trash and the disabled cars that had been parked there when the EMP had gone off. Windows were smashed, and the front entrance to the grocery was open, but Charlie couldn't see anything from his position in the parking lot.

Charlie remained hunched behind the tailgate of a pick-up, his eyes just above the back gate, squinting ahead. The overcast skies made the afternoon darker than it would have been, and a rain-scented wind blew from the west. He didn't want to get caught up in another storm.

"See anything, Boss?" Mario asked.

Charlie shook his head, and then lowered himself next to Mario. Both men were armed. "It's hard to tell if there is anyone inside, but the parking lot looks clear. No sign of traps."

"Should we look for another store?" Mario asked.

Again, Charlie shook his head. The past week had been a difficult one in finding food. "It's another fifteen miles to the next location, and there's no guarantee that it hasn't already been picked clean." Charlie turned to Mario. "Just stay low and quiet."

Mario nodded, and Charlie crept toward the front of the truck, checking the path toward the grocery one last time. He'd been careful on their approach, making sure to circle the place first. He just hoped that the long trip wasn't for nothing.

Charlie stepped from behind the truck and stayed low on his sprint toward the open front doors. He was mindful of his peripheral and the rows of cars that provided cover for him, and for anyone else that might be camping out and looking for a quick score.

But Charlie stopped outside the entrance, catching his breath as Mario was quick to join him. He squinted back out into the parking lot, still finding themselves alone. If there was anyone waiting, then it would be inside.

Once Charlie passed the threshold of the store's entrance, he was momentarily blinded from the store's darkness. He padded forward carefully until his vision adjusted and headed toward the aisles.

Charlie read the aisle signs, most of which were still intact, and moved toward the one labeled with canned food. But when he turned the corner of the aisle, Charlie stopped, lowering the rifle. "Shit."

The shelves were barren, the items already picked over. All that remained was dust.

"We can check the rest of the store," Mario said, though his tone sounded as defeated as his expression. "See if we can find anything people might have looked over. There are some vegetables that can last a long time without—"

Metal scraped across the ground, and Charlie and Mario raised their rifles in the direction of the noise on the other side of the store.

Charlie led the pair down the aisle, and then paused before he peeked around the corner, Mario still watching his back.

"We should leave," Mario said.

"We're not walking out of here empty-handed," Charlie replied.

And before Mario could protest, Charlie stepped around the corner, moving down the back aisle of the store, which used to hold all the meats and dairy, but what meat hadn't been taken had thawed and rotted and decomposed.

Charlie paused to check every aisle that they passed, making sure it was clear before they moved on. Both men kept low and hunched forward on their approach. The pair had already grown comfortable with maneuvering through areas with their weapons, and they never went anywhere unarmed. The rifle and pistol on Charlie's person were as much a part of him as his own beating heart.

The aisles were picked over, and when they reached the canned food aisle, Charlie lowered his weapon in defeat. "Dammit."

Mario kept his rifle up, turning in half circles. "There isn't anything here, boss. We should leave before—"

The gunshot forced both of them to their knees, and Charlie saw the shooter sprint toward the cover an aisle three rows down.

Charlie pursued and Mario followed close behind. He crouched at the corner of the aisle where the shooter had disappeared. He planted a foot forward and turned, the darkened figure already gone.

"Shit." Charlie pressed forward, moving fast and quiet. If that shooter wasn't alone, getting caught I in the middle of an aisle was like being stuck in a kill zone, plugged with shooters on either side.

At the end of the aisle Charlie found the shooter by one of the checkout lanes.

Both Charlie and the gunman fired, each missing their mark on the first shot, but it was Charlie who was able to realign his next shot first. He squeezed the trigger, and the bullet connected with the shooter's left arm.

The shooter ducked back behind the checkout lane for cover, dropping the rifle in the same motion.

Charlie moved toward the shooter quickly, Mario on his tail, and he kicked the rifle out of reach. "Don't move."

A bandana covered the shooter's face, and only a pair of eyes stared up at Charlie, studying him inquisitively. "You don't walk out with me alive, then you don't make it very far."

Charlie frowned then tore the bandana free, surprised by the woman staring up at him. She had short blonde hair, with a splash of faded purple on the tips of her bangs. The dirt around her eyes brightened their blue.

"How many of you are there?" Charlie asked.

She grimaced, readjusting her hand on the wound on her arm. "Enough." Finding no comfortable position, she finally looked up at Charlie, both eyebrows raised. "So what's it going to be, boss?"

Mario turned his back to the woman but leaned close to his partner. "Charlie, we—"

Charlie held up his hand, ignoring Mario and focused on the pair of blue eyes staring up at him. Most of the people that Charlie had encountered since the EMP had been folks looking for help. People who scavenged for food and water.

But Charlie hadn't run into too many individuals that could take care of themselves. And if he wanted to ensure the survival of his group, then he best start finding people that could.

Charlie turned around and looked at the rifle on the floor. He picked it up, examining the hardware. The weapon itself wasn't anything special, but the scope mounted on top was something to be admired. The fact that she was handling the weapon at all showed she had some competency with firearms.

Charlie raised it to his eye. The magnification was impec-

cable. Looking through the sight, it was hard to imagine that the woman hadn't missed on purpose.

Charlie lowered the rifle, then turned back to the pair of blue eyes still watching him, studying him. He crouched to her level, meeting the intensity of her gaze. "He's on the roof, isn't he? That's why I didn't see him when I walked the perimeter." Charlie nodded. "It's smart."

Blue Eyes drew in her mouth tight, struggling to maintain her stoic expression. The fact that his words affected her so much confirmed his theory.

"It also means that you had a line of sight on me for a long time," Charlie said. "More than enough time to have a good shot to take me out whenever you wanted. But you didn't."

"Yeah, well, maybe we wanted to follow you back to camp," Blue Eyes said. "Then take you for all you were worth."

"Maybe." Charlie mulled the words over in his head. "Or maybe you were looking for people to join." He looked to the bullet wound on her arm. "We have someone that can help you with that."

Blue Eyes laughed. "Is that how you make friends? Shoot them and then fix them?"

"It's how I make allies." Charlie extended a hand.

Blue Eyes held Charlie's gaze, then lowered them to the offered hand. She smiled, then raised her face toward the ceiling. "Jason! We're good!" Blue Eyes clasped hold of Charlie's hand and used it as leverage to heave herself off the floor.

She wobbled on both legs, lightheaded from the sudden rising, and then gave Charlie the once over. "I'm Shelly."

"Charlie," he said.

A few moments later, a door opened and another blond-haired, blue-eyed figure stepped from the shadows, rifle slung over his shoulder.

"That's my brother," Shelly said.

"You're twins?" Mario asked.

"Fraternal," Shelly and Jason answered at the same time.

Jason walked over, bypassing Mario without a glance, and examined the bullet wound that Charlie had given his sister. "I thought the deal was not to be seen."

"They got the jump on me," Shelly replied, wincing as her brother prodded the wound, then smacked his hand away. "It's not like I have night vision goggles on me."

"Those would be nice." Jason continued his examination of the wound despite his sister's protest, but eventually stopped, then looked Shelly in the eyes.

"I'm fine," Shelly said.

"We have a doctor," Charlie said, finally catching Jason's attention. "He's good on supplies, and he's dealt with worse."

Jason narrowed his eyes. "I bet he has."

"How far is your place?" Shelly asked.

"Eight miles," Charlie answered. "If we leave now, then we should make it back before nightfall."

"You don't want to be stuck out here at night." Jason adjusted the rifle to the next shoulder. "A lot of the people around here have started forming groups. Not all of them are friendly."

Charlie regarded the twins, knowing that his orchard needed fighters, "Then maybe we should build a group of our own."

THREE MONTHS LATER

*C*harlie lay still on the sleeping bag, Liz nestled in the crook of his arm, asleep. The night air had turned colder, and he was thankful for her body heat. She split her time with him in the tent and staying with Adelyn at Doc's place.

Staring at the tent's ceiling, Charlie knew it wasn't a shelter that would be adequate come winter, and if he wanted his family to be under one roof, then they'd have to make a change.

The twins had a bead on some trailers that they could haul over with the Humvee that Dixon had lent them. They'd offer a more permanent solution for their housing dilemma.

"Charlie?"

The voice came from outside the tent's entrance, and Charlie lifted his head, sliding out from beneath Liz, who remained asleep. He reached for the tent flap's zipper and pulled it open, a fresh breeze of crisp night air blasting him when he opened it, and found Jason crouched at eye level.

"We've got something," Jason said.

Charlie grabbed his boots, kissed Liz on her forehead, placed the blanket over her body, and then zipped the tent closed as he walked with Jason through their already-growing field of tenants.

Jason said nothing as he led Charlie toward the west guard post, passing the rows of crops that they'd put in the ground two months ago. Green had already sprout from the ground, and Charlie found it hard to look away.

The west guard post was Doc's place and when he and Jason arrived, Shelly and Mario were on scene. Mario was unarmed, but Shelly had a rifle aimed at the back of a man's head.

"We found him in the fields, trying to dig up seeds," Jason said. "He won't talk."

Charlie examined the thief. "Stand him up."

Shelly and Jason lifted the man to his feet and then shoved him forward so Charlie could get a better look at him.

He was a wiry man, tall. His clothes were tattered, his skin tanned and weathered. He looked like a man who had spent his life outside before the world went to shit.

Charlie checked the man for colors. "Are you with a clan?"

The clans had grown more troublesome for Charlie and Dixon lately. They'd formed in the weeks after the EMP and had become better organized, locking down territories in the different suburbs outside of Seattle. So far none of them had been tempted to come this far east, but Charlie knew that wouldn't last forever.

Squabbling over food, water, shelter, and medicine grew more intense every day. Anyone who had supplies was either absorbed into a clan, or they were killed, and the clans took their supplies. Most people chose to join, if nothing more than the fact that there was safety in numbers.

And while most of the clans were relatively small in nature, Charlie had noticed one clan growing at an exponential rate. They identified themselves with an article of blue on their arm. It was usually a bandana or a piece of cloth.

Charlie and his folks had already experienced a few dust ups with that clan, and out of all the people to fight, he feared them the most. Not because of their numbers, but because of their organization, their structure. It was like watching the rise of a tyrant.

But Charlie suspected that's exactly what others thought of him and Dixon. People with resources, trying to expand, trying to rebuild, gathering as many people and supplies as they could. It was as though everyone was preparing for a fight. No one knew when it would happen, but they felt it coming. It was as real as the hunger in their bellies.

"Did he have a weapon on him?" Charlie asked.

Shelly nodded and handed over a nine-millimeter Ruger handgun. Charlie ejected the magazine and found it fully loaded, then shoved it back into the weapon.

"Haven't used this today," Charlie said. "But what about yesterday?"

"You're asking me if I killed anyone?" The man kept his head down while he spoke. It was the first response that anyone had been able to get out of him. He raised his head. "Have you killed people, Charlie?"

"You know who I am," Charlie said, then stepped forward, bringing him a breath away from the thief. "Then you know that around here, stealing is a crime. And that crime is punishable by death."

"Haven't you stolen food? Haven't you done things to survive that were criminal?"

Charlie ignored the question. "Are you with a clan?"

"Yes."

"Which one?"

The thief smiled. "Afraid you might kill a member of the wrong one?"

"I just need to know what kind of pushback I might be dealing with."

"So you're worried that I'm with the blue boys." The thief nodded, rocking back on his heels. "They're making quite the name for themselves. They have a few rules like the ones you're talking about too." He shook his head. "I'm not with a clan."

The way the thief spoke, Charlie couldn't be sure if the man was playing games with him. If he was, then his people would undoubtedly come looking for him after he was gone, and the orchard would be the first logical place to check.

"Take him to the fields," Charlie said.

Shelly shoved the thief hard in the back and forced the man forward, everyone following, with Charlie bringing up the rear.

They dragged the thief out into the orchard, far enough away where Charlie couldn't see the house or the barn. All that surrounded them was blackened ash and death.

Shelly turned the thief around to face Charlie, and Charlie noticed that the man's eyes had reddened during the walk.

"So, you're the judge, jury, and executioner, huh?" He laughed, then wiped his nose. "Why don't you let me join your crew?"

"Hiring a thief is like inviting rot in the garden," Charlie said, and then held out his hand. Shelly placed the rifle in it. "You don't notice it at first, but it spreads. It comes at the plant from inside out, it's not until the plants are dead that you realize what's happened." He loaded a bullet into the chamber, then aimed the rifle at the thief's head.

"I just wanted to eat," the thief said. "I won't come back," the thief answered. "You'll never see me again. I promise."

Charlie adjusted his finger over the trigger. "People don't keep promises anymore."

"Boss—" Mario took a step forward, then stopped when Charlie cut him a glare. He held his hands up, then retreated.

"Is there no mercy left in you?" The thief frowned, his mouth trembling.

Charlie examined the man in front of him. A man who only wanted food. Food that had been so readily available for so long that he had forgotten what it was like to be hungry.

Hunger was an ache that carved you hollow, all the way down to your bones. It was a hunger that had spread, and Charlie knew that until he could get a fresh round of crops into the ground and get a harvest before winter, those seeds were the only thing keeping his people from going six feet under.

Charlie placed the end of the rifle's barrel against the thief's temple. "Not anymore."

The thief's scream was cut short by the thunder of the gunshot, the flash of the light from the muzzle brightening the carnage that ejected from the back of the thief's skull.

And while Mario winced from the gunshot and turned away from the blood, brain, and bone that was splattered across the dirt, Charlie didn't avert his gaze. He remembered his father telling him that the first time he ever went hunting.

You stared down your prey, all the way till the end. Because when you killed something, you owned it. But while this wasn't hunting, Charlie knew the same principles still applied. There was no going back. It was a line that once you crossed, you could never step back on the other side.

Charlie had murdered a man, willingly and deliberately. And he knew that he'd have to kill more before all of this was finished.

32

ONE YEAR LATER

*T*he sky was colored in the light blues and grays of early morning. In a few minutes when the first rays of dawn peeked over the horizon in the east, it would gleam off the roofs of the RVs that filled the once-empty acreage of Doc's property.

The mobile homes hadn't moved since their arrival. They'd trickled in over the past year, one, then two, then dozens at a time. They'd all heard the rumors of a haven with food, water, and the promise of protection.

And when they arrived at the stretch of land, they had all come to speak with the one man that had laid the foundation for such a place to exist.

Charlie Decker stood on the steps outside of the silver streamline trailer parked at the very front of the property. He looked east, enjoying the quiet of the morning before the village around him woke.

A thick beard concealed his face, and his hair was slicked back, nearly long enough to touch his shoulders. The wrinkles around his eyes had multiplied, the creases growing more worn from the sleepless nights that continued to plague him.

He had hoped that time would help ease the restlessness, but as the days grew longer, then shorter, then colder, then longer and warm again, Charlie found no such peace.

No matter how secure the orchard became, or how much food they had, or how many guns or supplies they stored, his restlessness plagued him like a nagging tic.

A pair of guards on patrol passed Charlie.

"Boss," the pair said.

Charlie nodded curtly and remained on the steps until they walked out of sight. He stepped back inside, doing his best to remain quiet, but the streamliner's age made it more prone to agitation, and Charlie couldn't prevent his footsteps from breaking the silence. But she was already awake.

Liz stood over the gas stove, boiling water and reaching for the coffee grounds in the small pantry next to their kitchenette. She turned to him, smiling. "Good morning." She kept her voice quiet, and then gestured to the tiny cubby where Adelyn slept. "She's still passed out."

Charlie smiled at the little girl curled up beneath her covers. He walked over and kissed the top of her head.

"We'll need to get a bigger trailer soon," Liz said. "She's growing like a weed."

Charlie nodded, then walked up behind her, sliding his hands around her waist. He nuzzled her neck, and she playfully shied away from him. He kissed her cheek and then walked to the trailer's rear, reaching into the closet of their bedroom and removing the Kevlar vest from inside.

Divots from bullet holes and knife blades riddled both sides of the vest. He strapped it on, and when he turned back to Liz, she was no longer smiling.

"I didn't know there was a raid today," Liz said.

"Dixon gave us some intelligence of a cell nearby," Charlie said. "It's inside our boundaries, so we're handling it."

Liz nodded. "Are you taking the twins?"

"Yup."

"Good."

The twins had become an integral part of Charlie's raiding crew. They'd proven their worth time and time again as effective soldiers, though neither of them had any formal training. They were another layer to the bulletproof vest that he took with him. It helped both him, and Liz, breathe easier.

The past year had seen several people come to join Charlie's growing township, especially after the emergency shelters in Seattle went under.

With the swell of people spreading out from the city, Charlie and Dixon helped as many as they could. And while Charlie and Dixon had helped one another handle the influx of survivors, Charlie wouldn't have called their relationship a friendship, but more of a mutually assured business venture. Dixon needed food, and Charlie needed guns and ammunition.

Plus, more supply shipments were coming from the east, and a trade/bartering system had grown commonplace between Mayfield and The Orchard.

"If everything goes according to plan, then I should be back by this afternoon," Charlie said, trying to wrap his arms around Liz once more, but she resisted, stepping away from him and toward the cabinet that held the mugs.

"Dixon has an entire base of soldiers," Liz said. "He should take care of those matters." She turned to him. "You're needed here."

"I'm needed wherever there is a threat to our home," Charlie replied, keeping his tone even-keeled and not wanting to spark a fight. "And if we don't take a stand against—"

"Okay." Liz held up her hands, then placed some of the coffee grounds in the strainer before she poured boiling water over it. She handed the finished product to Charlie.

"Thank you." Charlie leaned in for a kiss, and this time

was granted landing. His hands found the scar on her stomach, and he caressed it gently.

"Try not to come home with a souvenir, all right?" Liz asked.

"I won't." He kissed her harder, and then was out the door and weaving through the field of mobile homes, trailers, and RVs on his way toward Doc's place.

A few doors opened along the way, the residents inside offering a friendly wave or smile to Charlie as he sipped the coffee.

With the number of 'housing' units crammed into the tight space, Charlie would have thought that people would have gone stir crazy from being in such close quarters, Charlie included. After a lifetime of growing up on an orchard with open space and places to roam, he thought living in a tin can would be a difficult adjustment.

But it wasn't.

The only real time he spent in the trailer was when he slept. But a pleasant side effect of the close quarters was the fact that he knew everyone who lived with them. He knew where they had come from, what had pushed them from their homes, their skills, their fears, and what they hoped to do when the power finally came back on.

These were Charlie's people. Like Adelyn, they were an extended family he never intended to adopt, but one he inherited nonetheless.

Up ahead, Charlie spotted Mario coming out of his trailer, giving Maria a kiss, who saw Charlie before Mario did.

"Buenos Dias, Charlie," she shouted, no doubt waking up some of the neighbors.

Mario turned and offered a friendly wave. "Hey, boss."

Charlie nodded. "How's the new crop taking?"

"It's too soon to tell," Mario answered. "But I'll be checking on it again today."

"We have a short window to make sure it takes, or else the trees won't be mature enough to survive the winter," Charlie said, turning back toward Mario after he passed him. "Let's make that a priority."

Mario gave a thumbs up and headed toward the west fields, where he'd meet up with the field hands.

Charlie had christened Mario as head farmer, and the man had taken to it as well as Charlie had suspected. Mario never had the stomach for raids, and Charlie was glad to have someone he trusted work the land.

Charlie rarely walked the fields anymore. It made him uneasy. It made him remember.

Nostalgia was dangerous. Spending too much time living in the past affected the future. So, he kept the past buried.

The crew were already at The Shack, which was what everyone lovingly referred to as Doc's place.

The nickname for the house came after the Frankenstein patch job Doc and the others had done on the place. The old man had refused to move into one of the trailers, stating that if he wanted to live in a tin can, then he would have retired in Florida.

"Doc up?" Charlie asked.

"He's making breakfast," Shelly answered, cleaning her gun. "If you want something other than burnt eggs and bacon, then you better talk him out of it."

"How that old fart burns eggs I'll never understand," Jason replied, counting the bullets in his magazine. "I mean, you actually have to try and burn eggs."

The twins were always the first up when it was time for a raid. In fact, Charlie didn't think they slept at all. It was unsettling.

Shelly reassembled her weapon deftly, then rested the assault rifle along her lap and stared at Charlie. "You know what we're hitting today?"

"Yeah," Charlie answered, then sipped his coffee.

"How many?" Jason asked, retaining his leisurely post after he finished his bullet count.

"Dixon's intelligence says nine."

"Who else is coming?" Shelly asked.

"Nick and Lee."

Shelly rolled her eyes, and Jason smirked.

"That gonna be a problem?" Charlie asked, looking at Shelly.

"Not unless Nick makes it one," Shelly answered, her tone already riddled with stress, but then caught Charlie's lingering eye and changed her tune. "It'll be fine."

"Yeah," Jason said, laughing. "What could go wrong between two ex-lovers with automatic weapons?"

Shelly flipped the bird to her brother. Charlie headed inside, drawn in by the scent of sizzling bacon.

Doc was hunched over the gas grill that he'd transported into the kitchen next to a window, where the smoke funneled outside through a homemade chute he'd compiled out of portions of the air conditioning ducts that he'd salvaged from his own home.

"Breakfast is almost done," Doc replied. "You can tell those mongrels outside that they need to stop showing up so early. I make breakfast the same damn time every damn day."

"I'll let them know," Charlie said.

The twins were frequent house guests of Doc. And aside from Charlie and a few others, they were the only folks he talked to. It had been that way ever since his wife passed. She had suffered a stroke during the winter, in the middle of the night. And while his wife didn't suffer, the callous that formed over Doc's soul was only penetrable by a few.

Charlie didn't know why or how the twins had carved out a spot in Doc's circle of trust, but he suspected it was because the twins didn't know him before his wife had passed. He thought that maybe Doc liked being able to speak to people as he was now without them having the expectation that he was supposed to be something else. Charlie understood that.

"Another raid?" Doc asked, his attention still focused on the bacon and eggs, which Charlie noticed were just beginning to burn.

"Yeah," Charlie answered.

"Good." Doc flipped over the bacon, the grease sizzling and popping in the pan, his mouth down-turned in a grimace.

"You'll have the room ready in case we need it?" Charlie asked.

Doc grunted and nodded.

The "room" was what Charlie and his security detail called the operating table. While Doc had the supplies and tools needed to perform surgeries, it was hard to find a sanitary space. So the RV that Charlie had brought back for Doc to use had become that space.

It was always ready to go per The Orchard's protocol. But Charlie still liked to ask, because while Doc hadn't lost any skill from his job, he had grown forgetful.

Doc piled the burnt eggs and bacon onto a plate and then handed it to Charlie.

"Don't get shot out there," he said, then disappeared back into the shambled wreckage of his home. The home he refused to leave, even after it burned down.

Charlie headed back outside, Nick and Lee accounted for and ready to go. He looked for any sign of tension between Shelly and Nick, but other than a casual indifference, there was nothing else. He wished the pair had just kept it in their pants, but it wasn't his decision to make.

"We need to get moving, so I hope everyone can eat and listen at the same time," Charlie said, taking a scoop of eggs that he shoveled into his mouth before passing the plate around. "Dixon gave me intel on a local cell within our patrol radius. No more than nine, and Dixon's scouts didn't spy any heavy artillery. Commander Dixon and his men have been intercepting refueling supplies that they believed were intended for the local cell, which means that they're running low on ammunition."

"Nothing as dangerous as a hungry animal," Lee said, shoveling a bite of blackened eggs into his mouth, which was about all that was left on the plate, since he was the last to eat.

"They have guards on watch on the north and south sides of their house, which happens to be close to the clans, so we'll want to eliminate those targets quietly. We leave in ten."

33

---

*C*harlie rode shotgun in the rusted Humvee. Dixon had let them borrow one of their military vehicles once they started performing raids. It was all part of the symbiotic relationship that they'd formed over the past year.

Both men knew that they couldn't have made any progress without the other, and while they may have butted heads over a few items over the past year, they both had the same goal when it came to the terrorists: wipe them out.

Even without the use of modern technology and communication, Dixon and the rest of the military were still effective in their second round of assaults after the EMP strike.

The recovery time of their country's military was surprisingly quick, but even with their agility and adaptability, neither Dixon nor Charlie could have imagined the conflict against the Korean forces to last this long. However, part of their enemy's plan was to recruit and manipulate members of the local population. Once food and water grew scarce, anyone who was able to provide those life-sustaining needs found themselves in a position of power. And it was a power that not everyone wielded with the same responsibility as Charlie and Dixon.

"Heads up," Jason said. "We're near clan territory now."

Everyone kept their eyes peeled on the rundown houses that they passed on either side of the road. Windows had been boarded up, and the vegetation in the yards had grown to provide more cover for anyone looking to ambush, so it made any trip toward the edge of their safe zone more dangerous.

"Just keep moving," Charlie said. "The sooner we get to our stationary position, the sooner we can set up a perimeter."

"No complaints about that from me, boss," Jason said.

"You think that those fuckers would have the good sense to just join the rest of us in trying to rebuild society instead of clinging to the shitholes they've buried themselves inside," Nick said.

Shelly chuckled. "They don't have anyone to answer to, no one to tell them how to live their lives." She gestured to the crumbling houses and neighborhoods that started to pop up more frequently the farther they drove. "This is their world now, and you'd be crazy if you think that they'd just give up their freedom for chains again."

"Freedom?" Nick laughed, then poked his thumb at a few of the houses that they passed. "Are you serious? That's not what these people have."

"We're not here to start a philosophy class," Charlie said, cutting into the conversation before it became too heated.

Nick shifted in his seat. "I never liked school anyway."

Despite the heightened sense of awareness that accompanied a trip near the clan's territory, the unit arrived at their location without incident.

Charlie stepped out of the Humvee, the rest of his unit moving silently and efficiently behind him as he took point.

The house that was their target sat one hundred yards to the west. Charlie raised his scope to get a better look at the situation and found one stationary guard on the backside of the house.

Jason crouched near Charlie and then lowered his scope. "South side in the trees." He looked to the twin. "You think you can make the shot?"

Jason raised his rifle, which he had personally modified. He found the guard in the branches and then lowered it. "He has a lot of cover, but I should be able to get him."

"Wait for the signal," Charlie said, then spun around and found the rest of his crew ready to go. "Four-man standard. I want targets down in one shot. Let's make this quick and clean."

Nods reciprocated the orders, and Charlie turned and led his men through the overgrown jungle of the former neighborhood turned war zone.

Charlie weaved around the yards, staying low through the tall grass. The number of missions that Charlie had gone on over the past year had honed his senses. Whenever he was on a raid, the rest of the world ceased to exist. There was no orchard back home. There was no Liz, no Adelyn, no friends, no family, no other responsibility. The only thing that mattered was the rifle in his hands, and the men and women at his back.

Charlie had discovered that there was no greater equalizer than the battlefield. Race, gender, religion, each of them were pointless. War only cared for the offering of blood you brought to the altar of battle.

With less than thirty yards before the house appeared at the end of the street, Charlie held up his hand, the unit stopping in unison from the wordless order.

He raised the scope of his rifle and waited until he had a shot lined up against the side of the watchman's head. Then, keeping his aim steady, he flicked on the laser marker that highlighted the side of the guard's face.

The green beam was colorless unless you were either looking through Charlie's scope, or through Jason's scope stationed one hundred yards away in the tall grass. But their target, the man in the tree, had no idea he was being stalked up until the millisecond of consciousness that remained to him when the bullet from Jason's sniper rifle sailed silently into his skull and his body slumped lifelessly in the tree branches.

With the guard taken out, Charlie and the others stormed forward toward the house.

The group was so well seasoned that there was hardly anything that surprised them during a raid. And despite the terrorists' initial resourcefulness of sneaking into the country and disrupting their power grid, Charlie quickly learned that the remaining clusters of cells were highly predictable, which only made them easier to kill.

Charlie paused at the back door and then sent Shelly and Nick around toward the front. Once Nick and Shelly rounded the corner, Charlie counted to ten, and then he tapped the top of his fist against his helmet, so Lee knew what was coming next, because the moment that Charlie flung that door inward and breached the house, they became an avalanche.

Whatever was in their path, whatever they came across, was swallowed up and buried with an unforgiving and unrelenting force. And Charlie wasn't done until everyone inside was dead.

Charlie reached ten and kicked the door open. The element of surprise vanished.

With the windows boarded up, Charlie stepped into the pitch black, but the darkness was suddenly interrupted by the flash of muzzle barrels from the surprised enemy sitting around the kitchen table.

Charlie's heart rate skyrocketed, and the adrenaline

elevated his senses. He pivoted left, his heel grinding against the gritty surface of the dirty kitchen floor. A darkened figure appeared in his scope, the body silhouetted against the backdrop of the wall.

One squeeze of Charlie's trigger finger, and the familiar recoil of the rifle stock smacked against his shoulder. The darkened figure's arms flailed comically to their sides. Another gunshot pulled Charlie's attention to the right, and through the edge of his peripheral vision, he saw a body hit the floor.

A muzzle flash around the corner pulled Charlie toward the hallway that led him out of the kitchen and deeper into the house. After five steps into the darkness, Charlie's vision started to adjust, and when he turned the corner, he fired at the man sprinting down the hall and dropped him before he turned the corner.

Charlie paused in the hallway as he waited for Lee to join him.

"Two in the kitchen," Lee said.

Charlie added the one in the hallway to the tally. "Three! Three! Three!"

Charlie and Lee held their position in the hallway, waiting for Nick up front. They repeated the number of killed targets three times so they could keep track of how many they had left.

"Four! Four! Four!" Nick shouted from the front of the house.

In the same instant, Charlie and Lee dropped to their knees, rifles raised and primed to shoot, and then a dark figure darted from the end of the hall. Charlie and Lee squeezed the trigger.

"One! One! One!" Charlie shouted, once the second gunman that Nick had alerted them to vanished. Only one to go.

Charlie and Lee held their position for three seconds, waiting to see if a second gunman was hesitating and would charge around the corner, but they never appeared.

When the moment passed, Charlie pushed himself off his knee, his joints cracking from the momentary pause, and then rushed down the hallway, Lee right behind him. He paused at the corner, ignoring the corpse at his feet.

"Fuck," Lee whispered. "You think they're down?"

Charlie shook his head. "Negative."

No movement, no gunshots, no sound save for the breaths passed between Charlie and Lee as they waited anxiously for the final call out.

A minute passed. Then two. The seconds drew out into painfully slow motion. Finally, Charlie pounded his fist against his head and then turned the corner. If the last remaining terrorist was playing the waiting game, then they'd be here all night, and Charlie didn't have any plans on having a sleepover.

He turned the corner, which revealed another hallway, with two doors on the left and one door on the right. All of them were closed.

Charlie headed toward the first door, unsure if the remaining shooter was inside, but knowing that he couldn't pass without clearing them first. He positioned himself near the first door and waited for Lee to slide into position next to him, his rifle trained at the door crack.

Charlie reached for the door and counted down by mouthing the numbers. Three. Two. One. Charlie pushed the door inward and Lee rushed inside, Charlie following quickly behind him, as they cleared opposite sides of the room.

Both pounded their fists onto their helmets to signal that the room was clear and then returned toward the hallway. The next door was the one on their right, and again Charlie and Lee repeated the same fluid motion that they had in the first room.

And while they didn't find the enemies inside, Charlie paused before he stepped back out onto the hallway, his eyes fixated on the desks that lined the walls. It was hard to make out the objects that lined the desk in the darkness, but from what he could tell, they were work stations.

But with Lee already at the door again, Charlie didn't linger in the room, returning to the hallway, turning their focus to the last door on the left.

Again, Charlie and Lee assumed the same positions. Charlie mouthed the countdown. Three. Two. One. He swung the door inward and the moment Lee was exposed from the crack in the door, the hallway exploded with gunfire.

In Charlie's peripheral, he watched Lee fall, and then he pushed forward into the room. Ears ringing from the gunshots, Charlie scanned the corner of the room where the shots had come from and squeezed the trigger.

Four seconds of gunfire ended, and Charlie turned his rifle away from the last terrorist on the ground, his instinct and year-long training propelling him to finish the scan of the room, then lowered his weapon after he mentally counted the magic number of nine dead inside the house.

"Clear! Clear! Clear!" Charlie shouted, his voice hoarse from the sudden volume increase. He spun around in the same instant and dropped to a knee to examine Lee. "Where it'd hit?"

Lee rolled back and forth, grimacing in pain and clutching his stomach. "The vest, but I don't know if it went through— Mother FUCKER that hurts!" He kicked the door frame with his heel, rattling through the rest of the house, and Nick and Shelly rounded the corner of the hallway.

"Shit." Shelly joined Lee's side and helped Charlie remove the vest.

"If Dixon would just give us some new fucking gear, then we wouldn't have this problem," Nick said, spewing his frustration from behind them.

"What the hell happened up front?" Charlie asked.

"The living room fed into a dining room with a lot of open space," Shelly said. "They must have already been in the middle of the house by the time we busted through the front door and started shooting, so it gave them time to retreat toward you."

The Kevlar peeled off, and Charlie lifted Lee's shirt. Lee remained flat on his back, lifting his head up like a turtle trying to see its stomach.

"Is it bad?" Lee asked, his voice cracking from the nerves.

Charlie exhaled. "It didn't go through."

Shelly laughed and then smacked Lee's exposed and pale belly, which elicited a harsh smack.

"OW!" Lee grimaced, but started laughing.

But while the group relaxed, their objective complete and the targets wiped out, Charlie stood and returned to the hallway. He reached for the light on his belt and then flashed it inside the middle room he passed, scanning the work benches that lined the walls.

Charlie took a closer look at the poorly-shaped bricks on the table. "Hey, I need Jason in here now!"

Nick poked his head inside the room and let out a low whistle.

Charlie spun around, holding up the plastic explosive. "C-4." He gestured to the other tables. "They must have close to one hundred pounds in this place."

Shelly came in next, followed by a hunched-over Lee, holding his Kevlar jacket.

"Detonators, timing devices." Shelly picked up a few of the parts and examined the exposed copper wires and old cooking timers. "Christ, they've got enough C-4 in here to blow up Seattle."

Charlie flashed his lights toward the middle table where a stack of papers had been hastily scattered. He approached, plucking one off the top of the stack. "It's in Korean." But littered among the foreign jargon, Charlie saw the sketches of blueprints.

A pair of boots jogged down the hallway, and then Jason entered.

"Looks like our friends have been busy," Jason said, walking over to his sister and plucking a timer from her hands.

"Have you seen anything like this?" Charlie asked, holding up the paper in his hand.

Jason scanned it quickly. "Demolition plans." He set the paper down and then moved toward another pile of pages, picking them up one by one, scanning them just as fast. "Christ, this is for one big building."

Charlie stepped closer toward Jason. "Does it give a location?"

Jason studied the papers faster, then shook his head. "Not specifically. It's either one place, or several targets." He shook his head faster, no longer reading the pages and just picking them up and trying to put them in order. "Some information is missing."

"Let's pat down the bodies, see if any of them tried to run out with the rest of the plans," Charlie said, and on his order, everyone but Jason left the room. He inched closer to Jason then lowered his voice. "You think this could be for the power plant?"

Jason took a moment to look over the plans. "That would make sense, but until I have all the pieces, it's hard to say for sure."

"Right." Charlie tried not to jump to any conclusions, but with this cell's proximity to The Orchard and Mayfield, it was hard not to draw the connection. And there was no telling how many more of the cells out there had similar plans.

If they were lucky, this was it, but Charlie hadn't been lucky in a long time, and he didn't think that was going to change anytime soon.

ick took over as wheel man when they got back to the Humvee while Lee nursed his tender stomach in the backseat, enjoying the attention from Shelly, who doubled as their medic in the field.

"I supposed I should be glad your brother isn't the one taking care of me," Lee said, smiling, giving her a playful wink.

Shelly placed her palm over his wound, the touch tender at first, and then pressed hard, causing Lee to buckle forward and howl and squirm in his seat.

"Careful what you wish for," Shelly said.

Jason laughed and then gently caressed Lee's cheek. "I'm the one with the gentle touch, Lee."

Lee jerked his face away from Jason's hand, and Jason laughed again as Lee wiggled uncomfortably between the twins.

"Both of you are nuts," Lee said.

Charlie turned around, looking at Jason. "You decipher anything else from those papers?"

Jason cocked an eyebrow up and shuffled through the papers again, the motion ceremonial. "Negative."

"It has to be the power plant, right?" Nick asked, one hand on the wheel, driving the Humvee like it was a Z-28 Camaro.

"It makes sense," Shelly added. "Dixon's almost done with reconstruction."

But doubt swirled around Charlie's head. "Maybe." He tapped his finger along the side of the door, the glass against his arm rattling from the rough ride. He flicked his eyes at the rearview mirror and the pile of explosives in the back.

"What are you thinking, Boss?" Lee asked.

Charlie chewed it over. "We need to go to Mayfield."

Nick sighed. "I was afraid you'd say that."

"You think there are more bombs than what we found?" Shelly asked.

"I'm thinking we don't have the whole picture," Charlie answered. "And I want to know if Dixon has been keeping information to himself."

The rest of the trip to Mayfield was in silence, save for the occasional grunt from Lee as he adjusted himself between the twins.

Jason suggested that Lee go lay down on the plastic explosive, told him that they could make a nice bed. Lee flipped Jason the bird.

The road from The Orchard and into Mayfield had been cleared. A few other main roadways into Seattle had been cleared as well, which acted as the main supply routes between Dixon's unit and the other military posts that had been established to help sniff out the remaining terrorist threat and aid in the rebuilding efforts.

But seeing as how Dixon's unit was in control of one of the region's most critical support centers, the former lieu-tenant carried a lot of weight and was privy to information that most weren't. Dixon usually shared that information, which helped Charlie prepare for any shortages or conflicts that were heading his way.

And if Dixon knew something about this type of wide-scale bombing, Charlie was going to have a few words about what they had just walked into. And if he didn't know? Well, then Dixon and his people were sleeping on the job.

The first barricade they approached was a simple, two-man post with barbed wire and sandbags stacked on either side of the road.

Nick didn't bother stopping, seeing as how all of Dixon's guards knew Charlie and his unit. Their group had earned respect from the soldiers under Dixon, who lovingly referred to Charlie and his crew as The Mercs.

The nickname was short for mercenaries. Charlie and his unit were the only non-military combat crew that Dixon allowed on base.

The second barricade, which was positioned just before Mayfield's Main Street and the town itself, required a stop, for everyone. It was protocol, even for Dixon. The president himself wouldn't be able to get through without a badge.

Charlie fished his identification out of his pocket, which was a local sheriff's badge that Dixon and Charlie had found. Since there was a limited number of badges, and it was the only sheriff's station in the county, Dixon and Charlie figured they'd be good to dole out for security purposes.

"Hey, Charlie." The guard at the post took Charlie's badge with a smile, giving it the ceremonial once over before handing it back to him. "What brings you to Mayfield?"

"Need to talk to Commander Dixon," Charlie said, adding Dixon's title. He made sure to do that whenever he was speaking to one of Dixon's subordinates. Another part of their deal. The old lieutenant had grown accustomed to being in charge.

"You have an appointment with him?" the guard asked.

Charlie gestured toward the back of the Humvee. "Got a present for him."

The guard narrowed his eyes suspiciously at Charlie and then motioned for the second guard to investigate.

"Holy shit, Sarge." The guard stuck his head from out the back. "They've got enough C-4 to blow us all to kingdom come!"

Sergeant Scarborough briskly headed toward the Humvee's rear, and Charlie watched the man's face light up in surprise, as if his soldier had lied to him.

"Christ, Charlie," Scarborough said. "Is it stable?

Charlie looked to Jason.

"Yes," Jason answered. "Just don't touch it."

Scarborough retracted a finger and then placed his hands on his hips. "Let them through! And radio Commander Dixon that he has company."

The gate went up, and Charlie waved goodbye to the gate guards.

Over the past year, Mayfield had been transformed from a sleepy little northwestern town into a fully-operable military installation.

Most of the buildings that could be repaired after the fires last year were patched up, but the first several dozen houses and businesses that Charlie saw outside his window would most likely never be rebuilt again.

Charlie had asked Dixon one time why he didn't have his men clear the rubble at the front of the town once he started to get more manpower, and Dixon simply told him that it was because he didn't want his men to forget what the enemy could do.

Soldiers traversed the sidewalks, another transformation of the little town. Gone were the days of tourists visiting from different parts of the country, and Charlie never thought he'd miss them as much as he did now.

The farther they traveled into town, the more militarized it became, and just before they reached Dixon's office, which used to be the town's old hardware store, Charlie saw the hospital and then the power plant in the distance.

It was where Dixon had the highest levels of security.

Soldiers and watchmen were crawling over every square inch of space. Guard towers had been erected at the plant's four corners and were manned twenty-four hours.

Nick parked in front of the commander's building, and Charlie stepped out of the Humvee just as Commander Dixon exited the building, flanked by his staff.

"Charlie," Dixon said, no hint of joy or excitement in his voice at the sight of his old friend. "I was told you had a surprise for me." He shook Charlie's hand. "I wasn't told if it was good or bad."

"I'm not sure which one it is yet either."

Dixon grunted and then rubbed his freshly shaven face. While Charlie had grown his beard and shaggy hair, Dixon maintained his grooming habits.

Charlie opened the back of the Humvee and watched Dixon's face as the commander eyed the stacks of C-4 bricks.

"You found these at the cell you raided?" Dixon asked, focused on the enormous amount of bricks.

"And these." Charlie handed over the blueprints, and the lines of concern that covered Dixon's face deepened as he examined them closely.

Dixon shuffled through the papers, shaking his head. "Where is this?"

"I was hoping you could tell me," Charlie answered.

Dixon handed the papers to one of the men next to him, then ran his palms over his freshly-buzzed head. He faced Charlie. "Let's take a walk."

The pair of men headed toward the power plant, but they walked alone. Dixon was quiet for a while and waited until they were out of earshot of anyone nearby.

"We're less than three weeks away from having the power plant operational," Dixon said, ending the silence.

"I thought it was at least three months," Charlie said.

"That's what I've told people, and that's what I want them

to believe." Dixon kept his hands pinned behind his back, his posture rigid and unyielding even in motion. "Over the past year, we've wiped out more terrorist cells than I can count. The total kill number is sitting somewhere in the thousands." He stopped dead in his tracks, gazing out at the power plant in the distance, the shouts of the men on patrol drifting toward them. "And yet we still find more of them every week. It's like there's a leak in the boat and we just can't fucking plug it."

Charlie stepped around and blocked Dixon's view of the power plant. "What do you know that you're not telling me?"

Dixon hesitated, but finally nodded as though he concluded the argument in his head. "Intelligence coming in from Seattle is telling us that the remaining terrorist threat in our region is scaling up for an attack. We intercepted a few messages between some of the smaller parties, but we don't know when or where. Our best guess was they were going to hit the power plant, but the truth is we don't know."

"And you think the C-4 we found is a part of that?" Charlie asked.

"I don't know." Dixon shook his head, those worry lines on his face growing deeper and aging the young man right before Charlie's eyes. It was the smallest details that gave the former lieutenant away. The dark circles under his eyes, the drooped shoulders, the strands of gray that had appeared prematurely.

Charlie was sure that he'd aged over the past year, but it had been a while since he'd checked himself in a mirror. In fact, he avoided them as much as possible.

"If the terrorists are gearing up for something, then we have to assume there are another dozen places like the one we just raided, and better guarded," Charlie said. "I doubt that we just happened to stumble on the only cell manufacturing explosives. That stuff was homemade, which means that their recipe has more than likely been passed around." He stepped closer to Dixon. "Are you sure you're telling me everything that you know?"

Dixon's expression went from friend to commander in less than a second. "We have an agreement, Charlie. But I'm not obliged to pass along every piece of intelligence that I receive back to you. Our relationship has worked best by the pair of us staying in our lanes. So why don't we stick to that?"

"And you're sure that there isn't anything else I need to know?" Charlie asked, still pressing the issue.

Dixon remained stoic, but Charlie noticed the struggle just below the surface. Finally, the commander relented.

"The Orchard might be a target," Dixon said.

"What?" Charlie had expected a surprise, but this had come out of the left field.

"That is the only other large structural resource in the area," Dixon replied. "You and your team have developed a reputation, and it's no secret that you supply half the food for our military efforts."

"How long have you known?" Charlie asked.

"That's not your concern."

"It is if it means that my people have been open to a full-blown assault and you haven't told me about it!" Charlie's cheeks reddened from the sudden burst of anger, and his outburst was caught by a few nearby soldiers on their walk from the power plant.

Dixon leaned into Charlie's assault, the commander refusing to back down. "I didn't get the intel until yesterday, and it was only hearsay. We had zero credibility to believe it was true, and the schematics that you found prove that. Those weren't drawn up to attack The Orchard, those were buildings." He gestured toward the power plant. "Probably that one."

"What's the timeline?" Charlie asked.

"A week. Maybe two." Dixon shrugged. "The brass in Seattle and Washington are hoping it's a month, because by then we'll have the power up. The sooner we can get things back to normal, the easier it'll be for us to stomp out the insects. We shine a light on them, they scatter. But much of the country is still in the dark. We're the closest operation to completion, so brass wants to use us as a testing ground."

"I need more men for security," Charlie said.

"Can't do that," Dixon said.

"If the terrorists really want to disrupt operations out here, you don't think they've considered hitting the food supply? They've done it before."

"If we get the power back on, then it won't matter if the food supply gets hit, because then we'll have transportation, refrigeration, communications, all of it back online." Dixon pointed east. "Washington has truckloads of provisions just waiting to get to us, but until we have the power back on and refrigeration to store them, then they stay east of the Mississippi. Not to mention the medicines that are needed over here."

"So once the power comes back on, you think you don't need us?" Charlie asked. "You think that everything will just go back to the way things were—" Charlie snapped his fingers. "Just like that?"

"I'm just telling you what my orders are, and I need every man here to help defend this place if we're under attack. The only way the enemy gets through our defenses is if there's a crack, and I'm not going to willingly create one by giving you some of our men." He sighed, his voice softening. "I'm sorry. But the answer is no."

Charlie laughed, then nodded. "Well, don't blow yourself up with all of that C-4, all right?"

Charlie turned to leave, but Dixon called after him.

"Charlie!"

Charlie turned.

"I was planning to come tomorrow, so long as that's all right with you."

Charlie exhaled and then nodded. "See you then."

35

The ride back to The Orchard was quiet. The twins were upset that the C-4 was taken, the pair having a few choice words for the soldiers who unloaded it from the Humvee.

Lee was still wallowing in agony over his bruised abdomen, and Nick's contribution on the ride back were the heavy grunts and sighs as he shifted positions in the driver seat, unable to get comfortable.

Charlie stared out the window on the drive back, his mind racing over the different security nightmares that he'd have to deal with, struggling to come up with the resources needed to ensure the safety of his people.

Anytime resources were spread thin, it always made it easier for items to fall through the cracks, and that was something Charlie desperately wanted to avoid.

The sight of the orchard ahead helped ease some of the concerns, aided by the sensation of returning home, which had a new meaning for him. He suspected it had a new meaning for everyone.

It was late afternoon when they returned, and everyone

was on the back end of their work day. Charlie watched field hands work the crops along the Bigelow property, and then saw the clean-up crews still clearing parts of the Decker Orchard. Most of the trees had been removed, leaving only a few skeletons from the past.

Nick parked the Humvee in front of Doc's house, and one of the guards on duty was already heading over with a fresh can of fuel to replenish what they'd spent on their journey. It was protocol. Charlie wanted every vehicle they had ready to mobilize at a moment's notice. It was a worst-case scenario, but he wasn't going to get caught with his pants down again.

Lee waddled into Doc's house in search of some pain relief for his bruises.

The twins departed without a word, stomping off and still upset over the loss of the explosives.

"You good, boss?" Nick asked.

"Yeah. I'll see you tomorrow."

Nick pounded his fist twice on the Humvee's hood and then headed toward his trailer.

Charlie lingered by the Humvee for a moment, calculating all the possible scenarios the enemy could do to take them out.

But apart from driving cars lined with explosives straight into the homes and fields that comprised Charlie's growing village, he arrived at the conclusion that unless the enemy had drastically replenished their ranks, they didn't have the numbers to take them in an all-out assault. They were too well-defended, and too well-armed.

"Heard you found some bad shit."

Charlie turned around and saw Doc standing in front of his house, wiping his hands with a dirty rag, which he tossed over his shoulder when he finished.

"Explosives," Charlie said. "Enough to blow us up at least three times over."

Doc groaned and then joined Charlie at the Humvee's hood, resting his forearms on top of the rusted metal.

"You're sure it was meant for us?" Doc asked.

"I don't know." Charlie mirrored Doc's body language. "Dixon doesn't think so, but none of it feels right." He frowned. "Whatever intelligence that they think they're intercepting in Seattle might be bloated, outdated, wrong, or all three. The idea that there are enough cells still active in our region that possess the manpower to deliver such a coordinated strike doesn't make any sense. They know they're on their way out. The best thing for them to do would be to retreat. Head north and get the hell out of dodge."

"When I was still a vet, I had a farmer bring in one of his pigs," Doc said. "He told me that the animal wouldn't eat, barely even moved at all. Just stayed in one corner of the pen while the other pigs moseyed around like normal. So, I examined the pig, put it through standard physical procedures, and by the time I was finished, I was just as stumped as the farmer. I did blood tests, I pulled tissue samples, I checked for parasitic organisms and every disease in the book, but they all came back negative."

"So what was wrong with the pig?" Charlie asked.

"Nothing," Doc answered. "From a clinical and scientific standpoint, there was nothing wrong with the animal. A few weeks later, I called the farmer and asked about the animal's health, and the farmer told me the pig had died. So, still curious and wondering if I missed something, I asked if I could collect the remains for an autopsy, and the farmer gave me permission." Doc leaned forward. "I checked every square inch of that pig's innards, and still found nothing. But—" Doc held up a finger. "It made me realize for the first time in my veterinary career that some things couldn't be explained with reason and science, and from someone who used them every day, it scared the shit out of me."

287

"Either that, or you just couldn't identify what killed it," Charlie said. "It could have been something you've never seen before, something you hadn't encountered."

"Possibly." Doc pushed himself off the Humvee. "I suppose the same could be said for your predicament."

Charlie lingered by the Humvee long after Doc had walked back into the house. Maybe he was mis-identifying the situation. Maybe the reason he couldn't find the answer was because he didn't know the problem. Isn't that what the terrorists had done with the EMP? The weapon had existed, sure, but Charlie had never heard of it. Neither had half the country.

On the walk back toward the RV, Charlie made pit stops at the security posts, making sure that those on duty kept a heightened sense of awareness. He also made sure that they passed along the message during the shift changes.

He returned to an empty trailer, Liz still out in the fields somewhere and Adelyn with the daycare run by Sarah Bigelow.

Naked, Charlie stepped into the tiny shower, which drew water from a rain collector on the roof. It was nothing more than an upgraded garbage can, but it provided Liz and Charlie with the small comfort of having their own shower.

It was cold, and smelled, but soap helped take care of that. A few others had their trailers and mobile homes rigged up with similar setups, and those that didn't bathed down in the river. When they first started that trend, they'd made up schedules for men and woman to go down separately, but after a while, the village got so big that people went down when they pleased. Charlie had noticed that modesty was the first thing to fly out the window when times got tough.

The cold water drizzled from the faucet, and Charlie rinsed himself of the day. Once finished, he lingered in the shower, letting himself air dry. It was a nice reprieve from the summer heat, and once he was close to dry, he stepped out of the shower and lay on the bed.

The sheets still smelled like Liz.

After a minute, he stood and put on a pair of shorts just before the door opened and Liz stepped inside.

"Hey," she said.

Charlie wait for Adelyn to enter. "Where's the little monster?"

"Sarah volunteered to watch her for the night."

Charlie smiled and dropped his shorts.

Liz laughed. "Looks like you're ready for me." She peeled off her clothes on her walk toward him, the tan lines from her shirt darkened from her day in the sun. "Do you want me to shower—"

Charlie reached up and grabbed her, spinning her around and flinging her on the bed as he maneuvered on top of her, then kissed her neck.

"I'll take that as a no."

They made love, and when they finished, Charlie joined Liz in the shower. Both returned to the bed still naked, drying off on the sheets.

The pair lay side by side, facing one another. They were quiet for a while, content with only staring at one another before Liz finally broke the silence.

"What happened?" Liz asked.

Charlie reached for her hands and kissed her fingers, then gently massaged her palm with his thumb. "We found some plans at the house we raided. And explosives. A lot of them. Dixon said they have intel about an attack, but they don't know when or where."

Liz furrowed her brow, the light sunburn on her face causing the lines to crease white. "Do they think it'll happen at the power plant?" She paused. "Or here?"

"I don't think it's for here. But the plans didn't exactly match up with the power plant either."

"What do you think?"

Charlie hesitated, lingering on the question before finally giving his answer. "I think it's something new. I think they're using the last of their energy to hit us with something that we wouldn't expect. Like they did with the EMP."

"Well, that's a starting point, right?" Liz asked, trying to remain optimistic.

Charlie nodded, wanting a break from the subject so he could give his brain time to rest. "How are the fields going?"

Liz smiled. "Good. Really good. Mario says that we'll have crops for the fall."

It was the best news he'd heard all day. "That'll take pressure off us for any increases in demand we have heading into next year." He collapsed onto his back. "Thank God."

Liz crawled over and straddled his waist as she climbed on top of him and gave him a kiss on the nose. "Everything's going to be fine."

"I know," Charlie said.

Liz raised her eyebrows. "Do you?" She smirked. "Because right now you don't look like a man who believes that."

Charlie ran his fingertips down Liz's sides, keeping quiet.

"Are you nervous about tomorrow?" Liz asked.

"Yeah." Charlie spoke the words in a sigh.

The raid had provided Charlie the needed distraction from having to think about tomorrow's ceremony. He'd been dreading it since his mother brought it up three months ago.

Martha Decker wanted a ceremony for her dead husband, Harold Decker, and she wanted the entire orchard to come and pay homage. She told Charlie that if it weren't for his father that none of what they had here would even be possible. It wouldn't have been so bad if his mother hadn't requested he give a speech.

"Do you want me to go over it with you again?" Liz asked.

"No." Charlie frowned, shaking his head. He'd already

gone over it a hundred times, and reading the two pages he'd scribbled down was hardly going to make him feel better.

Liz pulled Charlie's face toward him. "Hey. You're going to do fine."

"Thanks."

But as Liz rested her head on Charlie's chest, he couldn't force himself to believe it. And as he drifted off to sleep, the nightmares returned.

Charlie was thrust back into the woods, running through the charred and smoking remains of the orchard the morning after the fire.

But this time when he made it out to the road and headed for Mayfield, there was no assistance from Dixon and getting a ride into town. He ran the entire trip, his feet pounding against the pavement. But no matter how fast he ran or how far, the road stretched to an endless horizon.

His sub-consciousness pushed his body past the point of fatigue, past the point of failure, but still his legs moved forward.

Muscles aching and his lungs burning, Charlie finally saw the sign for town, and above Mayfield were dark storm clouds. Lightning flashed and thunder rolled.

Charlie ran past the burnt wreckage of the town. Bodies lay in the street, disfigured and burned.

The hospital building towered up ahead, but there were no soldiers, no terrorists that surrounded the power plant as Charlie neared the ER's entrance on the first floor.

"Dad!" His voice had reverted to when he was a little kid. The same fear and uncertainty that plagued him as a child returned to him in the nightmare.

Charlie stepped over slain bodies, tripping over legs and arms on his path toward the stairs. He screamed for his father the entire journey up, and the closer he moved toward the top floor, the worse that anxiety became.

But while he strived toward his father, unsure of what he

would find, his body and muscles slowed the way they did in dreams sometimes. No matter how fast he tried to move, or how much effort he exerted, he couldn't move faster than slow motion.

Finally, after the grueling snail's pace, Charlie reached the top floor. He immediately spied the door where he remembered finding his father.

Charlie paused in the doorway, and he saw Harold Decker on his back, blood still pouring out of his stomach from the gunshot wound that killed him. He lay twisted and mangled, motionless. Charlie stepped toward him, and the tears began to fall.

He crouched by his father's side, examining the fatal wound that killed him, and then picked up his father's hand. It was still warm to the touch, and as Charlie sobbed, he struggled to speak.

"I'm so sorry, Dad," Charlie said. "I should have been here with you. I should have listened to what you were trying to do. Because you were right. You can't sit back and expect things to be taken care of for you. You have to do them yourself, or they won't get done at all."

Harold remained motionless, and then, slowly, he turned his head to face Charlie.

"You should have been here," Harold said.

Charlie squeezed his father's hand. "I'm sorry, I—"

"You were always weak. I tried to make you stronger, Charlie. I did. But I failed. You're still weak. You'll always be weak." Harold pulled his hand away from Charlie's grip. He stared at his son, but while he spoke and moved, there was no life in his eyes.

"Dad?" Charlie gently shook his father. "Dad!"

Harold remained unresponsive and motionless. He no longer looked at Charlie, his eyes staring off into some empty space in the corner of the room.

"I'm sorry!" Charlie sobbed, his cries intensifying. He

clutched his father's arm, squeezing tight, wanting another chance to right the wrongs, to make everything the way it was before. "Dad!"

But his nightmare wouldn't afford him such luxuries, and he was forced to mourn his dead father. Again.

---

*P*eople had known about the ceremony to honor Charlie's father for over a month. It was Liz who had done most of the preparation for the day, and Charlie helped where he could, but he distanced himself from the planning process.

From his position near the apple tree and the grave where his father was buried, Charlie had a clear view of the hundreds of people that had turned up. It was so packed that he couldn't even see the back of the crowd.

Many of them had shown up in their normal work clothes, but Charlie saw combed hair and scrubbed hands and faces. Shirts that could be tucked in were done so willingly. Flowers, candles, drawings, whatever offerings they could give were brought to the grave.

Charlie held the piece of paper that comprised the speech he'd written down. It fit on a single sheet, and the loose paper buckled between his fingers from the steady breezing coming in from the east. He stood there, waiting for the last offerings to be given, and when everyone had a chance to pay their respects, it was Charlie's turn to speak.

"Thank you," Charlie said, his voice cracking. He cleared

his throat then stared down at the paper, switching his glances between the crowd and his speech. "I didn't expect this many people, but I know that me and my family appreciate your time, and your gifts."

Smiles stretched the sun-soaked faces of the crowd. Every pair of eyes was concentrated on Charlie, and the longer he stood in front of their gaze, the more he sweated.

"My father grew up on this land," Charlie said. "It was the only home he'd ever known. He told me stories about him and my grandfather. The long days, the trials that they faced to keep this place growing, to keep everyone alive."

People nodded, the crowd leaning into his words.

"It's a fight that continues today," Charlie said.

A few grunts of affirmation accompanied curt nods. There wasn't a face among them that wasn't sun-soaked and lacking a few hours of sleep. And there wasn't one among them that hadn't experienced loss over the past year.

Charlie glanced down at his father's grave. It was the first time he'd been back to visit since the funeral.

"I used to take for granted the promise of tomorrow," Charlie said, his eyes lingering on the makeshift headstone that he and Mario had carved out on a slab of flat rock they found in the woods, then turned back toward the crowd. "We have new crops. We have food, water, shelter, we can protect ourselves from threats, but the only reason we've been able to do that is because we've done it together. And we'll continue to do it together."

Applause rippled through the crowd, and twice it looked like it was going to die out, only to be started up again with another raucous cheer that picked up the excitement like an earthquake rolling through the land. All save for one cheer.

Out of all the expressions Charlie would have expected to find on his mother's face, disgust would have been the last one on the list. He knew that she hadn't been happy with him for a long time, but he'd done exactly as she'd asked.

And still those hard lines were carved around her mouth and eyes, running along her forehead. It was hard to believe that she was the same woman who had raised him. The same woman who had always comforted him when he was scared, took care of him when he was sick, and was a patient and tentative ear whenever he needed someone to listen.

Charlie turned back to the crowd, unsure of how long his pause had lingered, lost in the order of his speech. He glanced back down at the paper, but the words might as well have been in a foreign language.

Mouth dry, Charlie glanced back up at the crowd and cleared his throat. "Anyway, I, um." He scuffed his heel against the dirt and chewed on the inside of his cheek, then nodded to himself. "My father was never one for ceremony. He woke up before the sun, and he worked long after it went down. He was a man of repetition. He was a man of conviction. He was the strongest man I ever knew. So, thank you all for coming here today." Charlie nodded. "Thank you very much."

The second bout of gratitude was enough of a signal for the folks to recognize that his speech was over, and Charlie stepped off his soap box and walked back over to join Liz, Mario, and the other workers clapping him on the back and telling him that he did a good job.

"How are you feeling?" Liz asked, planting a kiss on his cheek and then rubbing his back.

"I'd take a raid over doing one of these speeches any damn day of the week." Charlie plucked at his collar, sweat soaked through his shirt.

"I thought you were great!" Adelyn said, smiling up at him as she held Liz's hand.

Charlie couldn't help but return the kindness that the little girl had given him. "Thanks, kiddo." He looked to his mother, wondering if she would say anything, but she kept her attention focused on the approaching crowd, then smiled pleasantly at every person that walked over and shook her hand.

"Thank you so much for coming," Martha said.

And so it went for the next hour. Charlie, Liz, and Martha greeted the line of folks who had come to pay their individual respects to Harold Decker and his family.

By the time they reached the end, Charlie's cheeks hurt from the smiling, and he massaged his mouth to loosen up the random spasms that plagued him when they finished.

After the last person, Martha turned to Liz.

"I'm going to take a walk by the river," she said. "Thank you for your help this morning."

"Of course," Liz said. "Do you need anything?"

Martha smiled, shaking her hand as she hugged Liz. "No, my dear. You've done enough." She broke off the hug and then cupped Liz's face. "I just need some time alone."

Liz nodded in understanding. "Of course."

Charlie waited for his mother to finally acknowledge him, but she didn't even look his way as she turned and walked toward the woods.

In addition to the ceremony, Charlie had instructed that everyone get a half day off, and people were already taking advantage of the opportunity. It was a rarity, and while Charlie didn't like the lag in productivity, knowing that they were losing daylight, he understood the need for people to rest. It was why households received at least one leisure day a week. People needed time to reboot.

"Charlie."

The sound of his name and the tone in which it was called forced Charlie to spin around quickly, and his sudden motion made Commander Dixon smile.

The pair of men shook hands, and Dixon then leaned over and gave Liz a kiss on the cheek. "How are you doing? It's been a while since we've talked."

"Been a while since you've visited," Liz said, keeping

Adelyn behind her.

"I was hoping you and I could talk, Charlie," Dixon said.

Liz grabbed hold of Charlie's arm. "Every time you come here, Dixon, Charlie ends up having to do something dangerous. So if that's what you're here to do today, on the day that is supposed to be reserved for honoring his father, I hope you'll understand why we would decline."

"Liz—"

"No." The response was unwavering, and aside from stomping her foot in protest, Liz made her stance clear. "Not today, Charlie." She stared at Dixon, but the commander simply raised his hands helplessly and then looked at Charlie.

"Whenever you're ready," Dixon said, then nodded to Liz. "I'm sorry."

After Dixon walked away, Charlie took both of Liz's hands in his own, though she kept trying to pull away. "It might be nothing."

Liz picked Adelyn up off the ground, who had started to get upset, and locked eyes with him. "You've always been a bad liar, Charlie Decker." Her expression softened, anger replaced with worry. "But I suppose that's not a bad thing." She kissed him softy, warmly, and then let him go. "I love you."

"I love you too."

Dixon was surrounded by the company of his advisers when Charlie approached. Each of them had their own personality quirks, and none of them were bad men. However, there were two of them that turned Charlie's stomach sour every time they met.

The first was Sergeant Taylor Welkin. He was a tall man, thin and gaunt. Charlie wasn't sure if he'd always been that way or if lean times had turned him into that, but either way, he always looked one stiff wind from toppling over. And he never smiled. Good news, bad news, he always reacted the same. And it was that lack of emotion that made Charlie nervous. The man was too calculated. He saw people as nothing more than chess pieces to use as he saw fit in whatever games he played in his mind.

The second was Lieutenant Colonel Lloyd Bartrum. Unlike Welkin, Bartrum was short, stalky, and more warthog than man. A thick, bushy unibrow crawled over the man's eyes, which was always downturned in a frown. Charlie never knew what the man was concentrating so hard on, but he figured that it was nasty.

"Have you reconsidered giving us additional men?" Charlie asked, wanting to cut through the bullshit as quickly as possible. Bartrum and Welkin had an uncanny ability for bullshit, at least when Charlie was around.

Bartrum grunted. "I told you that's what he'd think."

"We need something from you," Welkin added, that nasally tone giving him a stuck-up persona.

"I'm not talking to either of you," Charlie said. "My question was directed to your commander."

Dixon held up his hands before Welkin or Bartrum could respond. "Enough. From everyone." He turned to Charlie and lowered his hand. "We need to talk. Privately."

Charlie led them back toward his trailer, knowing that they wouldn't be disturbed unless it was an emergency. Charlie wasn't sure how that came to be, but he figured it was because the people that lived in The Orchard respected him. And to a certain extent, they feared him. Because he was the man at the controls, and at any time, Charlie could pull the lever or change direction and throw any one of them out in the cold.

It was a power that he'd had to wield only twice, and neither occasion went smoothly. But there needed to be law and order if they were going to rebuild. And if people got away with breaking the rules without consequences, then that order and control would be lost.

Charlie let Dixon in the trailer first, and then closed the

door behind them. Charlie crossed his arms, staring at Dixon, who glanced around the small quarters.

"My grandfather lived in a mobile home," Dixon said, spinning around and smiling. "I'd stay with him for a few weeks every summer. He took me all over the country. Saw a lot of places that kids my age never would have dreamed. He was ex-military." He leaned against the pantry. "I think he's a big reason why I joined up in the first place."

"I've got a lot of items on my list today, and chatting with you wasn't one of them," Charlie said.

Dixon nodded. "We have a shipment coming in from Seattle. Computer chips. They're the last pieces to bring the power plant back online. The transport is considered a high priority by us, and the enemy."

When Dixon paused, Charlie shrugged his soldiers. "What does this have to do with me?"

"The intelligence you gave us about the bombs, and those schematics…" Dixon pushed himself off the pantry and rubbed his jaw, which Charlie now noticed wasn't shaven. "If they'd just approved my request for more men, then we wouldn't even be in this situation in the first place."

"What position?"

Dixon faced Charlie. "DC is aware of the threat that you found. It's a coordinated attack that's being planned at other utility installations around the country, though ours has the highest concentrated effort because the enemy knows how close we are to completion. The enemy wants to keep us in the dark. It's the only play that they have left."

Charlie stared at Dixon for a moment, mulling over the words, and then it started to hit him, and he chuckled. "You can't spare the men for the pick-up, so you need an escort team."

"I'm comfortable with you running the mission, Seattle command is comfortable with it, and so is DC," Dixon said. "It's already been approved. All we need is your cooperation."

Charlie raised his eyebrows. "Cooperation? Is that what you're calling it?" He tilted his head to the side. "And I suppose that if I were to turn down this offer, I'd suddenly find myself without any ammunition, weapons, and vehicles to help protect the orchard and the people who live here?"

Dixon's expression didn't change, and it told Charlie everything he needed to know. "We've worked well together for a long time now, Charlie. You do this, then I will ensure that your orchard gets your requested security upgrades."

Charlie shook his head and then spun around, trying to wrap his head around the situation. "And I don't suppose that Seattle command has a set route ready?"

Dixon hesitated. "They're working on clearing a path—"

"Oh, bullshit, Dixon," Charlie said, angrily spitting the words back at the commander. "Seattle is still a hotbed of terrorist activity, and the truth is you and the rest of your top brass bosom buddies have no idea how many hostiles you still have left in the city." He pointed west. "Seattle is a ticking time bomb, and if you're telling me that this transport run is considered high priority on both sides of the ball, then you can bet your ass that there will be trouble."

"We'll stock you and your team up," Dixon said. "Automatic weapons. Heavy body armor. Communications. I'm talking special ops gear. You'll be well prepared."

Charlie gnawed on the inside of his cheek and glanced out the front window of the trailer where his view was limited to the pair of RVs that were parked nearby. It still amazed him that even after everything he was able to accomplish, all that he was able to build, and how self-sufficient his people had become, Charlie could still be forced to cooperate at gunpoint. But he shook his head, not surprised by the commander's tactics.

"When is the transport coming?" Charlie asked.

"Tomorrow afternoon," Dixon answered, his reaction

revealing that he never expected Charlie to say no. "My men will deliver the supplies to you tomorrow morning."

Charlie nodded, but the math didn't make him feel any better. "If I do this, then I do it my way."

"You will have full autonomy," Dixon said, walking past Charlie and toward the door. "My men will be here at zero-seven-hundred. Make sure you're ready." He opened the door and stepped out.

"Dixon," Charlie said, catching the commander's attention and forcing him to turn around. "If I don't make it back, I have contingencies in place here. The machine will keep moving. You still remember those names I gave you?"

Dixon nodded. "I hope it won't come to that."

"Hope doesn't do much good out here."

"No. It doesn't." Dixon let go of the door, and it swung shut.

Alone, Charlie hung his head and then fell backward onto the hard bench that comprised their breakfast nook. He rubbed his temples, his mind racing through the hundreds of scenarios and alternate endings of his mission tomorrow.

If everything went well, then the country would be on their first real step toward reconstruction. If they failed, god knows how long it would set them back. And then his failure would no doubt have repercussions with his arrangement with Dixon and the military.

The limited amount of free rein that Charlie was granted would vanish, and he could already feel the constricting tightness of the short leash that accompanied his failure. And he also knew that his failure would affect anyone that lived in the orchard.

While Charlie had built a small and ordered civilization, it was still a new and fragile infant. It wouldn't take much to kill it, and Charlie dreaded being plunged back into that chaos again. Those first few months were hell, and he had no desire to relive them again.

The night passed slowly, but morning came quickly, and Charlie rose from the bed like a zombie, gently removing Liz's arm from his chest. He stared at her for a moment, studying the curve of her body, which lay naked beneath the thin sheet.

They'd argued last night, then made love, then argued some more, then made love again. And despite the back and forth, Charlie still couldn't rid himself of the anxiety that plagued his mind. It kept him awake, and after Liz had fallen asleep he lay there holding her, staring up at the ceiling and dreading the morning sun, which came quickly.

Charlie got out of bed, dressed quickly, then kissed Liz's cheek. She stirred, eliciting a pleasurable moan, but she didn't wake. He kissed Adelyn on her forehead then paused at the door, turning back to his girls, and struggled with either waking them or letting them sleep.

But they'd already said what they needed to say last night and well into the morning. And he needed to keep his mind right for the day ahead.

Charlie's boots crushed the grass covered in early

morning dew, and he quickly stepped out toward the road and out of his normal path through the RVs and trailers.

On the way to Doc's, Charlie stopped and spoke with the patrol commanders, telling them to start preparing for an attack. If they failed their mission, or if the terrorists decided to hit them early, he wanted to make sure The Orchard was ready.

"Full defense?" the commander asked.

"Yes. Up and running by the end of the day," Charlie answered. "Everyone's pulling overtime until I get back."

"Yes, sir."

By the time he reached Doc's house, his stomach was growling, and he took the hunger as a good sign. He found Doc awake and cracking the first few eggs into the skillet, then noticed the bacon already cooked on a plate on the side.

Doc turned around when Charlie entered, then followed Charlie's gaze to the bacon. "I heard about the mission today. Figured you and the crew would need the extra boost." Doc returned his attention to the skillet, scrambling the eggs up, steam rising from the pan.

Doc never made bacon except for holidays, but seeing as how this could be Charlie's last breakfast, he knew the old timer was doing his best to help make the morning easier. It was the old man's way of saying he cared.

Charlie grabbed a strip of bacon, which was still warm, and snapped it in half. It was the perfect consistency of crunchy and chewy, and Charlie's mouth watered as he quickly shoved the other half into his mouth and down his gullet.

It was the best thing he'd eaten in weeks.

Outside, the crew was starting to arrive, none of them dressed in their regular tactical attire. The twins arrived first, each of them giving Charlie a curt nod as they walked inside to grab breakfast from Doc.

There wasn't the usual bickering between the three of

them, and Doc actually came out and handed each of them a glass of orange juice.

"Squeezed it this morning," Doc said, not looking any of them in the eye and quickly returning to the house. But not before Charlie caught Doc wiping at the corner of his eye.

Nick and Lee arrived next, and Charlie waited for them to finish eating before he spoke.

"Everyone knows what we're up against today," Charlie said. "Pending Dixon will make good on his word though, we should be stocked with some pretty nice toys."

"Fucking better be," Nick said, crossing his arms. "We're going straight into the middle of the Devil's asshole, and you know that he's not going to be happy about it when we're done."

"I'd say to treat this like any other raid that we've been on, but that's just not true," Charlie said. "What happens today will have repercussions for years. We have an opportunity here, and I will not have us waste it."

Charlie looked at each of his crew, pausing and studying their expressions. He wanted to make sure they understood, that they really understood what today meant. And he was glad to see the fire and concentration in their eyes.

After that, they remained quiet, save for a few comments between the twins, until Dixon's caravan arrived with the promised equipment.

Contrary to what Charlie thought, Dixon didn't arrive with the men who brought the supplies, which worried Charlie at first. He thought that because the commander didn't come that they'd be short-changed on what was promised, but Charlie was happy to find that it wasn't the case.

Everything they could have wanted was in the boxes that soldiers pulled out of their Humvees. Full body armor, fully automatic weapons, communications links, ammunition, grenades, sniper rifles, everything that Charlie picked up looked brand new.

"Here." One of the soldiers extended a pair of keys to Charlie, who stared at them questioningly.

"What's that?"

The soldier walked over and then shoved the keys into Charlie's palm. "Don't make it harder on me than it has to be, man. Just make sure you don't blow it up." He then walked back over to another vehicle, and he and the rest of the soldiers drove off.

Charlie stared at the keys, then at the Humvee the caravan had left behind. It was for them. Brand new.

"Ho-ly shit." Jason walked over, sniper rifle slung over his shoulder, a string of ammunition draped across his chest. "How the hell did they get this beauty up and running?"

"Must have called in some favors from DC," Shelly answered, walking over and running her hand over the shiny armor. "Hello, little girl."

"Grab what you need," Charlie said, pulling everyone's attention away from the awe of their brand-new gifts. "We roll out in fifteen."

It didn't take long for everyone to pick out their favorite toys. Everyone gravitated to what they specialized in, and anything that was left over, Charlie had Doc stock it away with the rest of their supplies.

The new Humvee was a smooth ride, at least from a comfort standpoint. Seeing as how the Humvee was nearly brand new, or at least never been used before, it was like riding in a limousine.

And while the crew's excited chatter about their new toys continued after they left, it died down once they passed the marker for their safe zone.

"Heads up," Charlie said, straightening up in his chair as they entered clan territory.

Nick adjusted his grip on the steering wheel and then

tightened his grip. The road remained clear, but clans frequently put up road blocks in an effort to pick off any supply transports coming from Seattle and Mayfield.

"Anything?" Charlie asked.

"Negative," Jason answered, his eyes glued to a pair of binoculars that scanned the cluster of rundown suburban homes.

Even if there were some of the clans nearby, Charlie figured the sight of the Humvee would provide enough deterrent to keep them from trying anything stupid. But then of course there was always the terrorist cells to contend with as well.

Passing the broken homes, Charlie was brought back to the early days after the EMP. It was hard to imagine that at one point every one of those houses was filled with people. Families, friends, children, the elderly, people who weren't prepared for the shit storm that had come pounding on their doors and roofs.

Guilt flooded Charlie's veins as he stared at the broken homes, passing quickly as Nick kept his foot on the accelerator. He couldn't save everyone.

With tensions high, Charlie and the crew passed through clan territory without incident. But while they all would have liked to breathe a sigh of relief from still being alive, the sight of Seattle's skyline kept their lips tight.

Columns of smoke reached into the blue sky, the sights continuous and ominous as they continued their journey to the rendezvous point. It was a city in conflict, three sides struggling for control. The military trying to establish order, the terrorists doing everything in their power to disrupt that order, and the citizens stuck in the middle doing whatever they needed to survive.

Nick was forced to slow his speed when they entered the thick of the city. There were still a lot of vehicles blocking the road, and trash and other obstructions blocked their path.

"Watch the high windows," Charlie said, glancing up at the buildings that towered on either side of them.

"Looks like we're here," Nick said.

A soldier stood out front of a five-story apartment building, arm up and waving them forward. At first glance it looked as though he was alone, but a quick scan of the surrounding area, and the building he stood in front of, revealed at least two dozen other soldiers hiding amongst the street.

And while the sight should have evoked a sense of confidence that the perimeter was locked down properly, Charlie still couldn't shake the foreboding sensation growing from the back of his skull and slowly spreading throughout his body.

Charlie stepped out of the vehicle, Shelly, Jason, and Lee following suit. He approached the soldier who flagged them down.

"Decker?" the soldier asked.

Charlie flashed the deputy badge, and the soldier nodded, then motioned to another man inside the building through an open door.

Another soldier carried a small box out to Charlie, handing it over with great care. The exchange was so simple that Charlie wondered if he was missing something.

"Good luck," the soldier said, and then without another word, he returned inside the building with the rest of his men, leaving Charlie and his crew alone.

"All right," Charlie said. "Let's get out of here."

Charlie placed the box between the twins in the back seat, then checked his watch as he climbed back into the passenger seat of the Humvee. It had taken them three hours and seven minutes to drive from The Orchard to this location. But since they were taking a different route home, he went ahead and added another twenty minutes.

Charlie white-knuckled his grip on the rifle, eyes constantly scanning the changing landscape beyond his window. Every bump and kick that he felt on the road triggered the smallest of muscle spasms.

Despite his best efforts in creating a world where he would never be hunted again, here he was, performing Dixon's dirty work in an effort to keep his people safe. It was a job that never ended, and it was a job that Charlie didn't think he would survive.

And just when the tall skyscrapers shortened to the lower, squat buildings on Seattle's city limits, the first bullet hit the Humvee.

The progression of the gunfire was small at first, like drops of rain leaking from a cloud ready to burst, but then with a crack of thunder, all hell rained down upon them.

"Fuck!" Nick shouted.

"Go! Go! Go!" Charlie glanced out the window, trying to determine the origin of the concentration of gunfire, but it was coming from everywhere.

"There's too much shit on the road!" The Humvee jerked wildly as Nick steered them around the road blocks, hitting the gas and then slamming on the brakes on their hasty retreat.

"RPG! RPG! RPG!" Jason shouted from the back of the Humvee, and Charlie turned just in time to see the rocket jettison from the launcher, screaming toward them.

Charlie leaned over and jerked the steering wheel hard right, surprising Nick and crashing them into the side of a truck. But the maneuver caused the RPG to miss, and Charlie watched it explode into a sedan that sat in the middle of the street.

"Get us out of here!" Jason said, pounding on the back of Nick's seat.

Nick retook control of the steering wheel and floored the accelerator, the roar of the engine temporarily overriding the hailstorm of bullets raining down upon them, but while the engine revved, the Humvee didn't move.

"We're stuck!" Nick repeatedly slammed his foot on the accelerator, but it did nothing.

Charlie glanced around him, spotting three hostiles on their left, at least two in the back, and one he could see on the right. They were thirty seconds from being swarmed. "Secure the asset and head for the building on the northeast corner of the street at the crossing! We'll regroup there!"

"I've got the box!" Lee said, reaching into the back of the seat.

Charlie opened the door, using the steel plated door as cover, and then aimed his rifle at the approaching enemy on their right. He squeezed the trigger in one quick motion, and at least six bullets screamed out of the barrel, forcing the enemy back behind a mailbox.

The other doors of the Humvee were flung open and the rest of his team spilled out.

"I've got cover!" Charlie shouted, and Nick worked his way around from the driver side toward safety, followed quickly by Shelly.

Nick pounded Charlie's shoulder, which signaled to Charlie that Nick was on the move. Charlie stood, aiming for the terrorists across the road, and then opened fire.

Two of the four terrorists dropped to the pavement, bright crimson bursting from their foreheads as the bullets flung their skull backward.

He glanced over to the building and saw Nick in position, and one by one Charlie sent his crew to the building while he provided cover, the terrorists slowly inching forward.

Once he was alone, he waited for Jason to get into position either on the roof or one of the top floors and start picking them off one by one.

"Jason, are you set?" Charlie asked, pressing down on his communication link.

"Thirty seconds," Jason answered.

With his back against the Humvee, Charlie spun around and fired at the encroaching enemy. If they got any closer, then he'd be stuck. It was now or never.

"I'm set!" Jason screamed. "Go!"

Charlie turned tail, sprinting for the building, his crew providing cover fire on his mad dash for safety. Bullets nipped at his heels, trailing him all the way until he leapt inside the building, spinning around toward the wall.

"You all right?" Nick asked, clapping Charlie on the shoulder.

"Yeah." With all of them concentrated in the building, the enemy converged in formation in an attempt to wipe them out. Nick and Shelly fired sporadically from the broken windows that faced the street, while Lee inched toward the back in search of an exit.

"Got something," Lee said.

"All right, let's move!" Charlie waved his people toward the back of the building, the heat trapped inside the old and dusty structure sweltering from baking in the sun all day.

Sweat dripped into Charlie's eyes, and the salt burned. He swiped at the agitation angrily, his head on a swivel as his boots pounded the dirty concrete.

Everywhere Charlie looked, he saw the relics of the past. Microwaves, fridges, stoves, and toasters, all of them covered in dust. Must have been a show room in its previous life. Now, it might as well have been a museum.

Lee opened the back door, casting sunlight into the darkened storage room at the building's rear, and when Charlie burst outside, he was blinded with brightness, but that didn't stop his progression forward.

When his vision finally cleared, Nick and Lee were at his side, and Shelly and Jason brought up the rear. The exit had led them into an alleyway, which dumped them out to an adjacent street.

The five of them sprinted toward the end, Charlie eager to get out of the kill zone. If the enemy turned that corner before they left the alleyway, they were sitting ducks.

At the end of the alley, Charlie pointed to a building across the street, and the five of them hurried inside before the enemy grew wise and followed.

Charlie paused at the door to the restaurant, turning around and planting his knee into the pavement as he aimed his weapon at the end of the street.

Jason passed, then Nick, then Lee, and finally Shelly, and the five of them caught their breath inside the store.

After a few seconds, the first of the terrorists rounded the corner of the building on the street, and then three more emerged from the alleyway.

Using hand signals, Charlie pointed toward the back of the building, and the three of them quietly continued their retreat around the restaurant's tables, weaving through the derelict kitchen in the back, the floor littered with a litany of sound booby traps in the forms of pots and pans.

"Watch your feet," Charlie said.

The group walked gingerly through the kitchen and made it to the back door without incident. And so they continued their journey, Charlie weaving them in a crooked line on a path north and east. They never left the cover of buildings, and while they were forced to scan each one for anyone hiding inside, he knew it was better than walking the open streets like sitting ducks.

Once they escaped the downtown area and were out of the reach of the tall buildings and potential ambushes from above, Charlie moved them to the open streets.

With everyone's head still on a swivel, they pushed

forward out of the city limits and back into the first suburb of the city, which also happened to be home to the blue clan.

The sky darkened, threatening rain, and thunder rolled in the distance. Charlie knew that the rain would make the walk back miserable, but it might work to their advantage.

"Asset still secure?" Charlie asked, his eyes concentrated on the next alleyway, quickly pivoting around the corner to clear it before moving forward.

"Roger that," Lee said. "Package is snug."

"Nick, Jason, I want both of you to fall back, watch our six," Charlie replied. "Shelly, I want you up with me on point. That package gets back to The Orchard. No matter what."

Charlie kept them on their current path, but as he scanned the world through the eyes of his scope, a familiarity of the area washed over him. He couldn't quite put his finger on it, but it was like walking through a dream, and it felt like one that could turn into a nightmare at any time. And just when he had the answer to his questions and the cloud of the dream was lifted, it was Jason who pointed it out.

"Fork up ahead," he said. "I say we go right."

Charlie froze, then slowly lowered the tip of his rifle as he stared at the end of the road up ahead. It was the same intersection that Charlie had stumbled upon when he led a group out of Seattle on the day of the EMP.

"Hey," Shelly said, nudging him with her elbow, rifle still aimed upward. "What's up?"

Charlie shook his head, then raised his rifle back up to a firing position. "Nothing. We should head left. Clans are to the right."

"Left is a longer road," Nick said. "I think we'd want to get home as soon as possible, right?"

The first few drops of rain splashed against the pavement, and Jason turned his head up toward the sky. "Either way, it looks like it's gonna be a shitty walk back. I vote shorter."

Charlie paused, staring at the intersection ahead. Deep

down, he knew that going right was the correct move. And while he thought he had buried the past, he felt it crawling toward the surface, wanting to break free.

But he wasn't the same man that had walked this road before. He was battle-hardened now, and he wasn't going to fall back into old habits.

"We go right." Charlie marched forward, saying nothing else as his crew fell in line.

After the change in direction, the rain fell harder. It started off as a steady drizzle, but after a flash of lightning and a crack of thunder, it transformed into a downpour.

And while the rain offered a release from the heat, it added weight. With their clothes soaked, the heavy cloth added an extra ten pounds to their already-hefty load.

The deeper Charlie led them into the clan territory, the harder it rained. Wind whipped the water droplets against his cheeks, every single contact burning from the harsh wind. He squinted his eyes, staring ahead and barely able to make out the landscape through the wavering sheets of rain that blanketed the area.

"It's a goddamn hurricane!" Nick shouted. "I can't see a thing."

"Boss!" Lee shouted through the communications link. "We need to take a minute and regroup."

"Negative!" Charlie shouted. "We continue forward. This is the best cover we're going to get and—"

Lighting cracked, striking a nearby tree. Sparks erupted and the bark exploded, catapulting burnt shards of the trunk toward Charlie and his crew.

More lighting crawled across the clouds, appearing like veins and then vanishing in the blink of an eye, leaving behind the harsh pounding of thunder.

"Charlie!" Lee said, staring his boss in the eye. "We need cover."

Charlie glanced around and then pointed to a nearby

house on the other side of the street. "Let's go!" They entered the house, cleared it, and then settled in the living room while the storm raged on outside.

Lee walked over to a nearby wall in the living room and plucked a picture off a nail. He held it in his hands, staring at it for a moment, and then flashed the picture toward the crew. "Think they're still alive?"

"What does it matter?" Nick said, grumpy and still wet, taking off his boots and wringing out one of his socks. "They're not here anymore. And we are. End of story."

Charlie walked over and grabbed the picture frame from Lee's hands. He examined it, shaking his head. They were most likely dead. The past year had left little room for the weak or faint of heart. Most of the deaths happened within that first three months. And with the number of dead, especially from the city, stiff winds blew an unnatural stench of death into the countryside.

The smell lasted for three weeks. And while the scent wasn't desirable, it was the psychological impact of the smell that did the most damage. It was a reminder of the death that surrounded them.

"Lee, transfer those computer chips to your bag. That cardboard box is going to dissolve in the rain." Charlie hung the picture back on the wall and then left the living room to investigate the rest of the house. "Get your rest. Storm could be over soon."

He turned on his flashlight, exposing the darkened hallways that moved deeper into the house. He found a bathroom and grabbed a towel, wiping off his weapon. He would have used it to dry off his face, but the towel smelled terrible, and Charlie knew he'd dry out eventually.

Thunder cracked outside, and for the first time in his life, Charlie found himself wishing for the rain to stop. It was a rare request for someone who had spent most of his life praying for rain. Anyone that worked in agriculture had a fickle relationship with the weather.

"Boss, we've got something." Lee's voice was calm but quiet over the radio.

Charlie dropped the towel and hurried toward the front of the house. Everyone in the living room was up near a window, peeking outside into the rain, which had slackened.

Charlie knelt next to Lee, peeking above the windowsill.

"They're sweeping the houses," Lee said.

Charlie watched a cluster of the terrorists bust down a door across the street, filter inside quickly, and then move onto the next. He glanced as far to the left on their side of the street as they could and saw a similar team performing the same sweep two houses down, and another team, the bulk of their forces at twenty strong, marching down the street.

Charlie lowered his head, trying to think of a strategy, then looked to Jason and Shelly, who had already posted up by the back of the living room and the hallway that led to the back.

"What kind of exit point are we looking at?" Charlie asked.

"Fences in the back," Jason answered.

Charlie glanced back out at the street and saw the soldiers swarming the sides of the house and down the back-side to catch anyone trying to escape while the clear teams checked the interior.

"Fuck." Charlie slid down. "We'll have to shoot a path once they breach. Everyone find a good spot to hole up, and brace for gunfire."

Everyone moved quickly and quietly through the living room, keeping low to avoid any detection from the soldiers outside. Charlie maneuvered behind the couch, positioning it so it provided good cover for him when the bastards entered.

Nick jumped behind a chair, and Lee joined Charlie at the

couch, while the twins remained at their position in the hallway.

Once everyone settled, the world quietened into nothing but the sound of lightly falling rain and the foreign voices shouting in the street. Charlie glanced over to Lee, who still had the package secured.

Three terrorists crossed the front window, and Charlie tensed, placing his finger on the trigger and keeping his aim steady at the door. The voices outside dropped to a whisper as they prepared for their breach.

The rain stopped. Charlie held his breath. And just before the breach, gunfire broke outside.

Charlie glanced quickly toward the window, catching glimpses of the gunfight outside.

"What the hell is going on?" Nick asked, joining the retreat toward the back of the house, the five of them funneling down the hallway, Charlie bringing up the rear and getting a last good look out the window.

He frowned, trying to make out the commotion outside. And then it hit them.

"Clans," Charlie said. "Let's move!"

Charlie pushed his people toward the back, funneling them down the hallway, knowing that they had a limited window of opportunity to make it out of there alive.

They burst out into the light drizzle of rain and into the overgrown grass of the fenced-in backyard. Jason was on point and led them toward the gate's back exit, which led them out onto the side of the house, pinning them in a narrow, grassy alley between the crammed houses.

Jason planted his knee, aiming toward the street to act as cover should the fight in the streets be carried toward them, and as Charlie stepped from the backyard and into the alley, he witnessed the battle raging in the streets and noticed the familiar blue patches on the sleeves of the members of the blue clan.

Once they cleared the backyard, Charlie grabbed Jason and pulled him from his perch. The five of them hurried around the back of the next house and danced between the back yards, moving away from the fight as quickly as they could.

It wasn't until the sound of the gunfire was nothing more than a distant pop that Charlie and the group slowed to a crawl, catching their breath, dripping wet with sweat and rain, which had stopped.

Charlie glanced up at the sky and saw the sun struggling to break through the clouds, and as the temperature warmed, the air grew thick and muggy.

"The trek back is going to suck now," Nick said, noticing the same rise in temperature as Charlie.

"Everyone whole?" Charlie asked, ignoring Nick's words.

Everyone nodded.

"Good." Charlie turned, and when he set his foot down into the grass, he almost missed the faint click of a safety being turned off on a rifle. But by the time he tried to sound the alarm and raise his own gun to protect himself, they were already surrounded.

39

A total of seven blue patches surrounded them, all of them dirtied and wet, and stinking of body order despite the fresh coat of rain.

"Drop the weapons." The man who spoke did so through a bandana that covered his mouth. It was the same blue as the patch on his arm.

"We're just passing through," Charlie said, slowly raising his hands. "We're not looking for any trouble."

"Well," the leader said, a hint of a smile in his voice, which remained concealed behind his bandana. "You're shit out of luck."

Charlie kept an eye on the twins in his peripheral. Out of the crew, they had the itchiest trigger fingers. Charlie and his crew were in a kill box, and there wasn't a scenario that ran through his mind that didn't end with all of them dead.

"Those were your boys hitting the terrorists?" Charlie asked.

Blue leader stepped closer, his brow pinched together. "Drop your guns, and we might send you on your way with your lives."

"Fuck you," Jason said.

The blue patches lunged forward, but Charlie held up his hands. "Stop!" He lowered his weapon, which stopped the advancement. He turned toward the leader. "We have something that will end all of this."

"Boss—"

Charlie turned quickly and silenced Shelly with only a glance. He then reached for Lee's backpack, which held the chips. "What's in here can turn the power back on. For everyone."

The leader flicked his eyes back to Charlie, and for the briefest moment, Charlie saw hope flash in his eyes before he squinted, narrowing them into little slits. "You're from The Orchard, aren't you?"

"Yes," Charlie answered.

A murmur drifted between the blue clan members.

"We're working with the military in Mayfield. But we have to get there quickly." Charlie gestured back to the fighting to the south, the gunshots less frequent now, but none of them sure of who won the battle. "The terrorists who did this are planning another assault. And if they wreck the plant before we have our package installed, then it could set back the timeline for fixing all of this." Charlie took a generous step forward, letting himself believe the hope rising within everyone. "We don't have to do this anymore."

And just when Charlie thought the leader was going to lower his rifle and command his men to do the same, Charlie's stomach lurched when he raised it and positioned the barrel less than an inch away from Charlie's face.

"If the military wants what you've got, then I'm sure they'll be willing to pay the price. Now, drop the weapons, or I'll kill you and your men and then take your cargo anyway."

Charlie turned to his crew and nodded.

Jason looked at him. "Boss…"

"Do it," Charlie said.

The rifles hit the ground, and the crew raised their hands

as the blue patches swept over and grabbed their weapons, then patted each of them down, stealing the ammunition and whatever knives they had on their persons.

The computer chips was taken last, the leader holding them for himself. He opened the bag and peeked inside, his eyes widening like he was staring at gold or diamonds. He laughed, then zipped it closed and looked at Charlie.

"Let's hope the military like you as much as they like their computers." He laughed again, and then Charlie was thrust forward by the end of a rifle, falling into line with the rest of his crew as they walked toward whatever prison they'd be kept in.

The clan led Charlie and his people through the maze of houses, turning left and right at random points, and kept off the streets, using the small cutouts they created through secret doors in the fences of backyards.

The closer Charlie was shuttled toward the clan's main fortress, the more people he noticed along the way. It was nothing but guards and soldiers at first, but the deeper they traveled into the clan's territory, the more he saw of the citizens.

Women, children, elderly, all walks of life, a similar diversity to the people who lived in The Orchard. Curious eyes watched them, and Charlie held their gaze, surprised to find so many.

"How many do you have now?" Charlie asked the leader close to him.

"What do you care?" the leader answered, not bothering to turn around. "You and the military made it clear that you wanted nothing to do with us." He turned around. "A little too convenient that you change your mind now."

The deeper that Charlie was taken into the heart of the blue clan, the more that the houses blended together. They were attached with plywood and metal, any material that they could salvage. It was the biggest community he'd ever seen. Even bigger than The Orchard.

Charlie paused as he saw a garden that had taken over what was most likely a back yard. A pair of men picked tomatoes, peppers, and carrots, stuffing them into bags.

"Move!" The order was accompanied by a harsh shove of a rifle barrel into his back, and Charlie jolted forward into a nearby home.

He had always wondered how the clans fed themselves. After all, there was only so much pilfering that you could do before there wasn't anything left to pilfer.

Candles and lanterns, both wax and battery powered, lit the inside of what Charlie assumed was once a living room but had now been transformed into a cage. The windows and exits in the large barren room had been sealed off with bars, and the only entrance was guarded by a very large man, wearing no shirt, showing the scars along his protruding belly. Charlie tagged him close to six and a half feet.

Charlie and his crew were shoved inside, and Charlie winced at the clang of the iron bars that followed.

"Great," Nick said, scuffing his heel against the concrete. "Just fucking great."

"This was a bad play, boss," Jason said, pacing the floor and shaking his head.

Lee crossed his arms and leaned up against the back wall, the wiry muscles along his forearms accentuated by the dim lighting. "You think they'll kill us?"

"Why not?" Nick asked. "How many of them have we killed over the past year?" He gestured to the guard, who kept his back toward them. "They don't give a shit about us. We're expendable."

"They could have killed us before we got here," Shelly said. "That's something."

"They didn't kill us because they wanted more bargaining

power," Jason said, then pointed to Charlie. "That guy knows who Charlie is. It's the only reason we're not dead."

"The Orchard knows what to do in a situation like this," Charlie said.

When The Orchard started to grow and Charlie realized that they needed back-up plans in case a situation like their current predicament ever came about, he started to lay the groundwork for contingencies, which covered the gamut of scenarios.

From disease, to war, to mutiny, a select group of people were privy to the procedures that would ensure the orchard's survival. Because that was all that really mattered in the end.

For Charlie, the orchard represented something more than just a means of survival, it was the only thing that still connected him to his father. It was a legacy Charlie wanted to continue long after he had died, not for himself, but for Harold Decker. The man who had given his life to avenge the home and land that he loved.

The twins sat together against the back wall, whispering to one another, while Lee lay down on the adjacent wall and Nick paced the front of the cage like a tiger waiting to be let out.

"Fucking bullshit," Nick said, the anger continuing to simmer.

"Calm down," Charlie said. "We don't know what they'll do. Best to just wait it out now."

"I know what they're going to fucking do," Nick said. "They're going to either kill us, use us as bait and then kill us, or torture us until we tell them all about the orchard, and then kill us after they're done. Either way, it's going to be painful." Nick flapped his arms at his sides and gripped the iron bars of the front of the cage, twisting his palms around the old iron as if he could break it in half.

And while Charlie couldn't read the future, he knew that there was truth to Nick's words. Dixon had told him some stories from surviving soldiers that had run into the clans before. And while other clans had resorted to torture and barbaric methods of justice, anyone that was taken by the blue clan was never seen again.

"So, you're Charlie Decker." The voice came from the other side of the bars, though the man it belonged to was mostly concealed in shadow on the far wall and past the guard. "You're not a well-liked man around here."

"I couldn't tell," Charlie said.

The laughter that followed was more playful than Charlie expected, and the man that accompanied it from the shadows was even more unsuspecting.

Clean-shaven with a buzzed head and dark skin, a wide smile revealed sparkling white teeth. He was dressed in long sleeves, jeans, and boots, sporting the familiar blue patch insignia on his left shoulder. He crossed his arms and stopped just short of the bars.

Charlie squinted at the stranger. "Do I know you?"

He paced the front of the bars. "People talk about you around here like you're a god." He cocked his head to the side and shook his head. "But that's not what I see."

"What do you see?" Charlie asked.

The stranger grabbed hold of the bars and pressed his face between the long pieces of iron. The playfulness was gone. "A man who needs to answer for his sins." He pushed himself off the bars and left, eyeing Charlie the entire way until he finally turned and walked out of the house.

"What in the hell was that?" Nick asked.

Charlie's gaze lingered on the darkness where the stranger had hidden, and he shook his head. "I have no idea."

40

*T*he inside of their prison provided no windows and no air flow, and without the sky, Charlie and his crew lost all track of time.

Charlie wiped his brow, flinging the sweat collecting on his skin to the concrete floor, which darkened from the speckles of water that quickly evaporated from the heat.

"What the hell do they plan to do?" Nick asked, sitting on his ass and shirtless. "Cook us to death?"

"I do not give permission to any of you to eat me," Jason said, his voice lethargic.

Even Shelly had stripped down as far as she could go without forgoing her modesty, though if the heat continued to rise, Charlie wasn't sure how much longer modesty would last for any of them.

"I don't think we'll be in here long enough for that to happen," Shelly said. "They'll shoot us before they cook us. But they might cook us afterward."

Lee laughed. "A nice orchard crew stew."

"Yeah, well, I hope they choke on it," Nick said.

Voices and the steady patter of boots forced all of them to look toward the front of the cell where they were greeted by a dozen clan soldiers. The leader of the unit motioned toward the cell door with a single flick of his head, and the guard on duty opened it.

The leader stepped inside. He was grizzled, with a beard and shoulder-length hair, and he was so broad shouldered that he barely fit through the door.

"On your feet," he said, the words spoken like an order. "Now."

The crew looked toward Charlie, who remained seated on the floor. He locked eyes with the unit leader, and after a pause, he nodded to the others. They all stood.

They formed a single file line and were surrounded on their walk out of the cell and through the rest of the camp.

The bodies that surrounded them blocked Charlie's view of the rest of their compound, but he noticed that everywhere they passed, whispers followed.

People covered their mouths, leaning into their neighbors, their eyes darting back and forth between one another, pointing at Charlie as if he were a ghost.

They were eventually led to a small house at the end of a cul-de-sac where five houses sat in a semi-circle. They were led to the house in the dead center, the door closed, and guarded by two more armed sentries.

Charlie and his people were ushered inside, trailing dirty footprints along cool tile that was a relief against the soles of their bare feet. The leader of the unit pointed toward a room off the side of a hallway, and Charlie was the first to turn the corner.

And what he found inside was far different than what he expected.

"Please, have a seat." It was the stranger from earlier, sitting at the head of a dining table that held plates filled with meat, vegetables, fruit, and glasses of water, all of which was illuminated by candle-light.

Charlie frowned at the sight, clogging the narrow

entrance as the rest of his crew peeked over his shoulders. "What is this?"

The stranger picked up a fork. "It's dinner." He speared a cube of potato and popped it into his mouth, smiling as he chewed. "I'd eat before it gets cold." He reached for his cup and drank, focusing on his meal while Charlie stood dumbfounded.

But when Charlie didn't move, the stranger finally looked up from his plate, and that playfulness that was on display earlier vanished.

"We spend our days rationing, and this is a large amount of food to go to waste," he said. "If you don't eat it, then tell me now and I'll bring in someone who will."

There was a seat and a plate for each of them, Charlie taking the seat at the opposite end of the table from the stranger, who smiled when everyone sat down.

"There," he said. "That's better."

Nick, Shelly, Jason, and Lee all looked to Charlie after a thorough investigation of their food.

"If I wanted to kill you, then I would have done it already," the stranger said. "And I would have done it with something far more unpleasant than poison." He smiled at the words, and while the playfulness was charming, it didn't lessen the threat.

"What do you want?" Charlie asked.

"I want you to eat," he answered. "And then we will talk. But not before. Eat."

Once everyone had their first bite, nothing but the sounds of chewing and silverware scraping porcelain filled the room.

Belly full and plate cleaned, Charlie dropped the fork and knife and wiped his mouth with the back of his dirty hand. He stood, and a pair of guards rushed near him, but they didn't touch him.

"What do you want?" Charlie asked.

"It's just not what I want, Charlie Decker. It's what you want. It's what that commander in Mayfield wants as well." He stood. "It's what every single man, woman, and child still alive in this country have wanted for the past year." He leaned forward. "For the world to return to the way it was."

"If you want the world to return to the way it was, then you need to let me and my unit return with our gear home," Charlie said.

"Yeah, that's what we were trying to do before you fuckers fucked it up," Nick said.

The stranger didn't break eye contact with Charlie, the hint of a smile still curved upward on his face. "I imagine that you and Dixon have an arrangement with one another. I don't blame you. If I had the ear of a military commander, I would bend it a little too." He nodded. "It's a smart alliance."

"Is that what you're proposing?" Charlie asked.

The stranger leaned forward. "I propose we talk."

Another man walked past Charlie and set a box down on the table, which had been cleared of the stranger's plate. It was the bag that held the computer components for the power plant.

The stranger placed his hand on the bag. "I have to confess I peeked inside. I was always the kid that went looking for the Christmas presents after my parents had bought them. Curiosity always got the better of me, and it was a trait that I never outgrew." He tapped the lid. "I'd heard rumors that the military was nearly done with the plant." He stepped from the head of the table and walked toward Charlie, leaving the box. "The moment the power turns back on, things are going to change again, but I want to make sure that when things do change, that they change for the better." He stopped just short of Charlie, close enough for Charlie to strangle him with his bare hands.

"It will be better," Charlie said.

"Better for you, maybe," the stranger replied. "But not for the majority of my people."

Nick laughed, leaning back in his seat. "You're a real piece of work, you know that?" He stood, knocking the chair down behind him.

"Nick, stand down," Charlie said.

"No, because this self-righteous asshole thinks that he's got it all figured out, that we're just going to lie down and let you march in and control the narrative." Nick walked around the table toward the stranger but was cut off by a guard that slammed him to the floor, pinning his hands behind his back.

Lee calmly reached for his glass and shook his head. "You'd think he'd have learned to keep his mouth shut by now."

Shelly raised her eyebrows. "That's because he doesn't think at all." She peeked over the table and watched him squirm beneath the guard's boots.

"Why don't you and I talk without any distractions," the stranger said.

Outside, evening had fallen, and the stranger led him to a garden in the backyard, flowers in bloom, and everything a shade of gold under the light of the setting sun. It was beautiful.

"I always enjoyed coming out here," the stranger said. "Helps remind me of what we're really fighting for, especially when things get tough."

Charlie extended a finger, grazing one of the flower petals before retracting his hand. "And what exactly are you fighting for?"

The stranger shook his head and then collapsed on a bench between a pair of rose bushes. Deflated, Charlie felt like he was finally catching a glimpse of the real man behind the façade.

"I've fought for a long time now, Charlie," he said. "I've had so much bloodstains on my hands that I can't wash it off anymore." He stared down at his palms, wiggling his fingers. "I'm numb to it. And it scares me."

Charlie walked over, then took a seat at the man's side, his knees popping like an old man's. Whatever youth remained of him seemed to be locked away, and he couldn't remember where he put the key.

"I wanted to prove to myself that I could make this work," the stranger said. "It was why I had my men put you in the cell." He looked over to Charlie. "I did consider killing you. It was a thought that crossed my mind more than once."

Charlie nodded. "I would have done the same."

The stranger nodded, leaning back, relaxing a little bit as he gazed around his garden. "This wasn't my house before all of this started. It belonged to an old man. He was a widower, but the garden belonged to his late wife. He told me that he never had an interest in gardening until she was gone, and he'd always regretted not sharing that hobby with her. But he kept things growing after she died. He told me that it was a way for him to stay connected to her and the past that they shared with one another."

Charlie waited for a punchline, or a quirky remark, but when it never came, he figured that the man was speaking from the heart, and Charlie let the silence linger.

"The past is funny, isn't it?" the stranger finally asked. "It seems like half of us are trying to get back to it, while the other half are running for our lives from it." He turned to Charlie. "Which one are you?"

Charlie raised his eyebrows and shook his head. "I'm still trying to figure it out."

The stranger chuckled. "That's why you're in the position you find yourself in right now, my friend. If we let ourselves be torn in two by the past and the future, then we'll never be able to enjoy the present." He looked around and smiled. "I'd like to stay here when it's all said and done, but I doubt they'll let me do that."

"They?" Charlie asked.

"The people who want back in power," the stranger answered. "The government and police, all of the authorities that were stripped of their rank and title when the power got shut off." He pointed to Charlie. "Before people like you and me were able to build something for ourselves."

"I didn't build anything for myself," Charlie replied.

"No, and neither did I," the stranger said. "But if it wasn't for our ambition, then a lot of people would have gone hungry. And there would still be a lot more killing than there is going on now. We keep our people in check. We make sure that a skirmish doesn't escalate into a war."

Charlie paused. "And is that what we're doing now?"

"I hope so."

Charlie stood and turned to face the stranger. "Then let me go. The faster we get back to the power plant, the faster we can end all of this nonsense." He spread out his arms. "Isn't that our end game? Isn't that what we've all been fighting to get back?"

The stranger shook his head. "You're not listening, Charlie." He stood. "Do you know half the people that are a part of this community were living in poverty before? Barely had a roof over their head and went to bed hungry every night. The moment the power comes back on, that's exactly where they'll be returned to, hell, half of us will probably go on trial for murder."

"It's not about who was who when, or where, it's about saving more lives before they end," Charlie answered. "Because right now, the people who caused this are mounting an attack to keep us in the dark, and if they succeed this time, I don't know how much longer people will be able to hold it together. Hell, I don't know how much longer I can hold it together!"

The moment the words left his lips, they surprised both the stranger and Charlie. They had been tucked away in the back of his mind for a long time, and finally speaking them aloud relieved a tension in Charlie that he didn't even know existed.

Charlie wandered blindly back to the bench, collapsing, slouching and cradling his head with his hands.

The stranger let Charlie have his moment of peace, and after he rubbed his temples, letting the moment pass, he straightened up in his seat and turned toward the stranger.

"What did you do?" Charlie asked. "Before all of this?"

"Garbage man," the stranger answered, then waved his hand. "My official title was some sanitation engineer bullshit to try and help erase the stigma of telling people that you're a garbage man, but it didn't make you smell better at the end of the day." He laughed. "But it was good work. Steady. Pay was decent. And it gave me time to go back to school." He smiled. "I was going to be a math teacher."

Charlie reciprocated the smile, and for the brief moment Charlie wasn't talking to an enemy. He was speaking to a young man with aspirations to better himself for a future that was just around the corner.

"My family owned the orchard." The words poured out of Charlie unexpectedly. "I know it's not known for apples anymore, but when we did grow them, they were the best in the state." He smiled. "My dad always told me that it took a certain type of man to be a farmer. It was work that not everyone was suited for, and I always thought that was bullshit." He smiled, but it faded. "But then as I grew older, I realized what he meant. Not everyone has the patience, or the tenacity, to help something grow." He turned to the stranger. "Because that's all a farmer really does. We're not the creator of life, we're simply protectors of it, you know? Biology takes care of the hard stuff, and all we have to do is make sure it has a chance to flourish." He nodded. "I haven't seen a lot of that over the past year." He turned to the stranger. "Wouldn't it be nice to get back to the way things were? Before all of this? Before we had territories and clans and war."

The stranger nodded, but then stood and paced anxiously in the garden. The evening light had nearly disappeared now, and the day entered twilight. "I made promises to my people, and I'm sure you've made some of your own." He reached for a flower and plucked it from the bush. He twirled the stem around his fingertips and then turned back toward Charlie. "I want us to put things back together better than they were before."

Charlie shook his head. "We're far past ideals and hopes now." He stood. "There's a fight coming our way." He walked to the stranger, who was still focused on the flower in his hand. "We need to save the lives that we can. And if you're the man I think you are, then that's all that will matter to you and the rest of your people. If people really want things to change, then they will change them once this is over."

"You can lead a horse to water, but you can't make him drink." The stranger tossed the flower back into the bushes. He wiped his face and stepped away, muttering something to himself that Charlie couldn't hear.

"We're running out of time," Charlie said, hoping to coax the stranger toward a decision. "This is a window that's not going to open again for a long time. Maybe never. Generations would go through nothing but war. That's not a life I want for my people, and I know that it's not a life you want for yours. So let's stop it."

The stranger turned away and then finally nodded, spinning around in the same motion. "If I send you out of here alive, and with those computer boards, I want something in return."

"Name it," Charlie answered.

"I want a seat at the table," Stranger replied. "I want to have a say in the decisions that will affect my people moving forward." He raised his finger. "And, to make sure you hold up your end of the bargain, should you agree, I'll be keeping half of the computer chips with me. It gives me peace of mind, and it still gives your people something to work on while they consider my proposal."

With time running short and the possibility of a better proposition unlikely, Charlie knew that he had no other choice but to agree. But how Dixon reacted upon their return to Mayfield was a completely different story.

41

*C*harlie didn't look back once they were out of the reach of the blue clan's grasp, but he did hasten his pace. Charlie didn't think that Dixon, or what remained of the government and military, would take kindly to blackmail, but he wasn't sure how extreme their countermeasures would be. And truth be told, Charlie admired the stranger's boldness and tenacity.

It was a smart play, because both knew there wasn't another way for both of them to get what they wanted. Now it was just a matter of getting Dixon on board.

Charlie and his crew returned to The Orchard by nightfall. It was late, with most of the residents already asleep in their beds, save for the guards on duty and patrolling the area.

Not wanting to waste any more time, Charlie commandeered another one of their Humvees, and the crew piled inside. "Let's move."

Once again powered by diesel and steel, Charlie and the crew arrived at Mayfield quickly, once again crossing through the tight security, meeting Dixon outside of his office.

And it could have been the look on Charlie's face, or the fact that he got out of the Humvee so quickly, but something told Dixon that the plan had been altered.

"We need to talk," Charlie said.

Dixon looked to the back of the Humvee, where the box of the remaining components were being handed off to his engineers and rushed over to the power plant with an armed escort. He then led Charlie inside, Charlie waving for his team to stay put.

Once they were alone, Charlie walked Dixon through the events. The ambush, the capture, and his talk with the leader of the blue clan. To his credit, Dixon listened patiently and intently, and it wasn't until Charlie finished that he finally spoke.

"So he's holding the rest of the components for ransom until he gets," Dixon stopped himself, looking at Charlie. "A seat at the table?"

"He wants to act as the voice of his people," Charlie answered. "They want to make peace."

Dixon scoffed. "We were never at war with them!" He stood and paced anxiously. "They're citizens of this country, the same country that the terrorists invaded and attacked and brought to its knees last year." He spun around. "They chose to be outcasts. They chose to organize."

"And what else did you expect them to do?" Charlie asked. "You may not remember those first few months very well, but I do." He walked closer to Dixon. "No food. Water was in short supply, at least clean water. The terrorists were still running around, blowing people to bits, shooting anything that moved. People were scrambling and holding onto any type of order that they could get their hands on." He shook his head.

"So you would have preferred me to give what spare rations I had to someone else instead of you and your people?" Dixon asked, tossing the question like an accusation.

"No!" Charlie shouted, his patience running out. "But don't you think it's time that we make things right again? If there is a chance for peace, if there is a chance for redemption, then shouldn't we take it?"

"What do you think I'm trying to do, Charlie?" Dixon asked. "We have our chance, it's in the form of turning that power plant back on, and right now my engineers only have half the computer boards they need!" He kicked the side of his desk.

But while Dixon ranted, Charlie remembered the hundreds of faces that he passed within the clan territory. Not the soldiers, or the armed guards, but the people who lived and worked, just trying to survive. He knew nothing of their background, of their history, but the one thing he understood better than Dixon was the means of survival and the hard choices that must be made when your back is up against the wall.

"So you want to go to war with these people?" Charlie asked. "Against the people that you're supposed to protect?"

"I'm supposed to protect the nation," Dixon answered, spinning around, angry and defensive. "I have a duty to ensure its survival, and those people are preventing me from accomplishing my mission." He offered a grave shake of the head. "They're currently committing treason."

"They're trying to survive. If you can't see that, then you're no better than the people who did all of this to us." Charlie turned for the door.

"So what happens when I send a platoon to retrieve the rest of the computer parts?" Dixon asked. "They'll blow them up? Destroy everyone's chance to return to normalcy?"

Charlie turned back to Dixon, his expression soft. "You don't have to create another enemy to defeat." Short of dropping to his knees and pleading with Dixon, he didn't know how to make the commander see what he saw, and deep down, what he always knew to be true. "You march there with guns, and the only thing you'll come back with is more blood on your hands."

Charlie studied Dixon's expression, searching for any sign that the commander would listen to reason and compromise, but there was no such revelation, so he left.

Knowing the outcome before Dixon even sent his men to the clan, Charlie felt his heart sink into his stomach. He walked back out to the Humvee and climbed inside without a word to his crew, who followed suit when he slammed the door shut.

No questions were asked, and the ride back to The Orchard was one of silence and anxiousness. And while he knew that his crew wanted answers, Charlie offered them none as he made his way toward the trailer, kicking off his boots outside and stepping rather loudly, finding Liz sitting on the bed, tossing him an angry glare as she watched Adelyn sleep.

Charlie held up his hands, a gesture of apology for the hasty intrusion, then slowly crept toward the back bedroom and lay on the opposite side of Adelyn and across from Liz, who studied him for a minute before she finally spoke, their conversation an exchange of whispers.

"What happened?" Liz asked.

"We were captured by the blue clan," Charlie answered. "Everyone is okay." He gently ran his fingers through Adelyn's hair, the little girl undisturbed by Charlie's touch. "The clan took half of the computer chips."

"What? Why?" Liz asked.

"They're holding them hostage until they're able to speak with Dixon and the rest of the people in charge before the lights come back on." Charlie shook his head. "Dixon wasn't receptive to that idea."

"Is he going to retaliate?" Liz asked.

Charlie shrugged. There was a piece of him that clung to the hope that Dixon would have an epiphany before he pulled the trigger on something that couldn't be undone.

Liz reached over Adelyn and grabbed hold of his forearm, giving him a gentle squeeze. "What happens now?"

Charlie shook his head. "We have to wait."

The pair lowered their gazes to Adelyn, who remained undisturbed by their worries, by the world around her, and the general fear that plagued them on a daily basis. Besides Liz, the little girl had been the one shining beacon of light in a world gone dark.

Everything good that remained to Charlie was here with him now.

A knock at the door stirred Adelyn awake, and Charlie quickly answered it before there was another. But of all the people he expected to find him at this hour, it ended up being the person he least expected.

"Mom?" Charlie asked.

Martha Decker stood in an old shirt and jeans, wearing her work boots, her hair pulled back tight in a bun, nearly all of the gray turned to white. She had become frail, thin, and sickly-looking over the past year. The weight she'd shed hadn't been healthy.

The only attribute that remained to Martha was the piercing glare, which froze Charlie in his doorway.

"What's wrong?" Charlie stepped out of the trailer, closing the door behind him. She always got irked whenever Adelyn was around them. Despite her acceptance of Liz, she had never truly taken to Adelyn. Charlie never could figure out why.

And almost instinctively, Martha flicked her eyes toward the back of the trailer where Charlie had left Adelyn and Liz. She watched them for a moment, then glanced back to Charlie.

"Come with me," Martha said, and then left before Charlie had a chance to question why or where.

Charlie followed his mother through the maze of trailers and mobile homes, their course north toward the woods. He caught up to her, walking on her left, but she paid him no attention.

"What's going on?" Charlie asked. "Was there a breach on the perimeter? One of the guards see something?" He fired his questions at her, but she remained aloof and quiet. "Mom, you need to talk to me. You need to—"

Martha stopped, forcing Charlie to stumble forward a few steps before he caught his footing, and he realized they were both away from the bulk of the trailers. He turned around and saw that she'd led him to the barn.

"I don't understand—"

"Nick came to see me," she said.

And then Charlie understood. He knew that Nick had become a sort of surrogate son to her. The pair worked well in their new relationship. Nick needed a mother who could give affection, and Martha needed a son who was a blank slate, someone that she could remold into something other than the son that she was stuck with. The son who failed to live up to all the expectations that she had suddenly set within her mind.

"What are you going to do?" Martha asked.

"I'm going to stay out of it." Charlie tried to walk past her, but she snatched his arm, pulling him back into place, though the motion was more of his acquiescence to his mother's request.

"Did Dixon tell you what he was going to do?" Martha asked.

"In so many ways," Charlie answered.

"Then you need to stand with him. You need to keep the alliance with him strong. It's the reason we've lasted this long."

"The reason we've lasted this long, Mother, is because of everything that I've done," Charlie said, pointing to himself. "But you would have known that if you'd just pulled your head out of your ass long enough to take a look around you!"

Martha slapped Charlie, the strike quick and harsh. A flash of red appeared on Charlie's cheek, and the sting lingered as his mother stood her ground.

"And what do you want, Charlie Decker?" Martha asked, mocking him. "A parade? A monument erected for all of your sacrifices? You didn't wade through the shit of the past year by yourself."

Charlie's anger subsided, then transformed to despair as the sting on his cheek faded. He wanted nothing more than the mother he used to know. The woman who raised him, and who was kind and always had an ear to listen and a gentle hand to soothe.

"Why are you like this?" Charlie asked. "I know Dad died, but what happened?" He shook his head, unable to find the answer to that question for the past year. "Were you always like this before and I just never saw it? Why?" He stepped closer, tears in his eyes now. "Why?"

Martha stood her ground, and for the briefest moment, Charlie saw his mother return. The glimpse was brief, but real.

"Something broke, Charlie," Martha answered, her voice frail. She gently shook her head and lowered her eyes to the ground as if she could find the answers written in the dirt. "I don't know what happened, but it just disappeared… That little piece of me that was good and kept everything together." She looked to Charlie, her eyebrows pinched together, and looked as though she was lost. "I can't remember where it went, or what I did with it. It's just gone. It was like that EMP that stole our power and changed everything. You couldn't hear it, you couldn't see it, no smell or sound. It was just there, and then it was gone." She nodded. "That's what it was like for me."

And then, just as mysteriously as the kindness returned to his mother's face, it vanished, replaced by the cold exterior of the woman who'd embodied Martha Decker for the past year.

"Side with Dixon," Martha said.

Charlie shook his head. "I'm not going to get us caught up in a conflict with people who don't want to fight us in the first place."

"How many blue clan members have you killed? How many of them have killed our people?" Martha snarled. "Our alliance with Dixon is the reason we've lasted this long, and if we want to continue to ensure our survival, then it's a relationship we'll continue to need. What about the terrorists? What about the attack that has been planned? If it's the numbers you're concerned about, then we don't have enough. We need Dixon's men, and we won't get them if you don't stand with him now."

Charlie only shook his head. "They're not the enemy, Mom." He stepped away, pacing around her and looking out to the fields of trailers and RVs parked along their property. He saw what remained of their charred fields and the new growth that had attempted to push through the layers of death. "We're not meant to kill one another." He turned back toward his mother. "That's my final decision."

When he turned to leave, Martha stood her ground. "Whatever happens to this place and the people in it will be on your hands, Charlie. And if you're so willing to throw everything we've built away, then maybe it shouldn't be your decision!"

But Charlie didn't engage. He let his mother scream herself out, ignoring the painful cries and hurtful words. It didn't matter what she said anymore. She was never going to come back.

_I_t was a restless sleep, but when dawn broke, Charlie was glad for the few hours of rest. And the morning was made brighter by Adelyn's smiling face, who greeted him when he woke.

"Charlie!" Adelyn spread her little arms wide and then clapped Charlie's cheeks, giggling from the slapping sound between her palms and Charlie's skin.

Charlie smiled and puffed out his cheeks, Adelyn giggling again as she slapped the bulges of air, which rushed from Charlie's lips and blasted Adelyn's hair as she rolled back on the bed and to her side. Charlie tickled her, and she flopped around on the sheets, her laughter intensifying along with her little squirming body.

Liz appeared in the narrow doorway between the bedroom and the front of the trailer, smiling at the pair. "Hey, breakfast is ready."

Charlie finally ended his tickle assault, then looked at Adelyn. "You hungry?"

"Yes," Adelyn answered.

The pair rolled out of bed, and Charlie scooped Adelyn off the floor, carrying her to the little cubby where the trio ate their breakfasts together whenever they had the opportunity, which was rare. Usually, Charlie was up before either of them. Whenever they had a chance to enjoy a meal together, Charlie always took advantage of it.

Breakfast consisted of the unimportant conversations, laughter, and more than a few silly questions from Adelyn, who was going through a very curious phase of her toddler years.

"What happens if the chickens don't want to give us eggs?" Adelyn asked. "Can we get eggs from other animals? Like dogs? Or cats?"

"No," Liz answered. "Because dogs and cats are mammals, and mammals don't lay eggs."

"Did I come from an egg?" Adelyn asked.

"No," Liz replied, taking a sip of coffee. "You came from a person."

"Did I come from you?" Adelyn asked.

Both Charlie and Liz stopped. She hadn't asked about her mother since she passed. The pair had discussed how they would handle it when the inevitable happened, but now that it was staring them straight in the eyes, Charlie found himself unprepared.

"No," Liz answered. "You came from another woman." She looked to Charlie, then back to Adelyn, the little girl more focused on her eggs than either of them. "Do you remember your mother?"

Adelyn frowned. "A little."

"She loved you very much," Charlie replied.

"Why did she leave?" Adelyn asked, looking up from her eggs and right at Charlie, batting those long eyelashes that framed a pair of inquisitive hazel eyes.

"She didn't leave," Charlie answered. "She died. Do you know what that means?"

Adelyn stared at Charlie for a while, then nodded. "It means I don't get to see her again."

Charlie grabbed hold of the little girl's hand, his grip firm but loving. "You won't understand this now, but you'll see her when you're older." Charlie thought of his own father, all of his mannerisms and quirks, and how he found himself falling into the same habits. He saw more of his father in him in the past year than he had in his entire life. "You'll see her in all of the things that you do when you grow up. And because of that, she'll always be with you. Just like Liz and I will."

Adelyn looked between her adopted parents and then smiled. "Promise?"

Liz sniffled and then kissed the top of Adelyn's head. "Promise."

Charlie kissed Adelyn's hand, and the beautiful morning moment was interrupted by a hurried knock on the trailer door.

"Charlie!"

Charlie moved quickly, heading toward the trailer door and grabbing his rifle along the way. When he opened the door, he found Shelly and Jason, both of them already armed.

"Blue clan's heading our way," Shelly said.

Charlie turned back toward Liz and Adelyn and then reached for the bulletproof vest in the closet. He slid his arms through the holes, the front decorated with the scars of battle, and then kissed Liz and Adelyn on his way out.

The moment he stepped outside and put his boots on, the horns of war blared, signaling an incoming force from their guards on the perimeter. Charlie hadn't expected this, and for the first time in a long time, he was surprised.

After the talk he had with the blue clan's leader, he never would have thought he would charge into the attack, but the fact that the clan was on their way meant that they had either already run into Dixon's men and won, or Dixon had chosen not to advance. At least not yet.

Evacuation procedures were already in effect as Charlie

made his way through the retreating masses pouring between the crammed rows of trailers and RVs, all of them with their go bags in hand.

"Keep moving to the tree line!" The sentries in charge of the evacuation shouted above the crowds, and while there was a general sense of panic, there were no stampedes, no disorder. They had all prepared for this. It was a worst-case scenario, one Charlie hoped that they would be able to avoid, but it was also one that they were prepared to face.

Charlie made a beeline toward Doc's house, the military post where everyone who had been trained with a firearm should be headed. It had been over a month since they'd run a drill, but he hoped that everyone would still follow orders. And he was pleasantly surprised when he arrived to see the line of men and women filing into Doc's house to grab their weapons.

Charlie bypassed the line of men, marching inside and finding Doc helping with the logistics of arming their militia. "Do we have a head count?"

Doc passed off a fully-loaded magazine of ammunition to the next fighter in line, and then looked back to Charlie as he passed. "Seventy-three."

Charlie nodded. The two hundred fighters in their militia, plus the fifty full-time soldiers and guards that they had on duty, gave them a bulky force, but Charlie knew that the blue clan had double the numbers, though he wasn't sure of their training or the quality of their weapons.

Barriers were already set up on the road, sandbags loaded up, and guns aimed at the forest to their south in the direction of the enemy.

Charlie headed toward the main post at the front line, which stretched the entire length of their property all the way down to the Bigelows' farm.

The sentry who reported the activity was already on scene.

"What'd you find, Kip?" Charlie asked.

Kip wiped the sweat from his brow, still winded from the run from his post. "I counted at least three hundred before I left. But they were still coming." Kip shook his head. "I couldn't see the end of their line of men."

"All of them armed?" Charlie asked.

Kip nodded. "Shotguns, rifles, pistols. I counted a few automatic weapons and assault rifles, but most of the weaponry looked old. I didn't see any heavy artillery. They were moving quickly though."

Charlie nodded, then clapped Kip on the shoulder. "Head to your post."

"Yes, sir."

After Kip darted off, Charlie lingered at the main post, Nick and Lee joining himself and the twins, while the rest of their fighters filed into place. Everyone knew their job. Everyone understood their role. Now it was only a matter of execution.

Nick handed Charlie a pair of binoculars, and Charlie peered through the lenses

"I knew all of that talk about cooperation was bullshit," Nick said, then planted his elbows on the sandbags and dug in. "They made the wrong move."

Charlie lowered his binoculars, Nick's words stirring something in the back of his head. It *was* the wrong move. After everything that he and the stranger had spoken of, the need for peace, the desire for something better for his people.

War wasn't the smart choice, especially not if Dixon had attacked, which from Kip's report sounded unlikely. The stranger was doing the exact opposite of what he should do. It didn't make any sense.

"Shelly, Jason, send word down the line that no one fires unless fired upon," Charlie said.

The order was met with questionable expressions, and Charlie was forced to repeat himself before the twins did as they were told. The orders were echoed down the line, and while the fighters at their post might not be sure of his tactic, Charlie knew that they would be followed. Charlie's word was law.

A breeze brought with it the steady thump of boots against the earth, and Charlie dropped to a knee, rifle raised, just in case his hunch was wrong. He peered through the rifle's scope, the vision even better than what the binoculars provided.

Charlie lingered between a set of conifers, the crosshairs lined up perfectly perpendicular as he waited for the first figure to appear within the forest, and when they did, Charlie was surprised to find that they stopped.

"I've got a visual," Shelly said. "Enemy remains behind the trees."

Charlie pivoted the sight of the scope left, finding the rest of the fighters frozen in place. He peeled his eye away from the scope and frowned at the sight.

"What the hell are they waiting for?" Nick asked.

But while Nick was confused, that tiny spark of hope ignited in Charlie's chest, and he stood from the barrier, both Jason and Shelly looking up at him with concern. "They're not here to fight us."

"You sure about that, boss?" Shelly asked. "Because from the looks of it, they look like they've come for a fight."

"They have," Charlie answered. "But it's not with us."

A lone man broke through the trees, a white flag in his hand. Charlie raised his rifle, peering through the scope to find the stranger separating himself from his people, and almost immediately Charlie leapt over the wall of sand, Shelly and Jason the next to follow, with Nick and Lee bringing up the rear.

Charlie turned back to the other lieutenants within

eyesight and held up his hands. "Keep everyone on the line! And let's keep our fingers off the triggers!"

The stranger tossed the flag aside once Charlie was closer, and he turned around to the hundreds of men in the woods behind him.

"Felt like taking a walk?" Charlie asked.

The stranger nodded. "I needed to stretch my legs." He extended his hand, and he and Charlie shook, and then another man emerged from the woods, this one carrying a box.

Charlie raised his eyebrows. "I wasn't sure if you'd listen."

"I had more than just your voice advising me," the stranger replied, taking the box from the man who brought it out, and that serious expression returned to his face as he looked at Charlie. "We need a place where we can talk."

Charlie glanced to the armed men behind the stranger. "And what do we do with them?"

The stranger stepped closer toward Charlie and then clapped his free hand on Charlie's shoulder. "After you hear what I have to say, you're probably going to want them to stay put."

* * *

THE BOX of computer components was open in the center of the table. They were all accounted for, but now they were the least of Charlie's concerns. He sat at the end of the table, Shelly and Jason to his left, Nick and Lee to his right.

The stranger was at the end of the table, alone, void of advisers, and standing with both palms flat against the table's surface.

Charlie bounced his leg, a nervous tic that hadn't resurfaced since before the EMP. He finally peeled his eyes away from the box, that fucking box, the one box that was supposed to solve all of their problems, but instead only brought them more issues.

"How many?" Charlie asked.

The stranger shook his head. "Unknown. Should be here by this afternoon."

"Your scouts know where they're going, but they have no idea how many are en-route?" Shelly asked, her tone laced with skepticism. "Yeah, I don't buy that shit."

"You don't have to buy it, sweetheart," the stranger said. "It's already been paid for. All we have to worry about now is making sure that they don't reach Mayfield."

"Why wouldn't they just go to Mayfield directly?" Nick asked. "Hell, that's what I'd do. And I'm not even that smart."

"No argument there," Jason replied.

"I second that motion," Lee said.

"It's a diversion," Charlie said, furrowing his brow as he stared at the box and the table. "They know about our alliance with Mayfield and the military, and if they attack a citizen-heavy area, they think Dixon will send military forces to help, making it easier for them to overtake the plant." He nodded, running through the different scenarios in his mind. He looked up at the stranger. "You're confident that your territory is out of their path?"

"The scouts that confirmed the movement is far to our west," the stranger answered. "The terrorists aren't going to try and wade through our forces and waste resources. They have to know that Dixon is packing some heat, and they're going to want to train everything they've got on that town and the power plant. This is their last stand."

Charlie stood. "Then all we have to do is hold them." He glanced down at Shelly and Jason. "Have the post commanders coordinate with one another, and have the blue clan's men help them reinforce the line."

Shelly raised her eyebrows. "Charlie, blue clan has killed a lot of our people."

"And you've killed a lot of ours," the stranger answered.

"You tell everyone that the first person to throw even a nasty word to a blue clan member that they'll have to report to me," Charlie said. "Whatever evil we've all done to one another has to be put aside. It's the only way that we're going to have a chance at anything other than the shit we've waded through for the past year." He gestured to the box of components. "Let's get that to Mayfield." He looked at the stranger. "You're coming with me."

The stranger smiled. "I can't wait to see the look on Dixon's face when I walk through that door."

"That makes two of us," Charlie said.

He left instructions with the crew, leaving them in charge, with Shelly as his right hand. Lee led the stranger to instruct his fighters to integrate with The Orchard's forces. But while the stranger spoke to his people, Charlie headed for the tree line to make sure the evacuations guard were still on point. And after that, he found Liz and Adelyn.

"What's going on out there?" Liz asked, holding Adelyn's hand.

Charlie took note of the people that surrounded them, ears in the woods eager to hear anything from the front lines. He pulled Liz out of earshot to prevent any further panic or questions from arising. "The blue clan brought the components along with some intel."

"What?" Liz asked.

"The terrorists are on their way," Charlie answered. "They're going to hit us first and try to draw soldiers away from Mayfield."

The corner of Liz's mouth twitched, but it was born from frustration and anger. She shook her head, then after she regained her composure, she looked down to Adelyn and scooped her off the ground. "What are you going to do?"

"I'm heading to Mayfield now with the components," Charlie answered.

"And the clan?" Liz asked.

"They're joining us."

Liz paused, hesitating and voicing the one concern of doubt that lingered in the back of Charlie's mind. "And you don't think this is a ploy? We know they've had more fighters than us for a while."

Charlie nodded. "It's not." He kissed her and then kissed Adelyn. "Stay safe."

"You too."

Charlie turned, leaving the pair of girls he loved more than anything in this world, and he wasn't going to come back from Mayfield without more fighters from Dixon. They needed to hold the line. One way or another, the old world ended today, and the new world would be born tomorrow.

he conversation was kept to a minimum between Charlie and the stranger on the way to Mayfield, the box of parts between them. And when Charlie pulled up to the first security gate, he caught more than a few jarring glares from the guards on duty. But when he flashed them the computer components, they were granted immediate entrance.

Dixon was out to meet him once more, but the security that surrounded the commander was much more intense, and this time the guards trained their weapons on not just the stranger, but Charlie as well.

"Did you two have a falling out?" the stranger asked, the pair still inside the Humvee.

"More of a disagreement," Charlie answered, and then stepped out of the vehicle, bringing the box of computer chips with him. He walked over to Dixon as the rifles trained on him followed him the whole way over. "We didn't come here to pick a fight."

"No?" Dixon looked to the blue patch on the stranger's shoulder. "Then why did you bring him?"

"Because he brought me these." Charlie shoved the box

into Dixon's chest, and the grizzly commander opened the top portion of the box and peered inside. He stared at the contents for a moment, and then lifted his eyes. "What happened?"

"The enemy of my enemy is my friend," the stranger answered, maintaining the swagger that he'd displayed ever since the pair had met in the blue clan territory, and spread his arms wide. "It's nice to finally meet you, Commander Dixon."

Dixon handed the box off to one of the men by his side. "Get these to the engineers. And tell them I want them to speed up the installation process. Round the clock shifts." The soldier sprinted off, and Dixon pointed at the pair of men in front of him. "Let's go inside."

The trio headed to Dixon's office, and the stranger recited everything that he'd already told Charlie. Dixon remained quiet, soaking in everything the blue clan leader was telling him, and it wasn't until they were finished that he finally stood from his chair and walked around the desk.

It was just the three of them in the room, and the more the silence lingered, the less sure Charlie was of how the commander was going to react.

"They're on their way," Charlie said, watching Dixon take a seat on his desk, arms crossed and concentrating on a space on the floor.

Dixon remained silent, nodding to himself, and then finally raised his eyes from the spot on the concrete and looked to the blue clan leader. "You brought the computer components back because you were hoping to buy goodwill, but they were never yours to begin with."

"Dixon—"

"And if you and the rest of your military brothers had done their job, then we wouldn't even be here in the first place," the stranger said, stepping closer toward Dixon. "So I think we're way past pointing fingers. You need help. We need help. Let's help each other."

Dixon exhaled, nostrils flaring as he cleared his throat, then pushed himself off the desk. He kept his arms crossed. "You're sure that the terrorists will divert the majority of their forces toward The Orchard?"

"Enough to make you want to come and help us," Charlie answered.

"I can't give you any soldiers." Dixon stepped around his desk and opened one of the drawers. "But I will give you one of our fail-safe weapons."

"Fail safe?" Charlie asked.

"Six months ago, when the brass in Washington was able to establish better communications, they sent out packages to every major military unit across the states. It was listed as priority, and I didn't even know what the package was until it arrived." Dixon retrieved a small box from the drawer, which required another key to open it. "But because the second base to our south was wiped out, we received their package as well."

The hinges of the metal box groaned as Dixon opened it, and he plucked another key from inside. He pinched it between his fingers, staring at it with an almost longing expression, then headed toward the door. "Follow me."

Charlie and the stranger were led out of the office toward the back side of the hospital. Images of his father flashed in his mind when Dixon placed his hand on the handle and opened the door, but the anxiety that plagued him ended when he saw the innards of the hospital.

The halls had been cleaned out, the scent of bleach still clinging to the air, and Charlie followed Dixon down the dimly lit halls of the hospital, periodically stealing glances at the floor where so many corpses had laid after the terrorists had marched through and decimated everything in their path.

The trio traveled deep into the hospital, and Dixon finally stopped outside of a door that was guarded by two soldiers and had two sets of locks on it.

Dixon removed his key, and one of the soldiers on duty removed one as well. The pair inserted their respective keys into the lock, and then turned it, granting Charlie, Dixon, and the stranger entrance.

It was dark inside, the room void of any windows, and it wasn't until Dixon turned on a battery-powered lantern that Charlie saw the crates stacked around the room from floor to ceiling, leaving only a small space on the floor for them to step inside.

"What's inside?" Stranger asked, pressing his hand against the wooden crates, unable to decipher the meaning of the military-bequeathed moniker's seven-digit number plastered on the side.

"Something to give you an edge," Dixon answered. "It's my compromise for keeping my men here."

Charlie turned, forgetting the boxes that surrounded him, and shook his head. "We have over one thousand civilians at the orchard. If we break, then they won't be spared."

Dixon raised his eyebrows. "Then don't break." He turned toward the door, leaving Charlie and the stranger, but then stopped before he left and spun back around. "I appreciate you bringing the computer components back. But even after this is all done, I'm not sure you'll get what you want from my superiors."

Stranger nodded. "I'm sure a good recommendation from you wouldn't hurt." He cracked a smile, and even Dixon couldn't suppress reciprocating the charm.

"I'll have some of my men help you load the Humvee," Dixon said. "Good luck."

Dixon disappeared down the hall, the faint clack of his boots disappearing until they could no longer be heard at all.

Before the other soldiers came to help, Charlie pulled

down one of the boxes, which was heavier than he expected, and set it on the floor. He reached for a crowbar nearby and cracked open the lid. The stranger came over to look, and the pair both raised their eyebrows, eliciting a low whistle as Charlie hovered the lantern inside the box.

"That'll definitely help us out," the stranger said.

Charlie reached inside, grabbing hold of the rocket launcher that was broken into two pieces, while the stranger carefully picked up one of the explosives that rested inside.

With the help of Dixon's men, the Humvee was loaded up quickly, and they rolled out of Mayfield with a dozen rocket launchers and enough ammunition for them to make a very sizable dent in whatever forces the terrorists were able to throw their way.

But while the ride to Mayfield was quiet, Charlie couldn't quiet the questions running through his head on the way back to The Orchard.

"Why did you do it?" Charlie asked. "You had all of the cards. You could have done whatever you wanted so long as you had those computer components."

The stranger nodded, chewing the end of his nail. "Dixon would have eventually gotten them anyway." He turned to Charlie. "At least this way I have some goodwill with him."

"It's not going to get you as far as you think it will," Charlie said. "Dixon's a soldier. He takes orders and gives them, but he doesn't give himself a lot of time for free thoughts. It's a philosophy that's served him well over his lifetime, and it's not something he's apt to change any time soon."

"Then I suppose that's when these rocket launchers come in handy," the stranger said, gesturing back toward the crates, a smile spread wide across his face.

When they returned to The Orchard, Charlie was glad to see that his men and the blue clan had at the very least toler-ated one another, and the sight of so many men along the front lines helped Charlie believe that whatever evil was heading their way, they'd be able to handle.

Parked at Doc's, Charlie's crew greeted them upon their arrival, and without a word, Charlie opened the back of the Humvee and removed one of the rocket launchers, handing it over to Jason, whose eyes lit up like a kid on Christmas.

Shelly looked to Charlie, then to the stranger. "You should come over more often. Maybe we'd be able to get more cool shit like this."

"I want them stationed at every main guard post," Charlie said. "And let's make sure everyone understands how to use them before we load them, okay?"

The orders were followed, and Charlie and the stranger turned toward the line of men that stretched behind the makeshift barricade. The pair made it two steps before a noise caught Charlie's attention, heightening everyone's senses and sending a buzz of electricity through the entire front line.

Charlie peered into the woods, narrowing his eyes as the drums of war drew closer. "We shoot to kill! You find a target, and you bring it down!" He marched down the line, barking his orders like a general. "We hold this line!"

The stranger barked similar orders, and Charlie reached for a rifle when a harrowing whistling rocketed through the air. Charlie glanced toward the clear afternoon sky, unable to locate the object from the brightness of the sun. "Take cover!"

Charlie ducked near the front line, the surrounding fighters with their arms over their heads, and then the battle started with the shaking of the earth and the rain of soil and dirt.

$\mathcal{T}$he harsh ringing lingered in Charlie's ears, and he lifted his head once the vibrations stopped. He peered over the sandbags and scrambled for his rifle which he'd dropped into the dirt, his fingers fumbling blindly over the soil, searching for the familiar touch of metal and composite.

More explosions rocked the line of soldiers hunkered down on their side of the road, though Charlie couldn't hear the whistling that preceded the explosions.

Charlie planted his elbows on the sandbags, firing into the tree line, the scope thrusting him deep into the woods, and even with the cacophony of gunfire raining down upon him, he still managed to drop two enemy soldiers before ducking back below to check on the stranger.

"You need to get toward the east end of the line!" Charlie shouted. "That's where the bulk of your men are located. Hold the line, and save the launchers as a means of last resort."

The stranger nodded, then sprinted away. Meanwhile, Charlie took a moment to examine the surroundings. The first blast that landed near him breached a hole in the wall to his left, and body parts were scattered about the ground.

He stared at the severed limbs for a moment, the blood still pouring from the veins, the flesh and muscle and exposed bone all dirtied from flopping on the ground. Charlie couldn't pull his eyes away from the gore, and it wasn't until a hand slapped onto his shoulder that he finally turned away from the sight and stared into Shelly's eyes.

"You all right?" she screamed above the gunfire and the war raging around them, her face already covered with sweat, blood, and dirt, but the blood wasn't her own.

Charlie nodded. "Make sure the pressure points hold, and keep passing out those launchers!" He returned to the open space on the sandbag wall and planted his elbows, ready to take more of the bastards down.

The explosions had stopped, the majority of the fighting now concentrated to the exchange of gunfire back and forth between their forces and the terrorists.

A few more explosions rocked the asphalt and their line, but whatever devices they were using to launch the material seemed to have tapped out at a certain range, which meant so long as they held them to the tree line, they couldn't fling them deeper onto the orchard.

Empty shell casings littered the ground around Charlie's feet, picking off terrorist after terrorist who ventured too far to the front of the trees. After a dozen kills, he was forced to reload, and while he ducked down behind the protection of the sand-bags, another explosion rocked the opposite side of the wall and Charlie was bucked forward, landing harshly on the dirt.

His body ached, and his vision danced between darkness and light. He wallowed on the ground, disoriented from the blast. He struggled to get to his feet, falling back to his stomach twice before he managed to get to all fours.

More screams and more gunshots thundered in the

distance, but they all sounded so far away. Charlie finally managed to get his bearings and turned toward the front line, finding a crater where he had just previously been.

But there was more screaming now, the ringing in his ears subsided, and the harrowing cries for help grew worse. Charlie finally forced himself to his feet and scoured the ground for his weapon. He was naked without it, and he was weaker.

A rifle lay in the dirt. It wasn't his, but it would do the job. He snatched it off the ground, the particles of dirt sticking to his gloves, the layer of grit between himself and the weapon causing trouble for his grip.

Charlie wiped the dirt on his pants, and then wobbled to stay on both feet as he headed back toward the line, but before he reached his point of defense, a man sprinted through the column of smoke and darted past Charlie.

It was one of their men.

Not wanting the rest of the forces to break, Charlie sprinted forward into the chaos, coughing and hacking through the smoke, and blinking in astonishment when he finally broke through.

The terrorists had planted themselves in the ditch on the opposite side of the road, all the way down the entire line of defense, with more coming out the woods. Hundreds of them were crawling forward, trying to infiltrate his home, trying to destroy everything they had built.

One of the rocket launchers lay across the chest of a dead man, and Charlie dropped the rifle. He picked up the piece of heavy artillery. He made sure it was loaded, and then lined up the sight to the targets ahead.

The crosshairs lined up with a pair of faces, and Charlie squeezed the trigger. Smoke jettisoned from the end of the carrier, and the opposite side of the road exploded into a ball of fire and smoke. Charlie dropped the heavy piece of artillery and then charged forward, waving the rocket launcher as he caught the attention of the remaining fighters.

"Hold the line!"

Faces smeared with soot and sweat and blood turned toward him. Expressions of fear and uncertainty, of confusion and desperation.

"For the orchard! For our families! For our future!"

A roar of cheers erupted down the line, and the fighters cowering behind the lines rose from the depths of their fear and pushed forward, joining Charlie in his charge to engage the enemy head on. Charlie scooped the rifle back off the ground, keeping his aim as steady as he could muster on the run, and killed two men in the ditch before he felt a bullet strike his chest.

The hammer-like force of the contact slowed him, but Charlie didn't stop. He refused to slow, refused to be run out of his own home by people who no longer appreciated who he was. He needed to show them just how strong he could be. He needed to show them what he could do.

The stock of the rifle thumped against his chest, and Charlie pivoted his aim between the enemy in front of him. He didn't look left or right to the men who joined him, but he heard the explosions and witnessed the balls of fire rising from the rockets being launched into the enemy.

And the more they pressed the hostiles, the faster they retreated into the woods. Charlie led the assault, marching over the asphalt, closing in on the enemy until they were close enough for hand to hand combat.

One of the hostiles, who was still on the ground, lifted their weapon to shoot, but Charlie kicked the tip of the rifle away with his boot, sending it flying from the enemy's hands. He planted a hunk of lead in the terrorist's skull.

Charlie stole quick glances to his left and to his right, the wave of his assault cramming the enemy back into the depths of the forest. But they were retreating too quickly, running away faster than Charlie would have expected, even for their purpose of acting as a distraction.

After all, the stranger's intel told them that they were trying to draw troops away from Mayfield, and the battle hadn't even been going on long enough to call for aid.

Had they just overwhelmed them? Had they not expected this level of fight or resistance from a bunch of farmers? Charlie continued to push the enemy back into the woods, firing round after round, dropping body after body.

But Charlie slowed when he stepped into the woods, watching as the enemy cowered away into the thick of the forest brush. Something wasn't right. They were putting too much distance between themselves and the area.

"They're running from something," Charlie said, whispering to himself, the gunshots roaring around him, the screams of fear and anger and victory and death erupting everywhere. But something buzzed in the distance, catching Charlie's ear as he turned toward the west.

It was faint at first, and undecipherable, yet familiar. Charlie stepped toward the sound, and it grew louder on the horizon. Charlie shook his head. "That's not possible."

The branches of the trees blocked the view of the sky, and Charlie sprinted out of the woods, heading toward the open space of the street. The shade from the trees disappeared and the heat of the day beat down on him. Charlie lowered the rifle in his hands, staring up into the sky, shocked by the sight soaring above him.

"No," Charlie said.

They were still nothing more than dots on the sky, but Charlie recognized the planes heading their way. They were flying low, and the only thing that Charlie could think of were the schematics for the bombs that they found in that house.

Charlie turned, waving his hands as he headed for cover. "Run! Get to cover!" He turned back around, firing into the sky, a desperate attempt at trying to bring the enemy down. But his shots missed wide left and right, and the old prop planes retaliated with machine gun fire, the bullets raining down from the sky like hellfire.

All three planes zoomed past, and Charlie remained unscathed, but he turned to watch them fly overhead as they headed toward the bulk of his and and the blue clan's forces.

"NO!" Charlie screamed, his face reddening, as he chased after the planes, firing into their backside, but they were too far.

There was no cover on the road, and Charlie watched in horror as man after man was torn apart by the bombs dropped from the planes and the machine guns raining bullets from the sky.

Body after body dropped to the asphalt, their screams cut short by the vicious thunder of gunfire, leaving a trail of shell casings and blood along the pavement.

Charlie ran toward the wounded and knelt at the first man he came across that was still breathing. The bullet has torn through his stomach, and the man clutched at the wound, blood pouring between his fingertips and blood dripping from his lips.

"Just hang on," Charlie helped keep pressure on the wound, and the man trembled horribly beneath Charlie's touch. He glanced around for any of the medical staff, but it was nothing but a sea of bodies.

People crawled, they moaned, they cried out for help, but there was no help to give.

Charlie looked back down at the man in his arms, and the pair locked eyes. Charlie shook his head, unsure of what to say, but sure that the man would die. "I'm sorry I failed you."

With a bloodied hand, the man reached up and grabbed hold of Charlie's collar. His grip was weak, but forceful. He opened his mouth to speak, exposing the black hole of blood and darkness inside his mouth, but past the point of being able to produce any speech.

The final bit of strength went out of the man's hand, and he went limp in Charlie's arms. Blood continued to pour from the wound, spilling over the man's side and dripping onto the black pavement of the road.

Charlie gently lowered the man to the ground. He didn't know his name. There had gotten to be too many residents in the orchard for Charlie to keep track of everyone. And yet, he still felt responsible for the man's life. He didn't need to know his name to understand that he was a part of this place. He helped keep it running. Everyone played a part.

But now those parts were scattered across the pavement, bloodied and beaten, the bulk of Charlie's forces vanquished in less than a minute.

Charlie turned toward the forest, expecting the bulk of the terrorist forces to return in full stride, wiping out the rest of the survivors, and then continue their march toward Mayfield to destroy the power plant.

But the familiar whine of the prop planes grew loud again, and Charlie looked down the long stretch of road littered with the dead and dying.

As the noise of the prop planes grew louder and louder, Charlie saw them turning toward the trailers and RVs.

The ground rumbled, and more explosives were dropped from the planes, decimating not just the remaining survivors but The Orchard's land as well. Charlie watched as the trailers and RVs were consumed in the massive explosions, the plumes of red and black devouring their homes.

And as the explosions drew closer, Charlie closed his eyes, prepared to die along with everything else. He had reached the end. And it was time for him to atone for his failure.

45

*W*hen Charlie had shut his eyes, he never expected to open them again. So when a blinding light greeted him as his eyelids fluttered open, he was in shock. He wiggled his fingers and toes first, unable to move anything else. He coughed, and his chest ached, pained by even the simple motion of breathing.

He rolled to his side, his senses dulled, save for the pain that rippled through his body. Eventually the blinding light faded and the landscape took shape, though the more he saw, the more he wished he could have stayed unconscious.

Craters lined the street, and what wasn't turned to rubble was covered in blood. The bodies were scattered few and far between, but Charlie quickly realized that it was only because of the bodies had been torn apart from the blasts, pieces of the fighting core of both the blue clan and The Orchard scattered among the field of battle.

Covered in dirt and bits of asphalt, Charlie rolled off his back and propped himself up on his side. His heart pounded, and he blinked away the flecks of dirt that dangled from his eyelashes. His breaths sounded echoed and muffled, like he was underwater.

Charlie fingered his ears, but it didn't rid himself of the clog. He examined his immediate surroundings, searching for a weapon, unsure of how long he'd been out.

With nothing within reaching distance, Charlie forced himself to stand, the ground uneven beneath his feet. He drew in another ragged breath, still squinting from the brightness of the sun. He stumbled forward, away from the road and the forest, unsure if the enemy was still in the area, and headed toward the decimated land of the orchard.

The harsh slope of the terrain off the side of the road sent Charlie jogging off the pavement, and he slammed into what was left of the sandbag wall for their original defenses. He looked back toward the forest, noticing the hurried tone of voices, unable to understand them. He wasn't sure if that was because it was another language or his hearing just hadn't come around, but he wasn't in the mood for taking chances.

Charlie quickly leapt over the wall, landing awkwardly on his side. He rolled to his right, and a body lay in the ground next to him, a pair of lifeless eyes staring down at him. But a rifle was still clutched in the dead man's hands, and he removed it from the lifeless grip, the voices growing louder, clearer now. And they weren't speaking English.

Charlie made sure the weapon was loaded, flicked the safety off, and then peered through the cracks of the sandbag wall, where he spotted a pair of legs, and then hands gripping rifles themselves.

Charlie shut his eyes, trying to get his bearings, and trying to make the world not tilt to either the left or the right, but he couldn't keep his body straight no matter how much he tried. All he could do was wait until they were close enough for a shot. He didn't trust his body to keep steady to hit anything that wasn't point blank.

Boots crunched soil, and Charlie hung low, waiting until the enemy was directly on top of him before he aimed the rifle upward, firing the first shot into the nearest enemy's head, then lined up another while the second was still in shock from the sudden ambush.

Charlie fired, but his second shot missed the heart and connected with the terrorist's left arm, angering the enemy instead of killing him. He charged Charlie, fists swinging and blood spouting from the wound on his shoulder.

The pair collided then grappled in the dirt, both men forgoing their rifles and wrapping their hands around each other's neck. A pressure built up in Charlie's head, the flow of oxygen to his brain waning. He thrust his knees upward, ramming them into the terrorist's chest, and squeezed harder.

And while the terrorist had managed to roll on top of Charlie, Charlie knew he had the upper hand, seeing as how he put a bullet into the man's shoulder. Eventually, the terrorist's grip weakened, and from that Charlie was able to draw upon the rest of his strength, squeezing the life out of the man and tossing him to the side.

Charlie gasped for breath, choking and hacking, but forced himself to his hands and knees, even though he was still disoriented. He grabbed his rifle again and raised it quickly, unsure of how many others might still be lurking.

The quick patter of footsteps brought Charlie's attention toward the left. He reached for the trigger before he saw the faces. It was the twins.

"Charlie!" Shelly reached him first, Jason limping behind her, and she grabbed hold of his shoulder, her eyes so wide Charlie thought that they might fall out of her skull. "They're headed toward Mayfield."

"What?" Charlie scrunched up his face, shaking his head. Mayfield was the farthest thing from his mind. He looked toward the north and the forest that held Liz and Adelyn, but Shelly pulled his face back toward hers.

"They're fine," Shelly said.

"Nick already checked on them," Jason replied. "He

headed there first after the planes showed up. He tried to get Lee to come with him, but—"

Charlie frowned, then filled in the blanks from Jason's expression. He looked to Shelly. "How many are left?"

"I'm not sure," Shelly answered. "But it doesn't look good."

Charlie nodded, knowing that trying to pick through the field of the dead and injured would take time that he knew they couldn't spare. He turned to Jason. "Can you carry anything other than yourself on that leg?"

Jason smirked. "So long as they're not too fat."

Charlie looked to the south and found Doc's ER unscathed, though his house had been blown to bits. "You and Shelly start carrying anyone who's still alive and can be physically transported from the road to Doc's operating table." He glanced up to the sky, which was so blue and cloudless that it seemed incapable of raining down the hell-fire that Charlie and the others had just survived. "I don't know if they're coming back."

"There are still a few enemy stragglers left behind, picking people off down the road," Shelly said.

"Then the priority is to secure the area," Charlie said, separating himself from the rest of the group and heading toward Doc's house in search of a vehicle. "And when you find Liz—"

"I know," Shelly said.

"Thank you." Charlie turned on his heel, sprinting toward Doc's house, praying that a vehicle was still intact.

On the run, he tried to avoid looking at any portion of the ground, the field of death spread farther and wider than Charlie ever could have imagined. It wasn't fair. None of it was fair. But fair cared nothing of how Charlie felt about the events unfolding around him, and it cared nothing of the consequences that befell the world around it.

Charlie spied three Humvees destroyed, taken out by a

single blast, but when he rounded the damaged vehicles, he spied a fourth that had remained unharmed.

The engine roared, and the tires kicked up dirt as Charlie steered the hulking piece of armor around the dead bodies and craters that plagued his path toward Mayfield. The going was slow, and he saw no movement on the road, which only worsened the sour pit in his stomach.

Charlie weaved around the dead, making sure to hit nothing but asphalt and dirt on his way toward Mayfield. A few sparks of hope lit up inside of him at the sight of his people retreating toward the safety of the trees, but when he noticed that a few of them had blue patches, Charlie started to wonder.

He had no idea where the stranger was. He didn't even know if the man was still alive. And if the leader of their clan was gone, Charlie was unsure of how they would handle a succession. The thought made his foot hit the brakes, but he pushed past it.

All that mattered at this point was getting to Mayfield. Dixon needed to know about the planes, hell, he needed to know about the men that were marching their way. He pressed forward, unsure of what he'd do if he ran into the enemy along the way, but he knew that without the survival of the power plant in Mayfield, everything they'd done would have been for nothing.

Once clear of the carnage that the planes had unleashed upon the world, Charlie floored the Humvee down the road, the hillsides and greenery passing by him in a blur. He hugged the winding roads, only easing the brakes when it felt like the top-heavy vehicle was about to spill off the side of the road and tumble down the mountainside.

Charlie flexed his grip over the steering wheel, his fingers biting the wheel so hard that his skin peeled off like Velcro with every adjustment he made. His eyes were focused, his mind sharpened and his vision tunneled.

His heart raced in time and rhythm with the beating pistons of the Humvee, and when Charlie rounded the last bend that revealed Mayfield's sign, Charlie's eyes widened to the catastrophic and dismal display of destruction of the city ahead.

"No." The plea escaped a pair of desperate lips, and Charlie slammed the accelerator, rocketing toward Mayfield on the straightaway.

The guard post at the town's entrance had been destroyed, and the skeletal structures that the fire had left a year ago were demolished, fresh flames smoldering in the piles of rubble that dotted either side of the road.

And the street itself was torn up, forcing Charlie to stop and get out of the vehicle. He grabbed his rifle, slamming the door shut and running toward the power plant, the structure blocked by the still-standing hospital.

The bombs that had been dropped did a lot of damage, but like the orchard, there were pockets of areas that remained unscathed. Monuments left untouched, still standing tall above the rest of the rubble littering the earth.

Bullets kicked up dust to Charlie's left, and he veered right for cover behind a pile of bricks that had belonged to one of the buildings. Breathing heavily and his heart pounding, Charlie gripped his rifle with both hands, clutching it against his chest, and then slowly maneuvered his way toward the edge of the pile of rubble.

Unsure if it was enemy or friendly fire, Charlie tried to get a better look before he started to open fire. He knew that everyone was going to be on edge from the attack, and he didn't want to provoke an already-wounded bear.

"It's Charlie! From the orchard!" he shouted, his voice cracking from the effort after so much exertion. He waited for a response, hoping that if they were on his side, they'd reply with something in English, though he never considered the possibility of moles in the area working for the terrorists.

He'd run into that problem only once before, and he hoped that wouldn't be the case now.

"Come out with your hands up!"

Charlie exhaled in relief at the native tongue and accent and slowly did as he was told, weapon raised high and without malice as he squinted down the street. After a few seconds, a pair of men emerged from behind a rubble pile, both keeping their guns up as they jogged toward Charlie.

"Where's Dixon?" Charlie asked, keeping his hands in the air and spouting the question before either of them even got close. "Is he alive? Is the power plant—"

"Don't move." The lead soldier who arrived and stood in front of Charlie first stared at him through the sight of his assault rifle. He waited until his partner joined him before he lowered the weapon. "Drop it."

"You have to know who I am," Charlie said, keeping the rifle on his person. "Where's Dixon?"

"Wait." The second soldier lowered his rifle, squinting at Charlie in disbelief. "Holy shit, it really is you. What the hell are you doing here?"

Charlie stepped forward. "They hit the orchard." Charlie looked between both of them. "Is Dixon still alive?"

"Yes," the second soldier answered. "He's at the hospital."

"And the power plant?" Charlie asked.

"It got scorched a little bit, but it's fine."

Charlie exhaled. If the power plant was still intact, then they still had a chance at coming out of this with something good. "Listen. I think the bulk of their forces are on their way here. How many men do you have left?"

The first soldier chuckled. "You really are brain dead." He gestured around. "Take a look, Farm Boy. How many men you think we've got?"

"We still have our artillery," the second soldier replied, much calmer than his partner. "We took down two of their planes when they flew over. It's the only reason the power plant is still standing."

"Take me to Dixon," Charlie said.

Finally, though reluctantly, the soldiers led Charlie to the hospital at the end of the town. Along the way, Charlie saw the wreckage of one of the planes that they'd taken down, which crashed into a building, its final act of defiance before destruction.

But Charlie also noted that the second half of the town was in far better shape. The bombings had little to no effect on most of the structures leading up to the hospital, and Charlie stopped and stared at the power plant in the distance, unscathed, just like the soldiers had said.

And it was also where Charlie saw the bulk of Dixon's forces still crawling over the crater-infested fields that surrounded the power plant. He also saw the massive guns that had been wheeled out, along with the rocket launchers that Dixon had kept for himself.

Charlie followed the soldiers inside. He did his best not to get in people's way as the soldiers led him toward Dixon, but a room off to the left caught his eye.

It was filled with rows of tables, each of them with five stations manned by soldiers who held what looked like radios. Charlie stopped to stare, and one of the men inside the room noticed and quickly shut the door.

"Hey." The soldier tugged at Charlie's arm. "Let's go."

Charlie fell back into line and finished the short walk that remained to him back toward Dixon's new makeshift office. He found the commander hovering over a table with a large map spread out across it, his advisers flanking him on either side.

"The north is clear, we've already confirmed that with our scouts," Dixon replied. "The only concern we have from there is an air attack, so I want two of the guns moved to the structure's north side."

"There's heavy debris and the forest tree lines are quite high on that side, sir," the nearest adviser replied.

"Then start chopping them down, and tell them to double time it. We won't lose this fight because we didn't exert the effort." Dixon pounded his fist on the table to accentuate the point, and it wasn't until the advisers exited the room that he finally noticed Charlie near the door. "You're alive."

Charlie stepped toward Dixon. "They're on their way."

Dixon scoffed, returning his concentration to the map. "They're already here. I just need to make sure that we keep them away from the power plant long enough for backup to arrive."

"Backup?" Charlie asked.

Dixon looked up. "You don't think our air force doesn't have a few working planes? The moment those bastards bring back those tin cans, we'll blast them out of the sky, and then repay the favor to their ground forces."

"How long until the backup arrives?" Charlie asked.

"Undetermined," Dixon answered.

"Dixon, the orchard's been torn apart," Charlie said, leaning against the table with the map, his hands covering some of the region. "My people are open to attack."

When Dixon didn't respond, Charlie stepped around the table.

"Did you hear me?"

"I heard you, Charlie." Dixon sighed, then shrugged when he turned to Charlie. "But what do you want me to do about it? I need every last soldier here to defend the plant. We can't lose it now."

Charlie turned to the map. "How many hostiles have you counted?"

"Scouts have said it's near one thousand."

Charlie's jaw dropped, and he arched his eyebrows at the number. "How is that possible? I didn't even know there were that many left."

"Intelligence has confirmed it's the last of their men and resources on the western front," Dixon answered. "We win this fight, and we've won the war. The east has only a quarter of those fighting bastards left, and the rest are being snuffed out as we speak." He offered another heavy thud of his fist against the table. "It's the final hours, Charlie." He turned to him. "There's nothing for you to do here. Go back to your people. Keep them safe. Let me do my job."

Dixon tried to step around Charlie, thinking the conversation was over, but Charlie blocked the commander's path. "Your job was to send us backup. Your job was to make sure that The Orchard stayed out of harm's way." He frowned, staring at Dixon. "Did you know about the planes?" He tilted his head to the side, his mind and body becoming off kilter as he stared the commander down.

"Charlie, now really isn't the time—"

"Did you know?" Charlie stepped forward, getting in the commander's face, the pair of men one shove away from exploding into a fistfight.

Dixon clenched his jaw and balled his fists at his side. "I make a thousand decisions every day. And nearly every single one of them have life and death consequences." He frowned. "And while there are thousands of those choices to make every day, the only thing that I have to guide me are the orders that the facility under my command return to full functioning capacity. Because this place is more than just the sum of its parts, Charlie. It's the future. Future for my family. Future for your family and a million others." He cocked his head to the side. "So if you're asking me if I had to make the decision of keeping those cards close to my chest to prevent any panic or insubordination, then yes. I did."

Charlie wasn't sure how long he stood there, or if he said anything in the stretch of silence after Dixon had finished speaking, but before he even realized what was happening, he had his hands around Dixon's throat, driving the man backwards and pinning him up against the wall.

Dixon fought back, punching Charlie's sides, which weakened Charlie's grip and provided enough wiggle room for the commander to squeeze out of Charlie's hold and separate himself from Charlie just as a pair of soldiers flooded into the room to restrain Charlie and pin him up against the wall.

"Get him out of here!" Dixon shouted, his face and neck blood red as he readjusted his uniform, smoothing out the creases that Charlie had caused.

And while Charlie allowed himself to be removed from the area, he shoved the guards off of him once he was out of the room, the pair of men letting him walk out on his own accord, his anger still steaming out of his ears.

He was shoved outside and escorted all the way back to his Humvee, and the soldiers kept their rifles trained on him until he was completely out of the town.

A mixture of shock and rage flowed through him, and the more distance he put between himself and Mayfield, the more he wanted to turn around and knock Dixon's block off. But he kept driving toward home. Or at least what was left of it.

46

The bulk of the dead was still on the pavement, and Charlie slowed to finally look at the bodies scattered about. Every corpse on the ground was another stab to his heart. Every lifeless pair of eyes stared back at him with the glaring expression of failure.

Charlie stopped at Doc's, dropping the Humvee off and finding a trail of patients waiting for him to keep them alive. Shelly and Jason were helping a few more over, and Charlie moved in to assist, sliding the fighter's arm over his shoulders and helping him limp toward the queue of the dying.

Shelly and Charlie gently set him on the ground, propping him up against the shattered remains of Doc's house. Finished, the pair stepped back as Jason brought over another one.

Charlie counted thirty-two fighters wounded. And after seeing so many dead, he never would have thought he would have wished for more.

"What happened with Mayfield?" Shelly asked, wiping the sweat from her brow, smearing some blood across her skin.

Charlie stared at the crimson stain for a moment, and

then looked past Shelly to the road of destruction and death that had plagued them.

"He knew," Charlie said, shaking his head, a desperate laughter flowing through him. "He fucking knew about the planes."

"What?" Shelly asked, unable to hide the shock and anger in her voice. "That fucking cunt!"

"So what now?" Jason asked.

Charlie shrugged. He was in the dark and in unfamiliar territory. The only thing he could do now was wait to see if Dixon and his men could hold off the assault that was heading toward them and pray the terrorists didn't decide to come back to the orchard for another sweep. He glanced back out to the forest, his eyes scanning the horizon. "How is everyone else?"

"Scared, confused," Shelly answered. "God, and I still can't believe that asshole didn't say anything about the planes. We could have planned for—"

"I know," Charlie said, cutting her off. The anger had subsided, the rage carving out his bones, leaving him hollow. "We keep the rest of our people alive. It's the only thing left for us to do."

"Charlie!" The stranger called from down the road, helping carry one of his fighters, which he set down next to the rest of the wounded waiting for treatment.

"Wasn't sure if you made it out alive," Charlie said.

"Likewise." The stranger rubbed his fingertips, then noticed the blood staining his hands. He paused, looking back to the fighter he'd just dropped off. He lowered his hand then turned to Charlie. "I need to get back to my people. Make sure they're all right."

"How many men do you have left?" Charlie asked.

"A few dozen," the stranger answered. "That's all I could find." He exhaled, adjusting his footing, and squinted back

379

out onto the field of battle. "So much blood in such a short amount of time."

Charlie stepped toward the stranger, unsure if he should tell him what he knew about Dixon. The last thing he wanted was to make an already bad situation worse, but Charlie felt the man had a right to know what happened. He'd lost just as many men as Charlie did, but Charlie was unsure of what the stranger would do with the news.

"I understand," Charlie answered. "We'll take care of your wounded."

"Thank you."

"Good luck." The pair shook hands, and Charlie watched the leader disappear. Once he was gone, Shelly stood next to him.

"Why didn't you tell him?" Shelly asked.

"It'll only make things worse." Charlie turned back to the wounded. "And we don't need any worse."

Everyone kept an eye toward the sky for the next hour, Charlie included, as anyone who wasn't injured or hurt helped sift through the bodies of the dead. Charlie didn't request help from the tree line, knowing that many of the dead had family members waiting for them. There would be time for mourning and identification, but right now it was more important to keep the bulk of his community hidden in case the terrorists decided to come back.

While Charlie had hoped to find more survivors, they only discovered more death. The pile of bodies grew higher and higher as the day grew longer, and while he kept a close eye on the surroundings, he was surprised at the quiet.

No planes. No gunshots. Nothing.

Granted, Mayfield was some distance away from The Orchard, but with the kind of weaponry that Charlie had seen on both sides of the battle lines, he expected faint pops in the distance. But the more time passed and the longer that silence lingered, the more confused Charlie became.

Why were they waiting so long to strike an offensive? Surely they had enough men to make their last stand, so long as Dixon's number of one thousand was correct. But still the silence persisted.

"What in the hell are you waiting for?" Charlie asked, talking to the horizon.

"Charlie?"

He turned, finding Liz standing there in a bloody apron, gloves on her hands, her hair pulled back in a tight bun. She'd been helping Doc with the injured. She was one of the few Orchard members with professional medical training. He walked to her, wanting to kiss her, but knowing that it was only business that mattered now.

"We'll need more supplies from Mayfield," Liz said. "We're running low on morphine, and half of these guys aren't going to be able to handle surgery without it. They'll go into shock. Plus after treatment, we won't have—"

"We can't get it," Charlie said.

"What happened?" Liz asked. "Did—"

Charlie took a step toward her and grabbed her shoulders, and she shuddered from his touch. "We're on our own." He looked back to Doc's ER unit and the rows of fighters that still needed to be tended to. "Do what you can."

Liz nodded and returned to work, while Charlie returned to the pile of dead. The sun was already baking the corpses, the flies starting to circle. This wasn't how it was supposed to end. This wasn't how it was supposed to be, but again the world told Charlie that what he wanted and what he believed in didn't matter. What he wanted was irrelevant.

The sun dropped lower and lower in the sky, and by the time evening was upon them, Charlie and the remaining survivors of the attack had cleared the battlefield of their dead. Two massive piles had been erected on the side of the road.

"The plans of mice and men," Charlie said, whispering to himself.

"Boss," Shelly grabbed his attention, her sleeves rolled up and her body armor removed, though she still kept her rifle on her person. It was the unwritten law of the crew. "People in the forest are getting restless. They want to see what they can salvage from their homes." She hesitated. "And they want to know if their family members are still alive."

Charlie turned back to the piles of the dead. "Get a list of names of the injured from Liz. I don't want a stampede of people out here. It'll be easier to tell them who survived than who died." He looked to Shelly. "And don't let them come out. No one leaves until I know this is over."

And as Shelly left to carry out his orders, Charlie wondered how long they'd all have to wait until it was finished. Sitting on the sidelines after a year of being in the shit wasn't something that Charlie had grown accustomed to, and it was making him antsy.

Wanting to make himself useful, Charlie walked the list over to the tree line himself. He weaved through the smoky wreckage of the fields, examining the few bits of life that remained in the place. But like the field of dead he just cleared, what survived was few and far between.

Charlie heard the murmur of conversation from the rest of the orchard before he even arrived at the tree line. He kept the list of names in his hand, the short piece of paper folded over. He'd written the names down, but he already had them memorized. The list was short enough for him to do that.

He stared at the ground until the last minute, and when the world around him was so quiet that it was noticeable, Charlie glanced up.

The tree line was crammed with people, each one of them waiting with bated breath, hands clasped together, waiting on the man who would once again change their lives.

"I have a list of names," Charlie said, clearing his throat, his voice scratchy and raw, then repeated himself so everyone could hear. "I have a list of names! They're the survivors of the battle on the road. I didn't have time to write down if they were injured, or how they were injured, but as of my walk over, each one of these fighters was alive."

Whimpers rippled through the crowd as they held onto one another, dreading and hoping for it to be over quickly and to come out the other side unscathed. But when Charlie unfolded the list, a few burst into tears before he even spoke.

"Miles Cunningham," Charlie said. "Jared Levan. Carol Seethers—"

Charlie read from the list, keeping both hands on the flimsy piece of paper to help conceal the trembling of his hands. He kept his eyes on the paper, reporting each name as loud and clear as his voice would allow.

When he neared the end of the list, Charlie struggled to hide the quiver in his voice. Because the number of people that would be devastated when he stopped outnumbered those that exhaled in relief ten to one.

"—And Sharon Walker." Charlie's eyes lingered on that last name, and he waited for the rush of exhale from the held breath across the line of people. But when it didn't come, he folded the paper back into his pocket and addressed the crowd. "We've gathered the bodies—"

"That's it?" A man stepped from the crowd, eyes red and fists clenched. "That was less than thirty people." He shook his head. "There has to be more."

"There isn't," Charlie said.

"Are you sure?" A young woman stepped from back behind a cluster of people. Her hair was long and curly, tangled in knots, her joints too large for her small frame. "What if someone ran off in another area of fighting, or what if they're hurt and you just thought they were dead?"

Charlie watched the fear and desperation catch along the herd like wildfire. One after another they stepped forward, each of them clinging to the hope that Charlie was wrong, that the people they cared about, their fathers, and brothers, sisters, and mothers were still alive. But none of the ones they loved had survived. Charlie hadn't deceived them, no matter how much they wanted it to be true.

"Shelly will break everyone into groups," Charlie said. "You will be able to retrieve their remains—"

"Oh, god!" The skinny, wild-haired young woman dropped to her hands and knees in the dirt. She balled her hands into fists, clumping up patches of dirt, her entire body trembling. "Oh my God!" She spit the words out between horrifying sobs, and for a minute everyone around her just stood back and watched the grief and rage pour out of the young woman's soul.

Charlie had been the one to deliver bad news like this before. But he had never delivered so many names at once, or at such a horrific time. He turned to look back at their shattered homes, trying to think of anything that he could say to ease the pain, the fear, the uncertainty. But the wisdom eluded him.

"Dixon and the military are throwing everything they have left to defend the power plant in Mayfield," Charlie spun back around, the faces of rage and grief staring right back through him. "If they lose that fight, then all of this will have been for nothing. All of the loss we experienced, not just today, but over the past year. Maybe even over the course of our entire lives." Charlie shook his head, dropping his gaze to his boots. "I've tried to keep this place going. I tried to rebuild. And I will be damned if I'm going to let a bunch of assholes with machine guns ruin what future I still might have." He looked to the crowd, tears forming in his eyes, and no longer caring about acting as their leader, or being the man with answers. "It's a future that you can have too. But it only works if it's what you want. What you really, truly want. There isn't room for anything else anymore. And

384

if you want to honor the loved ones you lost today? If you really want to make sure that their memory lives on? Then you must live. You must create a future where their names are remembered. Because the only way they truly die, the only way that they really disappear, is when there isn't anyone left to remember them."

And as much as Charlie didn't want to, he knew that there was only one last path for him to take. And that was to fight the enemy at Mayfield. But not for Dixon, or the military, or even the crowd that had stepped closer, drawn to his words. It was for a nurse and a little girl who had become a daughter to him.

He would fight for two people. That was something he could manage.

*B*y the time Charlie had finished handing out the weapons, there was another seventy men and women at his back as they marched toward Mayfield. He hadn't expected so many, and he wasn't sure what they'd find when they arrived at Mayfield, but he knew that it was better than sitting at the orchard and just waiting to hear the news of their battle. At the very least they'd know whether there was any hope left at all.

It was an anxious hike, and while there was a plethora of new fighters, Charlie felt better about the decision to head back to Mayfield when the twins and Nick decided to join him. It didn't take much convincing. The fact that Lee had died and they knew the enemy who killed him was on their way or currently already at Mayfield, it was the easiest decision that any of them had ever made.

The sun dropped lower against their backs the farther they walked, bathing the world in that beautiful golden hue that Charlie loved so much. His eyes lingered on everything the light touched, his mind soaking in the beautiful sight as though he might never see it again.

It was a thought that crossed his mind several times.

Despite all of that big talk about living for tomorrow and creating a future, Charlie understood that he was walking into the lion's den. He was about to enter a world of blood and fire, and the only way out was to make sure that neither of those elements touched you.

Mayfield's sign came into view on that final turn around the bend, and Charlie's muscles and joints ached. It had already been a long day, and with night descending upon them, he knew it was only going to get worse.

"You think they already came?" Shelly asked, keeping stride with Charlie.

"Yeah, you think that anything is still left?" Jason added.

"They better be," Nick answered. "I didn't walk all this way not to fucking shoot something."

But while the crew chatted, Charlie kept his gaze ahead, squinting into the distance, the fading light making it harder and harder to determine the situation that they were about to encounter.

"Eyes up," Charlie said. "I want everyone to stay sharp."

The crew barked the orders down the line, and the greenhorns all nodded nervously, unsure of what they were even supposed to be looking for. But Charlie wasn't sure himself.

They entered the town at twilight, the dark reach of night reaffirming its grip on the world around them, and Charlie raised his rifle in preparation for a fight.

There were no signs that anything else had happened since Charlie had left earlier in the day. But that didn't mean they were safe. Not by a long shot.

Once they cleared the bulk of the rubble, Charlie stopped, causing the crew and everyone else that had followed him to stop too. The fact that they hadn't run into a guard or anyone on duty didn't sit well with Charlie. And the fact that it was so quiet didn't sit well with him either.

"Boss," Shelly said. "What—"

"You really do have a death wish, don't you?"

387

The voice came from somewhere in the darkness, and Charlie narrowed his eyes to get try and locate Dixon's position. "The fact that you haven't opened fire tells me that you need the help."

After a pause, a figure emerged from the shadows, and Charlie lowered the weapon when Dixon was finally revealed. He wore no smile or expression of gratitude for Charlie arriving with seventy armed fighters at his back.

"Planning on taking the town from me?" Dixon asked.

Charlie stepped closer toward the commander, a man who he had, at the very least, considered a peer. The pair understood that choices had to be made in order to ensure the survival of their people, and Charlie wasn't going to let their squabble get in the way of that.

"I know you had your reasons," Charlie answered. "If I were in your shoes and had to make that call, I probably would have done the same thing. But that doesn't mean you won't be judged for it one day."

Dixon nodded. "I suppose there will be a lot that both of us have to answer for." He finally looked behind Charlie to the armed men and women that had come to fight. "They know how to use those weapons they're squeezing just a little too tight?"

Charlie nodded. "Most of our fighters were taken out in the blast, but everyone on the orchard was trained to handle a weapon."

"Well," Dixon said. "We'll stick them in the back. They'll only see action if our front lines fall. God help us if they do."

Charlie followed Dixon through the streets, the pair moving quickly back toward the power plant, and on their walk, Charlie noticed the number of men that emerged from the darkness. They had snipers all over the place, and Charlie wondered how long he and his people had been in their sights.

"You got here just in time," Dixon said. "During the first

couple of hours after the initial attack, we had prepared for an all-out assault, but when that final hammer swing never came, we did a recon scout of the area and found it clear of the enemy. Nothing but empty woods and abandoned homes for miles."

"What about your intelligence?" Charlie asked. "You said they were mounting an attack, an offensive that was meant to be the final blow."

"They still are," Dixon answered, then gestured to the darkness and the night sky around them. "We shot down two of their planes, which means they've only got one left, and it's their best chance of obliterating the power plant."

Charlie frowned, but then caught on quickly. "It'll be harder to see the plane at night."

Dixon scoffed. "We've got everything but goddamn spot-lights." He shook his head, and the power plant and the hospital came into view. "We've tried to light up the ground, reflection and all that, but I don't think it's going to help."

"No, but it'll paint a hell of a target for the bomber," Charlie said.

Dixon stopped, placing his hand on Charlie's chest, forcing both men to stop. "I admire you returning. Especially after what happened. It takes a different kind of man to do that, someone who sees the bigger picture. It's one of the reasons our relationship has worked so well and lasted so long. But if you want to come back and help, have more of your people killed, then they'll be following my orders." He made a point to look to the heart of Charlie's crew, making sure that they understood it as well.

But Charlie wasn't fazed by Dixon's words. He simply looked back to the crew, and then turned back toward Dixon and laughed. "Well, they barely follow my orders." He clapped Dixon on the shoulder. "So good luck."

With their interaction over, Charlie allowed Dixon and his lieutenants to break up the fighters that had followed

Charlie to Mayfield, but while they were led to different sections of the town, Charlie headed toward the front lines by the power plant. If he was going to make a stand, then he was going to do it in the only place that he knew the enemy would want to get to. It assured him the best opportunity to make his journey a useful one.

Shelly, Jason, and Nick came with him, ignoring the orders of the military officers, and seeing as how they had another dozen or so to deal with, they let him pass without incident.

The foursome caught a few glares as they carved out their own patch of space around the power plant near the south side, which Charlie figured would be the most logical point of attack. And since it was where the bulk of Dixon's forces were, it helped reinforce that theory.

The energy that hummed through the soldiers was tense. It connected everyone to each other and heightened the anticipation of war. Everyone hoped for and dreaded the moment of the first gunshot. Charlie had never wanted something to start so quick and end so soon in his life.

The night dragged on, the level of anxiety remaining high through the trenches outside the power plant. Faces were glued to the night sky and chatter was low, knowing that since they were blinded by the night, they were forced to rely on hearing the planes.

It reminded Charlie of the boogeyman when he was younger. That faceless creature that lived beneath the bed, striking fear into the heart of anyone who gave it life. It was a phase that every child experienced growing up, but it helped instill a degree of fear about the unknown.

Perhaps it was just human nature, never truly knowing what lay beyond in the darkness. But while Charlie didn't know when the enemy would arrive, he knew what was waiting for him back home. Liz and Adelyn were the only things he had left. And who knows, maybe his mother would finally come around, but he wasn't going to hold his breath.

"Hey," Nick said, stirring from his motionless position. "You hear that?"

His words caught the attention of everyone in their area, and Charlie glanced up toward the night sky, squinting as if that would help him see more clearly.

"You're not fucking with us, right?" Shelly asked.

"Just listen," Nick said.

Everyone leaned forward, the night still as dead silent as Charlie would have thought, and the moment dragged on, but then Charlie heard it on the breeze.

"Plane!" The shout came from down the line, and the decree was immediately followed with a frantic panic of searching the skies.

The hum of the propeller plane grew louder, but Charlie couldn't pinpoint the section above. And with his focus on the sky, Charlie missed the first few gunshots from the horde of terrorists lurching toward them from the field of battle.

The gunshots were nothing more than firecracker pops at first, but after the first few bangs, the world dissolved into nothing but screams and gunfire.

Bullets darted through the night, most of them aimless, like shooting the fake monsters in the night. People were firing based off of fear instead of fortitude and action, but Charlie peered through the scope of his rifle, waiting until he had an enemy in his sights.

He pivoted left and spied a dozen men heading their way. "On the left!" He shouted the order right before he opened fire, dropping a man on the wing to the ground.

The cluster of terrorists hastened their sprint, spreading out and making it harder for Charlie to shoot, but he brought down one, then two, then three people. As he pivoted his aim between the approaching enemy, he realized that none of them held any rifles.

Charging with no weapons was suicide, but when Charlie pivoted between the fighters, he finally saw the bomb in one of their hands. Charlie adjusted his aim, the crosshairs bouncing left and right as he tried to adjust for the terrorist's sporadic, serpentine sprint.

He fired, missing once, missing twice, the terrorist less than thirty yards from him now. "Someone bring him down!" Charlie shouted as the terrorist screamed, one final cry before he would blow himself up, along with anyone in his path.

The terrorists raised the bomb high above his head and cocked his arm back in preparation to throw, while Charlie struggled to line up his shot, the man growing larger in his scope until he couldn't even find him anymore. He peeled his eye off and turned his head away just as a gunshot rang out, followed quickly by the explosion of the terrorist's bomb.

The earth rattled from the blast, shaking Charlie and throwing him off balance, but he turned back to the field and saw the crater carved into the ground. He looked to his right and saw Shelly, rifle still poised to shoot.

Shelly peeled her eye away from the weapon and then winked at Charlie. "We got your back, boss."

Charlie smiled and then returned his attention to the battle, picking off the enemy one by one. They were outnumbered, but with the open field in front of them, the terrorists had no option but to make a mad sprint toward the front lines to try and break through, and while they never stopped in their attempts, their pile of dead grew taller and taller on the field of battle.

Piles of shell casings rose on either side of Charlie, firing round after round into the enemy screaming toward him.

But eventually the enemy stopped.

Dripping in sweat and his joints aching, Charlie strained his eyes through the scope one last time, scanning the field of battle for any more hostiles that were trying to make their way up the power plant, but he found nothing.

"Is that all those bastards have?" Nick asked, panting from the adrenaline rush. "I expected more from them and their last stand."

But while Nick looked to the ground, both Shelly and Jason had their eyes toward the sky. "Dixon said they only shot down two of the planes."

And then a faint buzz echoed through the night sky. Every head turned toward the darkness above, the noise of the prop plane getting closer.

"This is it," Charlie said, quickly finishing his reload and aiming the weapon toward the sky. "Keep your eyes sharp!"

"I don't see anything!"

"Where's it coming from?"

"What if there's more than one?"

The questions were thrown from the mouths of nervous soldiers, but Charlie kept his attention toward the sky. The cloud cover made it nearly impossible to spot anything in the darkness, the world blanketed in nothing but pitch black.

"Eyes up!" Charlie said, the roar of the propeller growing louder and louder against the night sky. It was getting closer, and the louder it became, the more anxious Charlie grew. He knew that the moment the aircraft broke through the clouds, there would be only seconds before the enemy decided to blow up the power plant.

"On the left!"

Charlie pivoted toward the voice, scanning the stretch of darkness above, unable to spot the aircraft right away, but hearing the gunshots fired from the other soldiers. While they fired sporadically, Charlie waited for a shot.

Finally, he spied a blurred object less than one thousand feet in the air. He brought it within his crosshairs as it moved within five hundred yards of the power plant. He fired, the bullet screaming into the night, but still the object progressed.

"Fuck," Charlie whispered, again struggling to track the shot in the darkness.

"Boss?" Shelly asked.

"I've got it." Charlie lined up the shot again and pulled the trigger. The bullet screamed into the night, but still the plane kept coming. He lined up again. Pulled the trigger. Miss.

Less than two hundred yards.

He fired again. Miss.

One hundred yards.

"It's still in the air!"

There must have been thousands of bullets screaming toward it in the night, and twice Charlie heard the blast of rockets toward the sky, but still the engine of the plane continued to roar against the night sky.

Charlie lined up the shot again, this time waiting, continuing to track the shot. It was nearly overhead now, and the first bomb had dropped, landing on a cluster of soldiers, the ground shaking beneath Charlie and disrupting his aim. But he found it quickly and exhaled, letting his muscles relax. It was like his father had always taught him. Don't fight the shot.

"Charlie!" Shelly cried.

And then just as another whistling drop of a bomb came hurtling close, Charlie squeezed the trigger. But he never got a chance to watch the plane go down after the explosion went off.

He woke up with a pounding headache, but after his vision adjusted, he was glad to find a familiar face hovering above.

"Hey." Liz smiled and pressed a warm hand against his cheek. "Glad to see you up."

The fog of sleep hadn't fully been lifted, and Charlie wasn't sure how long it took for him to get up and off the ground, but he jolted up to his elbows, his body aching in defiance from the sudden motion. "The power plant."

"It's still there," Liz said. "The west end of the building got scorched, but the blast didn't affect any of the working components." She smiled, shrugging in almost disbelief.

The news washed over Charlie slowly. He rested his head back down on the pillow. He closed his eyes. It was done. He reached for Liz's hand and squeezed. When he opened his eyes, his vision was distorted by the tears that welled up in his eyes.

After the moment passed, Charlie cleared his throat. "What about the orchard?"

"Dixon made good on his promise with supplies," Liz

answered. "We got aid delivered this morning. Tents. Food. Water. Medicine." She nodded. "You did it."

"This morning?" Charlie asked. "How long have I been out?"

"Almost forty-eight hours," Liz answered. "Doc said you had a concussion."

"You should be thankful for that hard head your father gave you."

Charlie turned toward the door and saw Doc in the doorway. He had his arms crossed, still sporting that grizzly white beard and wild hair. He looked tired. But it was the first time Charlie had seen Doc smile in a long time when the twins weren't around.

"Thanks, Doc," Charlie said.

"Oh, don't thank me," Doc said. "It was your crew that pulled you out of the hellhole. I just made sure you didn't die on my table." He raised his eyebrows. "Liz would have killed me."

Liz laughed and mouthed thank you to Doc as he turned and walked out of the room, once again leaving the pair alone.

"So what's happening with—"

Liz pressed her finger to his lips and shook her head. "Rest. Business can wait. You've done enough." She kissed him again before he could respond and then left the room.

It wasn't until she left that Charlie realized that he was in a hospital room. The Mayfield hospital. He turned to the window and saw the trees and green of the world outside. It was bright, and Charlie tried to fathom getting out of bed and walking outside and realizing that things were going to be returned to the way they were.

But the longer he lingered on that thought, the more he knew that it wasn't exactly true. While he would still be able to get his orchard back and return home, his father was still dead. And his mother wasn't the same woman.

"I didn't realize you were awake."

Charlie's heart skipped a beat when he saw his mother standing in the doorway. She looked tired, older than even before Charlie left, which he didn't know was even possible. She crossed the threshold and walked to Charlie's bed.

He stiffened, inching away from his mother as she approached the bed. She folded her hands together, examining the bandage on his head. "Does it hurt?"

"What do you want, Mom?" Charlie asked.

A sad smile spread across his mother's face, and she nodded. "I suppose that's all that matters now, isn't it? Getting to the point." Her mouth twitched, and an expression of sorrow appeared on her face. It had more pain than Charlie realized. She twisted her arthritic hands, her eyes searching the white tile for help, but received nothing. "You've had a hard year, Charlie. It's been a life that has worn you down, and it forced you to be something that was unnatural to you." She looked him in the eye. "And I know I didn't help you steer away from that. In fact, I encouraged you down that path."

Charlie laughed, shaking his head. "And so what? You're telling me that I don't have to be like that anymore? Mom, it's not like turning a light switch on and off."

"No," Martha said. "It's not." She stepped closer, her waist pressed against the side of the cot. "But I know that while you think you can come back on your own, you can't. Just like I can't go back—" Her lips quivered, and she choked on her own words. She shook her head. "It doesn't matter now. Not anymore." She wiped her eye, but Charlie couldn't be sure if it was just for show. She looked at him, that familiar steel gaze returning to her face, and she raised her eyebrows. "You have a new family now, Charlie. Liz and Adelyn, they need you to be the man you were before all of this. The kind, forgiving man. Your father was that kind of a man. And I know that I can't be your family."

Charlie twisted the hem of the sheets. "You can't?"

Martha looked at him, her eyes watering. "I didn't think you wanted that anymore."

"Well," Charlie answered. "If I'm supposed to go back to the man I was before, then I'll need the woman who helped raise that man."

And with those final words Martha broke, twisting her face up in grief, the tears breaking free and rolling down her cheeks. "What if I don't remember?"

Charlie reached for his mother's hand and squeezed. "Then I'll help you. And you help me."

Martha nodded and then reached for her only son, her first born, and wrapped him in a tight hug, crying. The pair stayed like that for a while, and Charlie took his first step back toward the man that he had always wanted to be. And when he finally stepped out of the hospital, he'd be entering a world where that was a possibility.

ONE YEAR LATER

Charlie finished attaching the trailer to the truck, the rusted chains clanking together, his face red and sweat peppering his face from the awkward position. "All right!" he shouted, and then stepped out from between the truck and trailer, wiping his hands on his blue jeans. "You're all set."

Mario shook Charlie's hand, smiling. "Thank you, Charlie. For everything."

Maria kissed him on the cheek, and the kids wrapped their arms around Charlie's legs.

Charlie laughed. "Let me know when you make it home, and enjoy the time off. You've earned it." He stepped back, letting Mario and his family get into the vehicle. He waved as they drove off Doc's property, and Mario was the last trailer to leave the three homes.

He turned around, glancing at all of the open space. He'd forgotten what it had looked like without all of the trailers and mobile homes. It was like the earth finally had a chance to breathe again. And so did Charlie.

He walked back toward the house, reveling in the freedom. He veered toward the nursery of trees that they had planted in the spring. All of them had taken root, and Charlie touched the leaves of the new growth. It would be a few years before they were fully grown, but Charlie had managed to find a few already-grown trees to transplant to help supplement their income until they were mature enough to produce fruit.

Out of the fields, he passed the skeleton structure of the barn. He tore down the old one months ago, and Charlie was less than a week away from putting the roof on. After that, it was just putting up the siding for the walls and painting it.

Adelyn was out back playing with Martha, Liz watching them through the back porch. They had bubbles, and both were chasing each other with them. It was the most playful thing he'd seen his mother do in a long time. She was finally starting to get back to normal.

"At least I don't have to worry about you guys hurting yourselves with those things," Charlie said as both women turned their assault on him. "Besides getting some soap in your eye."

"It's fun!" Adelyn exclaimed.

"That may be, but it's time for dinner." Charlie kissed the top of her head and gave her a helpful shove toward the house. "Go get washed up."

"Fine." Adelyn slouched her shoulders, but Martha offered one last shot across the bow, sending a stream of bubbles against Adelyn's ears, and she giggled, sprinting toward the back kitchen.

Martha smiled. "She's got a lot of spunk."

"That she does," Charlie said, then looked to his mother. "Thank you for trying with her."

Martha nodded. "She's my granddaughter." The word had been easier for her to say over the past few months, and there was a hint of a smile whenever she spoke the title.

"Martha, can you come and get this out of the oven?" Liz said, stepping out from the back porch.

"Speaking of children," Martha smiled, heading toward Liz, who stepped down, well, more waddled down as Martha entered to help finish dinner.

Liz kept both hands on her growing stomach and squinted from the setting sun, which had bathed her in gold. "What are you looking at?"

Charlie walked to her, then placed his hands on her stomach and kissed her lips.

"Mm-hmm," Liz said.

Charlie laughed. "What?"

"You've got something up your sleeve, Charlie Decker." Liz examined him with a curious eye, but couldn't hide the smile. "What are you thinking about?"

Charlie looked back out onto the fields and the fresh growth. It was a new world, and Charlie was thankful to have survived long enough to see it bright and fresh. He turned back to the house and saw his mother and Adelyn setting the table, the pair still giggling about their bubble fight.

"Hey," Liz said. "You all right?"

"I'm fine," Charlie answered. "It's just nice thinking about tomorrow."

Made in the USA
Las Vegas, NV
25 August 2021

28908206R00223